Welcome

to

Mistywood Lane

REON LAUDAT

CHAPTER 1

Reese Sommers returned to her candlelit dining room carrying a tray with a second bottle of wine and a triple-decker strawberry cake. "I'm back!" she sang, placing the goodies on the table and admiring her shiny red nails. She'd splurged on a professional gel manicure for those *"this-just-happened"* engagement pictures to be added to her and Darren's joint Post-a-Pic. The couple had filled that social media account with fun, loved-up images of themselves: Darren and Reese on their first date at last year's Mayfair Fourth of July parade, Darren and Reese dressed as bacon and eggs for Halloween, Darren and Reese roasting their first "couple's turkey" at Thanksgiving.

"Your mother went all out." Reese admired the luscious cake, which she'd removed from a Tupperware container and showcased atop her best crystal platter. The treat was more elaborately decorated than Mrs. Reid's usual. Impeccable frosting swirls. Reverse shells. Rosettes. *Oh, my!*

When Darren had arrived with the cake, she'd given quite the performance. *"Your mother made this for little ol' me? To what do I owe this honor?"*

Reese had always adored Mrs. Reid, who would make a delightful mother-in-law. She envisioned the two of them swapping recipes, lunching at Marinelli's, shopping at farmers' markets, and baking sweet treats together.

"That cake looks almost as delicious as you, sweetheart," Darren crooned.

Reese's fiancé-to-be was so handsome with his sable brown eyes glittering in the candlelight, lean athlete's body, full sensual mouth, and adorable dimpled chin. She hoped one or two of their kiddoes—she wanted at least four—would inherit that dimple. Maybe Reese and Darren should get started on the baby making ASAP. She caressed his thigh. *Focus!* They had the rest of the night for nookie. First things first.

"Shall we get started?" Darren pointed to the cake and passed the knife to Reese. "You do the honors, Reesie."

Why of course! Reese grinned. Darren must've tucked the ring inside the cake with swirly jelly filling. A little messy, but super cute! Reese would scrub the ring until it burst with fire again in no time.

Time. She'd always dreamed of having a June wedding. If their official engagement kicked off that night, July tenth, she had time to get a ballroom at the Whittington Hotel for the wedding and reception.

"Oh, Darren! I'm so excited!"

"It's just cake. Mom made it, but—"

"Yeah, *just* cake, by your mom. I'm touched. This is so special. She's never baked a cake especially for me before."

"Well, you went nuts over the one she brought to the barbecue last weekend."

"Yeah, I did, didn't I? But I'm sure there's more to this cake!" Reese nudged his ribs. She couldn't resist hinting she was in on the Big Secret. After all, she and Darren had the rest of their lives to plan more surprises for one another. "One of these days I'll convince your mother to share her secret strawberry cake recipe." Maybe Reese would convince Mrs. Reid to bake a few goodies for the Sweet Spot, too.

"I doubt it. That recipe has been a closely guarded secret in the Reid family for years."

It would remain a closely guarded secret in the Reid family after they wed, Reese wanted to say.

Mrs. Darren Reid.

Dr. and Mrs. Darren Reid.

Reese Renita Reid. Now that had a nice alliterative ring to it. Musical yet as solid as reading, writing, and arithmetic. Yes, a real nice ring.

*Speaking of ring…*Where in the cake would she find the symbol of their betrothal? Reese studied the circular confection, inhaling its sweet-cream frosting. She'd remember every detail of this life-changing evening. Going with a hunch, she cut midway between what would be twelve and three if it were a round clock. The knife sank through the layers. *Nothing.* Twelve o'clock. *Nope.* Three o'clock. *Uh-uh.* Four o'clock. *Nada.* Five. Six. Seven.

Zilch. Zilch. Zilch. A fleck of diamond with a sliver of a base? She didn't care if Darren had fashioned the ring with bobby pins, rhinestones, and Super Glue. It was what it symbolized that mattered. Reese cut more cake.

"Hey, babe, it's just you and me. Why are you making so many slices?" Darren asked.

Reese let the knife sink in at the nine o'clock position. She was about to go for ten o'clock when banging and buzzing startled her. "What in the world...?" She hurried to the door, nearly tripping over Sinbad, her cat. A scowling woman paced on the other side of the peephole.

"Darren!" The woman jabbed the doorbell. "Darren! Darren! Get your lying, cheating ass out here! I know you're in there with some skank!"

Reese rushed back to the dining room. "There's a woman shouting and pounding on my front door!"

"Get rid of her." Darren popped a plump strawberry inside his mouth.

"Maybe you should get rid of her. She's calling your name!"

More banging. More buzzing. More shouting.

"What?"

Reese glared at him. "She said, and I quote, '*Darren*, get your lying, cheating ass out here.' "

Darren almost choked on the strawberry. "Um, er, does she have light brown hair with sun-kissed streaks and a mole on her left cheek? Is she about yea high?" he asked, holding his hand palm down and raised at a little more than five feet.

"Are you out of your flippin' mind?"

"She's supposed to be in Chicago."

"*Who's* supposed to be in Chicago?"

Darren's expression contorted with confusion and then mortification. Rushing to the front door, he stomped on Sinbad's feather-duster-like tail, causing the cat to hiss, spring, and swat at his ankles.

"Careful! You hurt Sinbad! Who is this woman?"

Darren peeked through one long window panel flanking the front door. "Oh, no!"

More banging and buzzing. "I know you're in there, Darren Reid! I recognize your license plate!"

"What's going on, Darren? I deserve an explanation!" Reese said.

Reese's neighbors would want one, too, especially Odette, who lived next door, to Reese's left. The house to Reese's right had been sold, but, as far as she knew, the new neighbor had yet to move in.

"Well, um, I didn't want to tell you this way."

"Darren! Darren!" More banging and buzzing. "Yes, there's a man-stealing skank in your midst, ladies! Watch out! She lives at 3456 Mistywood Lane! Watch your husbands! She's trying to steal my fiancé! But I'm not letting her get away with it!"

"Fiancé?" Reese gasped. "Darren! What is she talking about?"

"That's Sasha. I told you about her, remember?"

"Your *ex* named Sasha. You two had broken up *before* we started dating. And it was for the best, *according to you.*"

"I was frustrated and confused at the time, but we, um, sort of got back together."

"When?"

Darren winced and lifted his arms as if to deflect potential blows. "A little more than two months ago, I believe it was."

"Two months ago!"

"She's my best friend." Darren dropped his hands when no attack ensued. "You're great, too, Reesie. The best, but, but…" He heaved a heavy sigh. "I chose Sasha."

"Then what are you doing here!"

"When I showed up you'd made this wonderful dinner for us. Lobster fra diavolo is my favorite, and there was great wine. And you look fantastic in that red dress." With brazen lust, he observed her. "I got… distracted."

More banging and shouting on the other side of the door.

"So you're blaming this on me?"

"No, on the wine and the sexy red dress. And Mom had made the strawberry cake for you already. She didn't know we were parting ways. I figured you deserved to know first. And I thought you deserved the dessert."

"As a parting gift? Unbelievable!"

"I know how much you love it," he said as if it underscored what a gosh-darn nice guy he was. "I swear I was going to tell you tonight, Reesie."

"But you thought you'd get one last hump for the road, is that it?"

Guilt flashed in his eyes.

"You lying, cheating jerk!" Reese raced back to the dining room table, grabbed the cake, and hurled it at him. He ducked, and it hit the wall. "How dare you! Get out of here!" The crystal platter and the cake broke in pieces. Though he lacked a sweet tooth, Sinbad darted over to sample the mess on the floor.

"I planned to tell you sooner, but something always got in the way," Darren said.

"Yes! Your penis!"

"Reesie babe, I'm so sorry." Darren extended his hands and hopped from foot to foot as if dancing on hot coals.

Reese raced to the kitchen for the fire extinguisher.

"What are you going to do with that?" Darren asked when she returned.

Reese aimed it at him. "You'll find out if you don't get the hell up outta here. Now!"

Sasha pounded and ranted, "And he's the father of my unborn child! I'm seven weeks pregnant! Did you hear that, Mistywood Lane! Yes, your neighbor tried to separate my baby from its father!"

Darren's brows leaped. "Baby? I swear I knew nothing about that!" As if that made the news less stinging to Reese.

Reese sprayed the extinguisher, covering Darren with a powdery, fire-squelching agent. When he stumbled onto her front porch, Reese tried to slam the door. Sasha kicked it open. "Don't run and hide now, you home-wrecking heifer! Not woman enough to face me? Coward!" She hawked and spat at Reese.

Darren stepped between them and the loogie landed on his powdered shirt pocket.

"Get out of my damn way!" Sasha lunged and clawed at Reese.

Reese held the extinguisher between herself and the flailing woman Darren restrained. Why was Sasha directing her murderous wrath at Reese instead of the dirt bag fiancé holding her back? Darren was at Reese's house. He'd parked the Range Rover at the curb. Did Sasha believe Reese had abducted him and held him against his will?

"I knew nothing about you and Darren getting back together," Reese said. "Tell her, Darren!"

"Calm down, baby," Darren said to Sasha, who responded with an up-yours gesture before lunging at Reese again.

"Baby, please," Darren said again.

Hearing the former love of her life referring to this woman as his "baby" was like a kick in Reese's solar plexus.

"Let's go back to my place and talk this out," he said to Sasha. "I'll explain everything. It's not what it looks like."

"Go to hell!" Sasha burst into tears. She yanked out of Darren's grasp and stormed to her blue Lexus parked in Reese's driveway. She zipped into reverse and rammed into Reese's mailbox. Miraculously, she missed the neighbor's adjacent box. Sasha leaped out of the car, cursing and shaking her fist at Darren and Reese. Suddenly, she stopped raging. Her face twisted in a mix of pain and fear. "Something's wrong." She clutched her middle. "I'm, I'm...cramping. The baby! I think it's the baby!"

"Oh, no!" Darren sprinted to her. "Sasha, sweetheart!"

Sweetheart. A rotating double sidekick to Reese's midsection.

"Let's get you to the hospital!" Darren said. Sasha let him lead her to the Lexus. He held the door as she eased onto the passenger seat. Giving Reese a guilt-ridden look, Darren took the wheel of the car and backed out of the driveway.

Only after the Lexus turned off Mistywood Lane did Reese notice Odette, her friend and neighbor, standing on her own front porch. Brett and Brayton, her two-year-old identical twins, rode each hip. "Are you all right?"

Shell-shocked, Reese nodded.

Wearing a green reflector vest, Calvin, Odette's husband, who was back from his run with Ahmad, stood staring at Reese.

A crowd had gathered. Pitying and accusatory eyes were everywhere. So many eyes, curtains fluttering, blinds opening. The Swanigans, the Davises, the Wilsons, the Jacksons, the Johnsons, the Lopezes, the Rosenkrantzes, the DiMarcos, the Papadopouloses, and the Longmires. They'd seen it all. It was a beautiful summer evening. People were still out, walking, talking, and grilling. This sort of low-rent, pass-the-popcorn drama was never on display on Mistywood Lane or any other street in the upper-middle-class Granberry Ridge community. Even the most sordid, buzzed about scandals played out with discretion, whispered about at back fences.

Until now.

The entire subdivision would get a blow-by-blow account before dawn. It was just not enough that Reese was heartbroken. Oh, no. She had to endure public humiliation.

Odette left the twins with Calvin and rushed over to give Reese a hug. "Do you want to talk about it, sweetie? Come over to our place. I saw Darren, but *who* was that crazy woman?"

"I don't want to talk about it right now," said a trembling Reese.

"You shouldn't be alone," Odette said. "I can call your sisters for you."

Reese shook her head. She stepped out of Odette's embrace and gave her friend a grateful clap on the shoulder. Drawing a shuddering breath,

Reese trudged back inside her house and closed the door.

"If you need me, you know where to find me," Odette called through the door. "Come over anytime at all. We can talk, or I can sit with you if you don't want to be alone. I don't care how late it is. You know my door is always open for you, sweetie."

Reese blew out the candles on the dining room table and left the mound of crumbled cake on the floor. She reached for a wineglass and that second bottle of chianti on the table to drown her pain. On the family room sofa, she wept until her face and stomach hurt. What a disaster her love life was. *One-sided love.* She'd loved. Darren had lied.

After a year of dating him, Reese had believed Darren was The One. How could she have been so wrong? He seemed like such a stand-up guy. Intelligent. Witty. Kindhearted. Supportive. Sexy. Successful. He headed a thriving plastic and reconstructive surgery practice.

Trustworthy? *Not!* What red flags had she missed or reasoned away? The more she drank, the fuzzier her memories became. Soon, she passed out.

Hours later, she awoke as the room brightened with the rising sun. She glanced at the clock on an end table: 6:57. She'd fallen into a fretful wine-and-sorrow-soaked sleep. After an incoherent moment she remembered the previous night and her heart sank. *Oh, Darren, I loved you.* His deception packed quite a wallop. Nauseated and boulder-headed, all she wanted to do was stay on the sofa until the discomfort passed.

Pop an Advil and two Alka-Seltzer. Wash up. Get ready for work. Later for the flippin' pity party. But could Reese put last night's shocking ordeal behind her and get on with what promised to be a hectic day? Saturdays at her business, the Sweet Spot Cup Cakery & Coffee Shop, were always the busiest. But oh, the spectacle from the previous night. Sasha's over-the-top rage. Hormone induced? The woman's frightened expression haunted Reese.

What if Sasha miscarried? The circumstances were not Reese's fault, but the thought that she'd played a small role in such a loss was too much. She clenched her fists and refused to let that possibility take hold. The roses sitting on a nearby end table were also from Darren. She knocked the vase to the floor. She wanted to indulge in another good cry, but now fury stemmed her tears.

Her cellphone on the table vibrated. An image of Porsha flashed across its face. It was nearly 4 a.m. in Los Angeles where her close friend and former college roommate now lived. Porsha reaching out so early on a

Saturday morning meant one thing: Man issues, specifically Clinton Foster issues. But Reese had her own man problems. Would she have the patience to indulge Porsha, known for her long weeping screeds? Reese answered the phone and heard all about how Porsha had caught Clinton, aspiring actor and her longtime boyfriend, with his head buried between his acting coach's thighs.

"And he had the nerve to say it was an improv exercise!" Porsha told her. "Can you freakin' believe it? What kind of fool does he take me for? The woman wasn't wearing panties for heaven's sake!"

"I'm so sorry, hon. That *is* going far for his art," Reese replied, still stunned by a similar betrayal.

Nonstop, Porsha blustered for an hour about her and Clinton and then hung up, abruptly as usual. But she sounded less homicidal by the time the call ended. Reese had probably saved a life or two by listening.

"Sinbad." Reese needed to feel his fluffy warmth in her arms. "Sinbad." She patted a nearby cushion, all it usually took for her beloved fur baby to come running. "Sinbad. Come to Mama. I need you now."

Silence.

Five minutes later. "Sinbad!"

More silence.

"Sinbad!"

Nothing.

Reese sprang to her feet and raced upstairs. "Sinbad! Sinbad!" She searched under her bed and dashed to the two guest bedrooms to check all of Sinbad's favorite resting places. She called out again.

No patter of hind-leg kitty claws on the hardwood floor. This wasn't like him. A fresh swell of panic rose in her chest as the doorbell rang.

If it was Darren with another lame apology, she didn't want to hear it. Nor was she ready to confide in Odette. Sasha? Oh, heck no. She would not return to finish what she'd started last night...or would she? The visitor persisted with raps and rings. Reese called out to her cat again. After looking through the peephole, she opened the door to halt the racket.

It wasn't Darren, Odette, or Sasha on her porch. Instead, the most handsome man Reese had ever seen stood there. Sinbad quivered in his tan, muscular arms.

"Yours?" the man asked with a wide smile as he scratched Sinbad's ear.

CHAPTER 2

$\mathbf{A}$t five-foot-eight, Reese had to tip her head back to look at the stranger who stood well over six feet tall. Best guesstimate, six-foot-four.

"Sinbad! There you are! You scared the heck out of me, boy!" Reese snatched her cat out of the man's arms.

"So I found the right house," the man replied in a smooth baritone, bringing to mind a combo of fine leather and expensive brandy.

"Thank you for returning him," Reese said. Sinbad had obviously slipped out the front door during last night's commotion. *Oh, poor thing!* He must've been petrified outdoors all night long. For sheltered Sinbad, Mistywood Lane must've felt like the Amazon rainforest, teeming with deadly critters. She buried her face against Sinbad's soft coat and cooed, stroking his neck. She delighted in the sandpapery texture of his tongue licking her hand in gratitude and the feel of his hefty weight in her arms. "Sinbad, you scared me!" she scolded him, making a mental note to replace the fancy faux jeweled collar and ID tag she'd removed three days earlier when she'd given him a bubble bath.

"I'm moving in next door. My little buddy here was the welcome wagon I presume, but I thought his owner might get worried if he stayed at my place much longer."

"He could've been a stray. He's not wearing a collar."

"I don't see many stray Persians, pristine silver chinchillas, similar to the Fancy Feast cat. He looks pampered and well fed, *extremely* well fed. And I noticed his front paws are declawed and—"

"He came to me with his front paws declawed," Reese added, perhaps a

9

tad too defensively. She hated the mutilation. His paws felt like wool-sock-clad feet without toes.

The stranger acknowledged the additional information with a nod. "It was another sign he's not supposed to be an indoor/outdoor cat. So, his name is Sinbad. I'm Gabriel Cameron." He extended one large hand. "And you are?"

"Sorry! Reese Sommers." Still holding Sinbad close, she shook Gabriel's hand. "My manners are usually much better. It's just that..." She cringed. Had her new neighbor heard or witnessed last night's uproar? "It's been one of those mornings—"

"Already?" he asked, humor still twinkling in his brown eyes. "The sun is shining and the birds are singing. I think I'm going to love it here."

Thank goodness. He'd missed the show. The numbness in Reese's limbs ebbed, but her head and heart still ached. *Darren. Shake him off.* She'd try to chat up the new neighbor. It was the least she could do after he'd returned Sinbad. "Welcome. So, are you a townie or a transplant?"

"Townie. The truck's supposed to arrive in," he checked his watch, "oh, about an hour. Mayfair, North Carolina, born and reared."

"Me, too. I've lived in the Granberry Ridge subdivision for five years. You'll love it here. This particular street, Mistywood Lane, has a great sense of community. But I don't have to sell you on the place. You've already purchased the property. You're aware of all the assets and amenities."

"Yes, I did my research. And I have a good real estate agent."

Sinbad squirmed and pressed his front paws against Reese's arm, signaling he wanted down. Only after he'd leaped to the ground and scrambled toward the kitchen to seek his food and water dishes did Reese remember she was still dressed in her come-ravage-me red dress. A breeze carrying the scent of Odette's lush rose bushes brushed across her skin, triggering a reminder she wore nothing at all underneath the slinky number with a plunging neckline and not one, but two thigh-high slits. Now that Sinbad was no longer a warm cover, her nipples hardened, set on naughty. But she didn't dare look down to draw attention to them. From what she could tell though, Gabriel Cameron had been the perfect gentleman, maintaining eye contact the entire time. Nor did he ask why she was dressed for the Walk of Shame.

Odette tended to those prize-winning roses under a perfect blue sky. When her friend waved, Reese waved back, telegraphing she was (mostly) all right.

"That's Odette Carmichael," Reese told Gabriel, "my friend and head of Mistywood Lane's unofficial welcoming committee. She and her husband, Calvin, will visit you and bring a big basket of homemade muffins and a Thermos of coffee."

"I'll look forward to it," said Gabriel, who had yet to mention whether he had a wife for Reese and Odette to befriend. Did he have kids? Potential playmates for the Carmichael twins?

Reese glanced at his ring finger and found it bare. But, she reminded herself, some married men didn't wear rings. She'd find out sooner or later. Probably sooner if Odette, who was more adept at digging for details, made her way to his place today.

"It was nice meeting you, Gabriel, and thanks again for returning Sinbad."

"Nice meeting you, too. And though I did my research, I'm sure there's a lot more to learn from a five-year resident of the Granberry Ridge subdivision. I'd loved to pick your brain. I was thinking… Maybe, I, um, can talk to you and *Mister* Sommers?"

An innocent, awkward assumption or was he conveying a personal interest in her marital status? "I'll be happy to fill you in, but only on a-need-to-know basis. No gossip. Well, maybe a little."

"So whatcha got for me?" He'd moved those long legs of his into a wide stance, signaling he was in no hurry.

"Well, let's see." Reese wrapped one arm around her waist and tapped a finger against her cheek. "Our homeowners association is the gestapo. Ervin "Buddy" Wainwright is a stickler about other people's leaves flying over in his yard. So make sure you're on top of your leaf blowing come fall. Milo Papadopoulos's son, Aristotle aka Ari, will be a member of Harvard's upcoming freshman class. Milo is the proudest papa, as he should be. Ari's a great kid, but Milo will tell you all about Harvard at least a few dozen times. And Mrs. Longmire doles out stickers and clementines at Halloween, much to the kids' chagrin. And when the DiMarcos put up their truckload of Christmas decorations their house flashes like a giant pinball machine."

"Is that so?" Gabriel looked amused…and mesmerized, which caused an odd sensation in Reese's belly that had nothing to do with her hangover.

"Dottie Wilson claims it triggered her seizure once," Reese revealed. "I have my doubts about that, but the house sits right in front of yours so get ready. It couldn't hurt to invest in some blackout blinds for all those large windows." Reese's thoughts drifted back to last night's ordeal, but she attempted to chatter them away. "And by the way, *Mister* Sommers is my dad, Wallace, who lives in another subdivision across town with my mom, Mrs. Sommers, aka Diane Washington-Sommers before she dropped the hyphen to go in wholeheartedly with my father's surname."

"Is that so?" Gabriel's smile widened. "Then maybe we can talk over coffee at the Sweet Spot. The coffee's so good there, and it's conveniently located. I put it on my list of pros when I was sizing up the area. And in case you're curious, *Mrs.* Cameron, aka Vivian, is my mother, who never hyphenated and also lives in another subdivision across town with my dad, Mr. Cameron, aka, Martin Cameron."

"Not quite name, rank, and serial number—"

"But close."

Both laughed.

Though Gabriel had complimented the Sweet Spot, Reese wouldn't reveal it was her place. Yet. The man was flirting. Big time. But she was not in the market so soon after a messy breakup. And even if she were ready to put herself out there again, dating someone who lived so close was just asking for unnecessary complications. And while she didn't want to make snap judgments based on appearance and charming manner alone, she snap judged away. She wouldn't be the least bit surprised if Mr. Right Next Door had several lady friends and wannabe lady friends. How could he not? She was distressed about Darren, but not blind. This Gabriel Cameron was smoking hot — killer smile, sexy chocolate brown eyes, well-honed physique, and a panty-dropper of a voice. When it came to deep voices like his, Reese melted faster than microwaved chocolate. But not that day.

That Range Rover parked at the curb haunted her like a big black ghost. Maybe she should have that sucker towed away. A vengeful move, more Quinn's style than her own.

"So, coffee, then?" Gabriel asked.

Reese would leave the coffee klatch to Odette and Calvin. She would tread carefully with the hottie, but maintain a casual friendliness. After all, who could have too many pleasant, helpful neighbors? The previous occupant of Gabriel's home, Mr. Cohen, a recent widower, had helped Reese change flat tires and given her a jump when her car battery died on her. Before Mrs. Cohen had passed, Reese had cared for their plants and two parakeets, and had gathered their mail and newspapers when the couple had taken off on their frequent impromptu RV excursions.

"How about I fill you in the next time we see each other at our mailboxes?" Reese glanced where their two boxes stood together. How Sasha had managed not to plow into his was a mystery.

"The mailboxes?" The twinkle in Gabriel's eyes dimmed.

"Yeah, after you get settled in." Reese's mailbox leaned to one side, as if repelled by a stench. The stench of betrayal. So thick she could smell it.

"Reese." Gabriel broke her reverie again.

Pretending last night's ordeal hadn't affected her made Reese spacey. More than likely she smelled her own wine-laced morning breath. *Don't get too close, new neighbor. Might singe your nose hairs.*

"A little accident?" Gabriel asked about the mailbox.

"You could say that. But it won't happen again," she said, referring to her poor choice in men.

"So, about that Mistywood Lane debriefing—"

"Soon. Until then you'll be busy unpacking and settling in your new home." And it was a nice one. Actually, a lot of nice house for one person. She'd been inside numerous times and her oldest sister, Blaire, a realtor, had peeked at the listing and shared the comps and other details with Reese. Four thousand, five hundred square feet, open concept, two-level brick contemporary. Four bedrooms. Two and a half baths. Three-car garage. Lots of enormous sun-worshipper windows. Finished basement converted into a tricked-out media room. Patio. Basketball court.

"About that mailbox meeting…," Gabriel said, "When?"

"Soon. So nice meeting you, new neighbor," Reese said with a smile and a wave goodbye.

CHAPTER 3

Reese's heart might have taken a drubbing, courtesy of Darren, but she refused to let him interfere with her business, too. After Gabriel left, she showered and dressed, determined to get on with her day.

The Sweet Spot, nearing its four-year anniversary, was still her happy place, a close second to her home. Pride and accomplishment wrapped her in warm hugs each time she stepped inside the space that smelled like supreme yumminess. No nose blindness for her.

The homey bakery/coffee shop had fast become one of the area's hot spots due to her passion for creating quality products and providing the best customer experience. Even on her busiest days, she made time to chat with regulars and newbies. Taking a few minutes to extend hospitality was often the best stress reliever. Because she'd cultivated the current familial atmosphere among the staff, coming to work had never felt like work. That morning she whizzed through the hours in an over-caffeinated blur, too busy to ruminate over her raw pain as customers arrived in a steady stream.

Still, the hurt lurked at the fringes waiting to pounce. By noon, her sisters arrived. Blaire wore a low-cut, fitted, flower print Lilly Pulitzer dress, and high heels, one of her many preppy seductress ensembles. Tucked under her right arm was one of her many boxy designer bags that resembled carry-on luggage without the wheels. She stepped inside the shop yapping away with a Bluetooth headset attached to her ear. She gave a wave here and a nod there to acknowledge a couple of shop regulars she knew by name. Reese's eldest sister had a knack for making friends everywhere she went.

Reese's middle sister, Quinn, who'd finished making a video for *Natural Wonder*, had paired a dressy silk blouse with holey boyfriend-cut jeans and worn Chuck Taylors because the camera captured only her top half. Impeccably made up, she'd applied long faux lashes and something she described as "strobe highlighting," which was apparently all the rage. Her long hair was in a fresh, or rather, flatter than normal twist-out style.

Her sisters' smiling faces made Reese want to bawl.

Before a cluster of customers, Quinn reached for Reese's hand and examined her bare ring finger. "So, where is it? Oh, wait, you need to get it sized, am I right? Or did you request a different design? That's how it goes when you don't shop for the ring *together*. A ballsy move on Darren's part. I mean, you two had never discussed which type of ring you prefer and then bam! You find the jewelry store receipt in his pocket."

Why had Reese been so presumptuous? She could kick herself for spilling the Big Secret, which turned out to be an even bigger secret than she could've ever imagined. Now she felt like a flippin' fool.

"It wasn't the right style and size?" Quinn asked, dropping Reese's hand.

"Is that why you look so sad?" Blaire asked after ending her phone call and putting the Bluetooth away. "Are you ill?"

"Follow me," Reese said. Linda, the Sweet Spot manager and Danielle, another staffer, could handle the remaining customers.

Reese led the way through the kitchen to her office at the rear of the bakery/coffee shop and closed the door behind them.

"So, did Darren propose?" Blaire took one of the two seats positioned in front of Reese's neat desk. Quinn claimed the other.

"He did, but—"

"Congratulations, sis!" Blaire said.

"Woo-hoo!" Quinn pumped one fist. "Did you two set a date?"

"Will you rent that beautiful place by the lake for your reception?" Blaire asked. "Or are you going for the Whittington Hotel? It's pricey, but their ballrooms are fabulous."

Reese opened her mouth, but their rapid-fire questions overwhelmed her.

"For a newly minted fiancée, you look downright miserable," Blaire said. The cell in her purse sounded with the instrumental theme of the show Blaire hosted, *A Nest for Newbies*, which aired on the Home & Hearth Channel. When she wasn't taping, she had a thriving career in residential real estate sales. Blaire's attachment to her phone and various devices often bordered on obsessive, but this time she glanced at the face, silenced it with a swipe, and let the call go to voicemail.

"Darren proposed, but not to *me*." Reese fought back tears. She didn't want Linda, Danielle, and her customers to see her puffy and red-eyed when she emerged from the office.

"What?" Blaire said.

Mouth opening and closing, Quinn leaned forward. "But, but I thought you said—"

"I know." Reese paused and drew in a deep breath. She wanted to upchuck.

Quinn's brow furrowed. "So he proposed to…?"

"Sasha," Reese said.

"Wait. Sasha?" Blaire tipped her head to one side. "Why does that name sound familiar?"

"She's his ex," Reese said. "Well, she's his *ex*-ex. It's on again. In a big way. Obviously."

"Yeah, that's right." Blaire snapped her finger. "Sasha Jones. She was an account executive at the local branch of the prestigious James, Horton & Bower ad agency. Last I heard she'd accepted a promotion at corporate headquarters in Chi-Town."

"Yes, she and Darren broke up because of her move. And that's where they reunited when he attended a week-long plastic surgery symposium there. He made the trip to brush up on advanced techniques for laser and autologous fat grafting for vaginal rejuvenation. He rejuvenated a va-jay-jay all right. That ring was for Sasha, whom he also impregnated during that trip." Reese wailed.

"Oh, no!" Blaire said.

"I never liked him anyway," Quinn said. "Never trust a man who eats Buffalo wings with a steak knife and a salad fork."

"Because as a surgeon he's more comfortable with tools." Reese reached for a tissue. After everything he'd put her and his pregnant fiancée through, she justified his quirks.

"Good riddance!" Quinn huffed.

Reese blew her nose. "But a minute ago you said—"

"I know, I know." Quinn gave a dismissive wave. "I've had my misgivings about dude from day one, but before I knew it, you were in love. I had to trust your judgment and not meddle."

"Not meddle? Since when?" Reese asked.

"I was trying to turn over a new leaf here." Quinn twiddled with the cupcake-shaped knickknack container on the desk. "I believed you saw something in him I couldn't see. Something besides the obvious, I mean. He is very attractive… in a stiff-archetypal-department-store-male-mannequin sort of way. But he's a liar. He denied it, but I've always believed he's had work done. That Michael Jackson-esque cleft in his chin was always suspect."

"It's not a cleft," Reese insisted. "It's a dimple."

"More like a *climple*," Blaire said.

"Which doesn't appear naturally," Quinn insisted. "But I digress. You lit up around him, and you seemed happy so I had to trust your judgment."

"Same here," Blaire added. "Quinn and I talked about this at length."

"With each other, but you never said a flippin' word to me for a whole year!" Reese's face grew hot. "How could you not share what you really thought of him? We always have each other's back."

"Calm down. We didn't want to pee in your Perrier. And besides, would you have listened?" Quinn asked. "Seriously considered dumping Darren based on nothing more than Blaire's gut, my hunch, a suspicious climple, and his insistence on using utensils to eat finger foods?"

"Well, um," Reese sniffled and shredded the wad of tissue in her hands, "no, but maybe I would've looked a little closer, slowed down, and analyzed certain things to see what had given the two of you pause." Her tears flowed again and she choked out, "Oh, jeez, now look at me. I'm blubbering too much." She tried fanning away the tears. "He's not worth it."

"It's okay," Blaire said. "Let it all out, sis."

"It was a nightmare, y'all." Reese said. "Sasha stormed over to my house last night to confront me and Darren. That's how I found out. Like a fool, I'm searching for the ring in my cake, especially made for me by Darren's mother by the way, and Sasha's on my porch spitting, stomping, and shouting what a home-wrecking whore I am."

"What!" Blaire and Quinn bellowed at once.

"Yes. It was like something straight out of those wig-snatching, table-flipping reality shows." Reese shuddered. "Everyone on Mistywood Lane must know by now."

"And I'll bet Odette was right there gathering all the juiciest bits for one of her TMZ-style Mistywood Lane reports," Quinn said. "I can just see her now. Standing on her porch with the devilment twins, Brat and Satan, on each hip."

"I wish you wouldn't call them that," Reese said. "It's Brett and Brayton. One day you'll let that slip out when she's around."

"I'm sure it's not news to her. No matter what she says as she plays the proud alpha mom, deep down inside she has to know she spawned two little demons. Beware of their 'eyes that paralyze.' I'll bet they glow in the dark."

"Knock it off, Quinn," Reese said. "They're two years old. Just babies. "

"Yes, they're too young to be evil minions," Blaire added. "Wait until they're five."

"And Odette was great last night," Reese said. "After Darren and Sasha left, she came right over to comfort me. You're way too hard on her."

"I'm convinced she's the one who rats you out to that homeowners association when your lawn gets the tiniest bit overgrown," Quinn said. "And I'll bet she's the one who started that outrageous rumor that got around Mistywood Lane four years ago. The one about a sugar daddy providing the seed money for this place."

"You have no proof of that," Reese said. "Besides, she knows PawPaw gave me the money. Let's get real here. You've never liked Odette. Since our book club did a Secret Santa gift exchange that one year."

"The heifer gave me a ceramic flat iron!" Quinn had turned a hobby into a career with *Natural Wonder*, her popular hair blog and SeeMeTV vlog channel aimed at women with kinky, curly, coily, or wavy hair who preferred to wear their manes in a natural state, without chemicals or excessive heat. "That's like giving a vegetarian a side of beef, a pacifist an Uzi, Whoopi Goldberg a bra —"

"Odette meant well," Reese said.

Quinn still amazed her legion of followers with what she could do with one head of hair. Real hair. No weaves. No wigs. No clip-on pieces. No braided-in extensions. No direct heat. One day she was wore a wild profusion of coils and kinks teased *a la* Diana Ross and the next she was a Grecian goddess with uniform crimps.

Reese's phone pinged with a text from Darren. Shoulders shaking, Reese sobbed again. "Boy, did he ever pull one over on me."

Quinn reached for the phone. "Let me block that jerk."

"I can do it myself... later," Reese said, dropping the phone inside her purse.

"It's okay, sweetie." Blaire stood and moved closer to stroke Reese's shoulders and back.

"I'll hang around the shop and help you out," Quinn said.

"Bring Reese to my place after you close here," Blaire said. "I'll set up everything. We'll have a fun girls' evening in to help take your mind off the craziness."

Quinn stood and pulled Reese to her feet. Embracing her in what Reese liked to call "a Sommers sandwich with condiments of hairspray and expensive perfume," both sisters made her feel cherished.

"Wait. I can't go straight to your place," Reese said, before blowing her nose again. "I need to deliver the day's leftovers to Greenleaf."

"The hospice?" Blaire asked. "I thought you gave them to the homeless shelter."

"I donate to both, alternating days. I added Greenleaf a while back because the people there took such great care of PawPaw. It's my way of thanking them for making his last days…" Reese often choked up when she thought of her beloved maternal grandfather, who passed away six years ago. "And for all the good work they do there."

"We know." Quinn stroked Reese's back. "But can't you get Linda or one of the others to do it?"

"We have a schedule," Reese said. "It's my turn."

"Damn," Quinn said. "You're the boss. Delegate."

"Yes, I am the boss, and guess what? I know how to run my business," Reese retorted. "And I know how and when to delegate, thank you very much. So back off."

Quinn formed a cross with her fingers. "Okay! Okay!"

"After Greenleaf," Reese said. "I need to check on Sinbad. He's been at home by his lonesome all day. I need to see him, and refresh his food and water. He's experienced his own ordeal and needs extra pampering, too."

"His ordeal?" Quinn dropped back in her chair, huffing with the usual disapproval. "So he had to go a full day without those gourmet meatballs you feed him every chance you get? The way you spoil that cat…And all that ground filet mignon can't be good for him. He's too big."

"It's mostly muscle," Reese said. "Muscle weighs more than fat."

"Mostly muscle?" Quinn howled.

Blaire cackled as if she'd never heard anything so ridiculous.

"Okay, so he's a tad chubby," Reese said.

"A *tad* chubby? If he didn't have fur, he'd looked like a Butterball turkey," Quinn said.

"No, Humpty-Dumpty," Blaire countered.

As Reese had often done when they were kids, she pinched them both.

"Ouch! Admit it. You stuff Sinbad like a sausage." Blaire rubbed the area on her arm that Reese had latched onto. "He's not raiding the fridge and cabinets for a midnight snack of tortillas and Velveeta on his own."

"He doesn't like nachos," Reese said.

"Aha! So you have offered them to him before!" Quinn said. "Girl, you ought to be ashamed of yourself!"

Reese almost told her sisters Sinbad's ordeal had nothing to do with treat deprivation. An image of a tall, broad-shouldered, insanely handsome Gabriel Cameron with Sinbad in his muscular arms came to mind.

"You and Quinn do the Greenleaf pit stop," Blaire said. "On my way home, I'll stop by your place to pick up Sinbad—"

"Don't throw your back out." Quinn snickered before Reese whacked her. Their good-natured ribbing made her feel better.

"After I gather some things for you to wear, I'll pack his food, including the fresh gourmet meatballs I know you always keep in the fridge, if it'll make you and Sinbad happy," Blaire replied dutifully.

"Wait. I thought you and Hayes had tickets to the symphony tonight," Reese said.

"Not a problem," Blaire replied.

"I don't know," Reese said. "You guys already have trouble coordinating your schedules."

Blaire was in a long-term relationship with Hayes G. Reardon III, bank president and philanthropist.

"You're sure Hayes won't mind?" Reese asked Blaire. "I don't want to ruin your evening."

"I'll tell him you and Darren broke up, and you need extra TLC," Blaire said. "He'll be fine with it."

"Yeah, sisters before misters, *always*," Quinn declared. "We'll eat, drink, and trash Darren and that spiffy Range Rover of his." She removed her keys and brandished one as if it were a weapon. "I'll scratch all sorts of obscenities on both sides of his ride. And then I'll—"

"Rein in the crazy," Blaire interrupted. "Haven't you learned anything?"

Quinn did not take douche-bag deception lying down. Among past attempts to "even the score," she had subscribed to dozens of bizarre porn fetish e-zines (*Big Titty City, Boulder-Size Boobs, Tattooed Grannies in the Raw*) in one ex's name and had them digitally delivered to his place of employment's general email account. Reese believed messing with someone's livelihood was crossing the line. But that was Quinn. In her pursuit of vigilante justice, the punishment did not always fit the crime.

"Quinn, I know you empathize," Reese said. "And I appreciate it. I do. But I agree with Blaire. The sooner I try to put Darren behind me the better. Sitting around trashing him or thinking of ways to get back at him is not healthy or productive."

"But it could be cathartic knowing he gets what's coming to him," Quinn said.

"I want to forget I met the man."

"You sure?" Quinn asked. "Because you know I'll *get* him. I'll make him wish—"

"I'm sure you would," Reese said. "But promise me you won't do anything."

Quinn hesitated.

"*Quinn,*" Blaire and Reese said in a warning tone.

"Okay. Okay." Quinn put her keys away and raised her hands. "I promise I won't do anything, though he deserves it," she muttered.

"And don't instruct *anyone else* to do anything, either," Blaire clarified. "Promise."

"Okay! Okay!" Quinn said. "I promise. I won't do anything or hire someone else to do it."

"Besides, living and loving well is Reese's best revenge," said Blaire, ever the voice of reason, except when it came to her own love life. The sisters hugged it out again. How Reese loved these two. No one could nurse a girl through a devastating breakup quite like the Sommers sisters.

CHAPTER 4

When Reese wasn't working at the shop that weekend, she and Sinbad stayed at Blaire's house. It was just like old times, when the young Sommers sisters' nights had been one fun-filled slumber party after another.

They watched a slew of romantic comedies, which gave Reese hope that her own loveable hero was still out there somewhere. They guzzled wine and stuffed their faces with all manner of junk food. They gabbed and gabbed some more. Further discussion about Darren was off limits. Instead, Blaire and Quinn extolled the fleshly virtues of the men featured in a bundle of old *Glitz* magazine "Hottest Hunks in Hollywood" special editions that Blaire had stockpiled.

By Monday morning, Reese returned home to find Darren's Range Rover gone. Eager to get back on schedule, she tackled the first thing on her to-do list: a vet appointment to have that strange recurring dirt spot on Sinbad's chin examined. Like most pets, he hated vet visits. It was always a struggle getting Sinbad inside the carrier. He'd often steel his paws on each side of the opening to avoid sliding in. How he knew he was headed there and not to Blaire's, Quinn's or their parents' house was baffling. After Reese pried his paws off the opening and shoved him inside, she covered the grated carrier door with his favorite mackerel-print towel to calm his rattled nerves.

Inside the waiting area of East Mayfair Veterinary Hospital, she was met with the familiar scent of various pets and disinfectant cleanser, which made Sinbad more anxious inside his carrier. A few yowls and growls echoed from other rooms. "It's okay," Reese whispered to relax Sinbad. "I promise you, there are no shots today. And I'm sure they don't need to extract a urine sample, so you're good." She checked in at the front desk and took a seat. The place had separate waiting and treatment areas for cats and dogs. She and Sinbad had endured quite the harrowing waiting-area experience with a nasty, unleashed Rottweiler at the previous veterinary hospital.

In this cat-owners' waiting area, a woman on the loveseat held on her lap a striking Birman she called Binky. Binky, whose distinctive deep blue eyes were set in a dark mask and filled with condescension, stared at Sinbad as if to say "get a grip." Unlike Sinbad, Binky was not at all bothered by his (or her) trip to the vet.

"Ms. Sommers," the staffer at the front desk said. "Did you complete the new patient form online?"

"I'm sorry. No, I didn't." Reese had heard so many good things about this place she'd immediately booked an appointment. She'd planned to do more research on the doctors before arriving, but after the drama this past weekend, it had slipped her mind.

"Not a problem. You can complete the forms now, and we'll have," the woman looked at the sign-in sheet, "Sinbad's records transferred from his previous vet."

Reese completed the forms and peered through the carrier's grated door. As expected, Sinbad incessantly licked his lips. That and copious wisps of shed fur were signs he was terrified. "It's okay. It's going to be okay." She slipped fingers inside the carrier to stroke the area between his huge green eyes.

"We're ready for Sinbad," another young female staffer said soon after Binky and owner had been escorted to an examining room.

As Reese waited, she answered more questions about Sinbad. Removing him from the carrier was more difficult than getting him in it. Reese likened it to shaking a large cotton ball out of the narrow opening of a pill bottle. With the aide holding the carrier Reese tugged Sinbad out without dislocating his joints, which was quite a feat, considering he had managed to lock his legs against the sides. "Going for a weigh-in and temperature check," the aide said, reaching for him. "We'll be right back."

A short time later the young woman returned with Sinbad and Reese's hunky new neighbor.

CHAPTER 5

What a way to start a Monday morning! Gabriel stepped inside examining room B and laid eyes on the stunning Reese Sommers.

The vet tech departed.

Gabriel extended his hand for a shake. "Reese and Sinbad. Nice to see you two again." Without appearing too stalker-like, he'd kept an eye out and ears primed for her all weekend while supervising the movers and working to make a deadline for his side gig.

With men hauling furniture and opening boxes around him, Gabriel had been writing and illustrating his work in progress, the next installment of *The Adventures of Abraham & Zephyrus*, his middle-grade book series about the humorous exploits of a boy and his crime-solving dog. It was a wonder he'd made progress on it because he couldn't stop thinking about Reese. He couldn't help wondering if he'd been too forward, inquiring about her marital status and inviting her out for coffee. *But, oh, man!* He couldn't help himself.

He wanted to cheer after discovering she wasn't somebody's wife. However, he had to temper his excitement because the fact that she wasn't yet married did not mean there wasn't a significant other. Such a woman unattached? Could he be that lucky?

Reese had been welcoming, but was she interested in more than cordial, but brief interactions with the newest resident of Mistywood Lane?

When he'd arrived at his house early the morning of their first meeting, he'd found her frightened cat huddled on his porch. Because the cat wasn't wearing ID tags, Gabriel had planned to knock on a few Mistywood Lane doors to find its owner. If that had failed, he would've brought him to the hospital and scanned for a microchip. He hadn't expected to have his breath snatched away and his senses scrambled at the first house he'd visited. The way that skimpy red dress had skimmed over her body he knew there wasn't a damn thing but mouthwatering curves and satiny, café au lait skin underneath, which wreaked all kinds of havoc on his cool. It took everything he had not to ogle her lush breasts and the erect nipples pressing against soft fabric, taunting him: *Welcome to Mistywood Lane, Gabriel! Have a taste!*

Keep eyes well above the neck. Keep eyes well above the neck, Gabriel had willed himself as the two had swapped pleasantries about Sinbad and the neighborhood. His body had experienced such a potent reaction he feared she might have noticed, but she'd also kept her gaze above the neck. At that moment, he knew if she was available and the least bit intrigued by him, making love to her would be a goal. He'd do whatever it took to achieve it. Since, he'd lost his virginity at fifteen, he'd had his share of experiences with females, but he couldn't recall having such an instant and overwhelming reaction before. Even with his most recent ex.

Reese, however, had shown no sign the powerful physical attraction was mutual. It was a bit chilly that morning so he could take no credit for her erect nipples. But, hmmp, he could hope.

"Gabriel?" Reese interrupted his reverie.

"Sorry, I haven't had my coffee yet."

"What are you doing here?" Reese's gaze flickered to the stethoscope around his neck and then to the stitched lettering on his polo shirt, which read East Mayfair Veterinary Hospital. "You work here?"

"I do."

"You're the veterinarian?"

"One of them."

"You're not dressed like—"

"We're a jeans-and-polo-shirt-and-T-shirt kind of place. We believe it makes our clients— humans and their companion animals—feel more comfortable. First-name basis all around. There's no *doctor* this or *doctor* that. Though we have all of our veterinary medicine degrees and credentials of course, no formal labels. And no scrubs, no white coat syndrome. It's very casual. Coming to the vet is stressful enough. We do all we can to ease that, starting with separate canine and cat entrances, waiting areas, and holding sections."

"The day you returned Sinbad, why didn't you mention you work with animals?"

"I don't go around announcing that to every pet owner I encounter." He grinned.

"Ah, afraid they might try to coax free medical advice out of you?"

Gabriel rubbed Sinbad's neck and ears, but leveled his gaze at Reese. "Sinbad and I keep running into one another. And by extension, let's just say I think the universe is telling us something." Was he coming on too strong again? Too smarmy? Too Lance Donovan? *Don't unnerve the woman with forwardness too soon.*

"Oh?"

"Yes, the universe is telling us I'm the top-notch veterinary practitioner for Sinbad." Gabriel modified what he was about to say.

"And living right next door he's sure to expect house calls."

"I'd be amenable to that." Gabriel was glad Reese said what he was thinking. "So, it looks as if this is your first visit. Or have you seen one of my partners?" Gabriel had failed to check the chart before entering the room so he gave it a glance.

"Partners?"

"I'm one of four vets here," Gabriel said. "One is part-time. But my two best friends and I are equal, full-time partners."

It wouldn't have occurred to Julian to mention Reese. He was still struggling with his grief over losing his wife. However, it most certainly would have occurred to Lance. He mentioned all clients of the female, drop-dead-gorgeous variety. He would've catalogued and detailed this particular pet mom's many delectable assets.

"Yes, it's a first visit." Reese placed her big tote bag on the floor. With the motion, her necklace and its little cupcake charm swayed. The T-shirt's neckline gaped just enough to offer a peek at full, smooth cleavage. As the memory of their hardened tips in the morning breeze resurfaced, his pulse quickened and his jaw clenched.

"A friend recommended this place." When Reese sat upright again, the V-neck fell back into place, but the pendant rested between perfect twin mounds.

Fool, stop gawking like you've never seen breasts before! Gabriel gave himself a mental shake and then focused on her pretty eyes. "Mind if I ask who referred you? We give credits to clients who bring new business."

"Linda Anderson."

26

"Ah, yes, Tequila's owner."

"So how's the move coming along?"

"I'd say I'm settled in, except for a few boxes. It already feels like home."

"Good."

"I was sitting on my porch Sunday morning," he told her, but left out the part about how he had hoped to see her again. "Your friend Odette came by. She brought me a basket of warm homemade blueberry muffins and a Thermos of hot gourmet coffee like you said she would."

"Hope you two had a nice chat."

"She told me a few things about her family and the neighborhood. I told her a little about myself, but I'm afraid I'm not that interesting. The visit was short. Her husband...Calvin? He came to fetch her. Nice guy, by the way. He invited me to golf sometime. Cute twins, too."

"Yes, you'll like the Carmichaels. Calvin's laid-back energy complements Odette's gregariousness. The twins are prone to mischief, but oh, so adorable, with those dimples, big brown eyes, and gumdrop noses..." She hugged herself. "I just want to squeeze the stuffing out of them!"

"Do you have kids?"

"Not yet, just my fur baby here. You?"

"Not yet, but someday I want a starting lineup —point guard, shooting guard, small forward, power forward and center—"

"For your basketball team."

Gabriel's heart did a little skipping number. He'd assumed it would be a while before a woman made him feel that sensation again. Now all he wanted to do was pull up a chair next to Reese and get his full-out flirt on.

But this was his place of business. As best he could, he'd strive to keep this interaction professional, though her sweet fragrance stirred impulses to do otherwise. "So, what's up with Sinbad today?" He reached for the ophthalmoscope and otoscope on a nearby wall mount.

Reese took the next few minutes to detail what she described as "the recurring dirt spot" on Sinbad's chin. She'd scrubbed it several times only to have it return and spread.

Gabriel examined the area speckled with what resembled coffee grounds. "It's acne."

"Acne? Cats get acne?"

"Yep. They have follicles that clog with sebum."

"Sinbad's twelve. That's, like, what in people years?"

"Yes, we have a senior citizen here."

"I don't like to think of him as a senior. He'll always be my baby, but acne?"

"Keep in mind, people of all ages get acne, too. It's not limited to teenagers."

"Right."

"And it could be worse."

"Tell me about it. For a minute I thought he had fleas again," Reese said with a comical shriek, jolting an obviously antsy Sinbad.

"This does resemble flea dirt." Gabriel examined the area again, raking it with a flea comb he'd removed from a nearby drawer.

"I know it well. He got them when I went away for a week to vacation with my family and left him at one of those fancy boarding places. Huge mistake. He came home crawling with them. What is flea dirt?"

"You really want to know?" he asked, thinking of all the other things he'd rather talk about, such as the way sunlight pouring through the window highlighted her caramel-colored eyes, flawless skin, and thick dark curls. He admired her full lips with a deep, perfect cupid's bow he'd kill to kiss. Again, he gazed at curves accentuated by her form-fitting top. His groin tightened. Not the time nor the place so he told her flea dirt was feces, composed of blood digested, then expelled.

"Yuck." Reese screwed up her lovely face. "Sorry I asked. Let's go back to calling it dirt, shall we?"

Gabriel marveled at the way Reese managed to exude extreme hotness and goofy adorability at the same time.

"If it were flea dirt, he'd have it all over, not just on his chin, correct?"

Gabriel nodded as he checked additional areas for fleas. "You might see it around the neck or rectum. And he'd bite and scratch a lot more."

"So how do we treat this, doc?"

"Benzoyl peroxide gel or shampoo should keep it in check. You can purchase those at the front desk. And try to keep the area clean. Do we have Sinbad's previous records on file? Is he current on all vaccines?"

"He already had his thorough yearly exam. Everything's A-OK. Complete files to come."

Gabriel scanned Sinbad's new chart again. Though Reese said he'd had his annual exam, he checked the cat's eyes, ears, mouth, nose, skin, and other body parts.

"I didn't have his front claws removed," she repeated, still sounding defensive regarding the controversial procedure. "I adopted him when he was six months old. He came to me that way."

Though Sinbad didn't enjoy the exam, he remained pliable as Gabriel poked, stroked, prodded, pressed, and rubbed. No flattened ears, hissing, or tail thrashing. Just before Gabriel completed his inspection, he comically lifted Sinbad as if he were bicep curling a ton. "We need to discuss Sinbad's diet."

Reese groaned. "Aww. Not you, too. My sisters constantly tease me about indulging him too much."

"Did your previous vet talk to you about it?"

"He might have mentioned something a time or two."

"It's obvious you love Sinbad." Gabriel had to tread carefully. When it came to discussing pet obesity, owners tended to remain in denial after the problem was pointed out to them. Of all the dogs and cats he and his partners treated, a good fifty percent could stand to lose a few pounds.

"I don't think Sinbad eats that much," Reese said. "Yes, he has a good appetite. He's hale and hearty."

Roly and *poly* was more like it, but Gabriel bit his tongue.

"It's not as if he's raiding the fridge and cabinets, making himself towering sub sandwiches, you know."

"But you leave plenty of food out for him to graze all day whenever he feels like it?"

"Of course. I work long days."

Gabriel didn't want to sermonize. Instead, he kept it brief, emphasizing Sinbad's diet could go a long way in extending his good years, helping him avoid problems such as diabetes and arthritis.

"I'm not putting him on any crash diet," she said.

"No, that's not good for Sinbad, either." Gabriel passed her some nutrition literature from the nearby rack on the wall. "Read this. When I've seen his records from your previous vet we'll chat. Deal?"

"Deal."

"Anything else?" Again, he wanted to ask her to join him for coffee at the Sweet Spot. But he'd already made his personal interest in her obvious. He'd wait for their first mailbox meeting.

"That's it." Reese came to her feet and opened the carrier door for Sinbad, who scurried inside. If the cat could've slammed and bolted the door behind himself, he would have. Reese hitched her tote bag on one shoulder and held the carrier.

"I'll walk you to the front." Gabriel wanted to extend the visit until he met with his next client in fifteen minutes and run interception in case Reese caught Lance's eye. After Gabriel had staked his claim, Lance would steer clear.

While Lance was the big player of the three friends, he respected boundaries and followed "bro code" when it came to women. Gabriel and his two partners, who had run this hospital for nearly a decade, had met in their vet program at their alma mater and were now as close as brothers. These days Gabriel often felt more connected to them than to his biological brother who only made it back to Mayfair once a year, usually around Christmas or during one of his few breaks in a heavy work schedule.

As Gabriel strolled down the hall of the nearly 4,000 square-foot facility, he made note of various pet clients. A cat named Flash, with a head injury, was attached to an IV, which made Gabriel think of having seen Caesar on the canine side of the building. Caesar, a husky, had been sprawled on a rug, sleeping off anesthesia after having surgery for the herniated abdominal wall and fractured rib cartilage he'd sustained during a fight with a neighborhood dog.

The hospital had six vet assistants, seven licensed vet techs, and four receptionists. Staff doctors worked long shifts. Myles Novak, who specialized in advanced dental issues, worked with them part time. Julian often handled their abbreviated, early morning weekend hours. During off hours clients were referred to two of the area's emergency vet care facilities.

Lance left examining room D and strode down the hallway. He greeted both, but did a goggle-eyed take of Reese, just as Gabriel had assumed he would. Lance's voice deepened a couple of octaves as it usually did when he was around an attractive female. His eyes glittered with lustful interest.

"Ms. Sommers, this is one of my partners, Lance Donovan," Gabriel said.

"*Doctor* Lance Donovan, the charming and handsome one." Lance preferred to trot out the doctor designation for the hottest ladies as he unleashed his ear-to-ear—all white teeth and tonsils.

"So there are *two* charming and handsome ones," Reese replied gamely.

"Well, Dr. Phillips hasn't arrived yet," Lance said.

"Dr. Phillips?" she asked.

"Our partner, Julian Phillips," Gabriel clarified for her.

"Oh, but I meant Dr. Cameron here," Reese said to Lance.

Lance nodded and gave Gabriel a telling look. Message sent and received. Lance could can the lothario routine. The lady had made her preference clear. Well, her choice of veterinary practitioners clear.

All but pushing out his chest, Gabriel smiled. "Ms. Sommers here—"

"That sounds so formal when things are so casual here," she said. "Call me Reese."

"Reese is one of my new neighbors," Gabriel told Lance. "She brought us Sinbad and his feline acne."

"We appreciate your business," Lance said. "And hello, Sinbad." He lifted the towel and peeked inside the carrier. "And Sinbad's acne. Welcome to the East Mayfair Veterinary Hospital family."

"Nice to meet you, too," Reese said.

She and Gabriel continued making their way to the front, where she finished her business at the check-out window.

So, Reese had told Lance she found Gabriel "handsome and charming." A sign of personal interest? This gave Gabriel the confidence needed to go for a little more. He broke protocol and asked if he could escort Reese to her car.

"I'm over there." She pointed to a VW Beetle two-door coupe, as shiny and red as a maraschino cherry. The kind of cute car he expected her to drive. She activated its key fob.

Gabriel opened the driver's side door. When she turned, adjusted the front seat, and leaned inside to secure the carrier onto the back seat, he admired her curvy back seat. After she settled behind the wheel, he passed her the bag containing the shampoo gel and nutrition pamphlets. "As Lance said, we appreciate your business."

"I can see that," Reese lilted. "Going the extra mile, seeing pets and owners to their cars. And even carrying their bags and all."

"Not exactly a mile, a few yards." Gabriel closed her door and bent at the waist to lean at the now open window. "About what you said in there…I don't want to put you on the spot."

"But you will anyway," she said, lips tipping up at the corners. "The handsome and the charming thing?"

"If that was just a defensive move to deflect his—"

"Not just a defensive move."

"To be honest, though it's a place of business, I can't blame him for trying to unleash that 'Dashing Donovan charisma' on you."

"So *that's* what he was doing?" Reese played coy.

"His words, definitely *not* mine."

31

"Ol' Lance really needs to come out of his shell, huh?" Reese laughed, a sound Gabriel hoped to hear often.

"Yeah, so shy, that one."

"So what if you're playing up to me so I'll tell the rest of Mistywood Lane what a fine veterinary establishment you're running here." She started the engine.

"Anything to drum up more business and possibly get you to accept an invitation to join me for coffee at the Sweet Spot one day soon."

Before Gabriel could get a reply, a car resembling a box with wheels pulled into the lot. Mrs. Myers, his next appointment. *Damn her timing.* Muriel, her chocolate lab, had gobbled up a wedding ring set left on a coffee table. While Muriel was in no obvious distress, Gabriel would do an X-ray to calm Mrs. Myers' fear that the four-carat diamond had lodged somewhere that could cause serious health problems. After that, he'd advise Mrs. Myers to inspect all of Muriel's bowel moments. *She'll love that.* That ring set should reappear in approximately one to three days.

"Duty calls." Reese watched Mrs. Myers climb out of the car with Muriel. "Thanks for everything. See ya soon."

"At the Sweet Spot?"

"I'd prefer the mailboxes, for now," Reese said before pulling out of the parking lot.

So while the Sweet Spot was still a no-go, she found Gabriel "charming and handsome." And he hadn't missed that "for now" she'd dangled at the end. That left him brimming with hope. He couldn't wait for their next Mistywood Lane postal delivery.

CHAPTER 6

The next morning, Gabriel made a stop at the Sweet Spot. One of their vet techs was relocating to California so the staff had planned a send-off party. Their office manager had assigned the cupcakes to Gabriel because he passed the shop on his way to the hospital.

He found a parking space close to the storefront and stepped up to the counter. The delicious mingled aromas of coffee and sweet and buttery baked goods surrounded him. At least fifty types of cupcakes—everything from the traditional red velvet, carrot, cookies and cream, coconut, German chocolate, and banana split to the gastronomically audacious orange/chili/peppermint-mix and curry/salted caramel/ rum/pistachio-mix cupcakes— sat on display. A gluten-free section flanked them. All mini domes of art. Baskets of scones, muffins, and biscotti lined the area near the register.

He'd buy at least one of every cupcake flavor. He hadn't eaten breakfast and his stomach growled at the sight and scent of so many tantalizing treats. Then somebody called his name.

Linda Anderson, a longtime client, stood behind the counter waving at him.

"How are you and Tequila?" Gabriel asked the older woman. She had an infectious gap-toothed smile and often sweetened her speech with "honey" and "sugar," giving off that folksy auntie air.

"Fine, but it's almost time for his annual physical. Cup of coffee, hon? It's on me."

"I'd love it," Gabriel said. "Your darkest roast, please."

Reese emerged from the back of the shop carrying a big box she almost dropped when she saw Gabriel.

"Well, hello there," Gabriel said, still chucking cool out the window and putting his elation on full display. "All these familiar faces. This must be my lucky day."

"Hey, you!" Reese placed the box on a nearby counter. "Welcome to the Sweet Spot."

"So you work here, too?" Gabriel asked.

"It's her place, hon," Linda said.

"Oh, it is, is it?" Gabriel said, eyeing Reese.

"Yep. This is my place." Reese gave him a coquettish smile.

"Gabriel and I were just chatting," Linda added. "He's Tequila's vet."

"Remember, I told you, it was Linda who referred me to your vet hospital," Reese said.

"Yes, but you said nothing about being the owner when I mentioned the Sweet Spot, what, oh, about a dozen times," Gabriel replied with mock indignation.

"Not a dozen." Reese chuckled. "You exaggerate. Besides, a girl's gotta keep some secrets, for at least a minute or two."

"Ah, a woman of mystery," Gabriel said.

"So you already took Sinbad to his practice?" Linda said, passing Gabriel a tall cup of coffee. "Why, you never said a word."

"It slipped my mind," Reese replied breezily, her gaze still on Gabriel. "We've been so busy around here."

"Is that right?" Linda was now all atwitter, like a proud matchmaker, sure she'd provided the kindling for the obvious spark between Reese and Gabriel. A connection that went beyond a mutual interest in Sinbad's health. Linda's neck swiveled back and forth from Gabriel to Reese several times over in a matter of seconds.

"I'm sure to make this a regular pit stop for coffee on my way to work," Gabriel said. Reese looked more beautiful each time he saw her. That morning she wore a Sweet Spot T-shirt, lightweight white sweater, and black slacks. Her shoulder-length dark curls were in a ponytail. "This morning I'm stocking up on cupcakes. Six dozen. I'll take a mix of every flavor. We're having a little send-off party for one of the techs, but I'd like a few for the clients, the human ones of course."

"Oh? Which tech is leaving?" Linda asked. "Gabriel?"

"Huh."

"Which tech?"

"Oh, I'm sorry," said Gabriel, transfixed by Reese. "Brandi. Brandi's leaving."

"Aww. I'll miss her." With her attention zipping between Gabriel and Reese, Linda managed to fill boxes with his cupcakes.

"Throw in a dozen scones, too," Gabriel said.

Reese rang up the order. "I've already applied the ointment you gave me for Sinbad."

"Ointment? What ointment?" Linda asked.

"Good, you'll have his little acne problem cleared up in no time." Gabriel took a sip of his coffee.

"So that spot you mentioned was acne?" Linda pried.

"Yes." Reese said. She and Gabriel continued smiling at each other as if Linda and the rest of the world had faded away.

"Did you read those nutrition brochures, by chance?" Gabriel asked Reese.

"Not yet, but I will."

"Nutrition brochures?" Linda asked, finally breaking through again.

"Gabriel thinks Sinbad needs to lose a few pounds," Reese replied, still gazing back at Gabriel.

"Well, Sinbad is a little on the…" Linda started.

Reese tore her attention away from Gabriel to look at Linda. "Go on. Sinbad's a little on the… What?"

"Scones!" Linda said. "We need more scones. Now's a good time to go fetch them."

Reese and Gabriel laughed as they watched Linda scurry toward the back.

Gabriel tasted his coffee again. "This is damn good, lady. So how long have you been in business?"

"Nearly four years," Reese said.

"Great setup." Gabriel took in the gleaming commercial espresso machine, the long display case, and the large chalkboard menu busy with multicolored scribbling. Upholstered chairs, loveseats with pillows, wooden tables, and hardwood floors in the seating section brought to mind a cozy cabin living room. The fireplace, though not lit at the moment, would make the area especially inviting on chillier days.

The bakery's neutral palette and subtle lighting contrasted with the overly bright, juvenile cutesiness in another cupcake bakery across town.

Calming contemporary jazz flowed from the sound system. The setting ensured a variety of people, customers such as the thirty-something-business-attired man in the corner and the white-haired gentleman sitting in that plaid chair that matched his shirt, would linger over print editions of the *Mayfair Tribune* and coffee.

Gabriel walked to the corkboard tacked with assorted cards from various local businesses. "I'm very impressed with what you've done here."

"Thank you. Hey, put your hospital's card on the board."

As Gabriel added to the collage, he noticed the sign asking customers to vote for the Sweet Spot at a popular online site: DetoursMayfair.com annual Best of Mayfair list.

"We've been nominated for the Best Bakery finals category twice," Reese said. "Placed, but we've never won. The shop is still relatively new."

"Maybe this is your year." Gabriel removed his phone from his pocket and surfed to the contest site. "I'll show my support right now." He typed and swiped on the specialty bakery category. "There. You have my vote. If you have an extra flyer or two I'll put them up in the hospital. While you're at it, I'd like a little deck of business cards, too."

"Thank you. That's so nice of you."

"Since I moved to this part of town I've been in here at least a dozen times. Why am I just seeing you and Linda?"

"Good timing today. I have a decent-size staff so there's some rotation with the workers. I spend a lot of time out here, but there are plenty of office and kitchen duties, too."

"Right." Though Linda had returned and placed his order on the counter, Gabriel wasn't ready to leave.

An awkward silence settled among the three of them, all wearing silly grins.

"Well, I'd better get going," Gabriel said. "See ya around, neighbor."

"Neighbor?" Linda's asked, her eyes wider. "You two are neighbors? Since when?"

"Yes, brand-new neighbors," Reese said.

Gabriel gathered up his boxes of treats and attempted to balance his cup of coffee.

"Let me help you with those." Reese separated the boxes and placed them inside large shopping bags. She passed one to him and kept the other.

Linda gawked at the pair as they stepped outside. Among the many shops and eateries in the high-foot-traffic area were a barber shop, post office, a small concert venue, and a library branch. People shopping, tending to business, or heading to work hurried along the sidewalks.

"One good turn," Reese said as she followed him to his SUV. "Remember, you walked me to my car. And you voted for my shop. For future reference, there's free delivery for orders of one hundred dollars or more. And we do catering, everything from whimsical to elegant displays to suit any occasion. End of sales pitch."

Her willingness to help with his order, even as her shop filled with customers, was yet another promising sign. After all, she could've asked Linda to assist him, or she could've dispensed with top-rate customer service altogether and let him make two or three trips to his SUV.

As if self-conscious about the gesture, Reese launched into small talk. "Nice weather we're having, eh?"

"Yeah, it is."

"I enjoyed my run in to work this morning."

"You run here?"

"Some days I do. I had a shower added to my office restroom for that reason. But I count nothing less than a mile in my weekly tally."

"I run, too. Love it." Fearing he'd come off too pushy, Gabriel refrained from inviting her to join him.

"It's the perfect way to relieve stress and ensure I don't end up wearing all the sweets I consume daily. Occupational hazard. I have to keep these in check." Reese's hands skimmed along her curvy hips.

Another vehicle pulled in front of his and two women got out and entered the Sweet Spot.

"I'd better get back inside," Reese said.

"Hey, if you like, I can check on Sinbad's chin when we meet at the mailboxes."

"Sinbad would like that." Reese strolled back toward the shop.

"Just Sinbad?"

Reese opened her door, jingling the bell, and then looked over her shoulder. "Sinbad's mom would like that, too."

CHAPTER 7

$\mathbf{R}$eese had flirted. Shamelessly. But already?

This took her by surprise as she washed her hands, donned an apron, and prepared to whip up fresh batches of cake batter in the Sweet Spot kitchen. When she was with Gabriel, Darren's betrayal hurt a lot less. Gabriel radiated a perfect balance of confidence, persistence, kindness, and sex appeal she found impossible to resist. She welcomed the distraction.

While alone the past two weeks, she'd cried over crushed dreams. And the memory of Sasha doubled over in pain still disturbed her. Reese had to admit she was curious about the woman's condition. She wanted no harm to come to Sasha or that unborn child.

Instead of fighting back her emotion, however, she'd viewed her tears as needed cleansing, a mental purge of the life she'd dreamed of having with Darren. *Good riddance.*

Still, she thought about Gabriel a lot. Too much?

At 30, Reese was no fickle school girl. But she'd never been one to wallow in self-pity for long. After a boy or man had made it clear he didn't want her, she wasn't one to hang on or mope for months. The time a person pined or grieved for a failed relationship was not directly proportional to the depth of their love, but directly proportional to his or her sense of self. Confident and secure people were more likely to get on with life and not sink into a long, self-flagellating cycle of woulda-coulda-shouldas.

Or the death knell: *What's so wrong with me that he (or she) couldn't love me more?*

38

With a battered heart and bruised ego, Reese would bid adieu to a guy and keep it moving. Her sisters often joked about her unfaltering positivity regarding matters of the heart.

"You read way too many romance novels," Quinn would gripe.

But Reese refused to morph into one of those women, with hand to heavy heart, who declared, "I shall never ever love again" because of one, two, three…or even a dozen bad apples. She had friends and family members in successful, loving relationships. Reese would have the same eventually. In the meantime, the best way to get over one man was to get under another one. What about getting under Gabriel Cameron's hot bod? It was clear he was just as attracted to her as she was to him. Should she go for it?

***

The next day, a breathtaking sunrise painted the sky peach, red, and orange. Reese and Sinbad ate their breakfast on her patio. With her cat in her arms, she brushed and combed him. After checking and clipping his hind claws, she answered a text. Darren had left dozens of messages since that awful night. There was nothing more to say. He'd deceived her and offered tired apologies to boot. It was over. She'd already gathered up every gift and photo of him she'd displayed around her house and dumped them in the trash. She'd also deleted their joint Post-a-Pic account.

Reese's cellphone rang. Darren. Again.

She needed the answer to one question only so she texted it: *Are Sasha and the baby all right?*

When her phone rang Darren's number flashed on it.

Reese texted him instead: *I don't want to talk to you. Text the answer.*

Darren complied: *Both are doing well.*

Reese: *Good. If you ever cared about me at all don't reach out to me again. Please leave me alone. That's all I ask.*

Darren: *I am so sorry for the way I handled everything.* He attached that sad-faced emoji and a broken heart.

Reese didn't reply to his last text. *The nerve.*

Without listening to his voicemail messages, she'd deleted them and blocked his phone numbers as a knot swelled in her throat. *Shake him off. A good run would help.*

Reese put on her running gear and slathered on sunscreen. She had time for a three-to-five-mile run before heading to the Sweet Spot.

Standing in her driveway, she inhaled the cool morning air laced with a hint of Odette's roses and honeysuckle. Reese warmed up with a jog in place and maneuvered into a few hamstring and quadriceps stretches. Wearing earbuds attached to the iPod in her hand, neighbor Shireen Davis approached, her power walk form reminiscent of the North Korean military march. "Hey, Reese!"

"Hey, Shireen!" Reese quickened her jogging in place.

"We can count on your sponsorship again this year, right?"

Reese stretched her quadriceps. "Well, actually—"

"Your cupcakes were such a hit last year, girly! I'm sure they helped us reach our record-breaking goal!" Once again, Shireen reported to the penny how much money they'd raised.

Reese had donated cupcakes to the annual Mayfair Garden Club fundraiser for the past two years. It had started with an early morning conversation about a barter arrangement. Reese would provide cupcakes for the garden club luncheon and in exchange, Shireen, president of the club, would help Reese start and tend to a small flower garden.

Reese had done her part, but Shireen had yet to come to Reese's house with so much as a trowel and a single packet of flower seeds. Reese had not made an issue of it because the fundraiser was for a worthy cause, raising money for the care and maintenance of a memorial garden honoring local veterans. *"Still, a deal is a damn deal,"* Quinn groused when Reese mentioned Shireen had defaulted on their arrangement. *"So tell that heifer she owes you!"* But Reese didn't want to come off self-serving by pestering Shireen about it so she focused on the veterans, who had given up so much to serve their country. What were a few Lemon Lust cupcakes in comparison? And she liked Shireen, who had not once tried to pump Reese for details about that terrible night. She was sure their deal had slipped Shireen's mind. All she needed was a little prompting.

"Can we expect your help this year?" Shireen asked.

"Remember when we made the deal?" Reese did overhead stretches for the triceps. "You said you'd—"

"Can we get extra Lemon Lust?" Shireen interrupted. "Those went the fastest last year. I'll call you with the date and details for this year's event. You're such a sweetheart!" Though Reese had not committed to anything, off Shireen went, goose stepping to her usual Mozart playlist.

Dressed in shorts, tank top, and running shoes, Gabriel stepped onto his porch. Just when Reese thought the man couldn't look sexier. His mirrored sunglasses complemented his lean, angular face. *Hmmp*. Workout wear highlighted his broad bronzed shoulders, chiseled chest, and long, muscular legs. Her pulse, already elevated from jogging in place, kicked up a few notches. She almost didn't notice the two large dogs circling him.

"So you're in the camp who believes in stretching before a run," Gabriel called out to Reese.

"Not before a moderate warmup," she replied.

"I'm in the post-run camp, when the muscles are primed for a good stretch." Gabriel jogged toward her.

"Beautiful dogs." One of them rushed to Reese and nudged its wet nose against her palm.

"Reese, meet Apollo," Gabriel said. "Apollo, Reese."

A stunning golden retriever.

"And this is Maximus."

"What is he? Wait." Reese examined his distinguishing features. "A black lab. Wow! He's so handsome. Look at that gorgeous gleaming coat!"

Reese patted both dogs, whose tails wagged with enthusiasm.

"So what kind of run are you doing this morning, lady?"

"Short. About three-to-five miles."

"Do you usually run alone?"

"As in do I *prefer* to run alone? I enjoy the solitude so I can get into the zone with my iPod."

"Same here. But—"

"Company can be nice, too," Reese said.

"Yes. As long as—"

"Said company doesn't yak too much." She chuckled.

"Agreed. So what do you say?"

"I say, let's go! Give me a sec. Let me put my iPod away." She tucked the device, not much bigger than a postage stamp, inside her shorts pocket.

Gabriel put his away, too.

The pair took off. Maximus and Apollo ran beside them, only veering occasionally to chase squirrels. The loop around the subdivision's pond with ducks and frogs challenged them, but the well-trained dogs were not diverted for long.

As promised, Reese and Gabriel kept conversation to a minimum. They found a synchronized rhythm as if they'd been running together forever. After reaching her target heart rate, she flew over the sidewalks and grass as a light breeze caressed her face. *Paradise.*

Back on Mistywood Lane, both walked in circles on his wide front lawn as their heart rates gradually dropped to normal.

"Be right back." Buzzed on endorphins, Reese stepped inside her house to get two bottles of water from the fridge while Gabriel completed his thorough post-run stretching session.

"Good run." Reese collapsed on the grass beside him. She could get used to having a fine man running beside her. Though her father had enrolled the Sommers girls in mixed martial arts and target shooting courses when they were teens and the Granberry Ridge community had a low-crime rate, potential hazards lurked for a woman out alone. She never left home without pepper spray attached to the band of her shorts. She'd slip into a meditative state for a few seconds, but she never went so deep in the zone that she wasn't aware of her surroundings.

With Gabriel she felt free. And completely safe.

"So how often do you run?" With obvious appreciation, Gabriel gazed at her legs, muscles warm and joints oiled from their four-mile run.

"At least five days a week, but if I don't get outdoors, I use a treadmill in my workout room to get in my cardio, not my preference." Desire whispered through Reese as she admired the way his broad, sculpted shoulders tapered into a trim waist. There was most definitely a six-pack or eight-pack underneath that tank top. Cut granite thighs flexed above strong diamond-shaped calves as he stretched and released his muscles.

"Ever done a race?" he asked.

"Huh?" A bead of sweat rolling along the vein of his steel bicep had mesmerized her.

"A race? Done one?"

"I have. A few."

"Me, too."

They swapped details on their races and personal records as Reese checked the data about her pace and heart rate on her GPS sports watch. "You're incredible," she said of his race record.

"You're no slouch," he replied. "I enjoyed running with you."

"Same here. An occasional running partner might be what I need to take my training to the next level. Now that I know your numbers, dude, you were crawling with me."

"And so were you, apparently," he said.

"I'm not a show-off, but next time…"

Gabriel laughed. "I can't wait."

Before Reese could agree Ari Papadopoulos zipped by on one of those hoverboards banned by the HOA for use on Granberry Ridge sidewalks and streets. She'd endured her own HOA woes. No way would she snitch on Ari.

"I thought about getting one of those," Gabriel said of the self-balancing, two-wheeled scooter.

"What held you back?"

"Besides the HOA? Visions of a traumatic head injury, internal bleeding, and broken limbs."

Apollo and Maximus frolicked together until Reese and Gabriel began tussling with them. Reese rolled around on the grass as the dogs licked her face. Nothing like an onslaught of dog breath at your nose and ears. Big fun. Consuela Lopez waved as she strolled by with Conchita, her Malti-poo. Though Apollo and Maximus stared, eyes wide, ears high, the pair didn't bark, growl, or charge to protect their turf.

"They're very well behaved." Reese's voice hitched with awe. "I'm a diehard, card-carrying member of the feline fanatics club, but I love these guys already!"

"I'm happy to hear that. Sinbad is cool, too."

"I think he likes you. Not clicking with Sinbad is a deal breaker, ya know."

"Oh, really?"

"Yes, I once dated a guy who was so allergic his eyes swelled and welled up just looking at photos of Sinbad. He had to go."

"The guy you mean?"

"Yup."

"So you kicked him to the curb for that?"

"That and the fact that his mother used to spy on us, faking surprise and using the ol' 'fancy meeting you two here' ruse."

When Gabriel chuckled, Reese did, too. Both had fallen back on the grass. As Reese took in the blue sky with its loose weave of contrails, the customary personal space between her and Gabriel closed. He'd rolled on his side and propped his head up with one hand; the other rested on her hip as he looked deep into her eyes. "You're breathtaking," he said with heart-stopping reverence.

"I think that's an aftereffect of your run, but thank you," Reese replied as endorphins, now mingled with lust, careened through her body. "You're not so bad yourself." The butterflies in her belly descended, creating a warm, fluttering sensation between her thighs every time he was near. It was a potent, almost feral need, she didn't recall ever feeling with...*Darren who? Whoa.* She might have to thank Darren for the way things turned out. What was that old saying? Karma's only a bitch if you are. So she thanked God for the special delivery of Gabriel Cameron, the most appealing distraction, to the home next door. He plucked a blade of grass to brush along her leg. The tickle ignited a blaze within her. Were neighbors watching? Who cares? She considered tasting his lips, which she suspected had a sweet-salty deliciousness after their run. His eyes darkened as he stared at her mouth. He wanted to kiss her, too. Her heart hammered in her chest. The dogs played tug of war with a chew toy. Reese and Gabriel moved to close the last bit of space between them. A vehicle pulled into Gabriel's driveway, possibly a lost driver using the space for a convenient one-eighty.

Reese's anticipation escalated as Gabriel leaned closer. *He's going for it.*

Only millimeters away... *Oh, yes, the brush of his lips against mine...*

Interrupted when a gorgeous woman bounded out of the white SUV in his driveway. "Morning, Gabe!"

CHAPTER 8

Adriana!" When Gabriel shot to his feet, smoothing his tank top, and swiping at nonexistent grass on his shorts, Reese scrambled up, too.

"I tried to call first," this Adriana Out-of-Nowhere said. "When I didn't get an answer, I took a chance, thinking you hadn't left for the hospital yet."

Ears up and tails wagging, Maximus and Apollo bolted toward Adriana, jumping on her, licking her as if she'd bathed in meat drippings.

"Reese," Gabriel said, "This is Adriana. Adriana, Reese is one of my new neighbors."

"Hi, Reese!" Bubbly Adriana pumped Reese's hand with a vigorous two-handed grip. "So nice to meet you! Great neighborhood! And that pond I drove by is so beautiful and serene! I love the ducks and thick ridges of mossy trees! Perfect for dog walks and meditation!"

Adriana's over-exuberance...natural or over-caffeinated? She had that speech pattern in which each sentence ended as if it were a question, which Reese had associated with ditzy teen girls, who also littered their dialogue with "like" every three words or so.

Reese couldn't help sizing up this double-take beauty, who gave off a crunchy bohemian air with her clashing patterns and mishmash of bangles, beads, hoops, turquoise and...Reese continued her thorough appraisal. Gladiator sandals scuffed enough to have seen actual battle. Oddly enough, it worked for her. Adriana's billowy cotton (organic?) skirt and blouse did not hide the centerfold figure underneath. Her Botticelli curls—scooped up in a haphazard up 'do—flattered her high cheekbones, graceful neck, and lavish lips.

"Down, Maximus! Apollo!" Gabriel said.

The dogs got in a few more licks, slobber bombs, and victory laps around the striking visitor before obeying. Whimpering with excitement, they stayed close to this woman, whom they obviously knew and adored more than the branch-size chew toy they'd fought over before she arrived. It now lay abandoned.

"I have Sparky, a male basset hound, who needs a checkup." Adriana led Gabriel toward her SUV. "Back seat."

"You should've taken him to the hospital," Gabriel said, beckoning Reese to join them.

Reese wanted more information so she bolted right over. *Who is this Adriana?* Yes, Gabriel had shown he'd go beyond the call of duty, but did that mean clients could pop up at his residence with their pets?

"I know." Adriana laughed and nudged him. "But I was curious about your new digs, too, if truth be told. I wanted to see where you moved. I talked Vivian into giving me the address when we met for lunch at Pasquale's yesterday."

"Vivian is my mother," Gabriel repeated info he'd already shared with Reese.

"His mother loves the cannoli and calamari at Pasquale's," Adriana also explained to Reese as if she, too, didn't want Reese left out of the conversation. "We ordered both entrees and split them. But anyway, I have big news! I couldn't wait to share! I'm so happy!"

So far, Reese had gleaned Adriana could: call Gabriel's mother by her first name (without a courtesy title), share pasta entrees, and coax personal information out of "Vivian," dash over to Gabriel's house unannounced to share happy news *and* captivate Maximus and Apollo.

A longtime family friend? A cousin? Former neighbor? Significant other? Ex-significant other? Reese had to shower and dress for the shop, but maybe she'd linger a few minutes to gather more information. She'd already noted Adriana's bare ring finger, but that didn't mean she wasn't engaged, married, or otherwise spoken for. And Linda was opening the Sweet Spot today.

"Sparky" was anything but.

Gabriel regarded the brown, sad-eyed basset hound curled inside a large carrier secured to the back seat of Adriana's SUV. "How ya doing, boy?" he said to the dog as he opened the rear door.

"I think Sparky's in decent shape, but I want to be sure," Adriana said to Gabriel, who had unlatched the carrier door to pet the dog.

"I'll arrive at the hospital in an hour or so," he said. "Take him there. Now what's this big news of yours?"

"Guess who's back?" Adriana sang.

"Who?"

"Sasha!" Adriana was bouncing now.

Wait. Sasha? Reese's eyes bugged, but nobody noticed. Had she heard her right? *Sasha's not an odd name. Calm down.*

"That's great," Gabriel said. "I know how much you've missed her. You two were like two peas—"

"Yes, I was crushed when my sister moved to Chicago," Adriana politely filled in for Reese. "But she's moving back! The family is thrilled of course! And she'll run the Mayfair branch office of her agency." Adriana turned to Reese again. "My sister works in advertising."

Yup. Same Sasha. A sense of doom engulfed Reese.

Adriana whirled to face Gabriel again. "And get this, she's preggers! About ten weeks at this point, we think! I'm going to be an auntie! And I'm thrilled to pieces!"

Reese's belly dropped to her neon orange Nikes. What were the chances there was *another* Sasha, also pregnant? Another Sasha with plans to relocate back to Mayfair, North Carolina, from Chicago? Another Sasha who had not caused a scene on Reese's front porch two weeks ago? Another Sasha who had not tried to scratch Reese's eyes out while ranting to the entire neighborhood about a cheating fiancé and an unborn child before crashing into Reese's mailbox?

"That's wonderful news!" Gabriel smiled. "Tell Sasha I said congratulations."

"Tell her yourself. We're having a big party! You're coming, right?"

"A baby shower?" Gabriel said. "Already?"

"No, silly!" Adriana gave him a playful whack on the arm. "It's a welcome home and engagement party in one. Here's the rest of my news. She's getting hitched, too!"

"Somebody she met in Chicago?" Gabriel asked.

"No, she and Darren got back together!" Adriana said.

"Darren?" Gabriel's brow pleated. "Darren Reid?"

"Who else?" Adriana launched another don't-be-silly whack, and he pretended it actually hurt. Cutesy moves of an old married couple.

"I know you're happy about that," Gabriel said, now notably less jovial after hearing Darren's name.

What was *that* about? Reese studied both.

"I am. I love Darren. I always knew they'd get back together. Those two were meant to be," Adriana said as if she'd reached the happily ever after of her favorite fairy tale.

Gabriel's smile was about as warm and buoyant as a minus sign as he held something back. Reese had read him better than his visitor, who chattered on about her future brother-in-law.

Adriana's manner was not that of a woman informed of Darren's betrayal or her sister's public hissy fit that had led to a medical emergency. If Sasha and Adriana were close, why hadn't Sasha told her sister about that? Only one explanation made sense. Reese supposed sometimes women (or men) chose to keep such incidents a secret because somewhere, somehow, deep down they knew they would end up forgiving and taking back the person who betrayed them. Ergo, the betrayed wanted to avoid looking like a flippin' fool. Sometimes couples agreed to keep news about infidelity from their families, particularly if they'd chosen to work through the ugliness and rebuild trust.

Parents and siblings could make reconciliation more challenging if they clung to resentment toward the offending partner. Maybe Sasha had decided to try to make it work for the sake of their unborn child. Maybe she couldn't see herself as a single mother, and she'd come to care for Darren deeply enough to give him a second chance.

"Um, er, I'd better get going." Reese wanted to hurl the oatmeal and banana she'd eaten before her run.

"Nice meeting you, Reese," Adriana said. "So sorry I kind of horned in on you guys, but my news, I was about to pop!" She pivoted toward Gabriel. "May Sparky and I get a quick tour of the house? Before the drive here, I took him for a walk. He did his business, *both* businesses." She laughed. "Chances are slim he'll soil the floors."

Gabriel hedged.

"Pleeeeeassse!" Adriana pleaded.

Gabriel looked to Reese. "Why don't you join us? You can see what I've done inside."

"Maybe another time," Reese said. "I need to get ready for work."

"It'll only take a few minutes, c'mon," Gabriel said.

A sure sign he had nothing to hide. Reese checked her watch. Business before indulging her curiosity. "I can't. Raincheck, okay?"

When Adriana helped Sparky out of the SUV and walked to Gabriel's porch the three dogs behaved, no dueling for rank of alpha dog. They were content to share. At the front door, Apollo and Maximus romped around Adriana while Sparky trudged along and then plopped his butt near her feet.

"Go on inside. The door's unlocked. I'll join you in a minute," Gabriel said to Adriana, who gave Reese yet another flutter-of-her-fingers wave before slipping inside the house with her adoring canine crew.

"She seems...nice," Reese managed, choking on questions and her own mortification. The coincidental Darren connection was just too much. *Goodness, no!*

"Yes, she's good people, but sorry about the interruption." Without prompting, Gabriel explained Adriana was involved in animal rescue, dogs in particular. She owned four dogs, but usually had about seven dogs total at her Ashlyn Grove residence at any given time. At the moment most of her temporary boarders had special needs: Elliot, the beagle with one eye; Twiggy, the German shepherd with diabetes; Nugget, the boxer with arthritic hips; Chelsea, a mutt rescued from a crate minutes before being shipped to a research lab, had a noncontagious skin disease.

Over the past four years, Adriana had found homes for approximately 70 dogs. She was one of thousands of volunteers across the country who had committed their time and energy to rescue and home placement. She'd also taken in several cats and the occasional iguana, ferret, bird, and hamster.

"That's great," Reese said, still wondering why Adriana and Gabriel seemed especially close. "I've often heard shelter and rescue animals make the best pets because they know they've been rescued."

"Yes, they are grateful when they have a safe, happy home."

Okay, so now he was stalling with all the detail about Adriana's pet rescue endeavors, but Reese played along. "Is she part of a large network or national organization?"

"No. She has some support from small, local non-profits, but she works alone, using her own money and resources. Make that limited resources. She's a social worker by day. The animal rescue is a side thing."

"Such dedication," Reese said.

"I help her out with free physicals and meds. Some spaying, neutering, and other medical treatment when needed."

"That's generous of you. So how did she get the hookup at your vet hospital?"

"Adriana and I are old childhood friends. Our families have been neighbors for years."

"Oh!" Reese said, relieved. But why? She couldn't be *that* attached to Gabriel already. And wasn't she still (sort of) reeling from Darren's deception?

Before looking Reese in the eye, Gabriel appeared to focus on the hydrangea bushes in the Swanigans' front lawn. "And…"

"And what?"

"Adriana and I used to date."

CHAPTER 9

Her name is Adriana," Reese said.

"So let me get this straight. He used to *date* her?" Quinn asked Reese as they drove to Pump-it-Up, a hole-in-the-wall gym Quinn frequented. After a morning of making two new videos (A Three-Strand Twist-Out Tutorial and The Ten Top Drugstore Crunch-Free Hair Gels) for her *Natural Wonder* SeeMeTV channel, Quinn needed the release found in a good workout. She'd coaxed Reese, who always kept a bag of fitness gear at the shop, to join her for a lunch-break weight training session.

"How serious was it?" Quinn adjusted her rearview mirror.

"Not sure yet." Reese turned off the car's stereo and dropped the passenger side visor to block the sun shining in her eyes. "But they lived together for a short, a very short while, before they split, according to him."

"And when was that?'

"About a year ago."

"But they still see each other and act like BFFs?"

"Yes."

By the time Quinn pulled her Volvo S60 into Pump-it-Up's gravel parking lot, Reese had told her all about Gabriel Cameron, from their first meeting when he'd returned Sinbad to their invigorating run and near kiss that morning. For about ten minutes, they talked inside the parked car with the windows lowered. Then a wasp, the size of a bat, joined them and chased the sisters inside the gym, a slate gray building with blue trim, which sat between a pawn shop and a weathered storefront church. The clank of weight plates colliding like percussion instruments and the clink of re-racking dumbbells reverberated through what Reese estimated to be a 70-by-70-foot workout area, a veritable closet compared to the weight room at her flashier fitness center.

Pump-it-Up housed scads of mismatched weights and other equipment that looked like relics from the Jack LaLanne era. In one corner sat an old metal barbell with what resembled cannon balls on each end. To its left stood a spindly recumbent bike and a no-frills rowing machine that would break if a brawnier member broke wind in that direction.

"This place needs to get more cardio equipment," Reese said. "High tech."

"Why? There's a dirt trail in the wooded area out back. Get to steppin'."

Reese grabbed two rusting ten-pound dumbbells and sat on a cracked-vinyl bench. Working out here always proved challenging. It smelled like butt and sweaty socks. It was a wonder Reese hadn't passed out from lifting while avoiding deep inhalation. Despite three large blowing box fans, it must've been 100 degrees in there. Reese had yet to exert herself, but she already had a bad case of swamp bottom.

"So back to business, Adriana feels free to pop over to his house when she pleases, unannounced." Quinn, in baggy training pants, Chuck Taylors, and a faded Bev, Biv, Devoe concert T-shirt, stood before a streaky mirror and curled two fifteen-pound dumbbells. "And she still pals around with this mother?"

Reese relayed more details Gabriel had told her before she departed for work that morning. "Gabriel and Adriana grew up in the same neighborhood. Their parents still live in those houses. And their families socialize, enjoy barbecues, holidays, and vacations together. That short time they lived together confirmed that coupledom was not for them, according to him."

Quinn placed the dumbbells back on the rack, donned her thick leather weight belt, and passed the extra one she'd packed in her gym bag to Reese. She directed Reese toward the rickety squat rack.

Reese declined the belt. "I can't blast legs. I plan to do a long run tomorrow morning."

"Suit yourself. So okay, you've told me everything you know about Gabriel and Adriana so far."

"Oh, and they co-parent two dogs." Reese had learned why Maximus and Apollo were so taken with Adriana. After Gabriel's two senior dogs had passed away, the couple had adopted rescues Maximus and Apollo. After the most amiable split ever, the two agreed to share custody.

"Co-*parent?*" Quinn, scoffed, shaking her head. "You pet-obsessed people! But okay, I've heard enough." She shoved plates on the bar. "I have reached a verdict."

Reese watched her sister descend and ascend in a few warmup squats with deliberate care and focus. "Well?"

"Just a sec," said Quinn, whose toned musculature accentuated her bodacious curves.

Quinn placed the bar back on the rack and adjusted her lifting gloves. "You want to know the real deal? No holding back like I did with Darren?"

"Yes."

With a towel, Quinn wiped her sweaty face. "I can tell you already like this guy. *A lot.*"

"But I'm just thinking fling, keeping things simple."

"The friends-with, no, *neighbors*-with-benefits plan, giving whole new meaning to borrowing a cup of sugar."

"Yeah, exactly!"

"Bad idea."

"Some good times to take my mind off Darren. Why should I sit around alone and lick my wounds when the hottie next door can lick me." Reese chuckled at her own bad joke. "Don't I deserve some fun? I'm a big girl. I can handle it."

"Yeah, right."

"I *can.*" Reese pouted.

"Having a fling with someone who lives next door defeats the purpose. Flings work best when both parties agree upfront that's what it is, nothing more, and it runs its swift course, like say, when you're on an exotic island vacation. Treat it like a condom, fun while in use, but promptly discarded when the deed is done, never to be seen or spoken of again after you return home. How does that work with a friggin' neighbor?"

Reese shrugged, though she'd already considered the less than optimal logistics involved with this particular fling candidate. The setup was worse than choosing a lover at one's workplace, which was the reason many companies had strict rules against such fraternization. "We're both adults with itches to scratch," Reese said.

"And when you're done scratching, you'll carry on as if he's like the other men on Mistywood Lane?"

"Yes. When we're done, in my mind Gabriel will be Milo Papadopoulos with more hair, Buddy Wainwright without the beer belly, and Calvin Carmichael without the wife who is my Mistywood Lane bestie. That's the plan."

"Right," Quinn replied still unconvinced. "But he and this chick are still a little too intertwined in each other's lives."

"But it shouldn't matter if he's a fling."

"She might as well be his ex-wife sharing custody of two kids. And add Darren to the mix, too? Wait. If Gabriel and Adriana were together when Darren was with Sasha the first go-round, he probably knows Darren well."

"Darren never mentioned knowing a Gabriel."

"But what if they're buddies? Close buddies."

"I knew most of Darren's close friends and associates."

"Oh? So he couldn't have held back about Gabriel, because of the Sasha connection? We're talking about the bald-faced liar who, until he was busted, failed to mention he'd spent time with Sasha during that trip to Chi-Town."

"Because Gabriel and Darren were dating sisters doesn't mean they clicked as friends. And I get the feeling Gabriel doesn't like Darren. There was a definite shift in his demeanor after Adriana told him Sasha and Darren had reconciled."

"Will you tell him about you and Darren? It's bound to come out sooner or later. What if Adriana visits Gabriel's new place with Sasha in tow, instead of another rescue dog? They're all so chummy. He'll get her side of the sleazy tale and then assume you're some hoochie home-wrecker."

"Gabriel doesn't strike me as the type to jump to conclusions about people. He has a levelheadedness about him."

"Is he attending that welcome-home-engagement party?"

"He didn't say."

"I think you know what *I'd* do if I were you. I'd deal with him on a strictly platonic level. I'm talking ten-foot-pole platonic. Find someone else to lick you. Even without the besties-with-his-ex situation, let's say things heated up between you and Gabriel and then cooled off, ending badly. Or maybe he's a jerk, but does a convincing nice-guy opening act to lure in unsuspecting victims. Or worse, what if he's psycho?"

"I don't get the psycho-stalker vibe from him."

"That part's typically triggered *after* you dump them."

"He's Sinbad's new vet."

"There are lots of other qualified vets in Mayfair. Any entanglement with him, even a casual-just-for-fun one, is ill-advised, sis. I don't want to see you hurt again. I know you're good at bouncing back, but I still think it's too soon to gamble on this one."

Reese considered Quinn's solid advice.

"There's some strong lingering mutual affection between him and this Adriana. I smell unfinished business. Even the most secure woman might start to feel, you know, threatened by that. When I'm dating a guy, I set strict rules regarding female friends."

"Such as…?" Reese asked.

"When we decide to be monogamous, I share my manifesto upfront," Quinn said. "No making new female friends who aren't also friends with *me*. We hang out together."

"Cozy."

"Females who were my guy's friends *before* we met are keepers as long as they meet two criteria: One) My guy and his friend have never ever seen each other naked. Two) No weird vibes, as in I don't catch her making goo-goo eyes at him or shooting dagger eyes at me. If I ever get the eerie feeling she's keeping a voodoo doll and hoping to hasten my untimely demise—"

"She's. Gots. Ta. Go," Reese added.

"But I'm fair," Quinn said. "These rules apply to my male friends as well."

Reese retied the laces on her Nikes. "Adriana sounds so generous and caring with her social work and homeless pet rescuing. And she's beautiful. I must admit, I kinda liked her. Her first impression was the opposite of her sister's, that's for sure. Adriana was bubbly, warm…approachable."

"The nerve of that bitch!" Quinn said.

"Sommers, you know the rules," said a guy whose muscular thighs were so developed his feet couldn't possibly touch each other. He stopped loading plates on a vertical leg press machine to point to a cardboard sign. Red marker scrawl prohibited swearing, spitting in the water fountain, and flinging of sweat. The list included other obvious etiquette infractions one might assume would be unnecessary among adults.

"Sorry!" Quinn replied to her gym mate, before turning to whisper to Reese. "That's Sheldon Dorfman. He teaches topics in metaphysics and epistemology at Mayfair U."

"Cool."

"But around here he's known as Quad-zil-la, baby!" Quinn roared. She grimaced with veins popping out of her neck and flexed her arms and legs in that stupid bodybuilder pose known as "the crab" that made her look as if she needed a potent laxative.

"That's *Professor* Quadzilla to you." He laughed and shook his head at Quinn's antics. "You're a piece of work, you know that."

"This is my sister Reese," Quinn told him after she de-crabbed.

"Nice to meet you." Reese waved, and he took a deep bow just as a mouse scurried toward the half-eaten energy bar someone had left on the floor. The place was filthy as all get out, but, hey, members were sticklers about maintaining decorum.

"Your sister's certifiable," he said to Reese.

"Yep, I know," Reese replied.

Professor Quadzilla returned to grunting and grinding through his leg presses.

"Now, back to Adriana," Quinn said to Reese. "Don't you hate when the lingering ex is actually nice?"

"Said the rip-snortin' bunny-boiling ex."

"I've done things to jerks who deserved it, but I've harmed no animals in the process," Quinn said with pride.

"Still, you really need to stop watching those *Snapped* rerun marathons," Reese said, referring to her sister's favorite true crime series, featuring average women who'd offed their husbands or significant others.

"This Adriana chick sounds too good to be true if you ask me. Of course she's warm and friendly *now*. She's still *winning*! He's still doing free vet work for her. Any time she crooks her little finger, he'll go running back."

"You don't know that."

"She'll toss him aside when she's bored and call him again on a whim, for sport, and so on and so on."

"Sorry, but I don't sense mercurial diva there."

"You haven't seen all sides of her. Maybe mercurial diva comes out with a full moon."

"You're so cynical, Quinn." Reese tsk-tsked.

"And you could use more cynicism. When you tell Blaire I'm sure she'll side with me."

Quinn was right. Gabriel and Adriana were clearly still fond of one another. Unexpected disappointment washed over her. Despite what she'd told herself, she might have glimpsed a bit-more-than-fling possibilities with Gabriel Cameron when they'd run with Maximus and Apollo. However, the potential for soap-opera hijinks was far too great.

Despite their chemistry, she shouldn't risk it. As Quinn said, what if Reese fell for him, but he was emotionally unavailable to Reese because his heart belonged to someone else? She was ready to date again, but no more triangles if she could help it.

"Okay, so he's not significant other *or* fling material for me, but why can't he be Sinbad's vet? I like the setup at his hospital. He had a wonderful bedside, make that steel-top-table-side manner with Sinbad. His facility is spacious, clean, bright, and state of the art, from what I can tell, and has separate sides for dogs and cats. After receiving all required kitten inoculations, Sinbad has needed a vet no more than once or twice a year."

"Playing with fire, sis. Playing with fire. You've already undressed this man with your eyes."

Reese had done a lot more than that to him with her eyes.

"You've never been the sex-'em-then-X-'em type. What makes you think you can handle that now all of a sudden? Your heart *always* gets involved."

"I'm touched by your confidence in me," Reese said dryly as she slathered hand sanitizer on every inch of her exposed skin to combat whatever microbial cooties had attached themselves to her. She considered turning up the bottle and guzzling it for good measure.

Quinn moved to an uncluttered space on the floor to bang out alternating sets of pistol and half-burpee squats using her own body weight.

"Now, promise me you will," Quinn puffed between sets, "keep things neighborly, smile and wave, but ten-foot-pole platonic."

"I promise. Smiles and waves only." Reese pictured Gabriel's handsome face and tall, sculpted physique and crossed her fingers. "Ten-foot-pole platonic."

CHAPTER 10

After Reese returned to the Sweet Spot, she did inventory, paperwork, and then left Linda to supervise closing.

Soon, she had turned onto her tree-lined street with its eclectic mix of attractive ranch and two-story contemporary homes. Their lawns, resembling pro-golf turf, underscored the raggedness of her own, which seemed to have grown at least two more inches while she was at work. Where the heck was Rosvaughn? She parked inside her two-car garage and checked the scheduling app on her phone. Yup. He was supposed to do her front and back lawns... *last week.*

To help her ex-con cousin with his fledgling lawn care-slash-handyman business, Reese had been among the first to sign a one-year contract for his services. She'd even chastised Blaire and Quinn for not following suit. Both claimed to adore Rosvaughn, but had cited their cousin's often feckless ways as their reason for taking a more cautious approach. If he managed to operate two full years without incident or earned a good grade from the Better Business Bureau they'd use his services. If he received a sufficient number of positive reviews (at least 100, Blaire's arbitrary prerequisite) on at least two consumer review sites, Blaire promised to hook him up with some of her real estate clients and associates.

Reese, however, had wanted to help jumpstart his latest venture. The liability insurance alone was astronomical for ex-offenders. Now the joke was on Reese. *Again.*

Because of Rosvaughn her house had almost burned down after he'd turned a simple fuse replacement into some "minor electrical rewiring," which he was neither licensed nor skilled to do. She'd taken immediate action after noting a buzzing sound and a scorched odor coming from one wall socket. She'd hired an expert to investigate and correct the problem.

Because of Rosvaughn her air conditioner had blown out in 102-degree heat earlier in the summer.

Because of Rosvaughn Granberry Ridge Homeowners Association had fined Reese twice for her overgrown lawn.

Because of Rosvaughn Reese's downstairs toilet had not been right since he "snaked" it.

Reese went to her mailbox, the one Calvin Carmichael—not Rosvaughn—had replaced for her. She phoned her cousin, with whom she'd been close since toddlerhood. Of the Sommers sisters, she'd been the one to visit him regularly when he'd been incarcerated. Blaire and Quinn, who wouldn't be caught dead anywhere near a prison, even a country-club-style-minimum-security one, had never filled out the visitor application he'd sent to them.

Rosvaughn's crimes: bad checks, store price tag swapping, and shoplifting.

"Rosvaughn could take the shortening out of a ginger cake without breaking the crust," Reese's father had often remarked. Her cousin's sticky fingers and mastery of the hustle first surfaced during his days as a student at North Mayfair Academy, an elite boarding school in the area. But when Rosvaughn was paroled the last time, he had sworn at his release party, hosted by Reese, that his days as "Roguish Rosvaughn" were behind him. He would pursue a petty-crime-free lifestyle.

First, Reese would find out why Rosvaughn had missed her house last week. If he was off on another one of his infamous weed-smoking benders, she'd let him have it and terminate their contract. "Where the heck are you, Rosvaughn?" she grumbled aloud. A few rings later she reached his voicemail.

As Reese gathered her mail for the day, one envelope stood out. *Grrr.* Another Granberry Ridge HOA notice and a hefty fine for a third infraction.

"Hey, neighbor!" came out of nowhere.

Reese jumped and dropped her mail.

"Sorry." Gabriel, appeared, dressed in jeans and a red East Mayfair Veterinary Hospital polo shirt. He gathered her envelopes and passed them back to her. "I didn't mean to startle you."

Reese muttered, still preoccupied with thoughts of throttling Rosvaughn. She'd ended the call before leaving a message. No lighting into him until she was sure he wasn't dead in a ditch or something.

"Finally, we meet at the mailboxes," Gabriel said as he reached for his bundle and flipped through what appeared to be store circulars, magazines (*Runners World*, *Veterinary Medicine Journal*), and celebrity tabloids (*The Dirty Dish*, *Paparazzi Peepers*, and *The International Inquisitor*). He jammed the roll of tabloids back inside the box. "For the record, those are not *my* subscriptions so don't judge. They must've slipped through the change-of-address filter."

"I know, Mrs. Cohen used to read them before she passed away," Reese said, still preoccupied with thoughts of murdering Rosvaughn.

"Hey, you all right?"

Reese's skin tingled where he touched her arm. "Another HOA notice." Reese waved the envelope at him. "It's for the grass. My cousin was supposed to mow my lawn last week, but as you can see…"

"It's not that bad. They've sent a notice already?" Gabriel whistled. "Gotta stay on top of my grass-cutting game. Speaking of… I was about to do mine. I'll cut yours, too."

"I appreciate the offer, but I can't let you do that."

"I insist."

"I'll do it myself." Reese owned a mower, an edger, and a trimmer, housewarming gifts from her father. "I'd better get to it." She turned on her heel. "See ya!"

Reese spent a half hour spoiling Sinbad with cuddles and Salmon Supreme Yummy Tummy treats and her special ground filet mignon meatballs.

Since Sinbad was a kitten, Reese often played "Stray Cat Strut," that eighties rockabilly hit by Brian Seltzer and his band, the Stray Cats. She'd downloaded the song on her phone because Sinbad loved it. Sometimes he even caterwauled along as she cradled him in her arms to sing and dance. Sinbad would place his paws on each of her shoulders. His tail would sway with contentment as they moved together. She enjoyed the gentle scrape of his sandpaper tongue and the feathery warmth of his breath against her cheek. "*Yuck!*" "*Gross!*" Reese chuckled, recalling how she'd squicked out her sisters by revealing she actually liked Sinbad's ever-fishy breath. Reese and Blaire believed she was plumb nuts when it came to Sinbad. They didn't understand the depth of their bond because neither was a pet owner.

(Though Blaire had briefly fancied herself a hobbyist aquarist until her baby fantail goldfish outgrew its cute cantaloupe-size bowl to reach her shoe size.)

Reese changed into clothes more suitable for yardwork —denim cut-offs, sneakers, and a pink Sweet Spot tank top.

Gabriel's mower growled from his property.

Inside her garage, sat her own machine. Wallace Sommers had not only equipped each of his daughters with yard and boating safety equipment, but he had also gifted them with items from his vast weaponry collection. Though touched by the gesture, Reese had never been as comfortable around firearms as the rest of her family so she kept the handgun in a locked safe at the Sweet Spot. A former boyfriend had borrowed, but never returned the nunchucks. The Taser was in her car's glove compartment and the mini pepper spray, make that sprays, dangled from her key chain or the bands of her running shorts.

She surveyed the lawn mower. Pristine because she'd never used the darn thing. But how hard could it be? How many times had she watched her father and Rosvaughn operate theirs? Pull that thingy on the left, and she was off and running. But as always, safety first. No operating power tools without reading the owner's manual. Now where had she put that folder with the instructions for various home and yard equipment? In the file cabinets in her home office? The shed out back? The garage shelves?

Gabriel's lawn mower went silent as Reese climbed to the top of a step ladder and found the stack of booklets on a nearby shelf.

"Hey, you!" came from behind a few minutes later.

Reese whirled around to find… *Good googly moogly!*

A sweaty and shirtless Gabriel stood at the open side of her two-car garage. She nearly toppled off the ladder at the sight of his glistening bod, in all its tall and muscular glory. Her drop-jawed gape traveled from his scruffy work boots to diamond-shaped calves to the hint of cut quads peeking out of rumpled cargo shorts. Her gaze then advanced to chiseled pecs with a neat dusting of chest hair, which formed an inverted triangle pattern that narrowed over the deep ridges of his six-pack *(I knew it!)* before disappearing inside his pants. A white towel dangled from one front pocket. Mirrored sunglasses accentuated his gorgeous face. Just enough of an undies waistband showed to tease. Boxers, boxer-briefs or briefs? How brief? And how quickly could she get him out of them?

"It was so quiet over here." The five o'clock shadow accentuating

Gabriel's angular jaw only added to his manly yummiliciousness. "I thought I'd come and check on you. How's it going?"

Did Reese need to wipe the drool from her mouth?

"Reese?"

She cleared her throat. "Um, just getting started. Had to tend to Sinbad first."

"Your lawn mower doesn't have a blade of grass or speck of dirt on it," he said.

Rosvaughn had his own gear so he never used hers. Though Reese was not fluent in motorized-lawn-equipment speak, she didn't want Gabriel to assume she was an inept female homeowner, unable to handle house and lawn maintenance basics in a pinch.

"I do my best to keep it clean." As Reese descended the ladder, she felt him staring at her butt, but she didn't mind one bit. Turnabout, fair play, and all that jazz. No denying they found each other easy on the eyes. "I'll get started now. As you can see, all is fine here."

Gabriel's lips quirked up at one corner. "Yes, it is." His lustful gaze swept over her. When he shortened the distance between them, she inhaled his pleasing manly man scent—a mix of sweat, yardwork, aftershave, or cologne. And something distinctly Gabriel Cameron, which proved there was something to that pheromone business after all.

"So I'm good." Her polite way of telling him to *am-scray*. Pronto! Make like Lenny Kravitz's pants and split. Who needed the distraction of Gabriel's bronzed Adonis bod? The pressure of an audience and any potential mansplaining sure to follow while she figured out this contraption? *No thanks.*

Instead, Gabriel stood there, exuding extreme sex appeal. And the way he looked at her... His obvious appreciation of her assets... Sizzling.

"Are you finished with your own lawn?" She tried again. *Go! Vamoose, dude!*

"Almost. I did the front."

"Better get going on the back before dark." Reese hooked her fingers in the waistband loops of her shorts, which dipped in the front, exposing her belly button. What did she expect after knotting the edge of the tank top?

"I have plenty of time." Sensual mischief gleamed in his dark eyes. He knew she was giving him the bum's rush, but he refused to cooperate.

"Whatever." Reese proceeded to park the mower at the edge of her lawn. Seemed as if she recalled Rosvaughn fiddling with that spark-plug-like doohickey on his, an older model. Did hers have one of those, too? Maybe she could skip that step. A little sticker on the chassis promised a "fast start - auto choke system" and "easy drive." Easy peasy. Let 'er rip. She yanked the recoil starter – quickly and firmly—as she'd seen her father and Rosvaughn do to theirs many times. Nothing. Under Gabriel's watchful eye, Reese yanked again and again until her rotator cuff protested. Nothing.

"Did you open the gas line?" Gabriel pointed to a little button on the mower's left side.

"Right." Reese flipped the switch and pulled the starter again. Nothing.

"Do you have gas in it? Oil?"

Seemed as if she recalled her father mentioning the mower was gassed, oiled up, and ready to go. "Yep, there's gas and oil in it." *Duh!*

"What about the blade control lever there? Did you pull it toward the handlebar?"

"Huh?"

"May I?" Gabriel motioned toward the mower.

Because her shoulder hurt, Reese let him have at it. With a hint of prideful spite, she hoped it wouldn't start for him, either.

He held the handlebar and yanked the starter a few times. Those defined shoulder and upper back muscles of his flexed and enticed. The darn motor roared.

"There. Done." Gabriel flashed his toothpaste-commercial smile.

"Because I warmed it up for you." Reese massaged that aching shoulder of hers.

A few seconds later the engine sputtered and stopped. *Ha!* Reese couldn't resist gloating.

Gabriel crouched, unscrewed the fuel cap on the mower, and peered inside the hole. "Yep, it has gas in it all right."

"Told ya!"

"When was the last time you changed it?"

"Why do you ask?"

"Evasion tactic."

"It might have been in there a little while," she replied.

"Is that right?"

"Yes."

"A little while or a *long* little while?"

"I said a *little* while."

"Can you be more specific? Before or after Obama won his two-term presidency?"

"Ha. Ha," Reese said, unable to smother her smile. "Okay, so you busted me. I've never used the flippin' thing before. It was a housewarming gift from my dad."

"A housewarming gift? You moved here five years ago!"

"Darn that steel-trap memory of yours."

"No wonder it looks like gel and smells like varnish. It's degraded. It won't run without draining and refilling. And it could use a good tune-up because of the gunk inside. Tell you what, I'll use mine to do your lawn before dark. I'll take your mower, fix it right up, and have it back to you long before you, or somebody else, needs it again."

"I appreciate the offer, but again, I can't let you do that."

"I can't pawn it; you know where I live."

"It's not that. I paid Rosvaughn good money to handle lawn and handyman chores around here. We have a contract. He should do it." Besides, Gabriel cutting her grass so soon after moving in was juicy fodder for neighborhood gossip.

"I don't mind."

Reese considered Rosvaughn's spotty track record. Neighborhood tongue-waggers, screw off. "Well, okay."

"Cool. I'll be right back with mine." With long purposeful strides, he pushed her mower toward his garage.

"The least I can do is make you a cold drink for your trouble," she called out to him before heading back inside her house.

A few minutes later, Gabriel's mower roared as he tended to her front lawn. She raced to a window and gawked at him through parted curtains. His bare chest, arms, and shoulders flexed with each push and pull. Heat flooded her veins and pooled between legs. He had the ideal male physique as far as she was concerned. Tall and layered with well-honed muscles not so freakishly beefy they resembled the overstuffed fiberfill pads on a child's super hero costume. *Sorry, Quadzilla.*

Gabriel Cameron was too hot to resist.

"Ten-foot-pole platonic!" Quinn's strident voice rang in Reese's ear.

With a sigh, Reese released the curtain and got busy in her kitchen.

CHAPTER 11

After Gabriel finished the front lawn Reese served him refreshments, like a good little neighbor should. Two glasses of fresh-squeezed lemonade and a new cupcake she'd been testing sat on her tray. From across the street, Myra Swanigan, wielding clippers, filled a bucket with water to gather blooms from her massive hydrangea shrubs. How had she managed not to snip off a finger the way she gaped at Reese and Gabriel?

"So you're finally joining me for that drink?" Gabriel wiped perspiration from his face with his towel.

"No, both are for you. I wasn't sure if you'd prefer straight up or not. One is regular lemonade and, as you can see, the other has assorted berries and a sprig of mint. And this cupcake is double dark chocolate filled and topped with a light French buttercream frosting. It's a new twist on an old recipe I'm considering adding to the shop's menu."

"Thank you." Gabriel tucked one end of the towel inside his pocket and reached for the regular lemonade.

"You're welcome," she said, Reese noting her own reflection in his mirrored lenses. If her smile got any wider, she could count her molars. That morning's revelations about Adriana? Buried deep in a mental storage bin labeled denial. She was obviously his ex for a reason. And they'd been broken up for a year for crying out loud.

Gabriel chugged his drink until the glass was nearly empty. "Delicious," he said with a hammy slurp and lick of his lips to make her laugh. He polished off the cupcake in three large bites. He raved about the treat and lemonade until her heart fluttered. Oh, how she liked this guy!

"I'll let you finish," Reese said after he passed his empty glass back to her. "I'll leave this second glass on the porch. If the ice melts or you find a big bug doing a backstroke in it, I'll supply another glass, along with another cupcake."

"Yes, ma'am."

Reese left and then returned outdoors at dusk to find he'd cut her grass (front and back), edged the front, and shaped all shrubs.

"Wow!" Reese passed him another glass of ice cold lemonade and a cupcake. "I didn't expect the deluxe lawn care package. What about your own backyard?"

"It can wait." Gabriel propped the sunglasses at the top of his head. *(Goodness, his eyes)* He took the drink and wiped his sweaty face with the towel again. "I aim to please. And I always give it my all," he said in a husky voice. The tone coupled with the glint in his dark gaze suggested he was talking about a lot more than home-related chores, which induced a tropical rainforest effect between her thighs.

"I'm such a slacker, inside all this time in the air conditioning," she said to cut the tension. "You've probably noticed I have no flowers." She held up her thumb. "No green thumb at all. I even killed a plastic plant once."

With obvious skepticism, Gabriel lifted a brow.

"No lie. Long story for another time, but bottom line, I loathe yard work. I have since I was a child. I didn't mind other chores. Bring'em on. I never complained. We had professional lawn care service, but Dad would still make my sisters and me help out on lawn day." Reese chattered too much as antsiness got the better of her. It was all she could do not to spring and wrap herself around him like vine. "And when we reached our tween and teen years, Dad made us wear these giant straw hats, long-sleeved shirts, and coveralls. Lightweight ones in the summer so we wouldn't collapse from heat stroke and the heavier denim kind in the fall for raking leaves. Protection from the sun, or so he claimed. We looked like a trio of scarecrows."

Gabriel chuckled.

"Dad wanted to frighten the boys away after Quinn and Blaire wore Daisy Dukes while bending over to pull weeds, flashing butt cheeks for days."

"Daisy Dukes. Like what you're wearing today?" Gabriel's gaze dropped to her hips again, and he gulped his lemonade.

"I am *not* flashing butt cheeks." Reese punched his arm and then tugged at the fraying edges of her cut-offs.

"Almost, but don't worry." Gabriel wiped his mouth with the back of his hand. "I'm not complaining. But let's say I understand Dad's point of view."

"I still hate doing the yardwork, the grass part, but I would like to plant a flower garden to increase curb appeal."

"Your *curve* appeal is already on point, lady."

"Oh, you!" Reese said with faux exasperation.

Gabriel was fun and so easy to talk to. She longed to invite him inside and thank him with dinner and another kind of dessert. However, Quinn's advice still rang in her ears: *Ten-foot-pole platonic.* He wanted to kiss her from head to toe, no doubt. She stood nose level to his brick wall of a chest and flat round nipples so perfect she yearned to lick them as if they were chocolate-covered peppermint patties. Mere inches separated her from broad shoulders to grip as he had his way with her. But instead, Reese thanked him again and said good night.

"Wait." Gabriel's hand was on her arm and her skin goose bumped in pleasure. "Didn't you say your dad gave you an edger and a trimmer?"

"Yeah," she replied, her voice breathy.

"They need a good maintenance check, too. Are they electric or gas-powered?"

Reese shrugged. "Both are still in boxes."

"Why don't I take a quick look-see." Gabriel's voice dropped to a lower register.

"Yes, a quick look-see," she said, aware of would happen next, but helpless to stop herself.

It was dark now. She led him past her car to the shelves sitting deeper inside her double-doored garage. As soon as she flipped the light switch, moths played around the overhead fixture. With her back to Gabriel, she pointed to the top shelf. "They're up there." With only a whisper of space between them, his heady, masculine heat surrounded her. After he placed his empty glass on the shelf, she wanted nothing more than his strong arms holding her tight. He teased with a single fingertip tracing along the fringe edge of her shorts, creating a sensual tickling sensation at the under curves of her bottom. Left cheek. Right cheek. She shivered, loving and hating that all he did was taunt her. She'd been damp since she laid eyes on him shirtless. Now? Soaked after his intimate, feathery touch.

Gabriel's large hands glided over her hips to her trim waist and back again, as if admiring the flair.

"Somebody loves her some Stagg Chili, the steak house blend, according to label," Gabriel whispered against the back of her neck.

"Wha...?" Not exactly the sexy-sweet nothings expected.

"Sounds savory, but wait until you taste *my* chili. I make mine with black beans and a mix of mystery Caribbean-inspired spices."

"Um."

"Couldn't help noticing all these cases of chili on your shelves."

"Oh, that's part of my survivalist stash, courtesy of Daddy. He had to make sure my sisters and I were prepared in case of disaster. I also have enough water, batteries, flashlights, and other necessities to tide me over for a few months. A generator is in the shed out back. I added the cat food."

"Stranded with you? I should be so lucky."

"You might think again if I'm filling up on beans, beans, and more beans."

Gabriel snorted. "You're a goober, you know that?"

"I'll take that as a compliment."

"A very *sexy* goober." Then his hands slid around her waist and hips. "Want to know what else I'm thinking right now?" His voice rumbled in her ear, causing a pleasant belly quiver.

"About the trimmer and the edger?"

"I'm thinking how our bodies will fit when we get better acquainted," he said with a single nip to her earlobe. His self-assurance intoxicated her.

"Hmmm. Very, very nice equipment." Gabriel cupped her bottom and squeezed. Nerve endings sparked like live wires. He granted her silent wish and finally drew her into arms as strong as steel bands, an embrace that would make any woman feel protected from everything. Her breathing deepened as she melted against him. This bad idea felt so darn good, but wasn't that usually the case?

Gabriel's lips were on her left earlobe, tugging, nuzzling, and sending more pleasure shivers over her body. He planted kisses on her nape and tightened his grip on her. With his erection nestled at her bottom, she pressed against it. He released the knot to slip his hand inside her tank top. He cupped and squeezed one breast through the bra. They did a slow, grinding dance, delaying the next move. That inevitable first real kiss. She gasped when he cupped both breasts and teased her taut, sensitized nipples.

Their undoing.

A guttural sound of need thundered from his chest as he whipped her around to face him. Reese yelped when he slammed her against the wall. Her breasts pressed against his sculpted chest. Threading his hands through her hair, the lose ponytail holder slipped off and her hair tumbled around her shoulders. The muscle in his clenched jaw flexed as he yanked her closer still. His lips claiming hers was like mainlining hot buttered rum. High and heavy with longing, she stroked his tongue with hers. He sucked and bit her bottom lip. Their mouths mated, achingly slow and thorough at first then increased in intensity as hunger engulfed them. The kisses and touches turned desperate, bruising. He kept her pinned against the wall as one hand held her hip and the other unhooked her bra to fondle her breasts with greater ease. With his thigh parting her legs, she pressed herself against it. He dipped and drew a nipple deep inside his mouth. His lean cheeks moved in and out with a searing, damp suction. *Heaven.*

"I knew you'd be sweeter than those cupcakes of yours," he said between nips, licks and kisses.

"Cupcakes made of sweat and cocoa butter body lotion."

"Works for me. Nectar of a goddess," he said.

So hokey Reese couldn't help smiling. She released the top button of his shorts so she could grip his rock-solid bottom without a barrier. "So how's this for a welcome to Mistywood Lane, Gabriel Cameron?"

"Your hospitality is beyond measure, ma'am," he said before his lips skimmed over to kiss and lick the other breast. "And I'm much obliged." Gabriel unzipped her shorts and his hand delved inside and stroked between her legs.

Such delicious friction. And heck yeah, Reese would let him take her to the edge. *Sorry, Quinn!*

Reese moaned inside his mouth as he touched her, creating a sweetest ache at her core. She arched and strained against his hand which matched the thrust of his tongue. Steady at first. So luscious, so divine she wished they could stay like this forever. Pleasure ripples strengthened and radiated through her womb in rapid-fire succession. He groaned as if he could feel the vibrations. "You're going to come for me," he said in a thick whisper between kisses. "Now." Every pleasure nerve in her body had converged at one place – where he played her with perfect rhythm. His fingers skated along her slippery folds. One slipped inside, then two…three, coaxing her toward release.

Not yet. Here. Stay here. Suspended at this amazing place. No rush. No end. Panting, she placed her hand on his. "Just a minute." He waited a beat or two and then went in for the kill, fusing their lips with another thorough kiss as he resumed the beat. That moment of release closer and closer. She was almost there. She'd go with it. Scaling the peak with frenzied determination, she helped his hand along and went on a slick ride against it. She whimpered and bit her bottom lip, relishing the evidence of his desire. Her hand moved inside the band of his briefs and wrapped around his length. The man was as blessed as she'd fantasized he would be. She couldn't resist taking a peek at the hot steel in her hand. *Oh, yes.* It was a tantalizing mocha, deeper in hue than the rest of him and quite possibly even sweeter. She couldn't wait to find out for sure. As her eyes slipped closed again, she stroked him, tightening her grip, increasing her pace, and tearing a gratifying groan from his lips. *Yes.* Giving him pleasure, only increased her own. This would be a good one. *Oh, yeah.* No holding back now. She needed this. She deserved this after all she'd been through the last two weeks.

"Oh, Reeeeeeessssssse!" Not the sexiest orgasmic cry she'd ever heard.

High-pitched.

And sort of…

Faraway.

Wait.

Female?

Shrill even.

Sounded a lot like…

Reese's eyes snapped open.

CHAPTER 12

Odette.

Thank goodness Reese heard her neighbor and friend before she saw her. Gabriel, who had been supporting Reese's weight, jumped back. Her knees nearly buckled.

Reese and Gabriel tried to fix their clothing before wild-eyed Odette hurried inside the garage through the door Reese hadn't bothered to close before making out with Gabriel.

"Oh." Odette came to a skidding stop when she laid eyes on flustered Reese with Gabriel.

"Hello." Gabriel angled way from Odette. He zipped his fly and jammed both hands inside his front pockets in an attempt to adjust himself.

Odette gaped at the shirtless wonder. Reese could only hope Odette was too spellbound by Gabriel's pecs, six-pack, and mountain range shoulders to notice the ginormous bulge at the front of his shorts.

"What's up, Odette?" Reese's lips felt puffy from their vigorous smooching. Her thin tank top did little to camouflage the lumpy-bumpiness of the catawampus bra. She tried to right and secure the unhooked undergarment before giving up on it. She was a grown, single woman. And Odette had seen Reese's boobs many times before in their favorite spa's changing room. Odette could assume whatever the heck she wanted.

"I…I'm sorry, Reese. I didn't know you had company," said Odette, captivated by Gabriel's chiseled magnificence.

"Odette? What can I do for you?" Reese snapped her fingers before Odette's slack-jawed face. "Odette!"

Odette closed her flytrap and swallowed.

"Odette?" More finger snaps from Reese.

Odette blinked and stopped gawking at Gabriel. "Huh?"

"Why are you here?" Reese asked.

"I, um, well…I need you to do me a favor," Odette said.

"Are you okay? You don't look so good," Reese noticed Odette's tawny skin held a hint of blue.

Before Reese could respond, headlights flashed in her driveway. An engine stopped. A door slammed.

"Yo, cuz! What's crackalackin'!" Rosvaughn swaggered inside her garage. He wore his coiled hair in neat, pencil-thin dreadlocks gathered in a low bun. On his six-feet-plus, lean, cocoa-colored, densely tatted-up, muscled body: slim-leg Adidas soccer pants, Cesar Chavez T-shirt, Shit-kicker boots, his ready-to-work gear.

Rosvaughn had not seen Reese topless since they were eight and splashing around inside an inflatable kiddie pool. He didn't need to see her nipples poking against her tank top like buckshots. She reached for an old life vest her father had hooked on one of her garage shelves.

Then Calvin arrived with Brett and Brayton on each hip. "Is my wife over here? We returned from Gramps and Nana's to find the front door wide open, all the lights on, and the house empty."

Reese couldn't believe this. Two's company. Seven's a Neighborhood Watch Meeting. And just when she and Gabriel were getting to the best part, too. A near-climax flush coupled with stubble burn from ardent kissing left her skin inflamed. Her coochie still throbbed from a sensual promise not fulfilled. She was not in the mood. *Dig deep, real deep, into those nice girl reserves.* She stood there wearing a flotation device reeking of spoiled fish while Brett and Brayton pitched plastic Fisher-Price Little People figures at her.

One plastic projectile hit Reese in the eye. She counted to ten instead of ordering them all —except Gabriel of course—to get the heck out of her flippin' garage.

"Brett and Brayton, we don't throw our toys," Odette rebuked the twins. Then she attempted to scoop up their ammo, but appeared to have trouble bending and crouching.

Gabriel picked up the figures and handed them back to the twins who hurled them at Reese again, but she ducked in time.

"Cuz!" Rosvaughn said again. "I know I'm late."

"More than a week. *Again*," Reese snapped, hands on her hips. "I know you didn't come to cut the grass. My new neighbor helped me out." She gestured toward Gabriel.

"I'm sorry," Rosvaughn said to Reese before thanking Gabriel, who picked up the Little People again and returned them to the determined twins, who relaunched them at Reese, their prime target.

Reese bobbed, but one figure nailed her ear, making it ring. "Gabriel, this is my cousin Rosvaughn. When she picked up the Little People and stuffed them inside her pockets the twins began to cry. *Tough titty said the kitty when the milk went dry!*"

"Nice to meet you." Rosvaughn moved toward Gabriel. They bumped fists. "Thanks for helping her out, man."

"You already know Odette, Calvin, and the twins." Reese was talking to Gabriel, but Rosvaughn responded instead.

Rosvaughn gave Odette the stink-eye. "How can I forget the woman who called the cops on me."

"Reese wasn't home," Odette said, now hyperventilating. "I'd never seen you before. Your britches were hanging off your backside, and you had too many chains and tattoos." The chains and saggy pants were gone but Odette's accusatory glare dropped to the viper ink swirling around the length of his sinewy right arm, its head hidden underneath the sleeve of his T-shirt. "I thought you were one of those scammers who mowed people's lawns without permission and then demanded some outrageous payment for the unsolicited service."

"Clearly you were profiling," Rosvaughn said, indignation wafting off him. "And wrong, but you never apologized."

"I'm sorry, okay!" shouted Odette, who couldn't sound more unapologetic.

Jiggling the squalling twins, a saucer-eyed Calvin moved toward his wife. "You all right, honey bun? You don't look well."

"I'm, um, good." Odette bussed the twins' snotty cheeks and squeezed their tiny fingers when they reached out to her. "I need... Reese's help with... something. Girl stuff. You go... back with the boys. I'll... join... you shortly. I... made... your favorites." As if each word were a mile in a marathon, she paused and drew deep breaths. "Crispy... oven-fried chicken...b-b-buttermilk b-biscuits..."

"Honey!" With a flicker of alarm in his eyes, Calvin reached to steady Odette as she swayed and the boys clung to him. "You look as if you're about to pass out."

"I…I'm fine," Odette said. "Just a little winded from my workout. That… new Jillian Michaels'… DVD… is a killer."

The Odette Reese knew did not work out with exercise DVDs. Odette had deemed them mind-numbingly repetitive. The peppy small talk and banal jokes between squats and overhead presses often became a type of psychological torture after the first dozen views.

"As I was saying, the b-bi-cuits are made," Odette continued, "from… scratch of course, with honey…b-b- butter, also… from scratch…And, whew! That green… bean casserole… with… the little crunchy onions… also from… scratch of course…on top. I… know… how much… you love those… so I added extra this time."

"Yum!" Calvin smacked his lips, and Odette pecked his cheek.

"I'm heading home, Reese," Gabriel said. "Got to feed Apollo and Maximus. Good to see you again, Odette, Calvin, Brett, and Brayton." He nodded. "And nice meeting you, Rosvaughn."

"Reese…may… I… see… you… *in private*, please?" Still swaying, Odette pleaded when it was just the three of them. "Now?"

Rosvaughn's cell rang. "I'd better take this. It's Tasha," he said. "We need to coordinate particulars for later. Be right back" He turned and headed to his van.

"What's the matter?" Reese asked after she and Odette were alone in the kitchen. If Reese didn't know any better, she'd think her friend was inebriated.

"This!" Odette snatched open her over-size men's button-down shirt. "I'm… dying! And… I …can't get this… blasted thing off!"

The "thing" was one of those waist-trainer (aka shaper) devices. This one, fashioned from yellow neoprene, had an industrial-grade zipper with piranha-like teeth.

"Don't… just stand… there! Help! I'm… about to pass out!"

Reese tried to work the zipper free and said what she was thinking. "Hmmm. Seems to be caught. And you're wearing it cinched way too tight, girl."

"For *real???*" Odette replied in a simpering voice. "Is that… why… I feel… as if I'm about to… burp up my spleen?"

Reese shook her head at her friend's sarcasm. This was how Odette spoke to the person whose help she needed, but then Reese supposed near asphyxiation could make a person cranky. "Hold still."

"I don't want…Calvin to see… me in this!" For the past year, Odette had been experimenting with a variety of methods to lose those "last ten stubborn pounds" of baby weight using teas, wraps, diet patches, and ear stapling. Now this. All the while, not letting on to her husband. Calvin, at least a good decade from gaining a mushy-middle "dad bod," had the nerve to look forever boyish with his twinkling dark eyes and tall, rangy build. Though he had a couple of decades on the slew of teens he put in braces, he appeared to fit right in with them, making Odette feel as if she looked like "his mama." And Reese had never seen an orthodontist practice as hip as Calvin's Cherry Hill office, with its bright, trendy furniture; multiple wall-mounted screens for video gameplay; and rave-like atmosphere of loud rap music piped through a "bomb-ass," as he described it, sound system.

Still, why would anyone risk squashing or puncturing internal organs to temporarily project the illusion of a smaller, more youthful waistline?

Reese should've known something was amiss when her friend, who had exceptionally refined taste even in casual wear, showed up in a pair of threadbare leggings and a frumpy, stained men's shirt and with her face scrubbed free of her usual skillfully applied makeup. But this was a no judgment zone.

"I said, hold still." Reese gave the zipper another tug.

Odette wailed. "I'm dying!"

Brute force wouldn't work, but a good waxing might. Reese removed a tube of ChapStick from her kitchen junk drawer. "I once read about this in a magazine."

"Hurry!"

"Hmmm." Reese pursed her lips. "I should do a spot check first. I don't want to stain your trainer."

"I don't care! Get. It. Off. Me!" Odette sobbed.

"Please. Don't cry. It'll make breathing more difficult."

"I can't… help… it! My family… needs me. Reese, I can't… die like this… trying to regain my… hour-glass figure in… some tacky DIY experiment."

"You made this yourself?"

"Yes, how… gauche and desperate …would that read in my obituary? If I have… to die for… vanity reasons, I should at least… have the good taste... to do it on... a top board-certified plastic surgeon's... table. Darren's... table. At least... my bereaved family... can sue Darren's pants off... and expect a nice settlement for... my trouble."

"Stop talking, Odette." A sure sign her friend was nowhere near croaking, but acting out in her usual drama-queen fashion.

"Regardless of... what's said aloud... don't you think... everyone mocks... those people who die... from a nasty infection... after getting... commercial-grade silicone butt implants... from some... whack job... who calls... herself 'Miss Peaches' and... performs... cosmetic surgery... on a... soiled futon... in her dirty basement?"

"It's sad actually. And you're not going to die." After Reese rubbed the wax on the teeth and jiggled the zipper, it glided up and down. "There."

Odette jumped away from Reese. She yanked off the trainer and slammed it to the floor as if wrestling a gator. Winded, she collapsed over the marble island. "How will I explain this bruising to Calvin?" she said after peeking under her top. "I swear I'll never do that again! No more weight-loss-get-fit-quick madness for me!"

Until tomorrow. Odette had sworn the same thing after one of those "slimming teas" gave her the runs for a week.

"I'll get you a glass of lemonade," Reese said.

Rosvaughn entered the kitchen. "Hey, what's going on in here?"

After Odette's breathing steadied and her color returned to normal, she stomped that trainer again.

Rosvaughn mocked her, launching into a silly galumphing jig. "Call me Dude of the Dance," he said.

"Knock it off, Rosvaughn," Reese said. "Let her vent her frustration...in peace." She passed him a glass of lemonade and put one on the island for Odette.

"Starting a new fashion trend," Rosvaughn said, pointing to Reese's life vest.

The smelly thing had come in handy, though not as her father had intended.

"I noticed you called, but didn't leave a message," Rosvaughn said to Reese as she went to the mud room to remove the life vest and don a freshly laundered Sweet Spot T-shirt.

"Yes, too late. You're forcing me to terminate my contract for your services."

"Give me another chance, cuz," he said, after gulping his lemonade. "I promise I won't let you down again. On the real. Please. I overscheduled last week. Business has been good, but I should've called to let you know what was going on with me. I shouldn't have taken you for granted. And then Mom had the flu. I had to do some things for her. Ask her. I had a lot of balls in the air. Please. One more chance."

Reese should show some backbone for once and cut him loose.

"I understand if you must," Rosvaughn said. "But I want you to know I still appreciate you. You're one of the few family members who gave me a chance without making me prove myself first. You believed in me." He put his hand near his heart. "And that will always mean a lot. No pressure. I understand why you want out."

Oh, heck! He was giving her a wet-eyed-baby-seal face that had been effective since he was a kid coaxing that last watermelon Now & Later out of her. Or pleading for forgiveness after he'd scalped her Totally Hair Barbie with his Cub Scout lock-back pocketknife or given her the willies by chasing her around with a big fuzzy block of moldy cheese.

"But if there's anything, anything at all, I can do to make this right…," he said. "Oh, I almost forgot. I brought you something. It's out in the van. I'll be right back."

By the time he left, Odette's meltdown had passed, and she was sipping the lemonade.

"Hard to believe he's your cousin." She crinkled her nose. "You sure he's not one of those…What do they call them? *'Play'* cousins? You're from such a good, upstanding family, and he's so ghet-"

"He's blood," Reese cut off the slur teetering on Odette's tongue. "We're real *first* cousins. My dad and his dad are brothers, real blood brothers, not *brothas*, as in homeys or aces. And Rosvaughn is like a *brother* to me so watch what you say."

"Whatever," Odette replied with a dismissive wave. "I didn't mean anything by it."

"Just being your usual bougie self is all, huh?"

"Let's move right along, shall we?" Odette's lips tipped up in a sly grin. "I know something's going on with you and our new neighbor. I'm a happily married woman, but I've got eyes. O-M-G, the body on that man! He's so fine, it's spellbinding. Like, is he even real? There's something *very* familiar about him, though," Odette said, pursing her lips as if searching her memory. "I can't place it. I feel as if I've seen him before." She paused. "I *know* I've seen him before. I mean, before he moved over here. So what did I interrupt? Do tell."

"Gabriel just did some lawn work for me."

"That's not all he did for you, honey. I wasn't too oxygen deprived to notice how hot and bothered you two looked. Whew!" She fanned herself. "Maybe you can't talk now with Rastaman —

"Ros-*vaughn*," Reese told Odette for the umpteenth time.

"But I expect all the juicy details later." Odette sipped more lemonade. "This is quite tasty." She swirled the beverage and took more careful sips, sommelier style. "But if you want to take it from good to amazing, next time use Meyer lemons, a mandarin-lemon hybrid, if you can find them. They're pricier, but sweeter and juicier. Worth every extra penny. And for that dash of molasses flavor, go with raw sugar instead of refined next time."

"Gotcha," Reese chirped in her usual go-along-to-get-along manner. Besides, Gabriel had praised Reese's lemonade for its "perfect blend of tart and sweet" so Odette could suck it. And those Meyer lemons.

Rosvaughn returned, disarming Reese with a beautifully wrapped package.

"A gift for me!" Reese clapped.

"It's for Sinbad," he said.

Even better as far as Reese was concerned. Unlike Quinn and Blaire, Rosvaughn had always been super sweet to Sinbad, and he'd never once ridiculed his weight.

"I thought of Sinbad when I saw these," Rosvaughn said. "So I snapped them up."

Reese opened the package. Inside the she found a food storage baggy with two stuffed cat toys.

"How odd," Odette said. "Why is one shaped like a french fry and the other like a Japanese maple leaf?"

Before Rosvaughn could answer, Odette's hubby knocked on the door.

Bless you, Calvin. Reese invited him in, but he waved and stayed outside, next to the stroller with the twins.

"Hey, babe," he called to Odette. "We're starving. We don't want to start without you."

"I'll call you later, Reese." Odette left without that BDSM trainer.

Reese gave the toys to Sinbad. Whipped into a frenzy, her cat nuzzled, batted, flipped, licked, and lunged. Like a queen in heat, he rolled around the ceramic-tiled floor with the toys.

"Japanese maple and a french fry!" Rosvaughn howled at Odette's cluelessness. "Miss Priss would've called the cops on me again if I'd told her it's a pot leaf and a joint."

"Nothing you said would convince her it's catnip and not marijuana inside," Reese said, regarding him. "Hey, it *is* actual *catnip* inside them, right?"

"*Et tu, Brute?*" Rosvaughn often showcased his private high school education by quoting Shakespeare and Friedrich Nietzsche.

"I know you've never actually sold drugs, but you have—"

"Self-medicated in the past. But check this, I haven't been high in ages. Since way before my last bid. I swear. And besides, Sinbad's a cool cat, but I wouldn't waste primo ganja on him, that is *if* I still possessed and smoked primo ganja, which I do not because I'm running a respectable business now, completely clean, as in not under the influence of illegal recreational drugs," he said, lifting his hand as if taking an oath. "You believe me?"

Reese took a moment. "I do." He'd been clear-eyed and fragrant with his usual Ralph Lauren Polo Red. He had yet to raid her kitchen in a munchies tear or behave any loopier than normal. And he popped nicotine gum often, a sign he was also serious about kicking his Kools habit.

"I figured you and Sinbad would like the toys," he said, possibly chomping on a piece of Nicorette.

"They are funny, but…"

Rosvaughn nodded. "I know. I know. You don't condone illegal recreational drug use. So will you give me another chance? Please don't cancel our contract."

Reese regarded him for a few minutes. "Okay, one more time to miss a scheduled job for me or screw up something else. *Anything else.* One more time, Rosvaughn Tyrell Sommers Jr." She shook her finger at him.

"Uh-oh. She's using my full name. She means business."

"Darn right."

"Love you, cuz. You're the best."

"Wait. First up." Reese gave him the bill from her HOA. "It's my latest fine. Handle this."

"Handled." Rosvaughn accepted the envelope, wrapped her in a hug, and checked his watch. "I'm about to dip in a minute."

"Oh, got a hot date with Tasha?"

"Yup. I think she might be The One. I'll bring her to the shop so you two can meet. *Hmmp. Hmmp. Hmmp.* The things that woman does to me." He pumped his hips. "She makes *the* best oxtail stew, and we're both Capricorns."

Reese smiled. "A match made in heaven."

CHAPTER 13

Man, that was rough." Julian Phillips merged his black pickup truck into highway traffic.

In the passenger seat, Gabriel tried to purge unsettling images from his mind. "I'm leaving there wanting to bash some heads, man. The whole scene makes me sick to my stomach. I know we discussed grabbing a bite, but—"

"I hear ya. I'll run out and get some burgers for us later."

Gabriel and his close friend and partner were on their way back to their own facility, where Lance had agreed to see their morning clients and pet patients.

No matter how long Gabriel worked in their field, the evidence of pure evil perpetrated against animals still deeply disturbed him. "The inhumanity of all...the lack of respect..."

He and Julian had spent several hours at a special shelter, undisclosed to the public, and on the outskirts of town. They'd assisted a colleague who volunteered for a local animal protection association. Group members, along with police and animal control, had transported twenty pit bulls removed from a South Mayfair residence, where they had been used for fighting. The dogs had been kept in the most appalling conditions. Many had been beaten and undernourished. They bore the scars — broken teeth, deep bite marks, gashes, and other nasty injuries—consistent with involvement in the cruel and illegal activity.

One senior, used as a "bait dog" for training, was so mutilated by a pack of "fighters," he'd died that morning from massive blood loss. Several arrests had been made. This, however, did not guarantee a happy ending. Although the rest of the animals had received proper nutrition and medical care, many of these adult dogs, bred and trained to exhibit extreme aggression toward people and other animals, often could not be rehabilitated. When unadoptable, euthanasia was likely.

They rode for another fifteen minutes in silence until Julian turned on jazz music, which helped lighten Gabriel's mood. After another five minutes the friends discussed updates they planned to make at their hospital until Julian steered the conversation toward the personal. "So, Lance tells me you've met someone."

"I have." Gabriel smiled. "Her name is Reese Sommers and, man, wow. I'm talking *the* total package."

"You've met more 'total packages' than FedEx, UPS, and the USPS combined, bruh. So you're ready to move on, I take it?" Julian asked with a heavy dose of cynicism.

Gabriel didn't take offense. His friend, who often acted as the tight-ass buzzkill among them, meant well. The more methodical and practical Julian approached most changes at a slower pace, whether they pertained to entrees on a menu or a new piece of high-tech medical equipment. Julian also believed his wife, Josselyn, was his one and only. "My everything" or "the right one for me" as he'd often referred to her because she understood and loved him unconditionally. As far as Gabriel knew, Julian had dated no one in the year since Josselyn's death. He'd told his friends he simply couldn't envision making room in his heart for another woman.

No doubt, Josselyn had been the best. But Gabriel and Lance were sure Julian just needed more time to process his tragic loss before meeting that next "right one" for him. He'd loved married life too much to spend the rest of his days unattached in his spacious Greenwood Village home.

"What's it been? A year since you and Adriana broke up?" Julian asked.

"Yep. Split for good," Gabriel replied.

"Isn't that what you said the last time and the time before that and the time before that?"

There it was. Blatant skepticism. Again.

Okay, so Gabriel and Adriana had kept everyone guessing with their on-again-off-again track record. The first breakup had happened in seventh grade during spring break. They'd reconciled by summer vacation. Over the years, they'd had fulfilling relationships with other people before they found their way back into each other's arms.

"We're not meant to be a couple. We're way better as friends. We've come to realize that. Finally. Once and for all. And just wait until you meet Reese. She's something else, man. She has these pretty caramel-colored eyes…these full pouty lips." He licked his own as if he could taste hers.

"Sounds like Adriana."

"And Reese is a runner, a seasoned one."

"Didn't Adriana break her personal record in the Mayfair Go-for-Your-Gold marathon last year? And she did that… What's that one obstacle course called? The one where everyone rolls around in the mud and ends the race looking like swamp monsters."

"Tough Mudder."

"Yeah, Tough Mudder, the year before?"

"Man, Reese is sexy as hell. I'm talking scorching." Gabriel's jeans grew snug in the crotch thinking about how he had her pinned against that wall, his hands inside her skimpy panties as he caressed her to…He swallowed.

Standing in that garage with the gang, Gabriel damn near exploded from frustration and lack of release. He'd hobbled home to feed the dogs all right, but only after he'd jacked off in the downstairs half bath first.

"Ah." Julian nodded. "So you want to sleep with her."

"Hell yeah. I want to get down on it," Gabriel sang the chorus of the old Kool & the Gang song.

"Lance is rubbing off on you. Even his love of classic R&B tunes."

"But that's not the end game, my friend. I want her in my *life*, not just in my bed." With Reese a particular Internet meme rushed to mind: *I want to date you so hard and marry the hell out of you.* He'd never felt this way about anyone. 'She's smart. Fun. Doesn't take herself too seriously. I have no doubt the lady is strong and can take care of business, but something about her brings out a protectiveness in me. She has this gentle, unassuming way about her, too."

"Sounds like Adriana. You definitely have a type, my man."

Gabriel considered the comparison. "Okay so Reese and Adriana share a few qualities. I happen to like nice and easygoing. Shoot me."

"Gentle, unassuming, soft-spoken, nice, easygoing, huh?"

"She's so sweet and thoughtful, man. Before I left for the hospital this morning, I found the thank-you note she left after I mowed her lawn. Who still does that? Handwritten thank-you notes with little stickers and ribbons, in this day of text and digital everything?"

"And did she draw curlicues on them and dot her *i's* with little hearts, too?" Julian said in a mincing voice.

Gabriel gave him a shove.

"Do you hear yourself?"

But Gabriel was on a roll. "She did her research on dog-friendly ingredients and whipped up these cake-like treats with frosting for Apollo and Maximus and left them on my porch with the note. She called them 'pupcakes,' *pupcakes*, get it?"

"I get it."

"She's amazing," Gabriel said. Julian didn't need to know just how responsive, passionate, seductive and… *hmmp, hmmp, hmmp* spontaneous she was. Images of pinning her against that garage wall flashed through his mind again. His tongue teasing the skin beneath that little cupcake pendant nesting at her cleavage. He could feel her soft, insistent hands stroking his… "

"Gabriel."

"Huh?"

"Where'd you go just now? One minute you were going on about how amazing she is and the next—"

"Everything about her is sweet. I like her spirit."

"My late Great-uncle Cleavelle had a lot to say about those sweet ones with that 'unassuming and gentle' way about them."

Gabriel gave Julian a sidelong look. "You've told some strange tall tales about this Great-uncle Cleavelle of yours. Isn't he the one who used to gather you and your high school football teammates to watch porn and drink beer?"

"Yep, that's him, God rest his soul. He'd sit closest to the television, sloshing his tall can of Coors all over his Barcalounger and oxygen tank. Emphysema never slowed him down. He'd bounce, swear, and hoot the loudest at the porn starlet rocking on top. He'd shout, 'Riiiiiiide it, gal! You better bust that broncooooo!' He called it helping us 'man up.' Of course he thought I was soft because that type of macho male bonding didn't particularly appeal to me. Teenage Lance would've loved it, though."

"Now ease up on Lance, he's not here to defend himself," Gabriel said.

"I'll tell you, Lance couldn't say enough about this Reese."

"Nothing inappropriate I hope. I *will* kick his ass."

"Now ease up on Lance, he's not here to defend himself," Julian volleyed back with a grin. "But no, he didn't step out of line. Just said she's a real looker. And that her body is 'bananas, as in crazy b-b-bangin,' his words."

"She is the most beautiful, wonderful woman I've ever met, *inside* and out."

"Lance also said you're clearly smitten. Smitten is my word. I believed he used 'whipped'... and I added the 'for now.' "

"I sense this vulnerability in Reese. I could never hurt or betray her," Gabriel said with conviction.

"Not intentionally."

"She's special."

"Right," Julian replied, still unable to hide his sarcasm.

"Would you stop with the pessimism? It's getting annoying." Gabriel glared at Julian for a few moments, but brightened again. "Did I mention Reese is a business owner?" He even loved saying her name. Reese. Reese. Reese. Reese. He could write a song, a smooth melody, with a single word. Reese. Yeah, he was smitten. Already. "Reese owns a charming cupcake bakery and coffee shop in Briarcrest. The Sweet Spot. It's on the east end of Fremont Avenue. What she's done there is impressive. You should see it. And get this, most of the time she smells like cake. It's like a sugar rush being around her."

"But does she do pet rescue?" Changing lanes, Julian raised an index finger. "Now that's the question."

"No, but she has a cat. Good enough for me."

"Just one cat?" Julian said, unimpressed.

"Yeah, but he's a big one."

"A Siberian tiger, huh?"

"Not quite, but close."

"You lie."

Both laughed.

"Still, you've had relationships with other exceptional women *with pets* over the years. But not one could break Adriana's spell over you for the long haul."

"There's no spell, just the fierce pull of familiarity, force of habit, not to mention all the prodding from our families. Mom and Dad love Adriana, but they haven't met Reese yet. I'll admit it was comfortable and easy with Adriana, but if it were so damn right and we were so perfect together, would we have broken up so many times over petty things? Not exactly a hallmark of the healthiest relationship."

"True."

"Enough is enough. We're better as friends *without benefits*."

"I still don't understand how you two can turn the ol' platonic switch on and off so many damn times. How is that possible?"

"This man finally knows when to cut his losses. Adriana and I are in complete agreement. This time is different. I swear. It's been a year, a whole year already. A decade could pass with us apart, and everyone would still think we're getting back together. 'It's just a matter of time,' everyone would insist. Well, I'm done. We're done. Over and out—"

"But not really. The gentleman doth protest too much."

"I can't explain it." As Gabriel became more reflective his voice went low. "It's different with Reese. It just *is*, that's all. Our connection is…Not sure how to describe it. But it's like nothing I've ever felt before, *with anyone*."

"And you're so sure about it this soon?"

"All I know is I can't stop thinking about this woman. Even when she's not around I have a natural high looking forward to the next time I see her. And I couldn't be happier about it. I hope she's just as into me as I'm into her. Man, I can't shake this feeling I've met my wife."

"Whoa. That's fast!"

"Whoa indeed. It's clear why it never worked out with Adriana, as great as she is, or any of the others. Reese Sommers is The One. *My One*. And I moved right next door to her. What were the chances? It's fate, my friend."

"Your Fated One? This is the first time you've gone all woo-woo on me. I hope you're right, but only more time will tell."

Gabriel agreed. More time would tell. And he couldn't wait to prove Julian and everyone else wrong.

CHAPTER 14

That evening, Gabriel stood at Reese's front door, berating himself for not calling first. Was he turning into a pesky neighbor? Again, he'd been thinking about her all day long.

He had a rapidly approaching book deadline, but he'd lost the ability to focus for longer than a few minutes at a time. Picking up where they'd left off last night had crossed his mind, but even if that didn't happen, he'd be thrilled just to see her smile and maybe make her laugh.

Before Gabriel could knock or ring the doorbell, he turned away. *This is nuts!* He checked his watch. 8:35 p.m. He'd yet to make his daily word count.

He had arrived home after a long day at the hospital and gone to work on her mower so he'd have a reason to come to her house that evening, lest he deviate from gentleman caller to booty caller. But even though he was returning her tuned-up mower, he needed to let her make the next move, beyond the decorative thank-you note and pupcakes she'd left on his front porch. He had more than one thing on his mind, but she didn't know that yet. He needed to give her space. Before he could clear the property, Reese opened the door.

"Gabriel!" Reese, dressed in another pair of frayed, super short cut-offs and a T-shirt, stood in the frame. "I thought I heard someone on my porch." She opened the door to welcome him inside, but he didn't move. A loose ponytail sat high on her head. Her face, free of makeup. The dark top had streaks of white powder and mystery smears on it. Still, she took his breath away.

"Hi," he said, feeling like an geeky boy asking for a first date.

"Hi, yourself," she said as his heart leapt.

Gabriel could leave the lawn mower and go home now. Exultant.

"So you're leaving already?" she asked, her brows lifted.

"I, um, well, I know it's late to pop up unannounced, but I, well…I have your mower."

"I can see that."

"And um, thank you for the thank-you card and the pupcakes."

"And thank you for thanking me for the thank-you card and the pupcakes to thank you for doing my lawn and tuning my mower."

"And thank you for thanking me for thanking you for the thank-you card and the pupcakes… wait…I'm losing my train of thought here." Her long, shapely legs in those short shorts and her smile had that effect on him.

"You forgot to take the edger and trimmer yesterday," Reese said.

"Yes! I did, didn't I? So if you'll open the garage door, I'll roll in the mower, take the trimmer and edger and be on my way."

After one door ascended, he positioned the mower in a corner and went to the shelf with the lawn equipment.

Reese stepped into the garage. The sweet aroma of something baking floated out with her. From what he could tell from the outside, her floor plan appeared similar to his.

"So how was your day?" she asked

"Busy." *And I thought of you often.*

"Same here."

"What time do you close?"

"Seven p.m.," Reese said. "We used to close later, but after crunching the numbers, closing earlier made more sense. There's little foot traffic in that area after normal workday hours, unless there's a show or event at the auditorium nearby. What about you?"

"My hours? Long most days and all over the place." *The hours drag when we're apart.*

"Like an emergency room or Minute Clinic for animals?" she asked.

"Not exactly. We do hours extending into the evenings if we're extra busy, but we're not a 24-hour facility. Some patients stay overnight while getting treatment, but the staff leaves unless the animal requires close overnight monitoring. When needed, Julian prefers to take that shift since his wife suddenly passed last year."

"Oh, that's awful. Any kids?"

"No, but he likes to stay busy with work. And there's Myles, I mentioned him already. He's not a partner, but he works late sometimes, because he covers four hospitals in town. His specialty is dentistry—root canals, crowns, implants, and braces."

Reese laughed. "A dog with braces? Now that I've got to see."

"Business has been great for us all. And looks as if the Sweet Spot is a success."

"It is. Speaking of…I was experimenting with another cupcake recipe. As you can see, I'm covered with cake four and frosting."

Yum. Gabriel's dipstick twitched. *Yo, time to go!* He wanted to court her, but had he already sabotaged his more honorable intentions because he'd had his hands in her panties the day before? "I'll take these and let you get back to your cupcakes." He moved to lift the boxes off the shelf.

"I'd love for you to sample this one and tell me what you think?" Reese gave him that suggestive, glazy-eyed look.

"I'm afraid my opinion would lack detail, useful analysis, or anything else beyond the Cookie Monster brand of culinary assessment, 'Me like cupcake! Nom, nom, nom, nom!'"

"Maybe that's all I need. The thumbs-up or down." Reese let two fingers glide along his bicep, which made his dipstick twitch again. "And you promised to do a house call for Sinbad's chinny chin chin."

"Yes, I did, didn't I?" And Gabriel always kept his word, and so he followed her when she stepped inside the mud room.

Her house, also a contemporary brick with an open-concept design, was about a third smaller than his, but just as nice. The gourmet kitchen, like something out of a culinary magazine, was a bright, sizable, and modern space — all robin's egg blue, white, stainless steel, and marble. The cool Art-Deco-style *carpe diem* sign taking up most of one wall caught his eye. Despite the various baking bowls, tools, flour trails, and frosting globs on the countertops and the large island, the room was neat and arranged for efficiency, just how he'd imagined it would be.

"It smells damn good in here, lady." Her kitchen had a sweet buttery scent like that of her shop, but potent notes of peanut butter and vanilla replaced the aroma of coffee. He scooped up Sinbad who'd been lapping from his water bowl in the mud room. Gabriel checked the affected area. "It's clear. Good job." He dipped and lifted Sinbad, checking his weight. "But he doesn't feel much lighter."

"It's been less than a month. Remember, we don't crash diet."

"So you've been following the instructions in the literature I gave you?"

"Not yet, but I will."

When Gabriel relaxed his hold, Sinbad jumped down and went back to his water dish.

About a dozen chocolate cupcakes sat on one counter.

"I hope you like peanut butter," she said.

"I love peanut butter."

"They're our signature chocolate with peanut butter and cream frosting, topped with little chocolate bits in colorful hard candy shells. Cute, huh?"

"Sounds, looks, and smells like a winner."

"Taste one." Reese lifted the airy treat as if to feed him, but instead of pushing it all the way toward his mouth, she drew it to her own and took a bite, slowly chewing. "I'm waiting," she whispered.

Gabriel reached for the cupcake, but she placed her other hand at his nape and drew him close until her sweet peanut butter and chocolate-scented breath mingled with his. "Have a taste… here," she whispered, brushing her soft, full lips against his.

A husky groan emerged from deep inside his throat as she traced his lips with the tip of her tongue. He wanted to wine and dine her, show more of his chivalrous side to make his intentions clear. He didn't want a hookup. But now his groin was a lead pipe with two eight balls hitched high and ready for action. His mouth brushed across hers.

"Delicious," he said, licking his lips. "Definitely a keeper."

"Yeah?" Reese pressed her lush breasts against his chest and molded her hips against his. "So how does it compare?" Her tongue darted in and out of his mouth, teasing and lightly tangling with his.

"To what?"

"The double dark chocolate one with the light French buttercream frosting you had yesterday." Reese stroked him to near madness.

"Both are quite tasty," he said, sounding like a dork. But he had a plan, and he would stick to it. No matter how good she felt or how insistent she was. He wanted to bury himself deep inside her honeyed walls when he climaxed with her for the first time.

But that would not happen until they'd had a proper date.

"Do you think the frosting could use more chocolate to balance the nutty flavor? How about my adding a berry filling? Too PB and J?" Reese turned enough to reach a large, red mixer that stood like a gleaming steel sculpture on the counter. She dipped a finger in a mound of frosting and brought it to her lips. "Here, have a taste of this."

So Gabriel did, sucking her tongue and nipping at the frosting on her lips as she moaned and stroked him through his jeans. Their kisses deepened and grew more fervent. *Damn she tasted and felt good!* Then she went for the top button of his fly, but he nudged her hand away. He was barely holding on. Once his erection sprang free of confinement, sliding inside her soft, determined hands, there'd be no turning back.

"All doors are locked. No interruptions this time. Nothing can stop us now, but a fire, earthquake, or maybe Sinbad coughing up a hairball." Her teeth caught his bottom lip.

Reese wanted this. Wanted *him.* So why didn't he stop for a moment and tell her what *he* wanted? Would she think he was a cornball, somehow less manly for not taking what she was offering? Would he scare her off if they didn't agree on the type of relationship they'd have?

The day Adriana had shown up at his place unannounced, he'd revealed all he believed Reese needed to know about the situation with his ex. Reese asked no questions. Not one. Nor had she mentioned Adriana again for that matter. Past lovers with serious intentions had a thousand questions about Adriana and had found the continuing close friendship suspect from the get-go—*as they should have*—seeing how Gabriel had ended up reuniting with Adriana. His head hadn't been quite right at the time, and he'd known that all along, but now…

At first, Gabriel was relieved his friendship with his ex had not dissuaded Reese, but now her indifference bugged the hell out of him. What if Reese didn't give a damn because she only wanted sex? It was possible. Every woman wasn't hunting for a happily ever after when a hookup, a conveniently located one at that, would suit her fine. And he'd enjoyed his own share of mutual no-strings arrangements the past year. However, he wanted more—much more—with Reese, who went for his fly again. He gently brushed her hand away.

With his heart still hammering, he kissed her again and then put space between them. The pipe bomb with two eight balls was already damn close to detonation. *Ten, nine…*

"What's wrong?" she asked, reaching for his fly again.

Gabriel took her hand and kissed her fingertips. "Nothing, but I have to go. Thanks for the cupcake."

"You're leaving?" Confusion dueled with passion in her pretty eyes.

Gabriel couldn't look at her luscious lips, swollen from their kissing. *Eight, seven…* "Sorry, I have a big day at the hospital ahead of me."

"Okay. You have frosting near your left nostril." Reese tried to kiss it away, but he took a step back.

"I'll take care of it. I'll call you." Gabriel tapped her cute nose and gave her a dry peck on the lips, all he could handle. *Six, five, four…*

"Tomorrow?"

"No, tonight, right after I feed the dogs." Gabriel hobbled out of her place and crossed the swatch of lawn separating their houses, going right past eager Maximus and Apollo to his first floor bathroom. On the other side, the barking dogs scratched and thumped on the door. He braced one hand against the sink, opened his pants, and vigorously stroked and jerked his aching shaft. "Aaah." With an image of Reese in his mind and the tang of peanut butter and chocolate on his tongue, it only took three seconds to close.

CHAPTER 15

You what?" Quinn squawked, standing in Reese's kitchen on a Sunday afternoon after they'd attended a church service together. While Blaire was still dressed in a classic navy blue sheathe she'd worn to church, Reese had changed into a casual maxi dress and flip-flops. Quinn got more comfortable in a romper and Keds.

"I let him kiss me." Reese removed the pan of reheated leftover baby back ribs she'd grilled the day before.

"On the cheek? A peck?" Quinn mixed her specialty, a peach mango sangria with generous splashes of Grand Marnier.

"Nope, on the lips," Reese said, leaving out the part about his hand inside her pants. "And oh man! Can he kiss! *Muy caliente!*"

"I knew it," Quinn said, shaking her head in resignation. "I knew you were already gah-gah over this guy when you first mentioned him. And there was no way you could keep it ten-foot-pole platonic."

"And why am I just finding out about this guy and his pole?" Blaire pouted.

"Because you've been incommunicado lately," Reese said. Now that the Home & Hearth Channel had increased its episode order, Blaire was always taping *A Nest for Newbies,* taking care of the many duties required to maintain her real estate brokerage business, or attending one of her many networking events. "We invited you to join us that day at Pump-it-Up when I told Quinn everything, but you passed."

Quinn shared what knew about Gabriel.

"I'm with Quinn," Blaire said. "As if living next door weren't complicated enough, there's an ex still in the picture, too? Girl, you prefer loving dangerously, don't you?"

Blaire went on for another fifteen minutes, commenting on everything Quinn had relayed to get her up to speed.

Reese steeled herself for tag-team objections. "I like him, and I *will* have him."

"And you're ready to take a chance on such a potentially loaded situation, another triangle, so soon after the Darren and Sasha ordeal? Don't get me started on all the inter-commingling," Blaire rattled on in a sarcastic tone as if recapping the ridiculous plot of a soap opera. "So Darren has slept with you and impregnated Sasha, whose sister Adriana has slept with Gabriel who is probably close friends with Darren, who has slept with you, who will most likely sleep with Gabriel if you have your way. It's like a mash-up of *The Bachelor* and Six Degrees of Kevin Bacon." She shuddered. "I hope everyone has stocked up on antibiotics and is current on STD screenings. I smell trouble."

"Save your breath," Quinn said as she and Blaire helped Reese carry their food and drinks out back to the patio. "As Daddy would say, Reese still 'don't believe fat meat is greasy.'"

Reese left an opening at the patio door so Sinbad could join them when ready. He loved ribs and was sure to come running.

"You got angry at us for not sharing our reservations about Darren sooner," Quinn said. "Let the record show we warned you about this situation."

"So what's your plan?" Blaire asked Reese as she took a seat at the glass-top table. "What do you want out of this?"

"Fun," Reese replied. To better shield them from the sun, she adjusted the giant umbrella over the table. "Things at the shop are keeping me hopping so I'm living in the moment and having a good time when I can. I don't want to think too hard or project too much." Sinbad descended from his six-foot-high, faux-fur-covered kitty climbing tree in the family room to join them. Reese gave him a rib to lick, paw, and gnaw. When Sinbad ran off with it, she took a sip of her sangria and glanced at the fence separating her property from Gabriel's. While she'd played nonchalant with her sisters about her fling candidate, she couldn't help wondering what Gabriel was doing now. And with whom he was doing it. Was he still patching up homeless pooches with the winsome Adriana at his side? Was that *Adriiii-aaaaa-naaaaa?* All elongated vowels crooned like an aria.

Adriana, dressed in her sexy-peasant-girl outfit and beat-up sandals. Adriana, jingling with her many turquoise beads and bangles. Adriana with her wide gracious smile, born from a deep appreciation of the beauty and wonder of all God's creatures, Reese thought with more than a hint of... *What was that?* Derision. Yup. *Meow!* Such cattiness was so unlike her.

And Reese was not a clinger. Strong, confident men were attracted to strong, confident women, who also enjoyed satisfying lives outside their men's orbits. And technically he wasn't her man. Just a fling candidate. A sweet distraction from the pain of Darren's betrayal.

Strong, confident men were drawn to women sure of their own worth and what they had to offer. No perceived competition could rattle them. Strong, confident women weren't jealous and insecure about other women. Strong confident women were all about fostering girl power.

While Reese and Gabriel had chatted on the phone and texted several times, she hadn't seen him since that cupcake tasting in her kitchen. The same night, he'd phoned as promised and asked her out on what he kept referring to as "a proper date." He'd also taken the time to share and ask several thought-provoking questions so they could get better acquainted.

He told her about a harrowing experience in high school, a close call when he nearly had his left leg amputated because of a nasty infection that had been resistant to meds.

Reese could've told him about her recent breakup with Darren then, but instead, she went way back, too, confiding how difficult it had been navigating her early teen years. She'd been relentlessly bullied by a group of junior high girls. Her attempts at silencing her tormenters with kindness had failed. She'd internalized, feeling frozen out and stranded on her own emotional ice floe at school.

Quinn and Blaire hadn't been subjected to the same cruel taunts so Reese had assumed they wouldn't understand. And Quinn would've only wanted to beat up the queen bee for messing with Reese. A lot of good that would've done to resolve Reese's feeling of isolation, particularly when Reese herself wasn't sure who she was at the time.

"So when will you two see each other again?" Quinn asked.

Reese shrugged. For the past two weeks work had been so hectic, one or the other canceled their dates. She had invited Gabriel to her mother's birthday dinner, which had been a blast, but his schedule hadn't permitted it. Maybe that was for the best. His presence might have sent the wrong message.

Her family, especially her father and mother, would've read too much into it. Wallace Sommers would have spent the better part of the evening shooting Gabriel the flinty eye and pelting him with questions about his "intentions." Her mother would've fantasized about grandchildren. Reese could bring home Quasimodo and her mom would gush about "what pretty babies" they'd make.

On his end, Gabriel detailed what had derailed their plans. None of the ol' cryptic "something came up" crap Darren had pulled the last two months before their breakup, at which point he'd obviously been up to no darn good.

Before Gabriel could leave the hospital for one date, Adriana had shown up with two Chihuahuas from a puppy mill. One was suffering with a bout of mystery seizures and the other, ongoing diarrhea. Both required immediate medical attention. Lance had been tending to a Great Dane with a deep laceration sustained while jumping a fence. Julian treated a Yorkie who had two broken hind legs after darting in front of a moving car.

Meanwhile, Reese had supervised a few after-hours catering gigs. And on back-to-back evenings, a book club, a socialite mommy group, and a high school dance squad had arranged to meet at the shop for the Ladies Night event that included instruction from Naomi, the Sweet Spot's part-time baker and decorator.

Gabriel and Reese had yet to reschedule that proper date. "Gabriel and I will see each other again, when we see each other again."

"My, my, how very chill of you," Blaire said. "Maybe you can handle this particular situation."

"Of course I can," Reese said, thinking of Gabriel, who'd made her feel like the most desirable women in the world. He didn't trust himself alone with her at their houses. So he'd held firm on not seeing each other again until he'd "wined and dined" her or treated her to "a show or concert."

Nor did he want to do an early morning "buddy run" for fear he'd end up groping her in the bushes. He'd already sent several beautiful bouquets of flowers, and she'd sent cupcakes to him and the hospital staff and pup-and-kitty cakes to their pet patients. But wait! What if he was keeping his distance not because he found Reese irresistible but because of lingering feelings for Adriana? Reese deflated.

"So, Blaire, how are you and Hayes?" Reese asked to shift her downward spiraling thoughts.

"Our schedules are demanding, but we're still getting *it* in," she added with a shimmy on her seat.

"What? Once every two weeks? Meanwhile, BOB and I are still going strong every night," Quinn said, nibbling on a rib.

To foil another long-winded speech about BOB, aka battery-operated boyfriend, Reese asked Quinn about Sheldon Dorfman, the university professor. "He seems nice. He's handsome, and you two have such a good rapport. Is he single?"

"Yes, he's single, and I like him, but only as a friend."

"Why?" Reese sipped her drink and added another helping of potato salad to her plate.

"Hmmmm." Quinn chewed, tipping her head to one side.

"What?" Reese asked. "He's obviously intelligent, educated, and employed. I can tell he likes you. He likes working out in that hell hole. You like working out in that hell hole."

"All the boxes are checked," Blaire added.

"I hear he's too fresh off a divorce," Quinn said. "I'm not interested in a rebound situation. Too risky. And…"

"And?" Reese took another drink of her sangria.

Quinn scooped more potato salad inside her mouth, tipped her head to the side again, and took a few more moments to chew and reflect. "Don't you think he walks like his dick is too big?"

Blaire snorted, spraying her drink.

"Quinn!" Reese said. "Must you always be so snarky about everything? He seems like a nice man."

"What?" Quinn replied, unapologetic.

"Anyway," Reese said. "I thought it was due to his overdeveloped thighs, his quads, the walk, I mean. So? And what if you're wrong?"

"But there's only one way to find out," Quinn said, making poking gestures with her spoon to emphasize her point.

"Since when have you had a problem with big dongs?" Blaire wanted to know.

"There are acceptable levels of 'big.' " Quinn said. "Contrary to what most men think, too much of a good thing ain't always a good thing, just sayin'."

Sinbad abandoned the rib he'd licked free of sauce. As if his next meal depended on it, he stalked a frog. When Sinbad pounced, with reflexes like a spring, he had the prey under his paw. To Reese's surprise, he released the writhing creature and raced inside the house. She followed him. He rooted around his mud room litter box, one of four in her two-story home.

Reese made her own stop in her downstairs half bath. By the time, she returned to the patio, Quinn and Blaire wore mysterious smiles and sat at attention.

"Guess who's outside?" Quinn pointed toward Gabriel's property, where music, laughter, conversation, and dogs barking emerged with the exuberance of a party that had been going on for at least an hour.

Reese returned to her seat and food. A wooden privacy fence separated the properties so she strained to hear voices over the music. One voice was Gabriel's. She heard another guy and then a third. Why was she eavesdropping and feeling such relief when she didn't hear Adriana? Or any other woman for that matter? This. Constant compulsion to identify and classify all of his female guests was among the top five reasons fooling around with the guy next door wasn't the brightest idea.

When one song from Gabriel's property flowed into another, Blaire bobbed her head and waved her hand to the beat. "Hey, that's my jam!"

A ball bounced on the court. *Thunk* after *thunk* against the backboard punctuated the sound of speedy sneakers and muscle hustle. The usual testosterone-fueled trash talking between he-men playing hoops ensued:

"*Nasty dunk!*"

"*Puff a Marlboro, while I smoke you on the court.*"

"*Hit the shower, 'cause your game stinks!*"

Regressed to:

"*Bite me you panty-sniffing shithead!*"

"*Pussy-ass dork!*"

"*I got your pussy-ass dork swinging!*"

"Ah, what happened to good clean yo-mama jokes?" Again, Blaire reached for her vibrating phone.

That was a brick, asshat!

"Why, those cretins!" Quinn had the gall to act scandalized, her hand to cleavage popping out of her scoop-neck romper like canned biscuit dough. "I do believe I am disconcerted, my delicate sensibilities rattled."

"You haven't had 'delicate sensibilities' since you donned your first training bra and let BaeBae Bledsoe from summer camp give you three hickeys on your left breast." Blaire typed yet another text.

"I'm going to tell them to keep that vulgar racket down," Quinn said, eyelashes fluttering.

Reese tittered, assuming Quinn was only kidding. Then her sister popped up, snagged a patio chair, and dashed off.

Aghast, Reese surged to her feet. Her tube-style maxi dress made it impossible to give chase and tackle Quinn.

"But you've said a lot worse!" Blaire called to out to Quinn.

With a cheeky grin, Quinn stopped and glanced over one shoulder. "I know that. But I'm not about to pass up an opportunity to check out the man playing kissy-face with my baby sister!" She continued hotfooting it toward the fence.

"Quinn!" Reese stage whispered, flailing her arms. "Come back here! Come back here right now!"

CHAPTER 16

Gabriel jogged toward the woman peering over his fence. Based on the resemblance to Reese, especially the caramel-brown eyes and the wild curls, he had a good idea who this uninvited spectator was.

"Can you fellas keep it down?" she said. "We're trying to enjoy our lunch over here."

"Sorry for disturbing you. Sometimes we get a little too carried away with our game. I moved in a few weeks ago. I'm Gabriel Cameron." He extended his sweaty hand. She crinkled her nose and stared at it.

When he wiped his palms on his shorts and offered a fist bump instead, she acquiesced.

"And you must be Quinn, Reese's sister," Gabriel said. Including Rosvaughn, this was two down, with most of the Sommers and Washington clans still to go. He hoped to meet them all someday.

"I am," Quinn said. "Good guess."

Gabriel had heard all about the sisters from Reese during their long late-night phone calls, story after amusing story. After noting the mischievous glint in this woman's eyes and the sassy smirk, he had more than a hunch this was *the* one and only Quinn, who'd once scared off a would-be burglar by barking, *"Just what the hell do you think you're doing?"* after he'd placed one foot through the curtains at her family room window. *"I just dialed 911, but come on inside. While we wait, you can meet my pet Glock."* Quinn never got a look beyond that guy's one dusty Jordan because he took off like a shot before he got shot.

Gabriel turned to tell Julian and Lance to keep the noise down, but

100

Julian had plopped on a patio chair to talk on his cell and nosy Lance had already zipped over to join Gabriel and Quinn at the fence.

"Well, well, well, who do we have here?" Lance's eyes went dark with that familiar predatory gleam as he admired Reese's sister.

"Quinn, this is Lance Donovan, my friend and business partner at our veterinary hospital. Lance, this is Quinn, Reese's sister," Gabriel said. "It's Sommers, too, right?" Reese had mentioned her sisters were also single.

"Yes," Quinn replied.

"Beauty doesn't just run in your family, it does fancy footwork, a sexy, sexy samba." Lance laid it on too thick as usual and moved closer for a handshake.

Quinn appeared to restrain an eye roll, but offered Lance, also sweaty from playing ball, a fist bump.

"That's Julian, my other friend and business partner, over there." Gabriel motioned to where the other member of their trio sat using the phone. "Hey, Julian, this is Quinn, Reese's sister."

Julian nodded and gave a brief wave. "Be with you in a minute. Talking to Jaylon."

"His young nephew," Gabriel added for Quinn.

"You're a real *tall* drink of water on a hot day." For Quinn, Lance had shifted to his low melodic drawl, one of his lady killer moves. "I like 'em long and lean, too."

"I'm obviously standing on a chair." The *"you idiot"* at the end of Quinn's statement was apparent in the disdainful pucker of her lips.

"Just a little humor there," Lance added.

"Very *little* humor," Quinn replied.

Gabriel wanted a chair himself so he could eye Reese. Though Gabriel and Reese had kept in touch with copious texts, video chats, and phone calls, he missed her touch.

"I told Quinn we'd keep it down," Gabriel said. "Seems we were disturbing the sisters' nice Sunday lunch. And I offer my sincere apologies for the salty language. Had any of us known our voices carried over the music and that ladies were—"

"Lunch you say?" Lance sniffed the air and patted his middle. "What's on the menu? I'm starving."

"I was about to have pizza and Buffalo wings delivered for the game that airs in, oh," Gabriel glanced at his watch, "about ten minutes, *like we discussed.*" He glared at Lance for trying to wheedle a last-minute invitation to the sisters' lunch.

Lance ogled Quinn's generous bosom. When Reese popped up next to her sister Gabriel forgot all about reprimanding Lance.

"Well, hello there," Gabriel said, his smile stretched mile wide.

"Hi. Is my sister bothering you?" Reese asked Gabriel from her elevated position, possibly on yet another chair. "Sorry."

"Why are you apologizing for me? They were the ones disturbing the peace," Quinn said.

"Oh, hi, Lance." Reese gave him a little wave.

"Hmmp, you and your sister are a double vision of —"

"Hey!" Before Lance could complete what was likely another cheesy line, another head—one with long, shiny pin-straight hair—surfaced at the fence. "I'm feeling a little lonely over there all by myself. The party's over here."

"Gabriel, Lance, this is my other sister Blaire," Reese said.

"The *oldest*," Quinn added about Blaire, who gave her the evil eye before cheerily greeting the guys. She, too, possibly stood on a chair.

By now Lance could trip on his own tongue. "Did I say double vision? Scratch that. Triple vision. Wow, just wow."

Gabriel shook his head. *Wow* =*Woof*, in Lance speak. *Down boy*. Lance forged ahead with his plan to crash the sisters' lunch. "What's that delicious smell wafting from over there?"

"Weed killer," Quinn said.

"Is that so?" Lance replied, unruffled.

"We'll go order the pizza and wings now." Gabriel grabbed Lance's arm.

"Mind my asking what you ladies are noshing on?" Lance wouldn't budge.

"Barbecue ribs, greens, and potatoes salad," Blaire said. "We're washing it down with Quinn's special sangria mix."

"Hmmm, hmmm, love me some barbecue ribs, greens, and potato salad, especially mustard potato salad with those little bits of sweet pickle in it," Lance said, not taking into account Reese probably didn't have enough to feed three big-ass dudes with the collective appetites of the Panthers offensive and defensive lines.

"Ours is mustard potato salad with bits of sweet pickle in it. You guys should come over." Blaire's swift invite caught Gabriel off guard. "We have enough left, don't we, sis? When you grill you usually prepare plenty to store in the freezer for several meals."

Reese cleared her throat. "Well, actually—"

"We're willing to share the beer, pizza, and Buffalo wings, right Gabe?" Lance said.

Gabriel didn't like Lance putting people on the spot to get what he wanted, but damn, this wasn't the worst idea his friend had ever had. Gabriel would love to spend time with Reese, if she were so inclined to let the guys horn in on what was obviously bonding time with her sisters. And with others around, things were unlikely to get too heated between them again. They could talk and get even better acquainted without too much temptation.

Evidently, Quinn had her fill of Lance, but Blaire negotiated to make this happen. She nudged Reese. "C'mon, sis! Pizza and wings!"

Gabriel studied Reese, searching for hints of discomfort but found none.

"Are you okay with a change of plans, Gabriel, Quinn?" Reese asked.

"I'm game if you are," Gabriel said.

"Whatever," Quinn said noncommittally.

"Okay." Reese smiled.

"Cool!" Lance said.

"Everything's on me," Gabriel said.

"Because you three are crashing our lunch, we get to choose the pizza place," Quinn said.

"Quinn!" Reese chided her. "How gauche!"

"We like Marinelli's," Quinn said anyway. "It's the only place in town that makes authentic Neapolitan pizza. They use a wood-fired oven made from volcanic ash for that perfect light, crispy, and slightly charred crust. The dough is imported from Naples, Italy, and the cheese is traditional mozzarella, made from water buffalo milk, for that true Old World flavor."

"And would you like the anchovies specially flown in on the gossamer wings of angels?" Lance took a deep bow. "As you wish."

"You're awfully magnanimous for the tightwad contributing bupkis to the bill," Quinn deadpanned.

"Bupkis?" Lance scowled. "Tightwad? Hey, you don't know me like that."

Quinn gloated, obviously satisfied she'd zinged the cocky grin off his face.

However, Lance swiftly recovered, winking and smiling as he smoothed the front of his sweaty tank top. "Besides, I bring the charm, baby."

"Then I'll bust out the Rolaids," Quinn said before making a gagging gesture, finger to mouth.

"I see," Lance said, eyes still shining with interest. "Breaking bread with you promises to be quite the scintillating experience."

"Only if Reese whips out the knives," Quinn added. "The sharpest ones."

"You two better behave," Reese said. "Or you'll be banished to the kiddie table with plastic sporks."

***

Their group feasted, talked, and listened to music on Reese's patio well into the night. When the temperature dropped, Reese lit her fire pit and served mochas, hot cider, and an assortment of cupcakes. The chocolate/peanut butter ones made Gabriel think of those kisses in her kitchen. He kept it together, even when he and Reese were exchanging smoldering looks between bites.

Julian appeared more relaxed than usual with their comely dining companions. Blaire, who had mentioned she was in a serious relationship with a guy named Hayes, excused herself several times to go off with her phone. Lance homed in on Quinn, who spent the night dissing him at every opportunity. But it was clear Lance relished the challenge.

Odette crashed around 8 p.m. to complain about the music thumping over to her place, preventing the twins from falling asleep. But she soon took a seat, piled her plate with food, and commandeered the conversation. At one point, she mentioned how familiar Gabriel looked to her. He practically saw the light bulb pop on over her head.

"I got it!" Odette said, slapping her thigh. "Cameron! Your last name is Cameron. Any relation to Lucas Cameron, the actor?"

Lance and Julian looked at Gabriel to follow his lead.

"I get that all the time," Gabriel replied with a smile.

"That you resemble him and have the same last name?" Odette said. "I'll bet!"

"He's originally from these parts, you know," Blaire said, now studying Gabriel's face. "I read his memoir a few years back. Funny, he didn't write much about his family or reveal their names. Focused on his Hollywood escapades. But I'll bet dollars to doughnuts you two are related somehow."

"There are *lots* of Camerons. Check Mayfair's online white pages,"

Gabriel said.

"Now that Odette has mentioned it…" Quinn stared at Gabriel, too.

Damn. Gabriel reached for his drink.

"You do look like him," Quinn said.

"Then I'll take that as a compliment." Gabriel measured his words and forced a chuckle. As he feigned great interest in the natural stone fire pit, he could still feel Odette and the three sisters gazes bore into him. "But he's much better looking." He winked at Reese.

"I beg to differ," Reese replied with a flirty smile.

In deference to Gabriel, his two closest friends remained silent. Gabriel refused to confirm the speculation right now, especially after noting the potentially manic Lucas Cameron fandom glittering in Odette's and Blaire's eyes. Once Lucas Cameron, action film actor, was invited to a party (even in spirit), he never left.

The ladies dropped their inquisition when Lance came to the rescue by mentioning an article he'd read in a recent *Mayfair Tribune*. Odette took the bait and delivered an impassioned speech about the evils of unlabeled genetically modified salmon. After which Quinn and Lance took opposing sides, alternately muddying the waters with various straw man arguments and boring everyone senseless.

Party over.

The guys offered to help the sisters clean up, but Reese shooed them away.

Lance and Gabriel stood near the driver's side door of Lance's SUV. "That was jacked up the way you put Reese on the spot, pressing for an invite," Gabriel said as they watched Julian drive off in his pickup. "We crashed."

"But you're damn glad we did." Lance opened the door and climbed inside his ride. "Admit it."

"Yeah, I am." Gabriel grinned.

"And I'll bet Reese isn't complaining. Don't think I didn't notice the way you two were eye-fucking each other most of the time. Man, it was downright indecent."

"Indecent? That's rich coming from you. And don't think I didn't notice you trying to run your lines on Quinn, but she wasn't having it."

"Ah, yes, the beguiling Quinn," Lance closed his door, "with her rude-and-full-of-attitude self, so quick with the *bon mot*. But I dig her."

"Is that right?"

"Absolutely. Quinn, of the gorgeous face, ample bosom, mile-long legs, wasp-waist and ooooooh, nice firm-but-juicy ass."

"Firm? So you managed to cop a feel without drawing back a stub?"

"As a connoisseur of the female derriere, I can just tell." Lance sucked in a breath. "No need to touch...*yet*. But hers is a real showstopper." He shook his head as if disoriented by the memory. "All three of those sisters are... Hot. As. Hell. What man wouldn't want to dive in that gene pool, dick first?"

"I want more than that with Reese."

"Until you hit it and go running back to Adriana."

Gabriel groaned. "Not you too."

Lance clapped Gabriel on the shoulder. "Well, you know, there is a pattern that's hard to ignore, my man."

"Damn, it's been a year. That should tell you something. And Reese knows all about Adriana."

Lance lifted a brow. "Does she really? *Everything?*"

"Time for you to go now."

"Somehow I doubt you've told her everything. I mean, you failed to mention your older brother is a movie *stah*."

"You know I don't like exposing that Cameron connection so soon in a relationship."

"So you lie?"

"I didn't lie."

"Omission. Same as a lie when that Odette was grilling you."

"Okay an omission with the best intentions. When Reese gets to know *me* better, I'll tell her all about Luke. I don't like keeping things from her."

"Does she know..." Lance crooned the chorus of that classic Stylistics tune "Break Up to Make Up." "And just how many times you and Adriana have boomeranged back to one another? Does she know how on and off you two have been over the years? That's bound to make the lady skittish."

"Bye."

"I'll take that as Reese doesn't know that everyone has lost count. But back to Quinn. She wants me," Lance said as sure as ever. "She—"

"Just doesn't know it yet," Gabriel droned.

"In time, my friend, in time," Lance said, starting the engine. "And I'm a patient man when the right challenge presents itself, or rather, herself. Now don't you screw this up for me."

"Me?"

"Yeah, *you* and your cock blocking."

"I have no idea what you're talking about."

"Yeah, right. Dude, sometimes you're like a meddlesome old woman. Later." Lance gave Gabriel his usual two-finger au revoir salute and drove away. He had accused Gabriel of interfering on a few occasions.

Gabriel wasn't keen on his womanizing friend setting his sights on Reese's sister. Gabriel would stay in his own lane this time, but he would not aid and abet, either. On the upside, that Quinn was a pistol. She had Lance's number; that was for damn sure. And Gabriel had rather enjoyed their verbal sparring until it took that wrong turn into genetically engineered fish.

Lance liked to think he was the smoothest of the smooth, the mack-a-roni, the-mack-a-roon of all mack daddies. True, he had a remarkable success rate when it came to bedding women of his choice. Occasionally, he needed to meet a woman like Quinn, who was not in his thrall.

Gabriel stepped in his mud room and opened the back door for Apollo and Maximus to come in for the night. He overheard the Sommers sisters saying their goodbyes. After cars pulled away, he recalled that he'd left Reese's house again without the trimmer and edger. *Bummer*, he thought with a slow smile.

CHAPTER 17

Ten minutes after her sisters departed, Reese's doorbell rang. With Gabriel on the other side of the door, she couldn't open it quickly enough. "Hi there!"

"I forgot the trimmer and edger." Gabriel stepped inside, his nearness making her knees weak and her panties wet. *Goodness! The effect this man had on her.* "I came to get them. I also wanted to apologize again and thank you for being such a good sport. I know that was supposed to be a lunch with your sisters."

"I had a great time. I enjoyed getting to know Lance and Julian. My sisters did, too." Reese gave him a good show, seductively swinging her hips, as she led him to the garage shelves.

"I don't know about Quinn." Gabriel's muscles flexed as he reached for the lawn equipment.

Reese couldn't help moving closer, risking him jabbing her in the eye with an elbow as he placed the boxes at his feet. "Lance is the perfect foil for her."

"I like your sisters," he said. "You seem close."

"We are, but sometimes, because I'm the youngest, they forget I'm a grown woman with a mind of my own and the right to make my own mistakes. They're almost as overprotective as Daddy. Do you have brothers and sisters?"

"Yeah, an older brother."

"So you're the baby sibling, too."

"At thirty-six, I don't know about the *'baby'* part."

"You know what I mean." Reese reached to give him a good thump on the forehead.

"We don't see each other that often. He's on the road a lot."

"Oh? For work?"

"Yeah."

"What kind of work?" she asked, recalling that earlier conversation about Gabriel's resemblance to that actor.

"The kind that keeps him on the road and far away from family and Mayfair." Gabriel smiled and tapped her nose, possibly to take the edge off his sudden evasiveness. He paused for a moment and then pushed out a heavy sigh. "Okay, so the mystery older brother is….Drumroll please."

"Lucas Cameron."

"Yes, but I don't want to go into a whole lot about him tonight or explain why I didn't just come out with it at the party. I'd much rather talk about you and me." Gabriel wrapped his arms around her waist.

"I think the impromptu merging of parties was a smashing success," Reese said. "It also gave me a chance to spend some time with you again. I've missed you."

"I've missed you, too, but I meant what I said about enjoying a *proper* date with you before —"

"Today's party doesn't count?" Reese pinched his muscular tush. "So you came over just to get the trimmer and the edger and deliver an apology?"

"I did. And for this." Gabriel framed her face with his large hands and brushed his lips over hers, before slipping his tongue inside her mouth. No groping and grinding. Just the softest, sweetest kiss, so utterly perfect in its tenderness it left her swooning. After their lips parted, he tipped his forehead against hers.

"Good night, Reese Sommers," he whispered when he released her, "until we meet again." He chucked her under the chin. "I have a crazy week again."

"Me, too."

"But we *will* make that proper date happen. It's come-hell-or-high-water time. Saturday, okay?"

" 'Kay," Reese said with a little bounce because he made her feel as if she were back in high school anticipating senior prom. Everything he did or said gave her a bellyful of butterflies.

"We'll call, text, and video chat before then."

"Sure." Reese watched him open her garage door, gather the boxes, and disappear onto his own property. With what must have been the silliest grin on her face, she stepped inside her mud room, slid down the door, and dissolved into a puddle as she touched her lips and replayed that last kiss over and over again.

CHAPTER 18

As expected, the week had been demanding, and the days crawled by. Reese spent half the time fretting something would interfere with her and Gabriel's plan to rendezvous Saturday.

When noon on Saturday approached with no snafus, she relaxed. Their first proper date would actually happen. Though a steady stream of customers filled the Sweet Spot, things ran smoothly. Reese planned to leave early, around five, and let Linda supervise the staff and closing.

Reese had one catering gig to handle, but after that she was free to start her big-date-night prep with a long bubble bath. Staffers Danielle and Audrey loaded up the company SUV for the drive to the party. In her Beetle, Reese would trail them. She needed the privacy to touch base with her sisters, whom she owed return calls. Blaire wanted Reese to supply cupcake props for an upcoming *A Nest for Newbies* shoot. She juggled "a gazillion" things and kept the conversation brief. Quinn talked more, prying into Reese's dealings with Gabriel, as in how far she'd gone with him since that patio gathering.

"Nothing has changed." When they'd spoken on the phone Gabriel had asked about Reese's likes and dislikes, including everything from politics to favorite foods, which she'd found romantic. It was clear he wanted to know her. Reese Renita Sommers. She had dozens of questions for him, too. These exchanges had been enjoyable and enlightening. And she loved the sound of his rich, husky voice in her ear during calls, but she wouldn't have been disappointed if things had gotten a little raunchier during those phone calls and texts. Sexting? Hot video chat action, anyone?

But no. Gabriel wanted a chance to romance her, old-school style, without a focus on how bad they wanted to rip each other's clothes off. No question their chemistry was scorching, but a lasting relationship was not built on extreme horniness alone. As her anticipation soared, Reese mentioned the "proper date" to Quinn.

"So he wants to sweep you off your feet, is that it?"

"Yes."

"At the risk of sounding like one of those useless alarm clocks that shut themselves off after only sixty seconds of buzzing…"

"You're silencing the alarm?" Reese asked giddily.

"I am. Gabriel *seems* like an all right guy, *I guess*."

"So you like him?"

"I said he *seems* all right. Anyone can play a role for an afternoon. I still say proceed with caution. That stuff you told me about him and that Adriana chick still gives me pause. But you have my blessings regarding the 'proper date.' "

"So what's going on with you?"

Quinn took the next ten minutes giving Reese the rundown on what she'd been up to since the patio party. Though she put on a big front about how fulfilling she found her work and how happy she was with BOB (battery-operated boyfriend), there was a hollowness in her voice. Quinn enjoyed being part of a monogamous couple. She wasn't the type to hook up just to get her sexual jollies or to avoid being alone. And after receiving one too many (unsolicited) penis pictures, she'd given up on making a love connection through the dating apps on her phone.

"As if a girl's supposed to take one look, swoon, and go, 'Now *that's* the scrotum of my dreams. What the…?'" Quinn griped, her voice thin with disenchantment. "Whatever happened to breaking the ice by actually asking, 'Hey, what's your idea of the perfect first date? Dinner? Dancing? Darts? Even that can be fun with the right person at the right bar."

"Don't you think Lance is the epitome of tall, dark, handsome, and somewhat charming?" Reese asked. "It's clear he likes you."

Quinn harrumphed.

"And I think you enjoyed his company more than you let on."

"Girl, please!"

"C'mon now," Reese said. "Give it up."

"I will concede he is one of the most handsome men I've ever seen. And yes, he is a tall, beautifully sculpted chocolate hunk of man flesh. And he has incredibly sexy eyes."

"Ha! I knew it!"

"And he knows it, too. That's the problem. It's not all about looks with me and that man is way too impressed with himself. And I find his 'playa-playa-from-the-Himalayas' shtick hokey, disingenuous, and highly annoying so there's no way in hell I'd consider going there, even for fun."

"You sure?"

"I'd take my chances on a nice guy like Professor Quadzilla first. And don't even think about trying to play matchmaker. Besides, you need to focus your attention on Gabriel. I like him, but promise me you'll be careful."

"I will."

Reese ended the call when she arrived at Laurel Ridge, a lovely bucolic upper-middle-class neighborhood on the east side of Mayfair, which boasted lots of historically and architecturally noteworthy older homes.

The party was scheduled to start in an hour. At the Jones' Tudor, a striking middle-aged woman with a trim figure, gorgeous mahogany skin, and a chic, closely cropped afro, greeted Reese.

"Come on inside, I'm Markova Jones." She offered a warm shake.

"Nice to meet you, Mrs. Jones, I'm Reese Sommers. I took your order when you phoned the shop."

"We're not that stuffy around here. Please call me Markova," she said, her voice melodious as she opened the door wider. "Right on time. I'm glad. Honey, all morning I've been running around here like a chicken with my head cut off. A million different little details to handle. It takes only one, the wrong one, to tank the whole damn thing. This way, please." Reese followed her out to the patio. "They were predicting rain, but because it's such a beautiful, sun-drenched day we moved the party from the family room to outside."

Audrey and Danielle inspected the table assigned to the Sweet Spot. Lush flora filled the spacious, manicured back lawn. If this were Reese's place, she would not only hold every special event here, but she'd also grab her sleeping bag and camp out at every opportunity.

"Your home and lawn are lovely." Reese noticed the caterers handling the savory items on the menu had already set up at another long table. When Reese had asked if Mrs. Jones was interested in a particular theme, the woman had said she wanted something "beautiful and classic befitting a casual daytime party for grownups."

Audrey and Danielle carried in the cupcakes towers.

A middle-aged man with cornflower blue eyes and light blond hair, approached. "Looks as if everything is coming together."

"Reese this is my husband, Grant."

"Mr. Jones so nice to meet you," Reese said.

"Please. It's Grant," the older man insisted as they shook hands.

"You always do such a great job, honey." Grant kissed the hostess's cheek. "Like magic."

"And hiring the right service providers is a big part of it, even for a control freak like myself," Markova said to Reese. "You came highly recommended."

"Mind my asking who provided the referral? I'd like to thank him or her."

Before Markova could answer, the doorbell rang. "I'm sure that's bar service, right on time, too." She turned to her husband. "Will you get that, darling?"

Grant was too busy swiping samples from a meatball tray.

Two women came out with three casseroles and placed them on one buffet table. Reese didn't recall these dishes on the proposed menu. Markova read the question on her face. "It wouldn't be a Jones' shindig without potluck. Several friends are bringing homemade entrees."

Appetizing aromas floated from the other tables, making Reese's stomach growl, but she had to admit her table smelled and looked delicious, too.

Reese also complimented Grant on their beautiful home.

"Grant, stop stuffing your piehole and get the door," Markova said when the doorbell rang again.

"Please feel free to look around before the guests arrive," Grant said around a mouthful of meat. "My wife loves showing off her garden. Do check out the pergola. I built it for Markova for our 35th wedding anniversary," he said proudly. "You can't see it from here. It's around the bend with the maple trees." When Markova gave him a stern look, he speared another meatball with a toothpick before taking off. "I'm getting the door right now, dear."

Reese took his suggestion. Danielle and Audrey could handle prep without her. She strolled across the vast lawn and turned a corner to find the spectacular pergola, bursting with a breathtaking kaleidoscope of climbing vines and clusters of thriving blooms. She could only identify the roses, honeysuckle, and…

Sucker punch.

Gabriel and Adriana stood under the pergola beaming at one another.

CHAPTER 19

The pergola scene would provide more fodder for the bizarre dreams Reese had been having as of late:

In one, Adriana swelled up like the Goodyear Blimp, and Reese popped her with a harpoon.

In another, Reese sat in what looked like a haunted eighties arcade. She played a game in which she controlled Pac-Man goblins devouring images of Adriana's noggin flashing across her screen.

Then there was the one in which an insect buzzed around Reese, disturbing her sleep. When it landed, she whacked it with a giant bag of cake flour. The smashed mess had the body of a fly and the head of Adriana.

It didn't take a shrink to pinpoint the recurring theme.

Reese had U-turned and was about to scurry back to the Sweet Spot's dessert table when Gabriel called out to her. "Reese!"

Reese froze, sucked in a deep breath, and slowly turned to face the pair. "I didn't mean to interrupt. Grant, um, er, Mr. Jones thought I might like to see the pergola."

"You're not interrupting anything," Gabriel said.

"Don't just stand there. Get your heinie over here, girl!" said Adriana, who threw Reese off-kilter with such insta-chumminess.

Gabriel wore a goofy grin as his gaze locked with Reese's.

"So Mom decided to use your bakery for the party after all." Adriana pumped one fist. "Way to go, Mom! Sasha will love them!"

Reese's heartbeat thundered in her ears. Oh, heck, no! It couldn't be.

Fortune would not be so cruel as to have Reese serving dessert for the "big news" bash. Of all the Joneses in Mayfair, what were the chances she'd taken a party order for *these* Joneses?

But more importantly, was Gabriel Goodyear Girl's date?

"So you were the one who gave the referral?" Reese managed to plaster on something she hoped resembled a smile as she questioned Gabriel.

"Don't look at me." Gabriel lifted his hands. "I wish I could take credit, but I can't."

"You can," Adriana said. "I saw your vote-for-the-Sweet-Spot flyer. The business cards were in a little pocket on a cork board at the hospital. While picking up Apollo and Maximus, I pocketed your card, Reese. I dropped by your shop to check it out. Very nice place. I'd hoped to see you, but you hadn't arrived yet, according to the young lady working the register. I did, however, buy a dozen cupcakes to take to Mom, who loved them! We both did. I encouraged her to do something fun, like cupcakes, for this party. But at the time, she wouldn't commit to it."

"Thank you for suggesting the Sweet Spot." Reese's mind was still racing to put everything together.

"I think I owe Mom kudos for breaking out of her dessert comfort zone." Adriana flitted away like a sprite (of the rap video vixen variety), in another hippy-dippy, flower-print skirt and top.

Gabriel, who continued cheesing at Reese as if he couldn't believe she was there, reached for her, but she took a step back to avoid his touch.

"I'm working, though I took a little break for a self-guided tour of the grounds," she pointed to the pergola blooms, "I must look professional while goofing off."

"So good to see you. Believe me, I had no idea they were using the Sweet Spot."

"Clearly." Reese kept the edge out of her tone. And though they'd grown closer because of some intimacies shared, it wasn't her place to question him or feel some kind of weirdo way about why he was there. The reason was obvious.

But she still hadn't figured out Adriana. Her motives. Ulterior? Her explanation made sense. And if she was as thoughtful as Gabriel claimed, she'd simply thrown good business Reese's way. She wanted to ask him if Adriana knew about him and Reese getting better acquainted. How would Gabriel categorize his relationship with Reese? *She's my good neighbor, and I've had my tongue down her throat and my hands in her pants.*

117

"We're still on for tonight, right?" Gabriel's continued his bold appraisal of her body. "You always look so good to me. It's impossible to keep my mitts off you." He playfully gnawed one palm. "*Hmmp!*"

"Um, well."

"For the record, I had no plans to attend this party," he said.

But you're here with bells on. Reese's mouth opened, but she could not form an accusation or let him know she felt…What? Funny about it. She had no right. He owed her no detailed explanation. Didn't she tell Quinn Gabriel would be a fling only? So she just stood there with that strained smile, wilted at the corners by now.

Gabriel gave a detailed explanation anyway. "I went to the house to see Mom, who was on her way over here. My folks live next door. Remember? I told you that. She asked me to help her with some casseroles because she couldn't carry them all herself. So I leave the casseroles in the Jones' kitchen, then Adriana tells me she needs to talk about Apollo. It's urgent."

And she drags you out to the pergola to canoodle. "No need to explain."

"It's her time with the dogs," Gabriel went on. "So, she says Apollo's been dragging his backside on her carpet, leaving long 'poop tracks,' as she calls them. He's also biting his rear end and displaying discomfort during bowel movements. And she says he's extra smelly all of a sudden—"

"Gabriel you don't have to—"

"I need to examine him sometime today. It sounds as if there might be an issue with his anal sacs. And if there is, the stench will make your eyes water and knock you to your knees. It makes skunk smell like a cheap car deodorizer."

"I get it." Reese made a face. "But you don't have to—"

"We didn't want to gross out everyone so we moved to the pergola. In case you were curious."

In case she was curious… or the psychotically jealous type? Reese appreciated the explanation, but she wasn't sure how she felt about his practice of detailing his every move.

"Thanks for the blow-by-blow, but it wasn't required," Reese lied in her pipsqueak voice.

"I hadn't planned to stay, but now that you're here—"

"Don't change your plans for me. I'm making sure setup is done right, but I have another catering job to supervise," she lied again. Sasha and Darren, the guests of honor, had yet to arrive, but no way was she hanging around until they got here. Instead, she plotted her getaway.

"I'm looking forward to tonight," he said. "I hope you are, too. Is seven still good for you?"

"Um, yeah." Reese turned on her heel. "I'd better get back. Work, work, work, you know."

"Right."

"I'm counting the hours until tonight," Gabriel called out to her.

Good thing she'd driven her own car. No, it wasn't professional to leave a job she was supposed to supervise, but the alternative was unthinkable. Besides, Audrey and Danielle were efficient and reliable. Who knew what kind of hell would break loose if Sasha saw Reese again? And Reese did not want to see Darren, skinning and grinning, playing the perfect fiancé.

Still unsure of Adriana's motives, Reese chose to give her the benefit of the doubt.

Reese made her way back to the dessert table and relayed the change of plans to Audrey and Danielle. Dozens of guests had arrived at once, as if they'd all stepped off the same double-decker bus. Reese had to get the heck out of there so she concocted an excuse. An emergency at another booking required her attention. Danielle and Audrey exchanged befuddled (*other booking?*) looks. She would also adjust the bill for two workers instead of three.

"All looks good here," Markova said. "Thank you for doing such a wonderful job. The cupcakes are delicious! You asked who referred you. It was my daughter Adriana."

Great, now you tell me. "Oh, Adriana's a peach of a girl!" Reese gushed.

"Here, let me show you out," Markova said as Reese followed her.

Grant stepped outside, he clapped, and boomed to get everyone's attention. "Sasha, Darren, and his parents have arrived!"

Oh, no! Reese whipped around and searched for an alternate escape route. "I'd like to exit through the yard if that's okay. It'll give me a chance to admire more of your beautiful garden on the way out."

"Sure." Markova pointed left. "You can't see it from here. But there's an unlocked gate at the left side of the house."

"Thanks for your business!" Reese felt like the Road Runner, her legs spinning in place as she prepared to zip away.

"You will hear from me again. In a few months, we have a baby shower coming up!"

And Reese would make sure Linda supervised that catering gig. "Thanks again, Mrs. Jones!"

"Please, it's Markova."

"Markova! Well, better motor!" Off Reese went, dashing toward the gate only to find Gabriel standing there wearing a rascal's grin.

"I heard what you said to Markova." Gabriel blocked her escape when she tried to move around him. "Can you hang around a few more minutes? I know it's soon, but I'd love to introduce you to Mom and Dad."

"I can't, Gabriel. Gotta get a move on." Reese hated missing a chance to meet Mrs. and Mrs. Cameron because of Darren's messiness.

"You're off duty now, and we're out of sight, so how about a little goodbye kiss to tide me over?" Gabriel wrapped his strong arms around her and swept her off her feet.

Any other time, she'd be putty with such manhandling.

"Put me down, Gabriel!"

"C'mon, darlin', just a little kiss. No one can see us. I know you want to act professional, but you're too damn cute. I promise not to get too heated."

Reese couldn't deny him anything when he looked at her that certain way so she planted a peck on his cheek. "There! Now put me down! I have to go!"

Gabriel stole another kiss from her lips before opening the gate. "See you tonight," he said, "and dress to impress, my dear."

Reese made it to her car without running into Sasha, Darren, or Darren's parents. Talk about awkward. She imagined Darren's horror when he spotted the Sweet Spot SUV parked out front and then the relief flooding him when Audrey and Danielle told him Reese had already left. Then she imagined him fretting she'd laced the cupcakes with poison before concluding his "Reesie," too much of a goody-two-shoes, would not take out her resentment toward him on innocent people.

As she hightailed it out of Laurel Ridge, her anxiety escalated. These were the kinds of situations she'd wanted to avoid. And she was still a wee bit irritated at herself for being a wee bit irritated at Gabriel for…for…*what exactly?* Helping his mother deliver casseroles? Talking to Adriana about Apollo's poop tracks and anal sacs?

Should Reese keep her "proper date" with him? And was tonight the right time to trot out her history with Darren?

Reese realized she'd lied with too much ease. Maybe that was a sign she should get out of this thing with Gabriel before she fell in too deep.

CHAPTER 20

With the blinds drawn and multiple votive candles lit, Reese luxuriated in her bubble bath and listened to some plinky-plonky relaxation music. As tension eased its tight grip on her, she reflected on the surprises at the Jones catering gig. Gabriel had not appeared the least bit rattled to see her there. In fact, he was thrilled. Surely a man with something to hide would've had the opposite knee-jerk reaction. Gabriel and Adriana's little tete-a-tete under the pergola was innocent. Who would make up a stinky butt infection on the fly? And of course, Gabriel would help his mother carry those casseroles. Reese would waste no time pondering why Gabriel's father couldn't help with those casseroles. And so what if Gabriel was at that party as a guest? If he'd had a lifelong friendship with Sasha, he was allowed, right? With that squared away, she got dressed for her date.

She selected her slinkiest cocktail number and her sexiest high heels. She pulled out the statement jewelry, painted her face with more dramatic makeup, including a nice berry red lippy, and arranged her hair in a glamorous up 'do. As she cuddled and fussed over Sinbad, her doorbell rang and a uniformed man stood on her porch. A limo was parked at the front curb.

"Good evening," he said. "Ms. Sommers?"

"Yes."

"I'm your driver for the evening. Mr. Cameron awaits."

"Oh, my!"

"This way, please."

Reese gave Sinbad one more kiss before putting him down and then grabbed her wisp of a wrap and crystal cupcake-shaped minaudière. As she locked her front door, Odette rushed over with one twin on her left hip and a mystery object in her right hand. "Oh, Reese! Reese! I have something for you!"

Really, Odette? Now? Reese sighed.

Odette held the rotary cheese grater she'd borrowed from Reese three months ago.

Reese took the grater, chucked it inside the house, and locked the door.

"Hello!" Odette batted her lashes at the hunky limo driver, who nodded his greeting.

"Wowza! Look at you, all glitzed and glammed up!" Odette said to Reese. The twin was Brayton, who had a scar above his left brow, his only distinguishing mark, after a faceplant from his high chair. "So you have a big date, I take it."

"Yes." Reese checked Brayton's grubby hands for the Little People figures, Legos, and wooden blocks he and his brother liked to hurl at her.

"With our handsome new neighbor. I saw him get inside the limo first," said Odette, who trailed along as the driver led Reese to the car. Other neighbors gaped as if they'd never seen a luxury vehicle before.

"See ya later!" Reese said.

"Have a good time!" Odette waved.

Brayton snatched off one of Odette's chunky clip earrings and lobbed it at Reese.

And missed. *Ha!*

The driver helped Reese slipped inside the car, where Gabriel sat, looking dashing in an expensive suit and shoes. He smelled divine, as usual. And a box of fragrant, pink full-double bloom peonies filled the box beside him. She'd chosen the perfect dress because his mouth fell open at the sight of her.

"And I didn't think you could look more stunning and…," Gabriel paused and reached toward her. "But what's this?" He removed something from her mouth.

"Oops," Reese said of the remnants of that goodbye kiss for Sinbad. "Cat hair and lip gloss do not mix. Hope that doesn't gross you out."

"I'm a vet, remember?" Gabriel presented the flowers to her.

"Oh my goodness! These are hard to find in these parts even when they're in season," Reese said of her favorites. "Did you have these—?"

"Flown in."

"They're beautiful!" Reese lifted the box and sniffed the hearty, ruffled blooms. "And they smell wonderful! I'm sure roses would've been easier to get. Thank you!"

"Roses? No way did I want to chance selecting the wrong ones. Some varieties smell like old ketchup to you."

"Right!" Reese chuckled. "I forgot I mentioned that. That steel-trap memory of yours strikes again."

"Our proper date begins." He passed Reese a flute of champagne.

Gabriel had booked a private dining room at the five-star restaurant inside the Whittington, Mayfair's most luxurious hotel. As a jazz quartet played in the background, a fawning waiter served Gabriel and Reese's candlelit multicourse meal that included great wine, a scrumptious oyster-and-caviar dish, and the airiest soufflé for dessert. Afterward, he held her close for a rooftop dance underneath a blanket of stars. Then they left the restaurant for a carriage ride. Gabriel promised there was no chance of his mother showing up, unlike that carriage ride with her ex-boyfriend Tim.

At the end of the ride, there was a private fireworks display as they kissed. His veterinary practice was obviously doing much better than she'd assumed, because the entire evening had to set him back major bucks. A part of her fretted. Did Gabriel believe he had to spurge to win her over? *Nah.* If he wanted to woo her in style, have at it, dude. At no point during the well-planned evening would it have been appropriate to grill him about his finances or Apollo's anal sac issue. Nor would she shoehorn a mention of the drama regarding Darren.

As the limo headed back to their neighborhood, she snuggled in his warm embrace.

"I have to tell you," Reese said. "I've had some special dates over the years, but you've blown me away tonight."

"You deserve it and more." The overhead light illuminated his dark eyes and the lean, masculine lines of his face. "And I wanted to show you how much you've come to mean to me."

"You mean a lot to me, too."

Not too much. Not too little. She liked their heartfelt, but safe way of putting their feelings into words.

With the privacy wall between them and the driver, Gabriel drew her closer. She climbed onto his lap, her dress rising, exposing her thighs. She loosened his silk tie and nuzzled his neck, enjoying the mix of his natural scent and cologne. She tugged at his shirttails and undershirt and skimmed her fingers along his bare skin and the hard ridges of his torso. When he slipped his tongue inside her mouth, she trembled with need and sucked it hard. Their tongues tangled. Heated blood rushed, engorging her core. She'd straddled him and rocked against his hard shaft. He gripped her bottom as she slid against it, back and forth, panting and gasping. But it wasn't enough. She wanted him buried deep inside her. The thin straps of her slinky dress slid down her arms, exposing her full breasts, now straining against the frilly bra. When he cupped them, letting his thumbs brush against the hardened tips, she unhooked the clasp.

"I want you," she moaned. "Now."

"Whoa," he whispered in her ear when she attempted to lower the zipper of his fly. "We'd better stop."

"But why?" she said, woozy with passion.

"This is not going down in the back of a limo."

"He can't hear or see anything, right?" Reese said of the limo driver as continued brushing her lips against Gabriel's.

He submitted to another deep kiss, but cut it short.

"I'm not absolutely sure," he said.

Reese groaned.

"Lance has told me limo driver horror stories," he added. "Besides, I don't want another man, or anyone else for that matter, in the vicinity when we make love from beginning to end. I can barely tolerate Sinbad looking on. And don't think I haven't noticed him giving me the evil eye during our, um, more intimate moments. Truth be told, it freaks me out."

"He's not giving you the evil eye." Reese laughed. Though she wasn't thrilled Gabriel halted their heavy make-out session, he was right. Their first time pleasuring each other until completion should not include a limo driver mere inches away. "I forgot to mention," she added saucily, "Sinbad likes to watch. He's been known to take a ringside seat."

"Well, he can take a seat several yards away. From now on, he won't watch me. He gets the boot."

"Tonight?"

"I didn't go all out with the expectation of you putting out."

Reese scoffed. "But what an aphrodisiac. You knew exactly what you were doing." She rolled her hips against the bulge in his pants. "You want it bad, mister."

"I do, but I'm *romancing* you tonight. Will you let me?"

"Oh, all right." Reese pouted and slid off his lap.

"Man, you're not making this easy." Gabriel helped secure her bra. He tidied their clothing, and then shook a finger at her. "Behave, you hear?"

Both laughed, and she let him cradle her in his arms instead. Her stomach growled.

"Ah, sounds as if you're not just hungry for me," Gabriel said.

"Dinner was delicious…" Just light, but far be it from Reese to complain. As a never-ending-pasta-bowl-and-endless-breadsticks girl, she was a cheap date. She couldn't expect a buffet-style bounty at a chi-chi, five-star restaurant. But doggone it, she'd had appetizers at Applebee's that were more filling than that seven-course meal in Lilliputian serving sizes.

"For those prices, I expected a lot more food," Gabriel said with a chuckle.

"So that was your first time there?"

"It was."

"And you did that for me?"

"I did."

"I'm touched."

"And impressed?"

"Very much so."

"Good! Now we can get down to business." Gabriel rubbed his hands together and then pressed a button to give the limo driver an address.

"Where are we going?"

"You'll see."

CHAPTER 21

Fifteen minutes later the limo pulled into the parking lot of the neon lit 1950s style 24-hour diner in the Art Deco district of town.

"Yes!" Reese changed into the flats she kept rolled up in her minaudière when she wore skyscraper heels.

Holding hands, Reese and Gabriel raced to the entrance. Inside, a white-aproned waitress took their orders for the thickest, greasiest burgers, huge piles of hot fries, and milkshakes.

"I must say, I love a woman with an appetite," Gabriel said.

Reese tore off a huge bite of burger and chased it with a sip of thick vanilla shake. "I'll have to run a marathon tomorrow to make up for this. Want to join me?" she said, not caring that she talked with her mouth full.

"We'll have to do it early."

"Sunday's Julian's half day at the hospital, right?" She slipped in. Heaven forbid she come across as if she were prying for details about Gabriel's plans for the rest of Sunday.

"Yes, but I'm filling in for Julian. He wants to attend his nephew's baseball game." And on Gabriel went.

Again, she didn't like the relief flooding her body when he detailed his itinerary. Could he feel her mistrust?

"And after that, I have to hit my work in progress to stay on track and make a deadline."

"What kind of deadline?"

"I write, too."

"And you're just mentioning it?"

"What did you say that day I discovered you own the Sweet Spot? 'A girl's gotta keep some secrets, for at least a minute or two.' Ditto for the guy."

"Touché. So you write for veterinary medical journals or something?"

"I don't suppose you've heard of *Abraham & Zephyrus*, the *A to Z Double Dog Dare Detectives* books?"

"I have!" Reese said. "Why haven't you mentioned your writing and publishing before? That's huge!"

"I didn't want to bore you."

"Bore me? Not everybody can write a book, let alone write books that sell. Tell me more."

"The Bradford in my pen name is my mom's maiden name. I can't believe you know the books. Can't possibly be one of your book club selections."

"They're humorous comic-strip style middle-grade chapter books about a computer whiz kid, that would be Abraham, and his trusty mutt, that would be Zephyrus." Reese couldn't help showing off. "They solve neighborhood mysteries and petty crimes using Abraham's computer coding skills, apps, and social media clues and Zephyrus's good old-fashioned canine tracking ability."

"You don't have kids, and you're not a teacher, librarian, bookstore employee—"

"But I did give the Carmichael twins a trunkful of children's books for various reading levels as a Christmas gift last year. I had help from a bookstore clerk, but I perused every selection to make sure it was appropriate. Odette is so picky. She wouldn't want any middle-grade books with snarky, smart-aleck kids or too many references to boogers, farts, wedgies, and the like."

"The fun stuff."

"Right. You do those cute illustrations, too?"

"Yes."

"I can just see you with your giant sketch pad and easel. A black beret tilted to one side and a white smock."

"Not exactly. I'm a digital artist. I do my illustrations on a graphics tablet, and I'm usually wearing whatever I had on at the hospital. Or I might work in the nude if it's early in the morning."

"In the nude, you say? Oh, la, la. Then I'd love to watch you work sometime if it's not too much of a distraction."

"You would be a distraction, but a welcome one. It's a date."

"Gabriel, my, my, my, but you're multitalented. So how long have you been writing books?" she asked, before taking another sip of her shake.

"For publication? About five years—"

"Sorry to interrupt," said one of two pretty young women who had been staring at Gabriel from their booth a few yards away. The one who approached them wore her hair ombre-dyed pink at the tips, a mini dress, and high heels. She held up her cellphone. "Aren't you Lucas Cameron?"

"Kristy, I told you it's not him!" said her exasperated dining companion, who stayed behind in their booth. "Now get back over here and stop bothering those people."

"It can't hurt to ask, and it'll only take a second to snap one pic," Kristy said before turning her attention back to Gabriel.

"Sorry, I'm not Lucas Cameron," Gabriel said.

Kristy groaned. "Has anyone ever told you—"

"I get that all the time," Gabriel replied with a polite smile. "But thanks for the compliment."

The young woman teetered back to her table, tugging at her short skirt, and muttering about her failed celebrity selfie attempt.

"And with that, I think it's time I filled in a few more details." Gabriel discussed his side gig, giving most of the credit to his brother, whom he'd been reluctant to say much about earlier, and his brother's literary agent, Dominic Tobias.

"I hope I didn't annoy you when I didn't come out with it all straightaway," he said.

While Gabriel and Lucas resembled one another, they were hardly twins. And Cameron wasn't the most unusual surname. Leave to it Odette and Blaire to home in on a possible family connection.

Reese knew of the elder Cameron brother. Though she was a movie buff, formulaic films with endless car chases and explosions weren't usually her thing. But after Gabriel first confirmed the close family ties, she'd done some Googling.

A favorite of entertainment news shows and tabloids, the actor had a habit of getting into relationships that ended badly —allegedly due to his womanizing ways. If she recalled correctly, one former lover, allegedly, paid someone to ambush Lucas Cameron at a red carpet event, dump white powder on him, and tell him it was laced with ricin, a deadly toxin. (Subsequent reports revealed it was only flour.) At an award ceremony in his honor, another former lover had a plane fly over with a banner that read "CHEATING BASTARD." Reese took most of those tabloid headlines with a grain of salt, particularly those relying on "close anonymous sources." However, those reports with accompanying photos and TMZ video were harder to dismiss. Reese understood why Gabriel hadn't rushed into an exhaustive discussion about his older brother.

Gabriel also downplayed his talent. Lucas and his hotshot literary agent might have paved the way for Gabriel, but young readers enjoyed the books so much his publisher continued to offer him contracts. She marveled at his skill at balancing two jobs.

"I'm going to download your latest book right now!" Reese whipped out her phone that had at least three online bookstore apps on it.

"Oh, no you don't. Not on our first date. I'll give you your own autographed hardcover copies, how about that?"

"Deal." Reese put the phone away and chomped more fries.

"Now, I want to know more about Reese."

By the time they finished sharing a slice of lemon meringue pie, fresh from the dessert carousel case, she'd provided more highlights of her life, including details about her years working at the family sock company, Sommers Mills, Inc. As pre-teens, she and her sisters began doing odd jobs in the main office to earn their allowances.

The company, founded by her grandfather and a great-uncle, specialized in a patented athletic sock design with unique cushions for shock absorption and arch protection. The company had started in the USA and remained in the USA she was proud to say. The enterprise now sold products to several countries. After graduating from college with a business degree, Reese had gone to work for the company full time while studying part time to get her MBA. Though her father would've loved for his girls to run the family business someday, he knew socks didn't exactly inspire burning ambition so he'd encouraged them to set their own entrepreneurial goals. The Sweet Spot had been a lifelong dream.

"I'd love to say the shop came about solely through my own efforts, but it would've been a lot tougher to get started, hire adequate staff, buy top-notch equipment, afford a lease for such a great location, *and* survive that first year or two while getting the shop's name out there, without that seed money from PawPaw."

"PawPaw?" Gabriel's thick brows rushed together.

"My grandfather on my mother's side, aka the indomitable Jedediah

Washington," Reese said. "He was something else. Everyone says Quinn gets her fire from him. She was always his favorite, though he denied it. But anyway, my biggest fear was failing and wasting what was given to me."

"But you didn't fail." Gabriel squeezed her hand. "You've succeeded."

"Knock wood." Reese tapped their table with her free hand. "I'm not only operating debt-free, but we turn a nice profit. Knock wood again."

"Superstitious, huh?"

After adding salt to her fries, Reese spilled a bit. "I use whatever I can and take nothing for granted." She took a pinch of salt and tossed it over her left shoulder. "While deeply satisfying, small business ownership can test a person's mettle, but I'm sure you already know this. You run a vet hospital."

"I hear ya, but the risk associated with running my place is divided by three. And from what I've heard, the retail food business is not for wimps. The odds were not in your favor."

When Gabriel asked about her past romantic relationships, Reese glossed over the details. She repeated wanting several kids someday, but added she hadn't met the right guy. She had her opening, but now was not the time or place to drag out her history with Darren if she wanted to keep the conversation upbeat. Still trying to lock Adriana in the non-issue category, she didn't ask about her directly, instead choosing to let Gabriel tell her what he thought she needed know.

"I'm glad you took a chance on dating someone who lives so close to you." Gabriel released her hand to take a drink. "Our conversations are so easy. I feel as if I can talk to you about anything. Open communication and honesty head off a lot of problems, misunderstandings."

Tell him about Darren Reid. Now. But they were having such a great time on their first proper date. What if they couldn't salvage the evening after such an unpleasant topic?

While Reese didn't like the way Sasha had acted out that awful night, she understood the woman's fury. She also didn't want to put Sasha's business on blast. Based on what Reese had noted about the Joneses, she would bet they had no clue about Darren's infidelity. Did Reese want to put Gabriel in a difficult position by burdening him with such sensitive information?

"I want you to know I'm excited to see where this thing between us will lead," he said.

"Me, too."

"Good. I want you to continue to believe in me, *in us*, no matter what you might hear. And if you have concerns or questions about anything, anything at all, please ask."

Reese's spine stiffened. "And what might I hear? It would help if I'm prepared."

Gabriel looked down and took her hand again. "Well, you see… About Adriana and me…"

"Yes?"

Gabriel looked her in the eye. "We've broken up and gotten back together before."

"Oh? Once or twice?" This revelation put a new spin on things.

"A few times. Our families have been close for quite a while."

"So what you're saying is you've been on and off since you were kids?"

"Something like that. Since we were teens. But we've realized we're not meant to be a couple," he reiterated.

"What's the difference this time?"

"When we broke up last year I was ninety-nine point nine percent sure it was the right thing. But meeting you has sealed it for me."

The man was pouring his heart out. But was he trying to convince Reese or himself? Why was she in this position? Why did she have to put *it* out there, but even the most insightful men could act as if they'd been dropped on their heads as babies a few too many times. That ol' Mars vs. Venus chestnut.

Sex wasn't every-darn-thing. Many women could forgive a man's hot romp with a hooker a lot faster than a series of soul-baring lunches with a female co-worker. Too much talk about past relationships was a downer, but ignorance and denial weren't helpful, either. Reese all but felt Quinn giving her a firm whack upside her head: *Enough with this round and round nonsense! Just tell the damn man how you feel, already!*

"There is something I've been reluctant to admit," Reese said. "It's about Adriana…"

"And my friendship with her?"

"Yes. I'm not completely comfortable with it, especially now, in light of what you revealed about how often you two have parted and reunited. I've held back telling you because we've only been seeing each other a short time, and you've known her forever. I didn't want to come off controlling and uncertain, but —"

"Controlling? You?" Gabriel scoffed. "And you have nothing to be insecure about where I'm concerned. I know it might feel premature, but you're the only woman I want." He leaned over the table for a quick kiss, and she gave him one. "Believe me?"

"I, um, I, er… think so."

When Gabriel smiled, she forced one.

"We have to do something about all that stumbling. Turn hesitation into an abso-freakin'-lutely. I have something else for you." Gabriel reached inside his coat pocket, removed a black velvet jewelry box, and passed it to her.

Reese gasped. "Another gift?"

"Yes."

"You're spoiling me! You didn't have to…" Reese opened the box to find an exquisite silver bracelet with two sparkly charms.

"This," he fingered the cupcake charm, "matches the one you usually wear round your neck. That thing drove me crazy the first time you showed up at the hospital."

"It's beautiful."

"And this one is a…"

"Starburst."

"To commemorate our first proper date and the fireworks we enjoyed tonight and the figurative ones we generate when we're together. I know it's corny but—"

"Oh, Gabriel, I love this bracelet and what you said." Reese could heave the boulder of worry off her chest without playing the shrew or issuing an ultimatum. "Your continued thoughtfulness means more than you know."

"More charms to come when you least expect them."

"Thank you. I want to wear it now!" Reese extended her hand. He helped her secure it around her wrist and then kissed her open palm. "Now, I feel bad. I didn't bring anything for you."

"That lovely smile of yours is all the gift I need."

***

As fatigue claimed them, Gabriel and Reese rode home in companionable silence. While she snuggled close he stroked her hair and shoulders, both lost in their own thoughts. After he'd settled his business with the limo driver, Gabriel walked her to the front door and carried her peonies.

"Thank you for a lovely evening." Reese had her minaudière tucked under one arm and the high heels in her hands.

On her porch, Gabriel passed the flowers to her and took her keys to open the front door. She stepped inside, but Gabriel made no moves to join her.

"Thank you for accepting the invitation. I made a promise to be on my best behavior tonight. And I will keep that promise even if it kills me." When he reached down to adjust himself, she laughed. Then under a crescent moon, he pulled her back onto the porch and gave her a lingering kiss. "Ask me if I'm crazy about you," he whispered as he took her face in his hands and tipped her head back.

"Are you crazy about me?" Reese sighed when he looked deep in her eyes and caressed her cheek.

"Abso-freakin'-lutely."

"And I'm crazy about you...abso-freakin'-lutely." They shared another deep, silky kiss and an unhurried hug.

Gabriel didn't move until she was safely locked inside her home. She opened the window, thinking she'd call out to him and blow him another kiss. Instead, she smiled, watching him stroll back to his property, hands in his pockets and whistling a joyful tune.

Sinbad came running and yowled as if scolding Reese for staying out past curfew. But before picking him up, she twirled around the room, singing and pretending she was still in Gabriel's arms for a few minutes longer.

Their first proper date had been perfect.

CHAPTER 22

The next morning in her driveway, Reese jogged in place, stretched, and waited for Gabriel.

Odette appeared, pushing that double stroller with the twins inside. "I know you're Miss Serious Runner Chick and all, but care to join this hopelessly out-of-shape couch potato for a power walk? I'm trying more sensible methods to lose those last few stubborn pounds."

"Good for you!" Reese jogged over to Odette and patted her on the back. "Sorry, but I already have a running date with Gabriel. Maybe another time." She would've asked Odette to join them if Odette had a prayer of keeping up, but she kept that to herself. Instead, she checked the twins' hands for ammo. Their arms were too short to pluck potential projectiles (earrings, hair clips, sunglasses) off their mother. Both played with toys securely attached to their stroller.

"So everyone in Granberry Ridge knows you and the new neighbor are an item," Odette said.

"*And?*" Reese bent to stretch her right hamstring. "Why should anyone care? He's single. I'm single. No scandal. *Boring.*"

"You looked beautiful last night. Your hair and makeup. The smoky eyes and the perfect shade of red lipstick, even with that bit of cat hair only *you* could rock. Pow! Those supermodels have nothing on you."

"Why, thank you, Odette." Reese braced herself for the usual impending back-handed compliment.

"That no-secrets dress, though…"

"No secrets?"

"They say men are visual creatures, but I think they prefer it when you leave a little something to the imagination instead of, you know, putting it all out there for the world to see. When he takes you out for a night on the town, you don't want others to think he called 1-800-HotChick and you showed up," she added with a little laugh.

"Why call when there's an app for that," Reese said.

Odette had just told Reese she'd dressed like a ho, or rather, a *whore*, Odette's preferred pronunciation. *Let the slut shaming begin!* Reese took the high road. After last night's date, only a hurricane could dampen her wonderful mood.

"I think it's great you've moved on from the incident with that woman who spun out of control in a jealous rage. Her behavior was appalling. I hate to tell you this, but tongues are still wagging, girl."

No, it seemed Odette did not hate telling her because she'd done so at least a dozen times since the episode. And always with what almost looked like a hint of wicked glee...if Reese didn't know any better.

When Reese went to fetch the mail she'd neglected to collect the day before, she found a flyer in the tube below the mailbox. It was a solicitation: *Vote for the Sweet Spot in the best specialty bakery category in the DetoursMayfair.com competition.* "Where did this come from?"

"Oh, I made that one," Odette said. "I've been campaigning something fierce for your shop. I think I hit the entire subdivision and the next two over."

"Distributing these?"

"Yes. This is your year, girly!" Odette pumped one fist. "Woot! Woot! Woot!"

"Woo! Woo! Woo!" The twins echoed.

"Thank you. This is much better than the ones I photocopied for distribution." Just when Quinn's influence was about to take hold regarding Odette, her friend did something incredibly nice. Some experts claimed it took five positive actions for every negative action for a marriage to survive. One could say the same for friendships. Not that Reese had been keeping score, but she wanted to believe Odette maintained a decent five-to-one ratio that kept her out of frenemy or enemy territory.

Shireen power walked toward them with her shih tzu, Mimi. "Morning, girls!"

"Want to walk together?" Odette asked her. "Speedy Gonzales over here doesn't want Granny slowing her down."

"I didn't say that!" Reese jogged in place.

"You didn't have to." With a hard stamp of her foot, Odette released the stroller's brake.

"Sure, I'd love the company," Shireen said. "Oh, Reese, you haven't gotten back to me with a count for those cupcakes. The veterans' memorial fundraiser, remember?"

Nor had Shireen brought Reese a seed or bulb. "Sorry, my schedule has been nuts."

"But we *can* count on you as a sponsor, right? Those cupcakes are such a crowd pleaser. I know you haven't forgotten our dear, departed men and women in uniform. I need to know how many we can expect from you this year. The club has an organizing meeting coming up."

Before Reese responded her running partner sprinted in their direction. *Gabriel! Yes!* Her basic warm-up jog could've easily advanced to a couple of backhand springs of joy.

"Good morning, ladies!" Gabriel smiled, jogged in place, and then turned to Reese, who quickly shoved that flyer back inside her mailbox. "Ready to rack up some miles, baby?"

Each lifting a brow, Odette and Shireen exchanged a pursed-lipped look.

Reese and Gabriel shared three precious staccato kisses. As if they'd rehearsed the synchronized routine, the couple slipped on their too-cool-for-school matching mirrored shades Reese had purchased for them.

"You bet I'm ready, sweet'ems!" Reese said. "I'll give you a call later, Shireen! Buh-bye, Odette!"

Gabriel and Reese took off, matching paces.

"Where are Maximus and Apollo?" Reese asked when they made it halfway up the block. "It doesn't feel the same without them."

"At Adriana's place. And in case you're wondering, Apollo's anal sac problem has been resolved."

"Oh," Reese replied, keeping her expression and tone inscrutable. She'd told him how she felt about the Adriana situation last night. *Give the man time to make adjustments.*

Fifteen minutes in, Reese slipped into her zone. Though they did their miles with little conversation, she relished the bond they'd built through their shared passion for running.

***

136

Gabriel looked forward to his runs with Reese by his side. He glanced over at her profile. He could tell when she was in the zone by her steady stride, breathing pattern, and the light sheen of perspiration on her skin.

Earlier that morning as Gabriel had laced up his shoes to meet Reese out on her lawn, his cell had pinged with a text from Adriana, who had a medium-size, mixed-breed dog with a distended abdomen. The condition had worsened overnight and that morning the dog's breathing had become labored.

Gabriel had dealt with other rescue volunteers over the years. He'd seen it all, from cats put up for adoption because their shed fur clashed with pricey new sofas to dogs relinquished because they smelled…like dogs, but Adriana took in more than her share of rescues with health issues. Her instincts for determining which conditions could wait for treatment and those that were true medical emergencies were usually spot-on.

Gabriel had phoned Julian before responding to Adriana's text for help. He couldn't cancel on Reese again because of Adriana, not after what Reese had revealed to him the night before. Even though the aid wasn't *for* Adriana, but for what sounded like a very sick animal, it still wouldn't look right. Reese had been patient and understanding regarding his work schedule. He'd be a fool to press his luck with her. After he explained the situation, Julian agreed to handle the emergency for him. Gabriel texted Adriana back with the information.

Gabriel had made too many Adriana-related mistakes with women before, but he vowed to handle things differently this time. He cringed when he thought back to what he and his friends now dubbed "The Case of Carly and the Key Fob Fiasco."

Carly, his significant other at the time, had planned a surprise 35th anniversary bash for her parents. While rushing around, making sure everything was perfect, she'd sent Gabriel to buy more of the sparkler cake candles she'd misplaced. On his way to the party supply store, he'd received a distress call from Adriana. She and her teen mentees were stuck in the parking lot at Freddie's FunWorld and SkyPark because Adriana's keys had fallen out of her pocket while she rode the Lightning Loops Mega Coaster.

Though Gabriel and Adriana were no longer together as a couple at the time, Gabriel had her only set of spare cars keys because he'd forgotten to return them after they'd broken up. So he took a detour to drop off those keys. Not considering the heavy traffic in that part of town around seven at night or Murphy's Law, he figured he had plenty of time before the festivities at Carly's place.

Soon enough, he'd found Adriana and her three girls in the lot. A dead key fob battery, an impossible-to-locate emergency keyhole alternative in her push-button ignition vehicle, and a mad hunt for the right fob replacement batteries so Adriana wouldn't have to leave her car in the lot overnight had stretched what should've taken about 40-minutes, tops, into nearly triple the time.

When Gabriel showed up at Carly's place, the sparkler candle-less cake had been served and the party had wound down. Carly had taken him to a private room and listened to his heartfelt apology and detailed explanation about how he couldn't leave Adriana and those girls stranded in a dark parking lot.

"I see." Carly nodded and calmly as she pleased escorted his ass to the front door. "It's over. We're not a couple, but a trio. I wish you and Adriana the best. She's a cool girl. If I swung the other way, I'd go for her myself. Goodbye, Gabriel."

Soon after that incident, he and Adriana did get back together. *Again.* Only to break up three months later. *Again.* He'd botched his relationship with Carly because he'd failed to set the appropriate priorities and delegate. The lady in his life should come first. When helping a friend, whether male or female, he had to rein in his need to control, which meant occasionally utilizing an emissary. There was nothing wrong with that as long as the friend's need was met. Lesson learned.

CHAPTER 23

Later at the Sweet Spot, Reese sat in her office organizing supply orders and other paperwork. Jerricka, who owned Jerricka's Tea and Spice Shop next door, had left the Mayfair Fall Fest vendor application with a sticky note attached.

The pair had shared a table last year. Reese had filled out the application and paid the fee, but Jerricka had yet to reimburse Reese for the tea shop's portion of the bill. To square things, Jerricka promised to pay the entire fee this year. Had she forgotten their arrangement? Before Reese could phone her, Linda knocked and poked her head inside. "You have a visitor, sugar." Based on Linda's sassy expression, Reese knew her surprise caller was Gabriel. She hurried to the mirror on a nearby wall, where she checked her clothing for flour and frosting stains. She fluffed her hair and swiped on some fruity lip balm. Her plan was to drag him back to her office, lock the door, and smother him with kisses.

Except, it wasn't Gabriel.

Instead, an Armani-suit-clad Darren stood near the front counter. "Hello."

"What are you doing here?" Reese snapped in a stage whisper and nudged him to the front door.

"I need to talk to you," Darren said. "You blocked all my numbers, and I didn't want to just pop up at your house."

"So you pop up here instead. There's nothing more to say." Reese glanced around, keeping a smile on her face because she didn't want her staff or customers all up in her personal business.

"But there is. A lot more."

Reese regarded him, more irritated at his audacity than enraged over his betrayal, which further confirmed she was over him. His deception amplified every little imperfection that had never bothered her before, like the way she could always tell when his seasonal allergies got the better of him because his breath held a hint of sourness, as it did that day. And now as she studied it, that *thing* on his chin she'd long mistaken for a God-given dimple appeared suspect and possibly involved incisions and sutures. What had Blaire called it? *A climple.*

For a surgeon, Darren had always kept his nails a tad too long. His laughter sounded honk-like, not sexy and sonorous like Gabriel's. And Darren always scraped off the frosting, no matter the flavor, before eating cupcakes, which irked the heck out of her. And when she brought treats (cupcakes, cherries, strawberries, whipped cream, melted chocolate) to the bedroom, Darren would gobble them up with all the erotic creativity of a warthog. And she'd never let on how much she hated him calling her "Reesie," which was too close to the peanut butter cup.

"Please," Darren held out his hands, emitting potent notes of his expensive cologne which now caught in her throat, "just a few minutes of your time and I promise not to bother you again."

If Darren hadn't screwed up there would be no Reese and Gabriel. She had spent countless hours comparing and contrasting both men, reflecting on their interactions with her and how they'd made her feel inside. Though she'd believed she wanted a life with Darren, marrying him would've been a mistake. Sure, they'd shared good times. Lots of them in fact, if she were completely honest with herself. He'd been, or rather convincingly played the part of, the adoring boyfriend. The sex had been (mostly) satisfying and frequent, if a bit staid and standard-issue sometimes. Darren didn't particularly enjoy "taking orders," often carping that Reese wouldn't let him "be the man." A real man, comfortable with his masculinity, wouldn't hesitate to do whatever it took to please his woman. A real man— not a caveman—didn't mind using all the help he could get. Yes, Darren had a few bedroom tricks, and by gum, he was sticking to them.

Those things aside, Reese had never felt as if she were settling by being with Darren. He'd been exceptionally kind to her, actually. Things only got bad at the end. A reason-for-a-season relationship. That much was clear. Her residual rage had diminished to disappointment that they hadn't parted on better terms. She hated everything about grudges. They weren't good for the soul.

Maybe she could change that. "Follow me." Reese led him to her office, sat behind her desk, and put on her no-nonsense face. "You have five minutes. I wouldn't waste it with empty apologies. I've heard enough of those already."

"But I am sorry I hurt you," he said, taking the seat in front of her desk. "You didn't deserve that. If only I could go back in time. I've been sick about it all, about the way I hurt you and Sasha. I'd do a lot of things differently if I could."

Yada. Yada. Yada. Reese tapped a pencil against her desk, like the tick of clock. If he wanted to squander his five minutes, she could rest easy knowing she'd offered to hear him out, though she owed him nothing.

Darren's dark brown eyes welled up.

Oh, snap! Reese nearly fell out of the chair she'd tipped at an angle. She'd never seen him shed a tear, even when his beloved nana had passed away earlier that year. He'd handled his grief with macho resolve in Reese's presence.

"I mean it, Reesie. I am gutted, gutted I tell you." He choked up. "You're like an angel, always radiating positivity and wanting to think the best of people. I betrayed your trust in the worst kind of way." Then waterworks flowed, complete with heaves and shuddering shoulders.

Oh my goodness!

"I'm sorry. Say you believe me. Please. I hate that I hurt you."

Crocodile tears? Reese passed him a tissue from the box on her desk.

Darren blew his nose. "I think it might help if I explained some things in more detail, share how things played out."

"What's a timeline got to do with anything? You cheated on me… and Sasha. End of story."

"Just… Please."

Though it would make no difference, he had piqued her curiosity. "Go on," she said, sure his justification would start with the ol' *see, what had happened wuz…*

Darren told her about that business trip to Chicago he'd taken a little more than four months ago. He and Sasha had agreed to meet for dinner and drinks for old times' sake. Because he was in love with Reese, he believed he could keep lingering feelings he had for Sasha at bay. A few drinks and nostalgia proved too challenging, and they ended the evening in her bed.

Reese didn't care to ask if the condom had broken or if he'd dipped his dinker raw. She awaited the prickle or punch of pain. Stomach roiling with queasy yearning? Nothing. *Yup, she was done.*

"I didn't set out to deceive or hurt you," Darren said. "It was all innocent—"

"Until it wasn't. You should've told me what happened right away, when you returned to Mayfair."

"I was racked with guilt, Reesie."

"You've lost the right to call me that. And I've always hated it."

"I was scared. And it wasn't so simple. I wasn't sure what I wanted. I loved, *love* both of you. I do. I was truly torn."

"And it would've been so easy if we'd just agreed to be sister wives. So far, all you're offering is the cliché."

"So I took the time to think."

"And continue to play hide the sausage with both of us. And goodness knows who else."

"No. No. No. There wasn't anyone else. I swear!"

Though Reese had practiced safe sex with Darren, it couldn't hurt to call her ob-gyn to order an STD panel.

"It wasn't like that. I love you both, only you two. Even after I bought the ring, I wasn't sure."

"Unbelievable!"

Darren fidgeted, as embarrassed as he should be. "Both of you are so great. Then Sasha found the ring and assumed it was for her."

"And you let her run with it."

Darren shrugged. "I figured it was a sign."

"So why didn't you flip a coin!"

"Sasha decided to move back to Mayfair to accept a promotion and more money from her employer. I didn't have to move my practice to be with her. Everything fell into place."

"So the decision was made by circumstances."

"Something like that. So about that horrific night... Sasha flew in from Chicago to surprise me, found some incriminating things at my place, then tracked me down at your house using the GPS on my phone."

Another puzzle piece, but did it matter now? Darren, sounding like his usual animated self, had stemmed his tears now that he had her undivided attention. The big faker.

"Mom, who still adores you by the way, was so flattered by how much you praised her cake at the Fourth of July barbecue. She made one for you the same day I had planned to tell you everything. I showed up at your place and lost my nerve. It wasn't just about how hot you looked in that dress, I swear. You'll always have a piece of my heart, Reesie."

She glared at him.

"I mean *Reese.* You're a wonderful woman, but I have committed to making it work with Sasha."

"Especially now with a kid on the way."

"Well, yes." Happiness glimmered in his eyes that he tried to downplay. He'd always said he couldn't wait to be father and darn it, even after everything, she couldn't begrudge him that. A baby was a precious gift.

"I found out she was pregnant the same time you did," Darren insisted. "I swear I had no idea until that night. It's not the kind of news you deliver over the phone."

"Nor was it the kind of news you shriek through a locked door before trying to drop kick it down."

"Yes, well, er, Sasha…She's not usually like that. I take full responsibility for everything."

"Congratulations," Reese said with easy sincerity. *What a wuss she was!*

"Thank you. We're doing couples' counseling, inside and outside church, double duty. I wanted to be honest to move forward. I thought you deserved that. This was never easy for me."

Reese came to her feet. "Okay, I think we're done here."

"One more thing, I wanted to thank you for your, um, *discretion* at the party," Darren said. "I gather you were there, but left, slipped out the backyard when Sasha and I arrived."

Reese sat down as Darren's main agenda came to light: ensure Reese didn't squeal.

"I gather you know Adriana."

CHAPTER 24

Barely. She's the friend of a friend," Reese said.

"You impressed her. She's been praising the Sweet Spot, and I'm not surprised she likes you. People always take to you. You're so—"

"Cut the crap, Darren. About this visit and your toadying... You and Sasha want to keep your two-timing weasel ways from her family. Just admit it, since you're coming clean."

"Yeah, all right, even our therapist and church counselor recommended it, for now. We don't need additional opposition or judgment from her family or mine while we work through things. I was hoping...We'd appreciate your continued discretion. Sasha wanted to reach out to you herself, but I told her that wasn't a good idea."

"Horrible idea." Funny, discretion had been the last thing on Sasha's mind when she'd stood on Reese's porch, acting hysterical and humiliating them all.

"I won't waste my time asking you not to tell Quinn and Blaire because I know you tell those two everything."

"They're not gossips, nor am I vindictive or bitter. I'm not out to punish you or Sasha. I'm not rooting for your relationship to fail. An innocent child is involved now."

Darren appeared to unclench. He took a flyer off the stack she'd photocopied to drum up votes for the Sweet Spot in the DetoursMayfair.com competition. "Congratulations on your nomination. Third year in a row. This is your year. Remember, my friend Chip?"

"The expert in social media campaigns?"

"Yes."

"I'm doing my own social media campaign. The flyers are old school, but still effective."

"I know, you're on top of it, *as always* when it comes to Sweet Spot business. But Chip will be happy to help."

"Oh? He didn't help last year or the one before."

"He'll help *this* year. Pro bono. I can guarantee it."

Darren often did work at steep discounts for certain well-connected people so someone always owed him a favor.

"I plan to talk to him about this competition," Darren said.

"I don't need your help."

"I know you don't need it, but a little extra can't hurt."

Rejecting Darren's offer, even on principle, was not a savvy business decision. Winning this year's competition would help the Sweet Spot and push her closer to opening that second shop on the other side of town. Her long-term business plan also included expanding her Sweet Spot brand by offering franchise opportunities. Darren worked an angle, but he'd always been immensely supportive of her professional endeavors. His making this offer wasn't uncharacteristic, but it had the stench of a bribe.

"May I talk to Chip on the Sweet Spot's behalf?"

"It's a free country."

"I'll take that as a yes." Darren folded and pocketed a flyer.

"Take it any way you want, but let's be clear, *we* are *not* friends. And I refuse to lie or sacrifice my own best interest to keep your dirty little secret. That's the best I can do." Sooner or later, Gabriel would learn about Reese's past with Darren and connect the dots.

Now that she had Darren here, she could determine how well he and Gabriel knew one another.

"Adriana likes you, too. Are you two very close?" Reese asked.

"Yeah, when Sasha and I got together the first time *before I met you*," he clarified. "We often double-dated with her and Gabriel, her man at the time."

"Hanging out as a foursome can be tricky. It's easier when everyone gets along."

"I liked Gabriel well enough, but I always got the vibe that dude did not cotton to me."

"Oh?"

"Yeah, not sure why, though." Darren stroked his climple. "Maybe he was jealous."

Of what! Reese continued casually tapping the pencil against her desk.

"I'm a people doctor, and he's an animal doctor, a companion animal doctor at that. There is a pecking order, you know. He writes children's books. I'm told they sell, but I think he can't hack writing *real* novels for adults, a much tougher audience. Sasha also mentioned he has some huge hang-up about his older brother. I know you've heard of Lucas Cameron. One word describes that relationship. Rivalrous." He added an unsympathetic grunt. "Must be hard living in the shadow of a big-time movie star."

Reese had rarely glimpsed this condescending, status-conscious side of Darren. She wanted to tell him Gabriel had the smarts, talent, and resolve to achieve any career goals he set for himself, but she wasn't supposed to know Gabriel.

"But, then again, maybe it's not that at all. Adriana and I got along so well. You know women get a bad rap for competing with each other, but men have their issues with that, too."

"So you and this, what's his name, weren't friends?" Reese asked. Boasting about how close she and Gabriel had become would've been a purely retaliatory-but-ultimately-fruitless move. *Hey, now!* Instead, Reese plotted and pumped someone for info! And it felt darn good with the appropriate stoolie.

"Gabriel was, if overly formal and guarded, polite, probably as a favor to Adriana and Sasha, but he never took me up on invitations to play golf at the country club, shoot hoops, or any other type of bonding without the girls. Always talked about how busy he was. *C'est le vie.* I tried. But I might have to try harder with him."

"What do you mean?"

"I'm sure he and Adriana will get back together. They always do. Those two have been quite the pair over the years. In the Jones' family room, Markova, you met her, has this huge photo of them as kids holding hands. They're no more than four or five years old. They were the ring bearer and flower girl at a wedding. If they reconcile before our wedding, surely Sasha will want Gabriel to be a groomsman. Shoot, if they reunite in time, I wouldn't rule out a double wedding." Darren stopped rambling to stare at Reese when she snapped her pencil in two.

CHAPTER 25

Darren's prediction about Gabriel and Adriana's impending nuptials had fueled Reese's insecurity, but she managed not to work herself into a state. That was just Darren's opinion. What did he know? He had no clue Gabriel had a new woman in his life. Darren had no idea just how content Gabriel was these days.

Gabriel was delighted to be with Reese…or so Reese hoped. She wasn't just a backup or rebound chick until…She pushed the nonsense to the back of her mind.

With most of her paperwork done and only two customers left in the Sweet Spot by four o'clock, Reese asked Linda to join her in the office and let Danielle take over up front.

Eyes wide, Linda fiddled with the edge of her Sweet Spot T-shirt. "Is something wrong, hon?"

Putting on a blank expression, Reese paused. "Yes, something is wrong, but I aim to correct it. Have a seat, please."

***

Receiving a text message from Gabriel informing her he was taking the rest of the day off and delivering the good news that Linda had earned a promotion and a hefty raise went a long way toward brightening Reese mood after Darren's visit.

Energized, she changed into her fitness gear for a run home. Before taking off, she ducked inside Jerricka's shop to discuss the Fall Fest vendor fee, but her shop neighbor had left to tend to an errand.

As in Reese's place, a mix of appealing scents filled the air. Jerricka had stocked the amber walls with a wide variety of teas, herbs, salts, and spices from around the world, sold by the pinch or pound.

"I need to leave a note for Jerri." Reese passed Olivia, the sales associate, the envelope with the vendor application and a new sticky note, which read: *Your turn?*

Of course it was Jerricka's flippin' turn to pay, but a question mark and several smiley faces would soften what could come off as a mandate.

***

Reese arrived at her house and found a shirtless Gabriel leaving her front yard, pushing his lawn mower.

"I was doing my lawn and noticed yours was getting a little overgrown again," he said. "I hope you don't mind. I took the liberty. I know how upset you were when the HOA slapped you with that fine."

Though Reese always enjoyed the scent of a freshly mowed lawn, she bristled. "Thank you, but again—"

"I know." Gabriel lifted a hand. "Rosvaughn."

Reese, reached for her cell in her sports belt, but then decided against calling her cousin, which would only quash her endorphins rush. Instead, she ogled Gabriel's hard-muscled body. Pure splendor, glistening with perspiration.

"I had planned to finish the job and shower for our date before you arrived," he said.

"I like you all earthy and scrumptious," she purred.

"Same here." Gabriel wrapped his sweaty arms around her. He buried his nose against her damp neck and licked her.

"Some people would find that gross." Reese laughed, not caring who was watching.

"There's no accounting for taste."

If what Odette said was true, the subdivision, not just Mistywood Lane, knew she and Gabriel were an item. Why not give them something to talk about? She brushed her lips against his. Something sweet and chaste. When she went for a second peck, his hand curved around her nape, and he deepened the kiss with more tongue and lip action. Soon her body hummed with need. To ensure their PDA didn't detour to TMI...

"I'm about to take a shower, no, a bubble bath. I'd love some company," she said as if inviting him for a stroll around the Granberry Ridge pond.

Myra Swanigan worked on those hydrangeas of hers. Again. Blinds parted at two houses across the street.

"You go and put away that lawn mower," Reese said. "Wait a few minutes, then text me for further instructions when the coast is clear." She slapped his butt, made her way to her door, and then tossed over her shoulder, "Oh, and Gabriel, don't you dare clean up. That's my job."

"Yes, ma'am!"

Reese went inside and plucked Sinbad out of his litter box, where he spent a lot of time lately. "Come here, cuddlebug, Mommy misses you." After Reese and Sinbad did their "Stray Cat Strut" routine, she fed him, again ignoring the nutritional instructions on the brochures Gabriel had passed along. "We'll start your new diet next week. I'm sure that's okay with you." Sinbad chowed down on a big mound of grilled tuna in gravy. As she crouched to pet him her cellphone beeped with a text from Gabriel: *Coast is clear.*

Reese: *Wait five minutes. I left the back door unlocked.*

Reese gave Sinbad another ear scratch before heading to her bedroom. She removed her damp clothes and slipped on a silk robe and nothing else. Everything had to be perfect. They'd start with a bubble bath in her large Jacuzzi tub. Would Gabriel enjoy the scent of honeysuckle as much as she did? Dusk had arrived. Lowered blinds and dim lights gave the room a late-evening effect. Dark enough to be romantic, but not so dark she couldn't see every inch of Gabriel's amazing bod. She'd have him. All of him. *Finally!* Lit votive candles bathed the space in a warm glow. No new-age harp and piano music for this rendezvous. She brought out her old-fashioned CD player and a stack of old school R&B crooners. They'd start with one of her mother's favorites, the "Lady of Magic" track from *Maze Featuring Frankie Beverly* and then she set the player to segue to Luther Vandross and the sultriest tunes by Prince. Then she filled the tub with fragrant water and rich suds. Minutes later, Gabriel stood in her bathroom. Sinbad darted inside as if to nab a prime seat for the show.

"Oh, hell no." Gabriel picked him up, set him outside the bathroom, and closed the door.

"I told you not to clean up," Reese said.

"I didn't. Same shorts, but a half-dressed man slipping in your backyard might rouse suspicion and lead to a 911 call."

"True," Reese gave him a saucy grin, "more for me to strip off you." She moved closer to grab the edge of his shirt.

"Wait. I have some things for you." From his pocket Gabriel removed a small box and a rolled sheet of paper secured with a red satin ribbon.

"More gifts? You're spoiling me." Reese opened the box to find another sparkly charm in the image of a Persian cat. She unfurled the paper to find a beautiful ink rendering of Sinbad. "Both are lovely! And the detail in this drawing...You did this?"

With a modest grin, Gabriel nodded.

"I love them! Thank you!" Reese put the box and the picture on the counter and resumed pulling off his shirt. She released the top button of his shorts and then unzipped them, admiring his deeply cut abs and sleek, muscular thighs. He removed his shorts and grass-cutting boots. "You have no idea how many times I've fantasized about this." Reese stroked him through his boxer-briefs, slipped a finger inside the band, and snapped it. "Off. Now."

***

"Yes, ma'am." Gabriel rid himself of the underwear. "My turn." He trailed a finger along her silk robe, tracing the pebbled nipples until he heard her sharp intake of breath.

Gabriel slipped the robe off her shoulders, let it pool on the floor, and gasped as he took her in from head to toe. "You're so beautiful." More so than he'd dreamed. Toned legs for days. Luscious breasts. Curvy hips accentuated by a slim waist and sexy abs. All woman. His woman.

Gabriel's jaw flexed, and he drew in a shaky breath. *Pace yourself.* Make this slow and romantic for their first time. He could do it, though it seemed as if he'd waited an eternity for this moment. So he wouldn't pop just looking at her, he glanced around at the neat, ultra-feminine décor. He enjoyed the musky spice from a diffuser and the honeysuckle from the bubble bath. "I've wanted you since the moment I laid eyes on you," he said in low register, nuzzling her ear and running his fingertips along the curves of her incredible body. He would tell her how much she'd come to mean to him in such a short time. And how he envisioned them proceeding as a monogamous couple from this point forward. He'd rhapsodize about her beauty. And how she'd enchanted him with her warmth and thoroughly engaging personality. She needed to know no matter where he was or what he was doing, he thought of her at least a million times a day. He drew her into his embrace and brushed his lips against hers for a slow, deep kiss. But her tongue thrust and probed as she cast her hips against his. Okay, so he would follow her lead... for a few minutes. Her desperate moans spilled inside his mouth and reverberated through his body making him harder still. *Pace yourself. Pace yourself.* She held on as he swept her off her feet, cradle style, to place her inside the tub. Yes, he would wash her first. Get her nice and soapy, then he'd massage her back and delicate shoulders. Perfect after her long day at the Sweet Spot. And oh yes, he'd also massage her scalp with that coconut-scented conditioner he spotted on the counter. Maybe he'd apply lotion to her feet, and kiss her cute toes, one by one, and...

"Slap my ass! Pull my hair! Fuck me!" Reese bellowed along with several other X-rated demands.

Oh? If this were a movie, Luke would refer to the next moment as "breaking the fourth wall." Gabriel would look over his shoulder, directly into the camera, which stood for the viewing audience, and give them a cheeky grin and a waggle of his brows.

After everything Gabriel had learned so far, he had yet to reconcile *this* dirty-talking-Gumby-limbed-wild-monkey-sexpot Reese with the one who hummed bubblegum pop tunes, baked "pupcakes," and substituted "blankety-blank" or "flippin' " for curse words in everyday conversation. With gymnast agility Reese maneuvered and wrapped herself around him as if she were scaling a sequoia. With legs encircling his waist, she'd sandwiched his painfully throbbing erection between them, which excited her more as she writhed against it, bringing him near climax before he could make it to the tub. He adjusted himself to ease the decadent pressure. But with his erection free and homing in like a heat-seeking missile, she locked into target position. Now the engorged head bobbed tantalizingly against her opening. Whimpering with yearning, she gyrated against it, before he could get the damn condom out of shorts. *Shit!* The bare, slippery sensation felt good. Too good. He wanted to ram into her. Full-out raw. But fortunately his cooler head (on his shoulders) prevailed. He drew in a deep breath, paused for a moment, and counted the lit candles. *One. Two. Three. Four....*

Still balancing quite well, Reese lifted her breasts, cupping and squeezing them until the mocha nipples were distended points, reaching out him.

Eyes glazed with passion, she noted his hesitation. "Something wrong?"

"Hell, no."

"Good."

Well, alrighty then! Gabriel dispensed with his plans. She wanted it savage? Animalistic? Well, that's exactly how he would give it to her. There was plenty of time for the poetry-laced sweet nothings, classical piano concertos, and scattered rose petals. He shoved her toward her long marble, double-sink counter. After he plunked her luscious bottom on it, avoiding the candles, cat picture, and gift box, he reached for his pants to get their protection and wasted no time rolling it on.

"Now!" Reese would have none of that gradual inch-by-inch stuff. Oh, no. With both primed, his entry was smooth and fast like a well-oiled piston, though the fit was super-tight. Her heat seared through the condom. He paused momentarily to savor how unbelievably good she felt. After he filled her, their dance grew frenetic. He pounded into her with power. But with each wallop of his hips, she merely tilted hers as if they couldn't get close enough. Satisfied gasps exploded from her as she clung to him, coaxing him to go deeper, harder with more triple-X demands that pushed him closer to the edge. Her hands were every-damn-where. *Such a naughty, naughty girl.* His fingers tangled in her hair, so he gave it the firm tugs she'd demanded, without scalping her of course. He slapped her bottom, just enough to warm his palm. She moaned in approval. The reflection of her rolling spine and hips in the mirror as he drove in and out of her... beyond smokin'. Her most intimate muscles clenched around him, tightening then releasing quick and rhythmically, producing a decadent tugging sensation, like a honeyed Hoover. *Hot damn!* Where had she learned that trick? She scooched off the counter, so he gripped her hips as she rode him. Hard. Up and down. *Lower back, please don't fail me now.* Her breasts bounced enticingly close, a feast he couldn't devour. Instead, he focused on where they connected, the place where every pleasure nerve in him met. Soon her rising and sinking accelerated and her thighs clamped around him in a vise-like fashion. She came with a hoarse cry and an oath, her fingers digging into his shoulders. With a grimace and a growl, he soon followed. He clenched, his hot seed straining the condom as if blasted through a high-pressure hose. He'd never experienced such a knee-buckling-out-of-this-world release with anyone before.

Spent, he pushed them toward the counter and dropped her on it. They held on to each other, her head, resting against his damp chest. His heart rate galloped as if he'd sprinted for miles, while she was all bubbly and bright-eyed.

"Now *that* was peachy keen," Reese said.

Gabriel chuckled as he lazily stroked her hair and planted a kiss on her temple. *"Peachy keen"* from the woman who only minutes before had turned the air blue and stuck her finger in his ass. "Yeah, peachy keen," he replied, thankful his lower back, sometimes dicey from an old deadlifting injury, hadn't revolted and locked him into a stooped position. He disposed of the condom in a nearby trash can.

Shoop, shoop, shoop, shoop at the door. Sinbad attempting to pick the lock?

"I'm sure he wants another treat," Reese said. "I mean, his *first* treat of the day."

Gabriel shook a finger at her. "You haven't taken my advice yet."

"Sinbad will start Monday. I promise." Reese stepped down from the counter. "Sorry we didn't make it to the bubble bath." She stood on a wide, fluffy rug near the tub and dipped her fingers inside to play with the suds.

Gabriel's penis was now upturned and hardening as he admired the view. This had to be one for the record books. How in the hell was he ready to go? Again? Impossible. But nothing about his attraction to Reese Sommers was typical. *Don't question. Don't analyze. Flow, bro. Just flow.* "Don't move." He stroked himself.

Reese peered over her shoulder with a grin. Now aware of the effect she had on him, she shifted into more provocative positions, pulling her shoulders back, arching her back, accentuating the inverted heart shape of her slender waist meeting her curvy button as she scooped more suds. "Like this?" she asked with faux innocence as his hand quickened its pace, pumping his hardness.

When he was full-on steel again, he moved behind her. His erection nestled between her cheeks while he moved it up and down, and then rotated his hips. He molded against her to cup her breasts and enjoyed the feel of her beaded nipples against his palms. She held on to the side of the tub, moaned, squirmed and widened her stance. Ready for him. He grabbed another condom from his shorts. He gripped her hips and slid inside her, this time reveling in the feel of her firm bottom's rocking against him and the reflection of her swaying breasts in a standing mirror. She rose on her toes with fervent backward thrust. They moved together with perfect rhythm, as if their bodies were made for connecting just like this, and only with each other. Her inner muscles tightened, held him where she needed him most. *Hot.* This woman could fry them both alive. Every cell in his body sizzled as if made of magma. He gave his all until she climaxed with a rapturous cry that heightened his own excitement. After a few more focused, brute thrusts, he followed her over the fiery edge.

***

"Water's definitely tepid now," Reese said a few minutes later. "Come here." He joined her at the tub's edge. "I like it in here." They relaxed, stretching out on the large rug. The condom sagged on his flaccid penis as she caressed his thigh. He tossed the condom in the trash. When she scooped up a handful of suds, he let her give him a voluminous bubbly beard.

"Sexy Santa," she cooed. "I've been a bad girl."

"And I loved every minute of it." Gabriel propped up his head with one hand so he could admire her face, glowing with a fine sheen of perspiration. As the suds fell from his face onto her neck, he took in her high cheekbones, silky skin, the perfect arcs of her brows and those thick lashes. He could gaze at her for hours. He traced the contours of her full lips. He touched the small scar on her left knuckle he'd noticed while intertwining their fingers. He wanted to memorize every inch of her to make his fantasies more vivid when they were apart.

"I could still use a shower. I mean, I ran home from the shop, and we just had a heck of a workout."

"You smell wonderful." Gabriel nestled his nose against her neck and licked her there again. "Sweet and spicy."

"But could use a tad more salt, is that it?" Reese chuckled. "Sweat smells better on you." Reese rolled to nudged her nose between his pecs. "You're all man."

"I am, aren't I?" Gabriel grinned, wanting to beat his chest.

"So c'mon, *all man*, join me in the shower."

"Uh…"

"What? Would you prefer the tub? I can adjust the water temperature." Reese propped her head up with one hand. Their lips were mere inches apart so he enjoyed her warm, sweet breath against his cheek.

"Uh, depends. Are we bathing or banging?" Gabriel brushed the tip of his nose against hers.

"Don't tell me you're tired?" she asked as if he were a party pooper. Then she lifted his hand to swirl her tongue around his index finger as if it were a promise of pleasures to come.

"No. I have mo." Gabriel dusted the cobwebs off some ancient Mr. T bravado. "I gotta lotta mo."

Reese released his finger. "Is that right?" Issuing a challenge, she gave him a peck on the mouth. "Then show me." He tickled her middle until she erupted in a fit of giggles.

"Yeah, I, um—"

"What?"

"I need a minute first." Gabriel hated to admit it. "Men are built different, you know. I can't just slap on some lube and go."

"Could've fooled me."

Gabriel took her hand and planted a kiss on each of her knuckles.

"Well, you did do all the heavy lifting," she conceded, stroking his biceps. "But a shower sounds good, doesn't it?" Reese sprang off the rug as if she'd quaffed a week's worth of 5-Hour Energy drinks. She turned on the spray and summoned him, crooking her finger. When she stepped inside, she wet her hair. It became curlier, resting on her shoulders in loose, dripping ringlets. With a sultry gleam in her eyes, she blew kisses at him and shimmied, her beautiful body, inviting and glistening with water. He came to his feet, cracked his neck, and did a couple of triceps and lower back stretches, drawing a laugh from her. He reached for a fistful of condoms before joining her. They stayed in the shower long enough for him to give her a *whole* lotta mo.

CHAPTER 26

Later that night, Reese and Gabriel sat at the kitchen table eating the chicken and sausage gumbo leftovers she'd reheated for them.

"I'm glad your father and I are about the same size," said Gabriel, all yummy and shirtless, as he drank from his glass of wine. Reese had given him clean, drawstring athletic shorts, emblazoned with the logo from her father's favorite sports team. "Shame to take a shower and put on those same funky shorts."

"Aren't these too big for you?"

"They're Daddy's, but now they're yours. I'll buy him another pair."

Reese, who wore an oversize T-shirt and terrycloth shorts, sat next to him. Her hair, still damp, would dry in a voluminous pouf of spirals, like Quinn's.

"I think I prefer your hair wild and curly like that," he said.

"Quinn would love to hear you say that. She thinks curly-, coily-, wavy-, kinky-haired women should wear their hair in its natural state at least ninety percent of the time. I'm more fifty-fifty, so like Blaire, I have nothing against a flat iron. I like variety." She fluffed her spirals, plucked at his shorts, and then dilly-dallied between his legs.

"Now *that's* why I occasionally enjoy the freedom of going commando."

"There's something to be said for quicker access." Reese stroked him.

"Careful. Don't start something you can't finish, lady."

"Warning noted." Reese resumed eating. "I'm starving!" Gabriel's bare sculpted chest and chiseled abs never failed to evoke awe. "Not that you don't look irresistible right now." They swapped another deep tomato-and-garlic-flavored kiss to the sound of Sinbad digging in his mud room litter box for a second time in a half hour.

"This is delicious." Gabriel shoved a huge spoonful of gumbo inside his mouth. "How did you learn to cook?"

"I've been obsessed since I got my first Easy-Bake oven for Christmas. I had a little white one. This was back when they still came with an incandescent light bulb as the heating element. I soon moved on to dump cakes. For fun, I've had baking courses over the years, but I'm mostly self-taught, using books and bingeing on cooking shows. And a lot of trial and error. What about you? Have you always loved animals?"

"Yes, all sorts of animals. When I was a kid I thought I would become a marine biologist, but then one day I watched *Jaws*."

"And those marine biologist dreams—"

"Turned to nightmares."

"Aww, poor baby." Reese caressed his arm. "And the books?"

"When I was a kid, doodling and cartoon drawing was something that always cheered me up when I was having a bad day. The writing for the pictures came a little later." He stopped eating to settle back in his chair and gaze at her.

"Why are you looking at me like that?" Reese asked.

"Like what?"

"I often catch you staring at me, as if deep in thought."

"Truth? I'm trying to figure out why somebody hasn't snapped you up, beautiful lady, inside and out. You're perfect."

"I am *so* not perfect."

"Perfect for me."

"Are you flattering me in hopes I'll share my secret flaws?" she asked. "If somebody hasn't put a ring on it, I must be too good to be true? What's the dirt? Is that the angle? Maybe I clip my toenails, pick my nose, and sand my crusty heels at the dinner table, huh?"

"What I'm trying to say is I think you're amazing. You already know I've fallen for you. Hard. Fast. But I'm curious about your love life before us. I've told you all about Adriana and me. And a few others. Have you ever been in love?"

It was a fair question. Reese had only mentioned Timothy, the guy she'd dated, but had dumped after tiring of his helicopter mother and his severe allergic reaction to Sinbad.

"Ever been close to marriage? Tell me about the last guy you were serious about. What went wrong?"

There it was. Gabriel had asked. Point blank. No room for evasion. "I was seriously involved with someone before I met you. That morning you came over to return Sinbad…Well, we'd broken up the night before that."

"Is that right?" Gabriel sat up straighter. "So that's why you were out of sorts. You were pleasant and chatty, but I could tell there was sadness in your eyes, a little distraction, too."

"I'll say." Reese released a humorless chuckle before she told him everything, from expecting an engagement ring hidden inside that strawberry cake to discovering Darren had been unfaithful and with whom he'd cheated.

Gabriel pounded the table with a fist. "I knew it! I knew that joker was no good from the moment I met him. I got this vibe." His face tightened with rage. "I can't believe Sasha showed out like that! Believe me, that's not the Sasha I know. He brought that out of her. He pushed her over the edge. She snapped. He doesn't deserve either of you."

"I'm over it," Reese said. "I mean I'm *so* over it, it feels as if it happened to somebody else."

"But it didn't happen to somebody else. And I can't believe Sasha is giving that fool another chance." Gabriel shook his head. "Her family obviously doesn't know because if they did—"

"Darren and Sasha don't want her family to know. The fewer people who know, the better. I suppose I understand that reasoning. Yes, he deceived us, but—"

"No buts, he's a grade-A jackass!"

"For what it's worth, I believe he loves Sasha. He never stopped loving her. Somehow, deep inside a part of me has always known. But he tried to move on with me after she dumped him, broke his heart, and moved to Chicago."

"I can't believe you're making excuses for him after what he did to you."

"Not actually making an excuse, I'm calling it like I see it, without blinders or ego."

"So you want to give him a pass? Like Sasha obviously has. Damn! What do you two see in that asshole?"

Gabriel's judgmental tone made Reese defensive about her time with Darren. Well, at least the majority of it. "It's not always black and white," she said. "The relationship was not all bad. In fact, I cared about him deeply. I wanted to marry him for a reason. We had a great rapport, and he treated me well. He was kind… until… It's always so easy for people to demonize the ex. I'm talking about those who say the relationship was *all* bad and the ex mistreated him or her the entire time. I think that says just as much about the wronged ex. Such as, why did he or she *stay* in that abusive relationship for so long? In the name of love? Now *that's* whack, if you ask me. Nobody is worth that kind of pain. And enduring such agony doesn't prove how much you love that person, who doesn't commit to change. It's about how much you don't, or didn't, love yourself."

"Everyone isn't in a position to just walk away."

"I know. I'm talking about people who have options and financial independence, mind you. I know there are other considerations when someone's livelihood is dependent on someone else or when there are children involved and few viable alternatives. It's not always so simple."

"And you proved my point. So why in the hell is Sasha giving Darren another chance after what he's done? She doesn't *need* him. And she has financial stability on her own and a large, loving family for emotional and additional financial support if needed. They will help her with the kid."

"I believe Darren will try to do right by her and this baby. I know for a fact that he desperately wants to be a father. And I believe he will be an incredible, hands-on father. He talked about it constantly, but not just that, he worked with kids at every opportunity, mentoring underprivileged students, encouraging and advising those interested in medical careers. He regularly coaches in his community's youth sports leagues and—"

"Found a cure for chikungunya, located Elvis and Tupac, both alive and well, and invented the Internet." Gabriel thwacked his palm against his forehead as if he couldn't believe what a moron she was. "You're giving him a pass. You're *actually* giving the jackass a pass."

"I'm not giving him a pass! Even if I'm wrong about his intentions regarding Sasha, bottom line, he's not *my* problem now. I have moved on. I'm not wallowing in self-pity and pining. I've been enjoying getting to know *you* and spending time with *you*, Gabriel. I'm happy when I'm with you. I don't want to spoil it by obsessing about how things ended with Darren."

"So if all is going swimmingly in your world, you don't care about anybody else, is that it?"

"No! Sasha's a grown woman."

"Who is confused."

"And needs to be saved from herself? According to you?"

"I hate that he hurt Sasha *and* you. I can't believe you're not angrier."

"Looks as if you're outraged enough for Sasha and me. In what way would it enrich my life to continue seething about Darren's decisions? Would I be happier lobbing grenades at the relationship he's rebuilding with Sasha, who is having his baby? What's an acceptable length of time to marinate in bitter disappointment? Plot revenge? A month? Two months? Six months? A year? Vindictiveness would only block my blessings." Did Reese glimpse an eye roll from him?

Gabriel sat still and quiet for a few moments, as if he needed to choose his next words carefully after his outburst. "I get what you're saying about holding grudges and going for the get-back. But somebody needs to talk some sense into Sasha before she makes the biggest mistake of her life."

"That's not your call. I say leave them be. Couples have survived similar betrayals and moved past them to build stronger relationships."

Without looking at Reese, Gabriel grumbled something unclear.

"I hope it's understood what I've shared with you about my history with Darren stays between you and me." When he didn't respond she pressed for a promise. "Gabriel, this stays between you and me."

"Right."

"I think it's for Sasha to decide what her family knows," she repeated as if saying it enough times would get through to him. "And *when* they know."

Gabriel set his jaw and pressed his lips together in a tight line.

"I was reluctant to tell you everything because I know how much the Joneses mean to you. But only my role in the story is your business, sort of. Stay out of it. Promise me you won't say anything…yet."

"I won't say anything," he muttered, barely comprehensible.

"Good. And I appreciate how honest you've been with me. Now, can we move on?" Reese gave him a kiss on the cheek, but he was still distracted so she got up and brought over a Tupperware container of her latest experiment. She waved it under his nose. "Don't these smell heavenly? I'm thinking of adding them to the menu as a limited or seasonal offering, pumpkin cheesecake cupcakes. She placed the container on the table, choose a cupcake, and peeled back its paper lining.

He sulked like a big brat when she broke it and tried to feed him. "I don't have much of an appetite right now. I'm full," he said before clamping his sturdy jaw again.

"Aww, c'mon." Reese broke off another piece of the cupcake and teased him with it. "Open your mouth, here comes the airplane," she sang, borrowing the technique Odette used on her picky-eating twins. "You have to follow the one-bite-polite rule." She played with the piece of cupcake, putting it on her nose and trying to catch it with her mouth. Her failed attempt coaxed a reluctant grin out of him.

"Give me that." Gabriel reached for the cupcake and took a big bite. Maximus and Apollo are better at that than you are. They can catch anything balanced on their noses."

"You'll have to show me."

"But nothing is funnier than watching them eat peanut butter, organic peanut butter without xylitol, mind you."

"I want to see that, too. Let's go now!"

"We can't. Adriana has them."

"Oh." Now that they were talking companionably again, Reese hid her disappointment. "Hey, speaking of peanut butter. I have an alternate pumpkin cheesecake frosting I'm considering for these cupcakes. I'd love for you to try it." She went to fridge, removed a bowl, and set it before him. "Here you go."

Gabriel devoured the cupcake Reese believed was the perfect blend of density and moistness. "Hey, this is damn good. I didn't think your cupcakes could get any better, but this is my favorite."

"You said that about the last experiment I let you try."

"The raspberry champagne cupcakes you had delivered to the hospital. My staff loves you."

Reese passed him a spoon for the frosting.

Gabriel reached for another cupcake. "Eating a bowl of frosting is a bit much."

"Just a taste, silly. I didn't expect you to scarf it up as if it were an ice cream sundae."

Gabriel stared at the bowl of frosting until Sinbad darted by to go to the mud room. Again.

"He's running to that litter box a helluva lot. Have you noticed this before tonight?" he asked, looking toward the mud room.

"Yeah, so? I'm always thrilled when he goes to the box. We had this frustrating period when he soiled a corner of the rug in the family room and then kept going back and…"

Gabriel wasn't paying attention to her.

"Gabriel?"

"Have you noticed he's drinking a lot more water?"

"Yeah, he is. Lots of water now that I think about it. I can't keep his bowls filled."

When Sinbad left the mud room Gabriel stopped him before he could go back to his climbing tree in the family room. His expression turned serious as he scooped up Sinbad and ran his hand along Sinbad's back and belly.

"What?'

"Your vet never mentioned anything was off after Sinbad's last complete physical?"

"Not that I recall." But then Dr. Jamison had mentally checked out a long while ago, just going through the motions and looking forward to his approaching retirement.

"I'm wondering how *I* missed this before. Wait. I know. I was way too focused on how hot you were to do my damn job that day you brought him in. There's no excuse for that."

"What did you miss?"

"I'd like to investigate further before I say more."

"Investigate what?" The abrupt change in his demeanor startled Reese. "Nothing serious, I hope!"

"Doesn't have to be. Did your former vet send over his records?"

"I don't know, but I'll follow up." Reese wrung her hands. "Now I'm worried."

"I want to make sure we rule out something, that's all."

"Rule out what?"

"So you can run to the Internet and scare yourself to death before I have more information?"

"Well—"

"What's your former vet's name again? If we don't already have the records, I'll make sure we get copies first thing tomorrow. I'll send someone over there if he's not digital yet."

"What else do you have to do?"

"Some tests."

Reese gasped. "What kind of tests? Sinbad hates needles. And please, no scalpel!"

"Scalpel? That's the tool your tool of an ex prefers," he quipped.

Hands on her hips, Reese glowered at him.

"Sorry. Bad joke. But there are ways to check inside the package without opening it."

"What's the issue? Something's off, besides Sinbad's weight?"

"Bring him to the hospital tomorrow any time you're free. I'll work you in."

Reese's eyes welled up. "Sinbad looks fine. He's fine."

"Have you noticed a loss of appetite?"

"No."

Gabriel let Sinbad go.

"Don't fall apart, baby." Gabriel stood. With one finger he tipped up Reese's chin. "Look at me. We need to get more information, that's all for now, okay?"

"Okay."

***

Gabriel drew Reese inside his embrace with the plan to distract her with a kiss that left her dizzy with desire. He didn't like seeing her upset. Time to make her sing with joy. "Now, about that frosting sample." He nudged her toward the cabinet area and slowly removed her clothes. "How about I mix it with a piece of Reese?" He placed her bare bottom on the counter and spread her thighs wide. "And while we're at it, give literal meaning to sugar tits."

Reese chuckled. "Sounds like a splendid idea," she said, not worrying about the potential mess as he smeared the sweet mix on her.

Arching her back and circling her arms around his neck as he lifted each breast to suck and lick. He worked over her until her skin glistened, free of frosting. He would swallow her whole if he could.

He trembled with the need to ram into her. He'd better get a move on or lose the last of his tenuous restraint. He placed one of her feet on the counter. She locked one arm against the counter to stabilize herself. With the other hand, she ran her fingers through his hair. He kicked her clothing aside, and then positioned her other leg over his shoulder. He swiped more frosting from that bowl and smoothed it at the V of her thighs, where it melted into her.

Gabriel crouched and placed two fingers at soft folds protecting her most precious gem. He gently fluttered the tip of his tongue against it. She pressed closer, serving more of herself to him. He twirled his tongue against her and drew the sensitive bud inside his mouth. "Yeah, like that," she said, undulating against it, slightly lifting off the counter, squeezing one breast and the other and then plucking at her mocha tips. He loved this about her. His siren sweetheart. No holding back. No just letting someone *do* things to her. She was always an active participant when it came to heightening her own pleasure, and he fed on her unabashed way of telling him what she wanted and how to give it to her.

"Yes, there," she panted. "Don't stop."

Yes, ma'am. Hey, every woman was different. Each liking and disliking a variety of things. Reese took the trial and error out of satisfying her. He glimpsed the nearby bowl of candy-coated pellets of peanut butter and chocolate and reached for a few, slipping them inside her before retrieving them with his tongue. "Oh, baby," she whispered, both hands now raking through his hair. He relished her indulgent moans. Loved the soft gasps of delight as she careened closer to climax. His mouth was inundated with sweetness as he flicked and laved her without restraint, the pressure inside her building to that first tremor of release. He marked a circular path that tightened until he sank his tongue deep inside. With each thrust, her hands tightened around him, her hips moved with him in a fast, rhythmic glide until she cried out and came. The force of her orgasm vibrated through his mouth to his chest. With his heart rate rampaging, he stood to his full height, caressing her toned thighs as she rode out the waves.

"That particular version of the frosting gets two thumbs up…way up." Gabriel loved that drowsy smile and look of pure carnal satisfaction in her eyes. Nothing like loving her sadness away, but damn, he could barely move, his throbbing erection felt like a giant kickstand, anchoring him in place.

Reese noticed and stepped off the counter to stroke him where he needed it most. "Your turn. My specialty is unfinished business," she said, unzipping his pants and dropping to her knees.

CHAPTER 27

Reese had finished helping Linda replenish the supply of fresh cupcakes in the display case and steamed milk for lattes when Quinn and Blaire arrived. They requested the German chocolate cupcakes and the latest test coffee brew, before following Reese back to her office.

Quinn eyed Reese. "Hey Blaire, get a load of Hopalong Cassidy over here."

"What?" Reese limped across the room and eased down in her chair.

"Don't play dumb with us," Blaire said.

"Whatever are you talking about?" Reese asked, hand to chest.

"Milady," Quinn said with a posh inflection and faux eyelashes fluttering, "you're walking as if you've been soundly boned."

"I have a running injury. A groin pull," Reese said.

"Groins were pulled…and pushed all right," Quinn replied. "All night."

"You had sex with Gabriel, didn't you?" Blaire said.

"And from the looks of it, he *to' up* the coochie!" Quinn laughed.

Reese tried, but failed to smother a smile. The tenderness between her legs and the little love bites he'd left on her breasts, neck, and inner thighs were nice little parting gifts, pleasant reminders of what they'd shared and promises of things to come.

"I knew it!" Quinn leaned forward. "Deets!"

"Why do you always pump *her* for details?" Blaire sipped her coffee.

"Because you and Hayes generate about as many sparks as two wet socks," Quinn replied.

"Gabriel and I have exceptional chemistry," Reese said. "We can't get

165

enough of one another. That's all you'll get out of me on this topic."

"The way you're hobbling, I just hope you burned rubber on his peen," Quinn said, twirling her arm around as if working an invisible lasso. "Do us Sommers sisters proud. Put it on him. Slay!"

"You look fab, girls." Reese tried to steer the conversation away from her sex life. "Where are you two headed?"

"There's a regional natural hair show at the convention center tonight," Quinn said. "I'm doing one of the center stage presentations with a panel of six other popular bloggers/vloggers panelists. The tickets sold out in a day so they're expecting a huge crowd. And get this, Holland Gables, that reporter from WXBZ, called. She wants to do a piece on me! I'm so psyched!"

"Congratulations, sis!" When Reese gave her sister a hug, every muscle in her body protested, but she loved it. "Why didn't you tell me sooner? I made a date with Gabriel. I would reschedule, but he needs to see Sinbad."

"Sisters before misters, but not before cats," Blaire said, who'd modified her long straight hair with swoop bangs, the ends tucked behind one ear.

"Gabriel noticed something about Sinbad last night," Reese said. "I'm worried. I want to find out what's going on with him as soon as possible."

"I don't want you to cancel," Quinn said. "You've been to so many of my events and presentations, already. You and Gabriel have too much trouble coordinating your schedules as it is."

"Who would've thought a little vlog and blog you started for fun in your spare time would turn into this?" Reese said, bursting with pride for her sister. "Surely, *Natural Wonder* will get more followers."

"Speaking of getting new followers..." Quinn nibbled her cupcake, "You won't believe who subscribed to my SeeMeTV channel and is now following me on Post-a-Pic and FaceSpace."

"Who?"

"Lance."

"Lance Donovan?" Blaire asked.

"Correct. At first he tried to pretend he had all these questions about his hair. Yeah, right."

"You do have male followers," Blaire said.

"Ninety-five percent of *Natural Wonder's* followers and subscribers are female," Quinn said. "And you saw him. Lance needs no help with his hair. His waves are tight-cropped and well-maintained, not a hair out of place, even after hustling and playing basketball."

"Maybe he's thinking of going edgier with a really cool 'fro or short, hipster twists, or long dreads like Rosvaughn's," Reese said.

"Twists and dreads? Lance is the poster boy for Brooks Brothers." Quinn took another bite of her cupcake.

"How do you know this?" Reese asked. "He was all sweaty and wearing basketball shorts, compression tights, and a tank top when you met him."

"Er, um." Quinn averted her gaze. "I might have taken a peek at his social media accounts. I check out every new follower or subscriber with a public account."

"Is that right?" Reese smirked, enjoying Quinn's rare display of discomposure.

"I happened to glimpse a couple of pictures. Apparently, he's mostly into minimalism and neutral colors, with a slight edge, but we're basically talking classic cowl-neck sweaters, button-downs, tweed herringbone, loafers, and pocket hankies. What one might call a preppy dresser, when he's not navigating piss puddles and poop piles at the vet hospital, that is. And he's way too metrosexual for me. He actually exfoliates. Exfoliates, for crying out loud. Nope. I like 'em scruffier."

Reese settled back in her chair and regarded Quinn. "You took in *a lot* from a 'couple of pictures.' "

Blaire snickered. "You happen to know his shoe size and inseam measurement, too?"

"Okay, so I looked at a few pictures."

"I think you're more intrigued by him than you're letting on," Blaire said.

"Please!" Quinn added with a dramatic flap of one hand. "He is *so* not my type. And I told him so when he made his intentions known."

"He asked you out?" Reese reached for a piece of Blaire's cupcake.

"Yeah, via private message on my Post-a-Pic account. Of course I shut that bunkum down. No need to waste his time or mine. Besides, I was more turned off when I noticed who was following him and who he followed on social media."

"On his public account?" Blaire asked.

"No, his public account is attached to the vet hospital. It's perfectly fine, squeaky clean even, full of pictures of Baron, his long-haired German shepherd, and Thunder, his border collie. There are also pictures of other animals and the work they do at the hospital. He enjoys what he does and seems to be good at it, which I actually find laudable. But his private Post-a-Pic account," Quinn shook her head, "Ooooh, chile! A slew of what appear to be strippers, escorts and..." she made finger quotes, " Post-a-Pic '*models*,' the type you never see in fashion magazines, Target ads, or runway shows. These flaunt their Barbie-doll boobs and be-thonged badonkadonks in nonstop streams so there must be big bucks in it. The fool granted me access after he thought he was making progress, engaging me, drawing me in because I responded to a few of his private messages."

"Not too smart of him, allowing you access to his private accounts, when you were judging, digging for dirt, and counting his twinkle-dinkles," said Reese regarding the Post-a-Pic version of Facebook "likes," and Instagram/Twitter hearts.

"I didn't have to dig that far," Quinn said.

"Oh?" Reese and Blaire said in unison before tasting the bourbon vanilla smoked coffee, recently added to the Sweet Spot menu.

"Lance twinkle-dinkled damn near every horny-porny photo posted by some chick whose online name is...," Quinn reached for a sticky note on Reese's desk to jot down: Connie Lynn Gus.

Cocking her to one side, Blaire read it. "So? I don't get it."

"Read it again aloud," Quinn said. "*Fast*. At least three times."

Blaire did. "I get it now!"

"Claim to fame?" Quinn continued. "Apparently it's her '*lickety* splits' during girl-on-girl-on-guy action."

Blaire sprayed her coffee.

Quinn sat back and crossed her arms over her chest. "Classy, huh?"

"*Monsieur* is into the *ménage à trois*?" Blaire asked in an over-the-top French accent. With a napkin, she dabbed at damp spots on her outfit.

"I'm not surprised," Reese said, "based on some things Gabriel mentioned about Lance. But he *is* very much a freewheeling bachelor, down with just about anything between consenting adults from what I understand. Nothing wrong with that, I suppose. He'll settle down when he meets the right woman. That might be you."

"Oh, no. I do not need a project," Quinn said. "All signs point to unredeemable man-whore."

"I hear ya," Blaire said.

"So what did you think of Julian?" Reese turned her attention to Blaire.

"Why are you asking me that?" Blaire reached for her phone when it chimed with a notification. "I have a man. Hayes. 'Memba him?"

"Yeah, I '*memba him*, but you're not blind, either," Reese pressed.

According to Blaire, she and Hayes were "absolutely perfect for one another." Both plugged into the other's life without all the crazy highs and lows that plagued more passionate couples. And Hayes had never tried to clip her social butterfly wings. Blaire still lived for networking events, parties, and clubbing. Even when Hayes wasn't up for a night on the town, he would send her off with a kiss and well wishes. Unlike Reese, Blaire had been more pragmatic and less prone to indulge in romantic fantasies.

The couple's bond had been based on mutual goals, but with few sparks, from what Reese could tell. Hayes was sweet and steady. As reliable as Blaire's Rolex. Like Quinn's BOB, Hayes did not make demands. But unlike BOB, Hayes gave fabulous back rubs and could rock a tux like nobody's business for Blaire's more formal schmoozing events.

"Don't get me wrong," Blaire said. "Julian's handsome, and he seems nice, but even if I were unattached, he's a little too...What's the word? Too four corners. Square." She outlined the shape with her stiletto-nail-tipped fingers that should be registered as lethal weapons. "A little too guarded and brooding for my taste." She swiped the face of her phone to read messages.

"Brooding?" Reese said. "Hardly. Besides, he's a widower. Give the guy a break. I think he has this calm, quiet strength. A chivalrous way about him. He's my definition of a true Southern gentleman."

"Southern gentleman, huh?" Blaire affected loud wheezy snores.

"As if Hayes is the rowdy one, getting *turnt up in da club*." Quinn glanced at her watch and rummaged through her bag. "We'd better get a move on." She checked her makeup and reapplied her lipstick. "Enjoy your time with your... What is he, Reese? Your *bae*?"

"Yeah, is he officially your *'bae'*?" Blaire put her phone away when the conversation shifted back to Reese's beeswax.

"We haven't labeled what we are at the moment. But things look promising. He gave me this." Reese pushed up the long sleeve of her tunic top and extended her arm to show off the beautiful charm bracelet she'd been concealing until just right moment. "Bam!"

"Oh, beautiful!" Blaire said, fingers rippling.

"I like it." Quinn examined the charms and felt the weight of the chain "Hey, this isn't costume jewelry. This is serious bling. Check out the marking on that little tab there."

"Where?" Blaire leaned forward to read it.

"This isn't silver, but high-grade platinum, girl." Quinn's gaze met

Reese's. "So what do you want to bet these stones aren't Swarovski crystals, but quality pavé diamonds?"

"Not surprised," Blaire said. "I mean his brother is a movie star."

"Ah," Reese nodded, "So you confirmed it. I figured you or Odette would."

"And he finally told you?" Blaire said.

"Of course he did." Reese was pleased to share. "The night we had the gathering in my backyard. He told me after you two left."

"Good. I'm not sure how long he thought he could hide something like that," Blaire said. "He was acting real dodgy when Odette brought it up. I wasn't sure about the exact family relation, but I knew there was one. Besides, I know people."

"And you didn't say a word, being such a huge Lucas Cameron fan and all," Quinn said.

"I wanted to see how long it would take Gabriel to tell Reese. But even if I hadn't done some investigating... C'mon, look at the guy! And that family name. I, mean, really? Who did he think he was fooling?"

"Color me gobsmacked." Quinn pointed to herself. "Damn. And I pride myself on being the most astute among us."

"And I'm pleased to disabuse you of that notion," Blaire replied with a haughty air.

"You have a Hollywood connection, girl!" Quinn said to Reese. "And he's already showering you with diamonds. Take that, Darren!"

"I wouldn't call it a shower," Reese said, touching the charms. "If they were SweeTarts on a string, I'd love it just the same because Gabriel gave it to me."

"Are you sure you guys haven't labeled what you are?" Blaire asked.

"One cool point for him," said Quinn, still admiring the bracelet. "I'm cautiously optimistic."

"And he said he was falling for me," Reese said dreamily.

"And you're falling for him, so we're no longer talking neighbors with benefits," Blaire said.

"I know it was fast, but we're past that," Reese said.

"Good. I like him for you," Blaire said. "And I'm not just saying what I think you want to hear, like I did with Darren."

"Speaking of Darren..." Reese told them all about the Jones catering gig, her first proper date with Gabriel, and Darren's most recent visit.

"Cheater Cheater Pumpkin Eater has a ginormous pair, stepping to you so soon after what he did," Quinn said.

"But Darren did follow through on his promise to help the shop," Reese told them.

Blaire nodded. "I think accepting his help was a judicious course of action."

"I don't know about that." Quinn's voice held a warning note.

"Might as well use his superpowers for good," Blaire said. "Despite his faults, you have to admit Darren has always been supportive of Reese's shop. If guilt is eating away at him, he's probably sincere, wanting to help."

"I've heard from his friend Chip already," Reese said.

"Chip Weatherly, the social media marketing expert?" Blaire asked. "Tall, twitchy guy with the black Porsche Boxster Spyder?"

"Yes," Reese replied, still fiddling with her bracelet. She lifted her hand, admiring the way the charms caught the light in various positions.

"Damn Blaire, who *don't* you know or have on speed dial?" Quinn gave her a sidelong look.

"He's working on a campaign to help me win that best specialty bakery award this year," Reese added. "I thought I'd done a pretty good job with my website and social media presence. But thanks to Chip, and Darren indirectly, the shop now has a cool app available, a virtual loyalty card, and about a half dozen other high-tech, customer-friendly extras the competition is not using yet from what I can tell. And the shop's social media following has nearly tripled," she snapped a finger, "just like that."

"That an impressive uptick, sis," Blaire said.

"You're speaking of Darren as if it's been years instead of weeks since you broke up," Quinn said. "You've sprinted to let bygones be bygones."

"We're *not* friends, but we have an understanding and most importantly, closure," Reese said. "Things turned out as they should. Gabriel and I fit."

"But you thought you and Darren fit, too," Blaire said. "You wanted to marry him, remember?"

"I know. We did fit for a while. I wasn't unhappy during most of that relationship. But compared to Gabriel and me, Darren and I fit like right-size moccasins worn on the wrong feet, if that makes any sense. Something was askew. He never stopped loving Sasha. It took meeting someone I'm better aligned with to notice and appreciate different possibilities. With Gabriel," she released a wistful sigh, "I've never felt this way about *anyone* before. Ever. He makes my heart race, and I want to dance when I think about him. And we've finally cleared the air on a few things."

"Oh? Like what?" Quinn sipped her coffee.

"I told him I'm not completely comfortable with his continuing friendship with Adriana."

"That's a good start," Blaire said. "Good for you."

"But I didn't exactly get into the weeds on the subject," Reese said.

"Like how anxious you were finding them canoodling under that pergola?" Quinn asked.

"That was innocent." Reese reached for another piece of Blaire's cupcake, but Blaire slapped her hand away. "And I don't want him to think I'm Looney Tunes. I'm sure the bizarre dreams are behind me now."

"You're having the dreaded bizarre dreams?" Quinn asked. "This is the first I'm hearing about this. You only have those when you're stressed about something or someone. And suppressing it."

"Never mind. Let's just focus on the fact that I told him how I felt."

"So what's he going to do about it?" Quinn asked.

"Make sure I believe he's only interested in me, *us.*"

"How? Is he backing away from the friendship?" Blaire asked.

"I don't know his detailed plan yet."

"Gabriel and Adriana are tethered by those damn dogs," Quinn grumbled to Blaire.

"Whom I've come to adore." Reese played with the starburst charm. "And I will not ask him to give them up."

"Why the hell not?" Quinn asked.

"You're not a pet owner," Reese said, shaking her head at Quinn's insensitivity.

"But I came close once," Quinn said. "Gotta give me credit for that."

True. Quinn had fallen in love with a picture of a Pomeranian highlighted for adoption in a local community newspaper. She went to meet the pooch, who —at seven years old—had a flatulence problem and no teeth. After learning he was, according to a shelter volunteer, "just beginning to understand" house-training, Quinn couldn't run in the opposite direction fast enough, which made Adriana's commitment to her rescue work with ailing animals all the more extraordinary.

"You wouldn't understand," Reese said. "I feel selfish when I think of all the good Adriana does with those sick or homeless animals. Without Gabriel's pro-bono services, she wouldn't be able to afford… You get the point."

"The more I think about that pergola incident, the more I want to deduct that cool point," Quinn said. "Maybe that expensive bracelet is part of his strategy so he can have his cake and eat it too. Maybe he's like his brother who treats himself to whole bakeries of cakes, if you know what I mean, according to the tabloids."

Reese's ears grew hot. "Throw the monkey a shiny trinket to distract her. Well, thanks a lot, Quinn."

"He should know how difficult that situation is for you," Quinn said. "Men!"

"I need to tread carefully," Reese said. "I don't want to act insecure and jealous."

"Instead of the saint you need everyone to believe you are?" Quinn said.

"Quinn!" Blaire balled up a piece of paper and tossed it at her head. "That's enough!"

"What? Reese needs to know it's okay to put her foot down and demand he dial back with the ex if he wants to build something with Reese." Quinn swiveled her chair toward Reese. "And you *are* feeling insecure and jealous. You're entitled. Own it, girl. You think you're coming off so sensible and mature, but it's bordering on self-sacrificial and masochistic. You need to be clear—crystal— about what you expect of him. And while we're at it, you have a list of people you need to read, as in checkmate, pronto, in my humble opinion."

"Starting with Quinn," Blaire said. "Reese, tell her you refuse to be spoken to as if you're a child. Go on, tell her."

"As if you're not telling her what to do as well," Quinn volleyed.

"There's a difference between you and me," Blaire, said. "*I* know how to finesse it with Reese."

"Will you two stop talking as if I'm not here!" Reese shouted.

"So you agree with me, then?" Quinn asked Blaire.

"Yes, but not your tactless delivery," Blaire replied.

"But just a minute ago, you said..." Reese rubbed her temples where the beginnings of a headache throbbed. "Oh, never mind." Her sisters were exasperating, but well-meaning with their advice. However, she and Gabriel were still in that magical first-rush, first-blush place in their fledgling relationship. No need to turn badgering prosecuting attorney all of a sudden. Now that she'd shared her uneasiness regarding the Adriana situation, moving forward she wanted to trust he'd handle it in an appropriate manner.

CHAPTER 28

That Fall Fest vendor application made its way back to Reese's desk with yet another sticky note: *I've been so busy with the new tea shop opening in the Brookfield Galleria. We'll touch base soon. — Jerricka*

Still no check attached. Reese wrote another response on a sticky note after learning Jerricka was at her new shop that day. It read: *Congratulations on the second shop, girly! I want to be you when I grow up. But there's an online registration option. Only takes a few minutes and a credit card. Looking forward to sharing a table with you again this year. You always make it so much fun! —Reese*

After work, Reese went home to pick up Sinbad. When she pulled into the vet hospital parking lot, only two vehicles were there, including Gabriel's shiny SUV. He greeted her with a delicious kiss before leading her to the rear of the facility.

"Imani stayed to assist," Gabriel said.

"Assist?" Reese held the carrier, its weight shifting as Sinbad curled himself up in the tightest ball possible at one end. Poor, baby. The scents and sounds of other animals had terrified him as usual.

"The test I'm doing is noninvasive as promised," Gabriel said. "An ultrasound."

"Oh," Reese replied with an upbeat note though fear snaked up her spine.

A pretty young woman, possibly college-age, approached them. She was dressed in jeans and a red polo like Gabriel's and whimsical red cat-eye glasses. She greeted Reese, raved about those raspberry champagne cupcakes Reese had sent to the vet staff, and then whisked Sinbad to another room.

"Imani's going to prep him with a shave," Gabriel said.

Reese snapped to a stop. "A shave!"

"Relax. No chance of him returning looking like a Sphynx," Gabriel teased, referring to that alien-like hairless cat with huge, dark marble-like eyes and tent-size ears. "She'll only shave the areas I need to examine, leaving most of his luxurious coat intact."

Reese hit Gabriel with a flurry of questions as they continued down the hall. Soon Imani placed Sinbad on a table and held him steady as Gabriel applied a gel and moved a wand-like device he referred to as a "transducer" over Sinbad. It was attached to a nearby keyboard and a monitor. He explained every step for Reese to put her at ease while Imani whispered soothingly to Sinbad who did his usual vet-induced stress drooling and shedding. Wisps of fur floated in the air like dandelion fuzz.

"Ah, there we go." Gabriel studied the monitor and held the wand on Sinbad while the other hand tapped the keyboard.

"What?" Reese asked from a nearby chair.

"See the image here on the monitor?"

The black screen with white blobs brought back memories of Brett and Brayton at eight-weeks in utero and Odette's smiling face as she showed off the images. "I know this sounds ridiculous, but I'll roll it out there. Are you trying to tell me Sinbad is pregnant?"

Imani tittered.

"No," Gabriel said. "Those are his kidneys. And as I suspected, he has cysts, several cysts, a common presentation of PKD. Earlier today, his records were sent. I'm noting decline in renal function. Your previous vet didn't mention this?"

"I don't know. Maybe. What does that mean? Did I do something? Is this connected to his diet? Did my overindulging him cause this?"

Imani's eyes went soft with sympathy as she glanced at Sinbad and Reese. Why was she looking at them that way? Reese's mouth went dry. "So what do we do to treat this pesky PKD, doc?" As Reese came to her feet, she forced a bright tone, as if they were only discussing Sinbad's acne.

"PKD is polycystic kidney disease." Gabriel closed the distance between them. "This case is likely chronic, inherited. His breed and other long hairs are genetically predisposed. Progression varies. For some cats, it takes months, others years." In more detail, he explained PKD, the kidneys, and their filtering role in an animal's overall health.

Reese retrieved her cat and hugged him. "It sounds like a life-threatening disease."

"It can be," Gabriel said. "He's showing signs of renal failure. I need to do a chemistry panel and urinalysis."

Gabriel and Imani went to work to get the samples, his no needles promise, quickly forgotten. With that completed, Gabriel thanked her for volunteering to stay at short notice and sent her home.

"Good night, all." Imani shifted her pitying gaze to Sinbad and Reese before leaving.

"Is there a cure?" Reese asked in a wobbly voice.

"Not for this type, I'm afraid," Gabriel said. "And multiple cysts are in both kidneys so surgery is not an option. And at his age, that's not advised. We would treat this conservatively, altering his diet, which needs to be low phosphorus, low protein, and electrolyte-enhanced. We'll manage his fluids with SubQ treatments. And there's an injectable used to manage the anemia that comes along with his condition. We'll keep him as comfortable as possible. So what we're talking about here is," he paused, "palliative."

Palliative. In other words, lost cause. Reese shuddered. That word brought back heartbreaking and shocking memories of PawPaw's late-stage lung cancer diagnosis. Her eyes filled as her beloved cat curled up in her arms and licked her hand. "But, but... I don't understand. He looks and acts fine. You made a mistake!" Reese shouted at Gabriel. "If he's so sick his other vet would've told me so! And why did you miss it when I brought him to see you about the acne? You're wrong!"

"I know this is difficult."

Weak-kneed, Reese dropped on a chair. "But there has to be something else we can do!"

"We'll take good care of him and try to maintain his quality of life for as long as possible."

"But how long is that?" Reese's eyeballs stung.

"It's hard to say at this point, baby. Again, I need to do more tests."

Gabriel tugged Reese to her feet. With Sinbad still between them, he held her and stroked her hair as she cried.

"Let's get you and Sinbad home." Gabriel released Reese to get tissues for her. "You both will feel more comfortable there."

"Yes, you're right," she said drying at her eyes. "I'm sorry I snapped at you."

"No need to apologize. I understand. It's a lot to take in. I'm here for you and Sinbad." Gabriel scratched Sinbad's chin the way he liked it, drawing appreciative licks from him. "I'll do everything I can to help."

Gabriel offered to take Reese home, but she insisted on driving herself. On the way, she vowed whatever those additional tests revealed, she and Sinbad would fight. She wasn't letting him go.

After Reese arrived home, Gabriel came over with a big pot of his homemade turkey Caribbean chili, prepared especially for her.

"You're a cook." Reese helped him set the table for their meal.

"With my schedule, I'm strictly a Crock-pot cook. I throw a bunch of stuff in mine before I leave for work and dinner's ready when I get home."

"But you made cornbread, too." Reese tapped the Tupperware container with the bread.

"The turkey chili's from scratch, no canned beans, fresh mystery spices, the whole nine. The bread, Jiffy mix so don't get too excited."

"I love Jiffy! Tastes like cake!" Reese rustled up some cheer for his oh-so-sweet effort. At the table, he sat close in case she needed a hug. Though she had little appetite, the chili was delicious. "You have to give me your recipe. Just what are these 'mystery' Caribbean spices?"

Gabriel rested his spoon, rubbed his hands together, and twisted his handsome features into an expression common among cartoonish villains plotting world domination. "Zee cook, zee cook," he said in goofy heavily accented English, "vill never tell. I vill die virst. Mwahhhhaa haaaa!"

Reese laughed and decided to focus on the positive. Watching Sinbad eat heartily and romp around like a kitten made her feel better. Maybe the diagnosis was wrong. Even the best doctors made mistakes. Maybe Sinbad would beat the odds, and they would have a few more wonderful years together, singing and dancing to "Stray Cat Strut."

When Gabriel moved to give her time alone with Sinbad, she asked him to stay. The evening could unfold as it would have had she not learned of Sinbad's new challenge. She curled her arms around Gabriel's neck, molded herself against him, and pressed kisses on his lips. "Don't go."

"You sure?"

"I need this. I need you." Reese parted his lips with her eager tongue. He kissed her back until they were both hungry for much more. After she led him to her bedroom, he closed the door before Sinbad could join them.

"I hope you don't mind," he said. "I still don't want Sinbad watching us."

Reese couldn't help chuckling. She stripped him and let him do the same to her.

On her bed he covered her body with his, their fingers intertwined as their lips met. She writhed against him when he cupped one breast and sucked the nipple before moving to other one.

Only when he moved to slip inside her, did she mention the effects yesterday's overenthusiasm.

"Not a problem," he said before kissing a tender path down her torso, dipping his tongue inside her belly button before positioning his head between her open thighs. "Kissing you here is in my wheelhouse. I can't get enough of you. When you're turned on, you're mouthwatering," he said looking up to give her a wink, "like peaches in the sweetest heavy syrup. Must be all that sugar you consume on a daily bases." He waggled his brows.

"Could be." Reese grinned, her eyes slipping closed as he went to work.

His mouth was a balm moving over her as he loved her there with focus and gentle thoroughness. Reese whimpered in complete surrender with that charm bracelet jingling around her wrist as she clutched and tugged the sheets. Whatever discomfort she initially felt dissipated as sensations so potent, she had no name for what radiated through her core. It was as if she reached a new, unexplored plateau of pleasure with him. Since losing her virginity in college, overall, she'd had a satisfying sex life. But no one had ever made her feel like this. Her knees widened and her hips gyrated in an upward tilt as she wantonly opened to him. Her hands moved and her grip on him tightened with the relentless onslaught of hungry, penetrating kisses. She sobbed and came in scorching waves that seemed to last for minutes.

"But what about you?" Reese asked as she savored the last ripples of pleasure.

"Just relax. Enjoy the moment." Gabriel had moved to snuggle with her.

"I think you'll like this." Reese reached for the lubricant in the nightstand drawer and slathered it on his erection. She stroked and caressed him, drawing groans of satisfaction from him that aroused her again. "Here." She filled her hands with her breasts. "I want to feel you here." With his knees on each side her, he moved forward. His slippery, engorged tip skated along her under curves before nestling inside her deep cleavage.

Gabriel not only liked her suggestion, he loved it. He marveled at her skill at reading his mind. As she pressed the soft, warm flesh together, he slid inside the silken fold. His hands replaced hers, his thumbs caressing her nipples and pushing the weight of her lusciousness firmly around him. She squeezed his flexing bottom, then her fingers lowered to massage his balls with a feathery touch. He increased his rhythm, pumping, sliding in and out. Skin against skin. No latex barrier. This view of their bodies connecting this way and the feel of her so intensely erotic, he climaxed quickly and with such force, he pitched toward the padded headboard and held on so he wouldn't collapse on top of her.

Gabriel relaxed at her side, kissing her forehead and then reaching for tissues from a box on the nightstand to clean up.

"Thanks for not flattening me with your six-foot-three inches of solid muscle," she teased.

Gabriel chuckled. "Six-foot-three-and-a-half inches."

Reese's eyes were soft with affection that made him feel as if he'd do anything for her. Something powerful stirred inside of him. He didn't fear it. Wouldn't run from it. In fact, he welcomed it. Soul-deep certainty.

"I'm in love with you without a shadow of a doubt." Gabriel nuzzled her neck and dropped light kisses on her collarbone.

"I know you love having sex with me. And I love having sex with you. But love, love? You're sure you love me, not just the, um, fun we have together?"

"All of you, not just the sex, though that's pretty damn good. But there's more. I have felt there was more, something meant-to-be about us from day one."

"Meant to be? Day one?" She played with the charms on her bracelet.

"You're everything I've been looking for and then some. Right away I knew you would become very important to me. I even told Julian so."

"And what did Julian say?"

"I told you I love you, and you're cross-examining me?" Gabriel chucked her under the chin.

"Humor me for a moment." She stopped playing with the bracelet. "What did Julian say? Did he congratulate you? Question you? Did he believe you?"

Gabriel took a moment to consider his response. "Do you believe me? That's the question."

"Wouldn't you say he knows you well?" Reese intertwined their fingers. "You two are close."

"Who cares what he thinks."

"Ah, I have my answer."

"How do you feel about me? Us?"

"I'm in love with you, too, Gabriel," she took a beat, "but I'd be lying if I didn't admit you scare me. Everything is happening so fast, almost too fast, but I'm trying to go with it. Give it a chance. But —"

"No, buts. Let's focus on the fact that we love one another." With his fingertip, he traced her lips. "You have no idea how much it means that you're taking a chance on me, on us. You won't be sorry. I could never hurt you." He sealed his words with a soft kiss. "You believe me, don't you?"

"I want to." Reese pushed out a heavy breath. "I want to."

"I understand your hesitation after what you've been through with that…" He dropped her hand and clenched his fist. "No negativity. You love me, too, and want this to work. That's good enough for me. Now stop looking so serious." His fingers skimmed along her waist, and he tickled her until she thrashed about, laughing and begging for mercy. During the movement his hand brushed across something cold and hard at the edge of her pillow.

"What the hell is this?" He reached for it.

"Oh, that's my skinner knife," she said, as if referring to the satin sleep mask also tucked underneath the same pillow.

"Let me guess, another gift from dear ol' Dad."

"Yep, from Daddy." Reese chuckled. "If some intruder ever tries to attack me while I sleep, he says, 'Go for the gonads.' "

Gabriel wrapped his fingers around the skull-print handle he estimated to be four or five inches long. Its blade was an additional three or four inches that, fortunately, was sheathed. "I thought I couldn't wait to meet your father, but now I'm not so sure. I might want to invest in a bulletproof vest or something in case he finds out exactly what I've been doing with his youngest daughter."

"His 'baby girl.' " Reese mimicked her father's gruff voice.

Shoop. Shoop. Shoop. Sinbad was at the door. Gabriel passed the knife back to Reese, got out of bed, and let the cat inside the room.

"Now you may enter, my feline friend," he said to Sinbad, who ran, jumped on the bed, and circled his chosen space. Gabriel drifted to sleep with Reese in his arms and Sinbad curled up in a ball at their feet.

CHAPTER 29

Gabriel greeted the next day's golden sunrise with the bedroom windows open, sheer curtains blowing in a soft breeze, and Reese's hot tongue tracing a wet line along the under ridge of his shaft. Her full lips and tongue then swirled over, under, and around his sensitive tip as if she were ravenous and savoring the most delicious treat. And Sinbad was nowhere in sight.

"Good morning to you, too," Gabriel said before her skill and enthusiasm tore moans from his throat. He reveled in her appetite and all the ways she expressed her desire for him, which heightened his own. He'd never had such an instant, powerful emotional and carnal connection with anyone else. His fingers entwined in her soft hair as she sealed her lips around him and moved with rhythmic single-mindedness, gradually increasing the depth as she took in more of him. He clutched the soft sheets when her wet glide quickened and her grip tightened, nudging him to a fever pitch. As good as this felt, he held back. "Wait," he said in a plea hoarse with passion.

She released him. With a naughty smile on her lips, she paused and peered up at him through her curtain of curls. "Too fast? Too slow? Special instructions?"

Gabriel hauled her up until her full breasts pressed against his chest. "Inside of you. How are you feeling," he slipped his hand between them and caressed the juncture of her thighs, "here?"

"Much better," she said, her eyes glazed with passion.

"Better enough for…" He ground his hips against hers.

"I think so."

"Say no more." Gabriel flipped Reese on her back and reached for the condom he'd placed on the nightstand when he'd made a bathroom run in the middle of the night.

With the condom on, he settled between her open thighs, and pressed one of her knees high on his torso. She was ready so he eased inside her and savored the slow stretch of her body receiving him again. After burying himself to the hilt, he paused, almost in a deep meditative state of worship. "I could wake up like this every day for the rest of my life," he whispered as he stroked inside her, still mindful of her tenderness from previous lovemaking.

"For the rest of your life?" she said between a gasp and a moan.

"Yes."

"That good, huh?"

"The best," he rasped, moving out and easing back in.

"Every day for the rest of your life is a bit...of...an overstatement, don't you think?" Her breath now quickening to ragged little puffs of air against his cheek.

"No, I mean that. I want to be with you for the rest of my life. I don't care what we're doing."

"It would carry...more...ah...weight if we....weren't doing... this."

Gabriel tugged at her lip with his teeth.

"To give your words more credibility, you should say this during other activities."

Gabriel made slow circles before he gently sank deeper. "Such as..."

"Oh, I...don't...oh, yeah, *yeah,*" she sighed, clutching his butt tighter, "cleaning...tuning my lawn mower... cutting the grass, raking the leaves."

"Plowing a field?" He sucked her earlobe and licked at that delicate erogenous spot behind it.

"You're doing that now," she squirmed and chuckled, "very...well... I might add."

"Then why are we still chattering away like two grade school girls on brand new smartphones?"

"They wouldn't chatter, they'd text."

"Enough already."

Reese snickered. "You started it, trying to mack me up and all."

"I did start it, didn't I? Now I'll finish it." Gabriel gripped her thigh and tipped her hips up to apply more direct, but gentle pressure where she was most responsive, drawing a series of whimpering pleas. He then slid in and out of her with more focused effort, increasing his cadence until her breath quickened and her walls quaked around him. He followed her over the peak, burying his face and muffling an oath against her neck as he climaxed. He deeply inhaled, wanting to remember her scent and this moment as he hurried through his busy day at the hospital. Whether she believed him or not, he'd count the minutes until their next date, cutting her grass, trimming her shrubs, taking out her trash, or watching paint dry. He didn't give a damn as long as he was with her.

***

As Gabriel showered and dressed, Reese, clad only in an over-size T-shirt, went downstairs to feed Sinbad and make coffee.

"Do you have time for a run?" Reese passed Gabriel a steaming mug when he joined her downstairs. "If you do, here's a banana for fuel." She waved it at him. "But if you want to pass on the run I can whip up a heartier breakfast of blueberry pancakes, cheese scrambled eggs, and sausage."

"You're an angel." Gabriel kissed the tip of her nose.

"My way of thanking you. I appreciate your advice, consideration… and the bedroom distraction of course."

"Hmmmm, blueberry pancakes or a banana? That's a tough one." Gabriel brushed his lips against hers. "But as tempting as the pancake breakfast sounds I need to get to the hospital. I'm already later than I'd planned, but I'm not complaining." With a thanks and another kiss, he took the banana.

"Will you take a lunch break today? If you can, text me. I'll have a nice lunch waiting at the shop, or I can bring a picnic basket to you filled with your favorites. How does that sound?"

Gabriel released her to adjust the top button on his shirt. "That sounds great, but I have to squeeze in a tux fitting at noon."

Reese reached for her cup of coffee and took a sip. "A tux fitting?"

"Yeah." Gabriel made a face. "Sasha wants me in her bridal party, as a groomsman. I can't believe she's still going to marry that bastard. I thought for sure Adriana would…" His lips rounded with an exaggerated *oops!*

" '*Adriana would*' what?"

"Nothing." Gabriel was a terrible liar, which she hoped meant he hadn't had enough practice to perfect his technique.

"No. What were you about to say before you caught yourself?"

"I don't know what you're talking about," he replied with an uneasy chuckle.

"Yes, you do. So far, you've been aboveboard about you and Adriana; don't get evasive on me now. Your honesty has been part of the reason I've been willing to try to work through my hesitation and misgivings about some things. Now finish. You *'thought for sure Adriana would'* what?"

"Don't get mad, okay?" Gabriel negotiated like a small child trying to avoid a time-out.

"What?"

"It, um, sort of slipped out. You know, what you and I talked about."

"What did we talk about that *'sort of slipped out'*?"

"When Adriana dropped off Apollo and Maximus, she was going on and on about the wedding. I was still furious about what you told me about Darren. Of course she wanted to know why I had smoke coming out of my ears at the mention of his name. She knew something was up."

"Because she knows you so well," Reese said glibly. "And you cannot tell a lie, except to me, apparently. You told her after you promised me you wouldn't." She plunked down her cup, sloshing hot coffee over the rim.

"It wasn't planned. I didn't intend to, but… I…I couldn't could let that asshole get away with what he did to you and Sasha. I couldn't hold it in."

Hot blood surged to Reese's face. "Gabriel! How could you? You told her! You told her everything!"

"Not everything! I swear!"

"But you told her enough. Too much as far as I'm concerned."

"I couldn't just stand by and watch a close childhood friend make the biggest mistake of her life. I thought if Adriana knew she could talk some sense into her sister. Adriana promised not to tell the rest of the family."

Reese marched to the front door with Gabriel on her heel. "I need you to leave."

"What?"

"You heard me," she bit out. "I need you to leave."

"But—"

"I'm too angry to talk to you right now. I don't want to say something I'll regret later."

"But, but—"

"Please, just go."

"Okay. I'm sorry. I know I messed up."

"Yes, you did."

"We'll talk later?"

Lips drawn tight, Reese motioned for him to leave.

"I love you." Gabriel reached for the collar of her T-shirt and pulled her close. She didn't shrink when he pressed a soft kiss on her lips, but neither did she respond. "Please don't forget that."

CHAPTER 30

Reese was still vibrating with fury after she'd tended to Sinbad and dressed for work. She couldn't believe Gabriel had gone against her wishes and blabbed to Adriana. As she backed out of her garage, Odette approached the Beetle. Between Gabriel's betrayal and Sinbad's diagnosis, she wasn't in the mood. Still, she lowered her driver's side window. She would try her best not to take out her funky mood on her friend, but Odette had better watch herself.

"Hey, girl!" Odette waved an envelope at her. "The postman put one of your letters in our box." She passed it to Reese. "I just had a chance to go through the mail so this could've arrived a few days ago. Looks as if it might be from the HOA."

Looks as if it might be from the HOA? Reese bristled. Odette knew darn well it was from the HOA as it stated in bold black letters in the upper left hand corner of the envelope. Steaming it open wasn't beyond snooping Odette, the woman who had yet to tell her husband he'd inadvertently clicked a function that sent copies of all his personal text messages to her iPad. Fortunately, Calvin had been the perfect husband, but Reese shuddered at the invasion of his privacy. "Thanks. I'm running a little late."

"We haven't had girlfriend bonding time. We need to make a date to catch up."

"Okay. I'll touch base."

"Soon?"

"Soon."

"Oh, and Shireen says she's been trying to reach you, too. We're supposed to walk together this morning. Is it okay if I tell her to phone you at the shop?"

"Go ahead."

***

Reese's morning at the Sweet Spot had been so crazy-busy she had little time to fixate on her problems. Around 2 p.m. when the crowd of customers thinned, she took a much-needed break with a chicken salad sandwich and chips from the deli across the street. Linda, Audrey, and Danielle handled service. In the kitchen, Naomi, the Sweet Spot's part-time baker, and Glen, another staffer, placed cute customized fondant buttons on trays of cupcakes for an upcoming catering job.

Before tackling the stack of shop mail, Reese opened the letter from the HOA, expecting a receipt for the fine Rosvaughn had promised to pay for her.

Instead, she found the fee had doubled because the first notice had gone unpaid past the deadline. Now she had another strike in her file. *Grrrr.* Reese snatched up her phone to call Rosvaughn, who, as usual, did not answer. But she couldn't wait a second longer to do what she should've done a long time ago. She'd had it up to the yin-yang with him. Voicemail beeped with instructions to leave a message.

"Rosvaughn, this is Reese," she said in an ever-so-sweet voice. "Hope you're having a nice day. Oh, and you're fired. And in case that's not clear enough you're booted, axed, terminated, discharged, dismissed…our contract canceled… as in you're toast. And don't bother trying to smooth talk your way out of it because it won't work this time, *cuz!*" She jabbed at the end call symbol, missing the old days when she could snap close a flip phone. Her racing heart rate steadied with a feeling of profound satisfaction. A couple of minutes later her phone rang. She reached for it expecting Rosvaughn, but instead it was Shireen. Perfect timing!

"Hey, girly, where in the world have you been?" Shireen said. "The minutes are ticking away, and we still don't have a commitment from you for the fundraiser. I'm meeting with the committee today. I'd like to report that you're onboard. I know you won't let us down. So, how many cupcakes can we expect from the Sweet Spot this year, chica?"

"That depends."

"On what?"

"When I agreed to supply your garden club with cupcakes, it was a bartering arrangement if I recall correctly. Your idea, in fact. I'd provide the sweets for your fundraiser and in exchange you or a member of your club would help me start a garden and supply the right bulbs, seeds, instruction, supervision, and whatnot. So I've supplied your club with dozens of cupcakes two years in a row now. And still no garden assistance."

"Oh, I get it. You're holding the cupcakes hostage."

"I'd hardly call it a *'hostage'* situation seeing as I *bake and own* the cupcakes that are worth a lot more than what you were supposed to exchange."

"No need to get prickly. My memory's a little foggy regarding the first conversation about it. Why didn't you remind me?"

"Why did I have to? You never forgot to beg for the flippin' cupcakes. Don't turn your lack of follow-through on *your* proposed deal into my mistake."

"My schedule is packed."

"So is mine. When is your fundraiser? I suggest you come up with a time at least two weeks in advance to give the Sweet Spot scheduling room."

"You won't commit—"

"Until my garden is started."

Long pause.

"Tick. Tock."

"Okay, fair enough," Shireen said before they chose a gardening time and date that worked for both. "I'll pencil you in. Hey, you mentioned you're terrified of earthworms."

"And other creepy crawlers."

"You open to container gardening for now? How about some hanging pots with a few hardy ferns, Boston ferns, and some large pots with lots of annuals for extra pops of color? We can do some really creative things. I'll supply the pots that will complement your porch furniture. Come fall we'll get more ambitious and plant bulbs. How do daffodils sound?"

"Lovely."

"Eventually we can move on to Knockout rose bushes for the back, near the patio, very low maintenance as far as roses go."

"As long as they don't smell like old ketchup."

"What?"

"Never mind. Cool beans. I'm all for low maintenance. Talk to you soon."

Still driven by a delightful feeling of complete liberation, Reese cracked her neck, rolled her shoulders, and snatched up the vendor application that had made its way back to her desk. Again.

Reese marched over to the tea shop next door and slapped it on the counter, behind which Jerricka stood. "Hello, Jerri!" Reese warbled. "Having a nice day?"

"I am." Hip to the fact this was no ordinary pop-up visit, Jerricka warily eyed Reese, whose smile quite possibly resembled Jack Nicholson's in *The Shining*.

"Good. I came over to let you know you can reimburse me for your part of last year's table fee or pay in full for both of us this year. I'll check in again three days before the deadline. If it's not handled, I'll go solo on this year's table and take you to small claims court for your part of last year's fee. Oh, and no more free coffee for you, unless I get free tea for me. Quid pro quo. Enjoy the rest of your day. I'm out." With a cheerful click of her tongue and a deuces sign, Reese left Jerricka wide-eyed and speechless.

Rosvaughn had called by closing time. She'd told him all he needed to know that day. And she wasn't in the mood for his excuses so she swiped her finger over the *I'm-in-a-meeting* text option. By the time she'd settled behind the wheel of her car, her phone rang again. "Tsk, tsk. Rosvaughn, so hard to track down until you want him to get lost," she griped aloud and then noted it wasn't Rosvaughn, but Porsha, her L.A.-based friend and former college dorm mate. Though she'd phoned Porsha several times in the past few weeks to catch up, Porsha hadn't returned her calls until now.

The last time the friends had spoken Reese and Darren had just broken up, but Reese didn't get a chance to tell Porsha, who'd wept with rage about her own boyfriend. Reese related. She didn't hold it against Porsha for abruptly ending the call after venting for an hour about cheating Clinton.

"Hey!" Reese said, eager to confide in her now. "I've called you about a dozen times."

"Sorry, it's been insane on this end."

"Ditto. The last time we spoke, I meant to tell you—"

"Wait until you hear what that scumbag has done now!" Porsha cut her off. "Clinton has a new whore and she—"

"Porsha, stop, just stop."

"I know. I know. I should break up with him, but—"

"I *said* stop it."

"What?"

"You only call me when you want something, usually it's to rant about *your* problems, *your* job, *your* man, *your* life. And I always listen patiently. I offer advice, that you never take by the way, then you rant some more. And I listen and listen some more, patiently, because that's what friends are for, but before I can get a word in about what's going with *me*, suddenly you have to run. And you're lax about returning my calls. When I finally hear from you, you never pause to say, 'And how are *you*, Reese?' and then actually listen. No, it's all about *you* and *your* world."

"You're lecturing me now! With everything else I'm going through! I thought you cared about me!"

"There you go again. *Me. Me. Me.* I'm sorry. I can't talk to you right now, Porsha. Take some time to think about what I just said, *if* you managed to focus long enough to catch any of it. Then we'll talk. I mean *really* talk. Back and forth. A conversation. You share something about you. I share something about me, so forth and so on. Give and take. Goodbye."

"What!"

"I *said* goodbye." Reese ended the call and started the engine to head to the pet supply store.

***

When Reese pulled into her garage about an hour later, Odette crossed the lawn for a visit.

Good grief! After cutting the engine, Reese gripped her steering wheel and looked heavenward. "Is this gauntlet of the last two days a test, God? If so, how am I doing?" she said aloud.

"So, what did the HOA want?" Odette asked when she reached the driver's side window.

"I'm sorry, Odette." Hooking her tote bag handle on her shoulder, Reese climbed out of her car. "I'm exhausted. I don't feel like company right now. I'll try to come by tomorrow morning before I leave for the shop. Maybe before the twins are up. I'll skip my run for you. We can have coffee and catch up then, okay?"

"Are you all right? You look down." Odette stroked Reese's arm. The small gesture of kindness made her want to open up. After ending her call with Porsha, Reese had shopped for the new low-phosphorus and low-protein food Gabriel had prescribed for Sinbad. The purchases made the grim prognosis more real, and her heart squeezed. And Gabriel's neat boxy print on the script made her think of his betrayal. "Yes, I'm exhausted and sad."

"Did Gabriel break up with you?"

Reese didn't miss the hopeful note in her inquiry. "Sinbad's sick."

"Oh…" The *is-that-all?* painfully apparent.

"He has kidney disease. It's serious. The prognosis is not good," Reese said around the lump in her throat, assuming she'd get a compassionate response if she provided more detailed information.

"Well, he *is* a very old cat," Odette cheeped instead, examining her perfectly manicured nails.

Reese narrowed her eyes as years of Odette's unveiled snipes rushed toward her like a storm surge.

"Why are you looking at me like that?" Odette quipped as if Reese were a birdbrain. "I know you didn't expect him to live forever. *Hel-lo*, he's an octogenarian in cat years." She had the nerve to snicker and add, "Feline geezer. If he weren't born gray, he'd surely be grizzled by now."

"Get off my property," Reese hissed with simmering menace.

"What?"

Reese closed the space between them. "I *said*, get off my property."

"Girl, what is the matter with you?" Odette said with a condescending chortle. "You're acting very strange, you know. Is it that time of the month?"

"I want you to leave."

"Come again?"

"I *said* I want you to leave."

Instead, Odette dug in her heels, crossing her arms over her bosom.

Oh, no she didn't! Reese blinked.

"And if I don't?" Odette looked Reese up and down, as if sizing her up and concluding she could take her if push came to shove. Though Reese was no lightweight at five-foot-eight, Odette did have a few pounds and an inch or so on her.

Reese dropped her tote bag and reached for the sponge mop she'd left leaning against the garage wall after cleaning up the sticky coffee spill that had attracted an army of ants.

"What are you going to do with that?" Odette's lips twitched as she inched backward.

"You'll find out if you don't get the hell off my property." Reese slapped the mop's handle from palm to palm. She twirled it in front and behind her, and sliced the air as if it were a samurai sword. All moves from that mixed martial arts course her father had insisted Reese, Blaire, and Quinn take when they were teens.

"You're crazy!" Not taking her eyes off the twirling mop, Odette had backed herself to Reese's driveway.

"Wanna see just how crazy?"

"You've really lost it!"

And therein lay a major problem with Reese's usual approach of Susie Sunshining her way through other people's crap. When a person like Reese snaps—eventually even the most patient do—it's usually over something that would be perceived as trivial. The (frequent) offender, without considering his or her own history of crummy actions, feels justified to conclude that the person who lashes out is a certifiable lunatic. Reese no longer cared because the look on Odette's face was so amusing. Showing off, Reese assumed a lunging stance, extended one arm, vertical palm facing out before she reversed it with that taunting hand gesture made famous by Bruce Lee.

"You're scaring me!"

"Good!" Reese snarled. "Now haul ass! I'm giving you to the count of three. One…two…!"

Odette ran off shouting. "Calvin! Calvin!"

"You'd better run!" Reese shouted at her before dropping the mop. She was about to go inside her house when she felt eyes on her.

An open-mouthed Myra Swanigan stared at Reese from across the street.

Reese smiled, waved, and called out to her. "Well, hello there! Did you catch it all? Maybe take pictures for the Granberry Ridge newsletter? It's Reese with an S, no C. R-E-E-S-E. Got it?"

"Well, I never!" Mrs. Swanigan huffed.

"Oh, I just bet you have!" Reese trilled. "Now run and tell that!"

Mrs. Swanigan stalked inside her home and slammed the door.

Reese's behavior was childish, but, hey, after years of enduring Mrs. Swanigan's rudeness and brazen nosiness, that reprisal was preferable to flipping the older woman the bird or advising her to train those prying eyes on her husband. A recent retiree, Mr. Swanigan now spent the better part of his leisure days sneaking down to Elizabeth "Birdie" Hagenhaus's house when Mr. Hagenhaus was at work.

As Reese made her way toward the door leading to her mud room, Gabriel pulled his SUV into her driveway. She groaned. *Not now, Gabriel.*

Not now. You don't want a piece of this.

"We have to talk." Gabriel practically vaulted out and slammed the SUV's door.

"Not now, Gabriel." She turned her back to him.

"C'mon, baby. Please. I have something for you."

"Let me guess, another charm? A shiny trinket won't work this time." When Reese looked over her shoulder, he held up a plastic bag as if it were a peace offering.

"Vitamins for Sinbad." Gabriel stepped inside her garage.

"Maybe later. Right now is *not* a good time—"

"But we need to talk. We need to hash out some things so we can move forward. We don't want issues to simmer and get worse. I think that's best."

Why did everyone assume they knew what she needed better than she did? Reese dragged a hand down her face. "So you're going to come up in here and *force* the big talk after I told you now is not the time, is that it?"

Gabriel lifted his hands in surrender. "I've missed you. I'm disturbed about the way we left things."

"Okay, you want to talk now. Well, all right, then. We'll talk now. Come inside, but don't get too comfortable because this won't take long."

"What?"

When Reese stepped inside the kitchen Sinbad ran to her. "Hey, snookums! I love you," she cooed and held him close as he licked her face. "I can't squeeze you tightly enough, I love you so much, kitty of my heart, but our dance will have to wait just a bit."

Gabriel put the vitamins on the table and stood there watching her as she continued sweet talking her cat. Instead of treating Sinbad to the usual gourmet meatballs, she filled his bowl with the new prescription food.

"He's doing remarkably well, considering his values," Gabriel said as if he were mystified Sinbad still had a hearty appetite. "I have the results from the additional tests on his blood and urine. And I read his file from the previous vet."

Reese's heart sank again, but she didn't want to ask additional questions that would only make her feel worse. The initial diagnosis was indisputable.

"This won't work between us," Reese said instead.

"What? But last night you said—"

"I know what I said last night, but it's clear where this is headed, and I'd like to cut my losses."

"Is this a shoot-the-messenger deal? I brought you bad news about

Sinbad so—"

"No, this isn't about Sinbad. How dare you! I thanked you for being here for me and Sinbad, even offered you blueberry pancakes this morning. What you said makes no sense. But I get it. When you're still so emotionally invested in your ex, you can't see straight. Can't see the truth, but for me it's crystal."

"The truth?"

"Yes, you're still in love with her. Adriana. And when you have to choose, you will always choose her and by extension, the rest of the Joneses."

"That's not true."

"No? You made your choice clear when you went against my express wishes to do what you believed Adriana would want."

"So it was a test?"

"You figured Adriana would want to know about what really happened between Darren and her sister, so you said to hell with Reese. Or you assumed I'm so gutless I'd let it slide, because, hey, so far Boo-Boo the fool has rolled with everything else. Not only did I take all of your Adriana's-my-bestie crap, but I also hung around for seconds and thirds!"

"No, you have it wrong, babe."

"I…must…please…Adriana," Reese droned as if under a spell and lifted her arms in a robotic fashion. "That's you, by the way. But no more. I've had enough."

"It wasn't like that at all. I loathed that Darren, the, the… pretentious asshole, was getting over! Again! He shouldn't get everything he wants with no adverse repercussions after hurting you and Sasha!"

"So you appointed yourself the judge, jury, and executioner?"

"Maybe I did, but the bottom line here is this isn't about pleasing Adriana or wanting her back."

"Even if that's the case, I don't believe you, Gabriel, so it doesn't matter."

"You want me to give up Apollo and Maximus? I'll give up Apollo and Maximus. Done," Gabriel announced with a dramatic sweep of his hands. "No more Apollo and Maximus. No more shared custody with Adriana."

"So this is the part where I melt because of your grand sacrificial gesture? No way. I don't want you to give up your dogs. You love those dogs. You'll only come to resent me for that."

"Then what do you want me to do? What do you want from me? Tell me! I'll do anything!'"

"I'm not liking who I'm turning into with you." Reese scrunched up her face as if smelling something foul. "I'm all whiney, jealous, and insecure. Obsessing, like some basket case, when I shouldn't. The point is, loving someone is supposed to bring out the *best* in a person, not the worst."

"I've seen none of that."

"My sisters have. I was playing a role with you, while all sorts of petty thoughts were seeping into my dreams. With harpoons I'm popping Goodyear Girl, swatting at flies with human heads, and conjuring up flesh-eating Pac-Man goblins."

"What! Goodyear Gi—?"

"Never mind," Reese said with a wave of her hand. "I don't think a healthy relationship, *healthy* love, is supposed to feel this way. We had some fun and made each other feel good sexually, but there's no way we can build a long-lasting relationship on that alone. We must have mutual trust."

"What we have is not just about sex!"

"You're right. It's the sex and proximity."

"You don't believe that. Last night we said we loved—"

"Yup. We sure did. Right after we banged each other silly and came hot, hard, and often enough to fry brain cells."

"Cut the act. I'm not buying it was just sex for you, not after sharing what was in our hearts. If sex was all you cared about, you wouldn't give a damn about my staying in contact with Adriana as long as I saved some dick for you, correct?"

Reese flinched. She didn't have a comeback for that.

"And why didn't you make it clear just how much distress my friendship with her was causing you?"

"I did tell you I was uncomfortable with it. Why did I have to go into a lot of detail, Gabriel? Duh! Are you that dense? Or do you like playing that role and rationalizing to get what you want? This is a pattern, you and her, breaking up and making up, you even admitted it yourself."

"You're absolutely right." Gabriel pressed a hand to this temple. "I should've known better. I screwed up. Again. But I can fix this!"

"We need to take a break. Everything is moving way too fast."

"No."

"Yes. We need a break."

"All this because I told Darren's dirty secret. Is this about protecting Darren? Maybe you're still hung up on *your* ex, ever considered that?"

"You're projecting." Reese leaned against the marble island as she regarded him. "So do you keep Adriana around as backup booty when other relationships crash and burn? Or maybe she's your meant-to-be deal, and you take occasional breaks to sow more wild oats, knowing your happily ever after will be with her?"

Gabriel shook his head. "You have it all wrong, baby. You're so wrong this time. Yes, I've handled some things poorly. But you're the one I love now…and forever. And if I have to spend the rest of my days cleaning up this mess of my making, I will."

"Go home, Gabriel," she said wearily. "Please, don't make me sorry you moved next door. No means no. And persistence will get you a brick upside the head."

"You don't mean that."

"Maybe not, but right now I'm furious with you. Going against my wishes—again—will drive home the point that you're not listening to me, not hearing me, not *respecting* me. But only thinking of what *you* believe is best."

"Just a break, not a permanent breakup?" Gabriel's voice hitched with hope.

Reese shrugged and left things vague because she didn't want to hear more pleading and empty promises.

"Okay. I'll take this as giving you some space, time to think. But don't go back to your former vet. I know there are other capable vets in Mayfair, but I can guarantee Sinbad will get stellar care at our hospital. You don't have to work with me. Julian is excellent with this kind of case. You and Sinbad can see him on Saturday or Sunday mornings. You don't have to worry about running into me. Will you consider that?"

Again, Reese shrugged, now too emotionally drained for words.

They stood in silence for long minutes. Sinbad had finished eating and drinking. He came to meow and do figure eights around her feet.

Reese picked him up, stroked, and cradled him. "Will you go now? Sinbad is waiting so we can do our thing, right, buddy?" she said with forced cheer for her cat. "Our song is coming right up! Yay!"

"All right, I'll leave. But if you and Sinbad need anything, anything at all…"

"I know where to find you."

Tears pooled in Reese's eyes as she reached for her phone and tapped the app with "Stray Cat Strut." As she sang to the music and swayed, holding Sinbad, Gabriel quietly left.

CHAPTER 31

The next morning, Gabriel drove to the hospital wondering how in the hell he'd make it through the day on zero sleep. He wanted to believe the break between him and Reese actually was just a brief time-out, but he couldn't count on it. He went for a long run after leaving Reese's place, hoping exhaustion would calm the regrets replaying in his mind, along with Lance's accusation: *Dude, sometimes you're like a meddlesome old woman.*

Why did Gabriel keep making the same boneheaded mistakes over and over again? He loved Reese and wanted to build a life with her. That much he knew was true, no doubt about it. Yet as was his MO, he'd bungled things once again because he couldn't keep his big-ass mouth shut and couldn't stand the thought of Darren, the no-good, lying bastard, pulling one over on the rest of the Joneses. But despite what Gabriel believed, Reese was right. It was Sasha's choice and mistake to make. If he'd just accepted that, he wouldn't be in this mess now. He would've been comforting Reese or planning their next date instead of praying she'd forgive him and consider giving him another chance. As he gripped the steering wheel, desperation took hold, causing a stinging in his throat.

What he had to do crystalized. Maybe giving up the dogs was best. He clenched at the freakin' gut blow. He'd miss them like crazy, but they were safe and loved with Adriana. *Yes.* He'd take this step if it meant winning back the woman he loved. *But oh man, my dogs, my guys.* Pin pricks behind the eyes. *Suck it up, man. Suck it up.* He swallowed the lump in his throat and set his jaw in stoic determination.

Gabriel parked in his assigned space at the hospital as Adriana pulled up next to him for their usual dog drop-off.

"Morning!" Adriana looked as pretty and vivacious as ever as she bounded out of her SUV. But Gabriel's heart had stopped racing for her, and hers had stopped racing for him a long time ago. He and Adriana had mutually ended their on-again/off-again romantic relationship because it had come to feel like a comfy, old sweater. Reliable, but dull and passionless. They'd been nice and thoughtful to one another, but had been going through the motions of daily life together out of habit and family expectations. There had been no screaming, yelling, cheating, or mistreating. Each had revised what they'd wanted in a life partner, why he'd known the last time they'd broken up had been different.

Final.

The romance had simply run its course.

And that was a problem for most people. Gabriel and Adriana had put the *ex* in exceptional, baffling the hell out of everyone who knew them. He'd never uttered a bad word about her to anyone. And as far as he knew, she had never bad-mouthed him, either. They liked and respected each other a great deal, therefore, they must be in love. Still. Or so most people had assumed. Somebody *had* to pine. Somebody *had* to want the other back. Why were they still in one another's life? Just in case? The only scenarios that made sense to everyone.

Everyone but Adriana and Gabriel.

The two swapped warm greetings as the dogs circled Gabriel, pawed him, and butted their heads against his shins.

"I need to talk to you about something," Gabriel and Adriana said at once.

Adriana laughed and passed Gabriel Maximus's and Apollo's leashes. "You go first."

"Ladies first." Gabriel tried to hand back the leashes in preparation for his big announcement, but Adriana wouldn't take them.

"I appreciate that you confided in me," she said. "You know, about Sasha and Darren. At first I was angry with both, especially Sasha for not coming to me for emotional support during such a devastating time. And I wanted to throttle Darren for what he put my sister through. But," she looked down at her sandals, then back up at Gabriel, "crazy as it sounds, I believe those two still love one another. Sasha realized she'd made a huge mistake breaking up with Darren in the first place. And he had a right to try to move on with someone else. He was confused and handled things all wrong."

With great effort, Gabriel bit back disparaging comments about Darren's so-called confusion. Clearly Gabriel was no match for the bullet-proof mojo Darren had over the women in his life.

"Sasha doesn't want to deal with the family's objections. She wants the rest of her pregnancy to be calm, no drama, especially after that one scare. She begged me not to tell Mom and Dad what I know. I have to respect her wishes, but I pray it all works out, especially for the sake of my little niece or nephew. Sasha doesn't want to know the baby's gender yet."

"I, too, hope it all works out for Sasha and the kid's sake." Gabriel felt like the biggest fool for letting his dislike for Darren instead of his love for Reese drive his decisions. While his intentions were good, he'd didn't think it through. He'd put his own relationship in jeopardy and acted like a judgmental, gossipy twerp with no life of his own. And for what? Darren, the colossal asshole, had come out on top while Reese had pushed Gabriel away.

"And I wanted to talk to you about something else," Adriana said. "I've been doing a lot of thinking lately. I know how much you love Maximus and Apollo."

"You love them just as much."

"Yes, I do, but I'm thinking it's time one of us let them go."

"I was thinking the same thing," Gabriel said.

"We can dispense with these frequent drop-offs and have a cleaner break. I've lost count of the times we've broken up over the years. But even when we're done, we've never really been done."

"Until now." Gabriel needed to clarify.

"But are we really done?"

Whoa, Nelly! Gabriel's brows hitched and dread tore through his body. The last thing he wanted to do was reject her. The dynamics of their friendship worked because the split had been mutual. "Is this your way of saying you want to try again?"

"Oh, gosh no!" Adriana a made face, mocking his momentary display of inflated ego. A sign he'd been hanging around Lance too long?

Still, Gabriel tried his damndest not to look as if her adamant denial brought him so much relief.

"That's not what I'm saying at all. Relax," Adriana said. "I think we're still a little too involved in each other's lives. That's why our family and friends aren't taking this last breakup seriously, even after a year. And why are we still orbiting one another? I mean, think about it. Have we ever gone longer than two weeks without touching base with an email, text, call, or visit? Are we using each other as a crutch? I admit that was my mindset a few times when we broke up, but I feel different now. I don't need that. I'm confident in our decision. But quite frankly, all this orbiting makes moving on with someone else challenging."

"Oh, is that right?" Gabriel had to chuckle at the observation. "Is there someone in particular in your life who's challenged?"

"Yes. His name is Nathan Reeves. We met at the Mayfair Walk Against Canine Cancer last year. You remember it? You had to cancel for an emergency at the hospital."

That four-mile walk to increase awareness about the disease and raise funds for research had happened a few weeks before he and Adriana began their last discussion about breaking up for good. Was there a connection? Had sparks flown between Nathan and Adriana in Gabriel's absence? Gabriel absorbed this news without the slightest prick of jealousy or poke of possessiveness. "I know Nate," he said. "He's a damn good attorney and does a lot of pro bono work for the Mayfair Animals Rights and Protection League."

"Yes, that's him! His dog was diagnosed with a mast cell tumor about two years ago, but is now cancer free." Adriana's lips quirked up in a girlish grin. Nate and his dog had either captured her heart or were well on their way. "Nate doesn't quite understand or appreciate my relationship with you. He thinks we see each other way too often for former lovers who are *supposedly* done. He's been tossing around the *supposedly* more and more lately with extra emphasis. He teases and jokes, but it's clear this bothers him to no end."

"I get that not everyone understands us or this thing between us. It hasn't exactly made my life easy, either."

"Oh, no. You and Reese had a tiff?"

"More than a tiff." Apollo tugged at his leash to get closer to Adriana while Maximus licked Gabriel's hand. "I pray Reese gives me another chance." The ache in his chest intensified each time her words rushed back to him: *No more. I've had enough.*

"Don't tell me she broke up with you?"

"She did. I hope it's just a temporary time-out, wishful thinking on my part," Gabriel said. Reese's sayonara had not been as definitive as Carly's, but it sure felt as if she'd kicked his ass to the curb for good.

"I'm sorry, Gabe. Want me to talk to her?"

"No! Please don't do that. I can see her interpreting it as me running straight to you."

"Give her some time." Adriana patted his shoulder. "I'm sure she'll come around. I mean, she's right next door. That has to work in your favor."

"Ever the optimist."

"So about the dogs, you should have them," Adriana said as if she needed to blurt it out before changing her mind.

Gabriel blinked. "What? But I was about to… You're giving them up? You love them, and they love you."

"Yes, but giving them to you means I can make room to adopt two or three more dogs who need a good home. I'll miss Apollo and Maximus, but I know they love you, too. I won't worry about them because you care about them as much as I do. It feels like the right thing now."

"I, I… don't know what to say." Gabriel patted the dogs. Apollo whimpered as if he understood Adriana's sacrifice, while, Maximus, as hyper and blithe as usual, wound his leash around Gabriel's shins for fun until Gabriel gave him a stern look and his leash a firm tug.

"I'd better let you get to work. I've held you up long enough. Speaking of work, I'll try not to bother you with the rescues. Lance and Julian have agreed to help as my backup team."

"You spoke to them already?"

"Yeah."

"What do you mean by backup?"

"Nate has several veterinarian friends. A couple have agreed to help me as my first-string team, so to speak. Isn't that great!"

"With a little arm-twisting from Nathan I'm sure they agreed to be first-string." Gabriel smiled. Good for Adriana. She deserved the best. And he hoped she'd found The One in Nathan, who clearly meant a lot to her. Over the years, Gabriel had heard only good things about him.

"We've already said our long goodbyes, haven't we, fellas?" Adriana's eyes glistened with tears. She crouched to give both dogs hugs and vigorous neck rubs, as they whined, jumped, and licked her face.

"Thank you." Gabriel watched her climb back inside her SUV and start the engine.

With a watery smile, Adriana secured her seatbelt and blew a kiss to Gabriel and his dogs.

CHAPTER 32

At the Sweet Spot, Reese had settled at her desk, ready to focus on the shop's books, when a decorative canister with a red ribbon caught her eye. Inside she found a receipt for a Fall Fest table and printed confirmation for the Sweet Spot and Jerricka's Teas & Spices. Reese's favorite tea blend and a note from Jerricka were also inside: *Looking forward to another great year as tablemates! Come on over when you get a break. The cup of Moroccan mint tea is on me! —Jerricka*

"Now you're talking, Jerri." Reese put the note away as someone tapped on her door.

"It's open."

Rosvaughn swaggered inside her office.

Reese sighed. "You should've called first. Some of us have a business to run, the *right* way."

"Ouch." Rosvaughn brought one hand to his lean chest. "I deserve that and more. I'm so sorry, cuz."

Reese gave him the talk-to-the-hand sign before swiveling her chair to face her computer. "Now, if you don't mind, I have orders to make and books to do."

"You have every right to be pissed. I let you down—"

"*Again.*"

"I apologize for not paying that fee as I promised. You see, it slipped my—"

"Among many other screw-ups, but no more." Reese kept her eyes on the monitor and typed.

"And I don't blame you one bit for feeling that way." Rosvaughn passed a piece of paper to her.

"What's this?"

"A check. It's what you paid in advance for my yearly service, a full refund, and all the HOA fees, and a little extra for your trouble."

The old Reese would've taken one look at his wet-eyed-baby-seal face and the check that included token financial restitution and then buckled. Refusing the funds meant offering him more license to take advantage of her.

But this was the *new* Reese. She swiped the check, held it up, and inspected it. Had it been a gold coin she would've tried denting it with her teeth to authenticate its value.

"Don't worry. It's a cashier's check. It won't bounce."

"Good." Reese mean-mugged him as she folded the check and slipped it inside her shirt pocket.

"That was easy enough," he said.

Again, Reese focused on the computer screen.

"But I know I can't regain your trust with a single check. I hate that I didn't appreciate one of the few people who always believed in me, no matter what. You mean the world to me, cuz. I always want to do better, but doing better still doesn't come as easily for some of us. I want to keep trying for you."

Reese faced him again. "No, it can't be for someone else. It has to be for yourself, Rosvaughn. And if you want your business to succeed, you have to do the hard work. Keep quality service and reliability at the top of your list."

"I...I have no excuses, but on an up note I have enrolled in some small business night courses at the community college. I want to learn how to do better. And I'm reading books about time management and organization for entrepreneurs."

"All steps in the right direction. Good luck with that." Reese turned to read the spreadsheet on her screen and type.

"And I want to work for you."

Reese faced him again. "Have you lost your flippin' mind? N-O. *No.*"

Rosvaughn lifted his hands. "Wait. Hear me out. I'll do a full year for free. I want to prove myself. I *need* to prove myself to you. At the end, you can judge my commitment and services, then decide if you want to do another year with a contract. How's that? What do you say? Deal?"

"No."

Rosvaughn's shoulders slumped.

"I don't think it's a good idea to mix family and business right now," Reese said, her tone softening.

"With me you mean? But—"

"Goodness knows I've given you more than enough chances to prove yourself, but I can't continue right now. I'm sorry, but let's face it, your handyman skills are not up to par. Maybe you need to take some handyman classes or something, too. In the meantime, focus on the lawn side of your business. You're very good at that, when you actually get around to doing a lawn. Maybe expand your services in that area. Maybe, emphasis on *maybe*, at some point I'll reconsider letting you do my yard again, but with no up-front payments or contracts. I'm not saying never or forever, but I don't want business to come between us. We're better as favorite first cousins. Deal?" Reese extended her hand.

Rosvaughn hesitated. "You sure I can't convince you to change your mind?"

"Not even if you chased me around with a big fuzzy block of moldy cheese," she said.

"You still remember that?" He smiled.

"Yup," she said. "Now, give it up. Don't leave me hanging. You know I'm right."

"Yeah, okay, but I'd still like to do a few things at your house so—"

"No. We're just favorite first cousins."

He paused and sighed. "Favorite first cousins it is."

Reese and Rosvaughn did the customary shake that soon shifted into the choreographed dap they used to do as teens: four back-and-forth hand slaps, three palm slides, two fist glides, three finger snaps, two arm flaps, with a high-five ending with peals of laughter.

***

Later that evening, Odette rang Reese's doorbell.

"Instead of the white flag, I'm waving a furniture duster." Odette held a rectangular piece of light blue fluff and carried a box. "May I come in? I won't stay long."

"I'm busy with something," Reese said, referring to the lasagna she'd been eating. How many times had she made it clear she wasn't up for company only to have Odette sweep inside her home anyway?

"Okay. Give me a call when you have time," Odette said with unexpected deference before turning to leave.

"Wait." Reese's curiosity got the better of her. "Come on in."

"You're not cleaning your floors, are you?" Odette asked with a nervous titter. So she could joke about the mop Reese had wanted to whop her with the day before. No accusations yet. No attacks questioning Reese's mental stability. All positive signs. She followed Reese to the kitchen. Sinbad came over to sniff Odette and rub against her shins, with his tail high. She took a seat only when Reese invited her to do so.

"I'm sorry about what I said yesterday." Odette placed the box on the floor. The duster sat on top until Sinbad nabbed it and proceeded to drag it across the floor. "It was so insensitive and inexcusable, knowing how much you love Sinbad."

"And what about all that other passive-aggressive stuff you've said to me?" Reese sat beside her. "You've changed. You seem...I can't put my finger on it. I guess the word is I sense this festering resentment radiating off you lately."

"I'm sorry about that, too. To tell the truth, I've been a shitty friend."

In all the time Reese had known Odette, she'd never heard her swear or utter so much as a damn.

"Bottom line, I haven't been feeling like myself. And sometimes I was mean and took it out on you. I know what you're thinking. To everyone on the outside looking in, I have it all. Big beautiful house; cute-as-buttons twins; devoted, handsome husband, who is running a thriving orthodontics business. We're financially stable. I have good friends like Shireen, Melina, Birdie, and you. I hope I can still count you as a friend. Not a care in the world, besides deciding which elaborate homemade Halloween costume to design and sew for the boys, which organic vegetables to buy, which blooms to plant."

"Would you like a drink?" Reese reached for her bottle of merlot.

"Don't mind if I do."

Reese took another glass from the cabinet, poured wine for Odette, and topped off her own.

"So you're probably thinking, 'What could Odette possibly have to gripe about, besides a few extra pounds'?"

"And even that's questionable. Honestly?" Reese sat beside her. "Yeah, what's the darn problem?"

Odette took a big gulp of wine. "Everything I've tried to do for *me*, to feel good about myself as a businesswoman with something on the ball, besides her husband and kids, has failed."

Odette listed every direct sales rep/consultant business she'd experimented with since marrying Calvin. To support her friend, Reese had amassed a vast collection of unnecessary items Odette had hawked, including, but not limited to pizza stones, extra tote bags, lipsticks, costume jewelry, fragrance diffusers, and rolls upon rolls of scrapbooking/planner stickers and washi tape.

"And I know I probably didn't do as well as I'd hoped because I didn't stick with anything long enough. I monkey barred from one thing to the next with no real commitment, because they didn't excite me. And then I'd see you so focused, fulfilled, and motivated when you worked so hard for your family's company. And then you reached your goal, opening your own successful bakery. I felt like a big loser. Where was my drive? What did I do with my college degree? I studied business at a top school, but what did I accomplish? And I'm already over the hill."

Reese scoffed. "You're only 39, Odette."

"But I'm getting those AARP membership solicitations, and the other day I had to pluck a gray hair," she cleared her throat, "*down there*. And when I took the twins in for their most recent checkup at the pediatrician, that new receptionist asked me if I was their mother."

"So?"

"As if she wasn't quite certain if I was their *grand*mother, get it?"

"Maybe she makes a habit of asking everyone that because she's *new* and wants to be sure. Maybe she thought you were the aunt or the nanny or something. And Audrey, who's twenty-seven, said she'd received that AARP mailing. Doesn't mean a thing."

"I know. I know. And you're only as young as you feel."

"You said being a great wife and mother were your ultimate goals. Remember how hard you worked to get pregnant? My heart broke for you while you struggled through multiple fertility treatments. You kept saying over and over, 'My life would be complete if only I had babies and—' "

"I know I'm blessed to have Calvin and the boys, but is it so wrong to want a little more, for me, before I'm too old to enjoy it? Is that too much to ask? Or am I one of those pathetic women destined to be dissatisfied no matter what?"

"Calvin has been supportive."

"Yes and he tells me to do what makes me happy."

"Sounds as if you haven't found that *thing*, yet. But you will. I admire your tenacity."

"You do? So you don't think I'm just some dumb ol' boring, desperate housewife?" she asked softly, so unlike the self-congratulatory, know-it-all super wife and alpha-mom image Odette usually presented to the world.

"No. That never crossed my mind. Not once." Odette's frankness and vulnerability took Reese aback.

"So you think I'm as interesting as your sisters and other friends? You don't think I'm too clingy? You *like* spending time with me?"

"Yes, I like spending time with you. When you aren't zinging me, you're incredibly sweet and generous. Every time I have a bad cold or flu, you cluck over me like a mother hen. You keep me stocked up with the tastiest homemade chicken soups, tissue, with aloe no less, mint tea, and a stack of the juiciest *International Inquisitors*. And when I thanked Calvin for snow blowing my driveway and front walks or power washing my windows, he said you sent him over. Every time I've had to fly out of town for something, you volunteered to drive me to the airport *and* pick me up when I return. My sisters will do it if I beg, but neither has ever volunteered. They hate driving to the airport. And you helped me redo my ugly backsplash last year. And just recently, what you did with those beautiful promo flyers for the shop. Not only did you design them, but you distributed them. I could go on. These are the things I'd focus on when your behavior was more, um, challenging. And you're funny as heck, smart, and downright boss with a tile saw, lady."

"Really? You think I'm *'boss'*? You actually think I'm smart?" Odette's cheeks flushed.

"C'mon, Odette! You *must* know this already!"

"Back when we used to do book club here, I'd mention I was a stay-at-home mom and watch the light of interest go out in the," Odette made air quotes, " 'career women's' eyes. It was like flicking an OFF switch."

"Are you sure? I can't imagine my sisters or any friend of mine acting in such a snobbish manner because you're a stay-at-home mom, homemaker. Is it possible you misinterpreted that reaction?"

"Well…" Odette twisted the four-carat sparkler on her ring finger.

Actually, Odette had flicked Reese's guests' OFF switches because of her tendency to hijack the book club discussion. As if she were a college lit professor taking center stage at a lecture hall, Odette would deliver long-winded discourses on author intent, subtext, theme, and narrative structure while tossing around dozens of five-dollar words. She'd lost the last of her audience (Reese) after "*pusillanimous*" and one particularly rambling tangent on Newtonian mechanics. Who knew insecurity had fueled Odette's annoying display? And Odette had first made Quinn's crap list after the flat iron gift blunder.

"I've asked your opinion on several business matters regarding the shop, and I've taken your solid advice," Reese said. "And Calvin brags about how shrewd you've been with the family's budget and investments. Your decisions will finance that addition to your house next summer."

"Calvin told you that?"

"You know how that works on Mistywood Lane. He told Milo, who told Buddy, who told Ahmad, who told Shireen, who told me."

"I care what you think. You're such a ray of light, Reese, always smiling and not sweating the small stuff. And I love being around you, even if we're tearing down backsplash tiles or driving to the airport."

Reese squeezed Odette's hand.

"But," Odette had more, "You've been so busy, busy, busy lately. I thought that was your way of dumping me or 'ghosting' me as Melina said Ari calls it."

"Ghosting? It was a time management issue. Nothing more. So, what's next month's big project?"

"I'm hosting a Boudoir Delights party."

"You're going to sell sex toys?"

"Yes!"

"Wow."

"Hey, it jumps off in the Carmichael bedroom. No problems there. We get it in."

"But what will people think?" Reese teased with Odette's familiar refrain.

"That I'm one red hot mama. Might as well spread the knowledge. And make a little dough on the side. I swear by the Boudoir Delights products. I can really get behind them. Calvin adores the Gold Bullet Ball-Cock Ring & Chain. It's taken our lovemaking to a whole new level. It's like Viagra in jewelry form so he can go all night when he wears it." Odette sniggered.

Calvin's ornamented privates. A mental visual flashed that, unfortunately, was impossible for Reese to un-see, but she was excited about her friend's new business venture.

The women slapped high fives and laughed.

"One more thing," Odette said, sobering. "Because I want us to have a fresh start, I need to come clean about everything. Please don't hate me, Reese."

"What?"

"During your grand opening people on our street were buzzing about it. Shireen wondered how the shop was financed. Birdie an Melina thought maybe you received help from your parents or some older gentleman. I knew you'd inherited some money from one of your grandfathers but I didn't exactly rush in to correct some erroneous speculations. And I might have agreed, yes an older gentleman was involved, but I didn't explain who that older gentleman was to you, your... What did you call him?"

"PawPaw."

"I never said it was your, uh, 'PawPaw' so it might have left the impression that—"

"It was a sugar daddy-type deal straight out of the gold-digger's playbook," Reese interrupted. Quinn's hunch about the rumor's origin had been right. "And Shireen, Melina, and Birdie probably mentioned it to someone else and so on."

"I'm sorry, Reese." Odette's eyes filled. "That was wrong. You've always been so good to me, even when I was in one of my pissy moods, which have been way too frequent lately. I wish I could take back everything I've said or insinuated to hurt your feelings or reputation."

"I'm disappointed."

"I tried to make up for the shop misrepresentation with the flyer distribution. A small thing, but a start."

Reese should be infuriated, but she believed Odette's remorse was sincere. And Odette had revealed more about herself in the past half hour than she'd done in five years of them living next to one another. "One more thing. Have you ever reported me to the HOA?"

"No! I swear! I wouldn't unleash that tyrannical HOA on my worst enemy."

"Not once?"

"Not once. I do love you, Reese. I haven't been good at showing it lately. I've been comparing our lives, like one of those stupid Who Wore It Better columns in *The International Inquisitor*. But I promise to do better and not make my issues your issues. You deserve a much better friend. I want to be that friend."

Reese paused and studied Odette before speaking again. "We'll spat and disagree sometimes. We all make mistakes, but if I question your loyalty or sincerity again, you're O-U-T, out. And I refuse to let you get away with saying just any ol' jacked-up thing to me. No more chances. I mean it."

"I know you do."

"Darn right."

"And girl, you and that mop! I about peed my pants!"

The friends laughed again and hugged it out.

"This is a gift for Sinbad." Odette dried her eyes with a napkin and pointed to the box.

Reese opened it to reveal a large puffy pillow with a zippered side.

"It's a Pet Pocket. When he's having a bad day because of his condition, I think he might feel a little better resting in it." Odette unzipped the pillow.

"This is beautiful! And extravagant!" Reese ran her hands over butter soft fabric. "Silk and …Is this what I think it is?"

"Yes. Cashmere," Odette revealed with pride. "I went shopping first thing this morning and spent all day working on it while the twins were at their grandmother's house."

"You made this yourself?" Reese held it close before placing it on the floor. "Look, Sinbad! Look at the nice gift Auntie Odette brought for you."

"Auntie Odette to a cat. And I can't believe I like the sound of that."

Sinbad abandoned the duster to inspect his gift. He sniffed and pawed at it before crawling inside and curling up.

"He likes it!" Reese said.

"I'm glad. And thank you for understanding."

"Nobody's perfect, but true friends should uplift one another, not tear one another down or compete—"

"Or get spiteful when something good happens for the other one. I will admit I really got a bug up my behind when you started dating Gabriel."

"But why?"

"Because Mr. Right Next Door was horning in on my," she jabbed a thumb to her chest, "time with you. You already had your hands full with your shop, your sisters, and the rest of your family. And you were with Darren for a while. Though I knew I'd miss those complimentary Botox shots," she touched that area between her brows that double creased into what Darren had called The Angry 11. "I must admit I wasn't too broken up when that didn't work out for the two of you—"

"Odette," Reese huffed. "Really?"

"Hey, I'm not proud, but I promised complete honesty so we can start fresh. You were free and single again. But then, boom! Gabriel moves in. And just like that," she snapped her fingers, "you're canceling our early morning coffee confabs and running with, um, *'sweet'ems.'* I thought you preferred to run alone. Then he's wining, dining, and limo riding with you. All I could think was uh-uh… *majorly intrusive*! I'm your main Mistywood Lane connection. He's got to go, or I'll never get my time with you. I know it was selfish, but—"

"Aww, Odette," Reese said, not ready to discuss her and Gabriel's breakup. "I promise to do better with that, especially now that you and I have talked."

"I interrupted your dinner." Odette noticed Reese's plate of lasagna, now cooled. "I said I wouldn't take long. I'll let you get back to your meal. I'm glad you agreed to hear me out. You're such a sweetie. Well, a sweetie who will kick my ass if I get out of line. Oh, I almost forgot to mention, I know for a fact that Gabriel is Lucas Cameron's brother, thanks to good ol' Google. And I knew I'd seen him before. He was on the inside back cover flaps of those *Abraham & Zephyrus*, the *A to Z Double Dog Dare Detectives* books you gave to the boys. I remember thinking he looked more like a Calvin Klein underwear model than a children's book author. In my mind, a male children's book author should look like Mr. Rogers, Steve Urkel, or Santa Claus."

"I missed those photos," said Reese as she walked Odette to the front door, where they embraced again.

"Coffee tomorrow after your run… if you have time?" Odette asked. "I don't care how early."

"Coffee tomorrow. I'll look forward to it."

CHAPTER 33

The following month, the Sweet Spot won the DetoursMayfair.com specialty bakery award, but Reese couldn't bask in the honor. She missed Gabriel, but held firm to her decision. He'd respected her wishes, only coming over twice to retrieve Apollo and Maximus's Frisbees that had glided over the fence and landed in her backyard.

They'd seen each other several times, possibly more than when they were trying to connect. Funny how that worked out. Starting what was supposed to be "a fling" with the neighbor had been such an idiotic idea.

Gabriel and Reese would swap brief morning greetings when they happened to roll their trash and recycle bins to the curb at the same time on pickup mornings. They'd been exceedingly polite. No need to behave like bratty kids who hated one other. After all, she still loved him, but simply did not have faith he'd always love her. Surely, Gabriel would eventually cut out on her the way Darren had when he realized he loved Sasha more than he loved Reese. Had Gabriel reunited with Adriana? If not, it was just a matter of time. Because Reese was still plagued with unwavering doubts, breaking up with him had been the only sensible thing to do.

Sometimes before doing their miles, they'd give each other the customary fellow "runner's wave." After watching Gabriel sprint in one direction, she'd dash in the other, careful to avoid areas where they might intersect again. But...

What if Reese's growing insecurity had skewed her reasoning? What if she'd been too hard on him and overreacted? After all, she'd forgiven others' various offenses. Rosvaughn, Jerricka, Shireen, and Odette...

And even Darren, the person who'd committed the whopper of a betrayal.

How nice it might have been to enjoy the first chill and the awe-inspiring range of autumn colors with Gabriel. She'd anticipated weekday lunches with him, engrossing conversation over light-as-air biscuits and rich butter bean and pumpkin soup with a side of fried okra at Lula-Bell's, the little ma-and-pop restaurant five doors down from the Sweet Spot. Finishing the day, cuddling up with Gabriel and a cup of hot cider in front of her fireplace also topped her list... before all hell broke loose.

Reese spent what free time she had caring for Sinbad, whose condition had rapidly deteriorated over the last few weeks, as Gabriel had predicted it would.

One week, Sinbad was spry and gobbling up everything in his bowl, the next week he'd stopped eating on his own altogether.

Sinbad wedged himself in a dark place between a shoe rack and a wall in her walk-in closet every chance he got. He'd sit inside the Pet Pocket Odette had made for him and stare at that wall for hours on end, when he wasn't sleeping or making multiple trips to his litter box or water bowl. He didn't yowl or make other sounds of distress. Was he in pain?

Reese had taken Gabriel's advice and not returned to her former veterinarian. Researching a new one was not a good use of her time. She stayed with East Mayfair Veterinary Hospital, but met with Julian about Sinbad's condition.

***

"That's a difficult question to answer," Julian said during one of Sinbad's frequent checkups.

Reese had asked how much time Sinbad had left.

"What kind of lasting memories of him do you want to have?" Julian asked, his delivery gentle, but frank. "I have to be honest with you, end-stage kidney disease can get pretty gruesome, Reese, because the body becomes septic. You said he's spending most of his time in a dark closet looking at a wall. He's not responding to affection. You have to force feed him. You're doing fluid therapy and pumping him with meds. What does that tell you about his quality of life?"

"You think I should put him down?" Reese asked.

"You're his owner. It's ultimately your decision, but sometimes when weighing everything, it's the most loving thing to do."

Once again, Reese drove home in tears.

Early the next morning, she took one look at her beloved companion as he trembled and labored to breathe.

Today is the day. Reese had to let him go.

She'd been clinging to him, hanging on because she wasn't ready to say goodbye. That choice wasn't about what was right for Sinbad, but all about her. She shouldn't have let him weaken to this point, she berated herself. Then she phoned Julian, who was already at the hospital. She told him about her decision. He promised to work them in and not make them wait.

When Reese ended the call, she desperately wanted to talk to Gabriel. She wanted him there, but what kind of mixed message would that send? Her sorrow was making her erratic. She scooped up Sinbad, who had lost so much weight his ribs and spine protruded against her fingers. The fishy breath she'd come to adore now reeked of ammonia. Another sign of his extreme deterioration.

"Oh, Sinbad." She wept, cradling him. "I don't want to let you go. But I have to. For a dozen years, you've given me so much love and joy. And now I have to be strong and do this last thing for *you*." She dried her tears when he looked up at her with bleary green eyes as if he knew. He understood. As if to agree, he licked her hand again with that scratchy little tongue of his. Yes, he was ready to say goodbye to her and his pain.

Reese wrapped him in his favorite towel, the one with the multicolored mackerels on it, and gently placed him inside his carrier. This time there was no fight from him. To have other loved ones near, she phoned her sisters and Rosvaughn and asked them to meet her at the vet hospital.

Under a shroud of smoke-colored clouds, so cliché in their bleak appropriateness, Reese drove to the hospital as if on autopilot. Soon, her loyal triad joined her.

As promised, Julian did not make them wait. They gathered inside a sterile room. Reese sat and held Sinbad in her arms and spoke to him sweetly, without tears, as Julian delivered the injections. Blaire and Quinn stroked Reese's shoulders. Rosvaughn gave Sinbad's head a gentle pat. Reese fought breaking down herself as she heard all the sniffling and nose blowing around her. She had to be strong for Sinbad. During his final moments, she didn't want him to feel fear or her anguish, only her fierce love and devotion.

For their last dance together, she stood, swayed, and softly sang "Stray

Cat Strut" to him. She scratched his left ear, and stroked the bridge of his nose, the way he liked it, as he peered up at her through slow blinking green eyes until the last bit of life in them vanished.

"Goodbye, my sweet boy." Reese kissed his head and cradled him for a few minutes longer. Then the vet assistant took his motionless body, wrapped in the towel, its colorful fish pattern now blurry through her tears. At a window on a second door, she thought she saw Gabriel. She blinked, and he was gone.

Quinn took care of the business at the receptionist desk. Reese had opted to have Sinbad cremated so she could have him with her. She'd considered preserving his body, but keeping a freeze-dried, glass-eyed Sinbad around like a trophy was just too creepy, even for an ultimate pet lover such as Reese. And no, she would not try to have him cloned. Also possible these days, but even creepier.

Imani, the assistant who had helped with Sinbad's ultrasound, pressed a folded green sheet of paper in Reese's hand.

"Why don't you let one of us drive you home?" Blaire asked after they stepped outside, under even darker clouds.

"I don't want to leave my car here." Reese dabbed her wet eyes with a tissue. "I'm capable of driving my own car."

"But you're crying," said Quinn, who was also as red-eyed as Blaire and Rosvaughn.

"You are, too," Reese said.

"I am not. It's my seasonal allergies," Quinn insisted, blowing her nose.

Right. Trash-talking Quinn who'd always found Reese's devotion to Sinbad "weird" and "exasperating," was just a big ol' softie. She carried Sinbad's empty carrier and placed it inside her own car to spare Reese the agonizing task.

"I'm good," Reese said. "I swear!"

"I can drive your car back to your place." Rosvaughn curled his arm around Reese's shoulders. "Blaire or Quinn can bring me back here to get my ride. Not a problem."

"No. I want to drive myself, guys."

"You and your hard head," Quinn said.

"Hey, everyone come to my house," Blaire said. "I'm free the rest of the day. I'll make a big breakfast."

"Sounds like a plan," Rosvaughn said.

Reese wasn't eager to get back to her own house with all of Sinbad's things she hadn't had time to put away. "All right. I'll see you guys in a few minutes." As drizzle fell, she watched them drive away. Before she climbed inside her own car, she removed that folded sheet of paper from her pocket. Inside was a miniature baggy with a snipped tuft of Sinbad's beautiful shaded silver fur. She held it against her cheek and then put it away. She scanned the title on the page. "Rainbow Bridge." As the rain softened the crisp page, she read the poem and then heaved and bawled.

Strong arms wrapped around her.

Gabriel.

Reese let him hold her.

"It's going to be okay, sweetheart," Gabriel said, his voice low and hypnotic, as she buried her face against his broad chest.

Gabriel soothed her, stroking her damp hair. He held on tight, her sobs muffled against his warm body. She trembled, but then something unexpected happened. As the heart-rending words on the page echoed in her mind, her sobs shifted to soft chortles.

"Are you," Gabriel loosened his embrace enough to study her face, "laughing?"

Reese nodded, lips drawn tight in an effort to stifle another chuckle.

"You're actually laughing?" he asked, obviously flummoxed.

"I guess I am." Reese couldn't restrain a snort. "I think it's called laugh-crying."

Gabriel looked at her as if she'd lost her mind.

Reese snorted again, covering her mouth.

"I'm confused," he said.

"C'mon, you guys actually give *this*," she held up the green paper, "to newly grieving pet owners? Seriously?"

"For your information that poem is popular. Look online."

There was no way to soft-pedal this so Reese came out with it. "But it's so, so, over-the-top sad. I mean in a twist-the-knife-in-your-gut-maudlin sort of way. It's downright masochistic to read."

"Some people actually find comfort in those words."

"Oh, yeah? Well, pluh-leeeease don't comfort me anymore. Not like this! I can't take it!" Reese hooted, waving the paper around, enjoying the respite brought on by her own hearty laughter.

Gabriel's grave expression gave way to a small smile. "You weren't supposed to read it right away. Didn't Imani tell you that? You were *supposed* to wait a while before you read it. Had you followed instructions the effect might have been different."

"No, she didn't tell me or maybe I was too distracted to hear her." Reese dried her eyes with the tissue he'd pressed in her hand and chuckled some more. "I thought it was a copy of the receipt after Quinn paid the bill."

"I'm sorry about Sinbad," he said softly.

"I know." Oh, how she'd pined for Gabriel. She wanted nothing more than to tuck away her grief for a little while and get lost in their lovemaking. But though Sinbad was gone, nothing had changed between her and Gabriel.

"I tried to stay out of sight. I told Julian to call me if...I wanted to be there."

"I know. I appreciate that."

Imani came to the door. "Gabriel, Julian needs your help. He wants to consult about Tink."

"Tink?" Reese asked.

"Tinkerbell, our pot-bellied pig client. I have more experience with them."

Reese sniffled. "Oh, I guess you'd better get back in there. Tink needs you."

"Yeah. You sure you're okay?"

Their gazes locked as he caressed her arms.

Reese nodded. "Thank you."

"If you need anything later, you know I'm—"

"Right next door."

CHAPTER 34

By the time Reese arrived at Blaire's house, not only were Quinn and Rosvaughn there, but her parents had left church to attend what was now a brunch. Those she loved most had gathered so she wouldn't spend the rest of the day crying and moping about Sinbad. Still, she couldn't get Gabriel off her mind. Seeing his face, inhaling his scent, and feeling his strong arms around her again had sparked a ferocious longing that made it difficult to concentrate on the spirited conversation and camaraderie around her.

"We're so proud of you, baby girl!" her father said as they sat on stools around the large island in Blaire's kitchen.

"Best specialty bakery in Mayfair!" her mother cheered. "What an honor! Of course I made copies of the article posted on the DetoursMayfair.com website to pass out to all my friends and church members."

"The *Mayfair Tribune* is doing a big story in its weekend entertainment and food supplement," Blaire added. "Be on the lookout for it. And Reese has a plaque to display at the Sweet Spot. It's huge."

"Why didn't you take a picture and post it?" Quinn asked. "The first thing I did was check your Sweet Spot Post-a-Pic feed, but it wasn't there."

"I plan to add it. I've been, well, distracted lately, tending to things that couldn't wait."

Blaire, who sat near, patted Reese's back. "She'll get to it soon."

All were aware Reese was unattached again so her parents quizzed Blaire about Hayes and asked if Quinn had met any interesting dating prospects. No one asked Reese about Darren or Gabriel. But she couldn't count on her nosy sisters to give her a reprieve for long. After a week or two, they'd get back to pumping her for information about the breakup. At the right time, and not a second before, she'd tell them Gabriel had consoled her in the hospital's parking lot.

Both sisters, however, asked about girlfriends. Without divulging details about Odette's secrets and personal struggles, she shared that the two of them had taken the time for wonderful, no BS, heart-to-hearts that had strengthened their friendship. And Reese announced that she would no longer tolerate Quinn and Rosvaughn ridiculing her friend. Both agreed to be more respectful.

"But if Odette gets out of line again, all bets are off." Quinn gestured with her fork.

"Word," Rosvaughn said.

"I, cautiously, believe that some people can change," Quinn added.

Because Reese wanted to keep the mood as light as possible under the circumstances, she had little to share about Porsha, whom she hadn't heard from since that day Reese had revealed she'd been dissatisfied with their "conversations" of late and why. Reese, however, had heard from a mutual friend who'd reported Porsha was "enraged" about the way Reese had "callously let her down" during Porsha's "time of personal crisis." Porsha didn't think she would ever forgive Reese, even if Reese flew to L.A. to grovel.

Don't hold your breath, Porsha. Now that Reese had had time to think about it, Porsha had been the most self-absorbed, soul-sucking, so-called friend of all, only calling when she wanted something or an ear to bend with no consideration for anyone else. Why hadn't Reese realized this sooner? Score one for hard-won wisdom.

Hard-won wisdom. Now where did that leave her and Gabriel? Unlike her split with Darren and a few others before him, time apart had only made Reese yearn for Gabriel more.

***

When Reese turned into her driveway late that night her headlights illuminated a burst of color on her front porch, a beautiful crystal vase of cheerful wild flowers. Someone had propped an envelope beside it.

Gabriel had put the blooms there. She sniffed the fragrant flowers and touched the soft petals. Maybe Reese had been too hard on him. Yes, he'd made a mistake, but was her reaction too harsh because she no longer trusted her own judgment? Her self-esteem had been battered and dragged. Yes, she'd tried to move on. But what had happened between her and Darren had affected her more than she'd wanted to admit. And learning of Sinbad's bleak prognosis had contributed to her downward emotional spiral.

As Reese removed her clothes, she considered what Quinn had said about Reese bottling up her feelings and needing everyone to think she was "a saint." For as long as Reese could remember, she'd been a people pleaser. She had needed everyone—no matter how brief the encounter— to like and accept her.

Revealing her authentic, flawed self to the outside world, beyond her family who loved her unconditionally, had been daunting on far too many occasions. Yes, she, too, could be just as impatient, bossy, mean-spirited, uncertain, selfish, and petty as the next person when provoked.

And that was okay.

Lapses in righteousness? Bring 'em on. Her most recent flicks of the so-called bitch switch had been freeing and therapeutic, even. No more accepting botched restaurant entrées because she dreaded troubling the waitstaff and sending orders back to chefs.

With aplomb, Reese now navigated one particular minefield, aka her corner Brimble's grocery store. No more saying yes to the multiple solicitations for the Children's Make a Dream Come True to Save the World charity out of fear clerks would think she was stingy when it came to helping kids in need. One generous donation a year was enough.

Reese also refused to eat another misshapen slice of toast. Now she demanded that Tanya, Brimble's worst cashier, stop pitching the 28-ounce cans of stewed tomatoes inside the bag with the loaves of bread.

Reese had also refused to continue providing detailed reviews on personal items in her cart as male shoppers in same check-out line, listened in and snickered. If Tanya was so flippin' curious about the Eve's Garden Oasis Paradise Va-va-voom Vanilla feminine hygiene wash in Reese's cart, she could darn well Google it.

Hindsight? A high-powered microscope. As Gabriel noted, Reese had not been completely honest about the extent of her anguish about his ongoing friendship with Adriana.

Reese went to her kitchen sink to refresh the water for the bouquet and read the sympathy card, which was from Odette, who'd likely found out about Sinbad's passing from Gabriel. The message was beautiful (and more subtle) than "Rainbow Bridge." Inside the card was a printout. In Sinbad's honor, Odette had made substantial online donations to a local no-kill animal shelter and to Mayfair University College of Veterinary Medicine's Pet Friends Fund, established to study diseases and disorders affecting companion animals.

Reese curled up on the family room sofa, clutching one of Sinbad's catnip toys and the Pet Pocket to her chest. She appreciated Gabriel's and Odette's gestures of compassion. Still, her home felt colder, darker, and emptier than ever.

CHAPTER 35

On a Sunday about a month later, Reese headed out to collect Sinbad's ashes. They'd been ready for pickup since the third day after his passing. However, when the hospital had called her to collect them, she'd emailed Julian to ask if she could wait. He'd agreed to keep them for as long as she needed.

Now that she'd had time to grieve and could shop for the perfect keepsake cremation urn without bursting into tears, she was ready.

As Reese sat in Julian's office, he gave her a blue, velvet box with a smaller rectangular one inside marked Sinbad Sommers. "Time to take you back home where you belong, my sweet boy." His jeweled collar and ID tag were inside a drawstring bag.

"There was no rush," Julian reminded her.

"I appreciate that." Reese looked up at him. "Sometimes I feel horrible because I refused to let go after it was obvious Sinbad didn't feel well. I let him suffer too long."

"The timing varies from pet owner to pet owner. Sometimes it's difficult to know when to say goodbye," Julian said.

"The house is so empty without him. I feel adrift. He was just one cat, but he filled my house with so much life and love. I miss that. I miss being a pet mom, but I feel guilty even thinking of looking at another cat. Is it too soon?"

"There's no one-size-fits-all answer. Depends on the individual. You can be a pet mom again as soon as it feels right to you. Only *you* can decide. But my advice is to start fresh with a different species altogether, such as a dog or maybe a bird. If you must stick with cats, try a different breed so you're not as tempted to compare him or her to Sinbad, a competition another cat simply can't win. And remember, you are not replacing Sinbad. As far as feeling guilty about getting another pet, don't. Nobody should judge. It's actually a testament to how much that relationship with Sinbad meant to you. You want something that's the same, but different, if that makes any sense, in your life again."

"So when should I move forward?"

"Again, only you can answer that. Some people struggle with that empty feeling and move ahead in a few days or weeks. Others take longer, but I don't believe either approach is a direct correlation to how much a companion animal was loved, just an individual choice."

"Thanks, Julian. You've been great."

"How is everything else, if you don't mind my asking?"

Obviously, his way of inquiring about her and Gabriel. "My shop won a big award on that popular DetoursMayfair.com site," she said instead.

"Yeah, I heard about it. Your cupcakes are great. And Gabriel is so proud of you, downright effusive. You would've thought our hospital had won something, the way he was going on and on about it." Julian chuckled.

"Yes, he was always supportive of the shop," Reese said, and then swerved. "So, you think I should steer clear of Persians for a while?"

"That's my advice, but if you feel strongly about it and have a passion for the breed you can move forward. Just remember what I said about comparison."

"Will do."

"I know I'm butting in where I shouldn't, but I have to say this. About Gabriel, I was the biggest doubter of them all when he talked about what he felt for you. But now, after getting to know you, I understand. And I have to say I believe him. He did fall hard. And for what it's worth, I think it's real and lasting for him. I have never seen him like this...about *anybody else*," he added pointedly.

Reese fidgeted on her seat. That *anybody else* was clear.

"He's crushed that you broke things off with him. As one of Gabriel's closest friends, I want him to be happy. Life's too short. And boy, did I learn that the hard way. I'm still struggling to move on myself."

Reese nodded, recalling what Gabriel had told her about Julian's devastating loss.

"I don't want to get too mawkish here. Again, for what it's worth, you made Gabriel happy," he added. "Deliriously happy."

"Deliriously, huh?" Though Julian was getting all up in Reese's personal business, she still liked him. He had a warm but no-nonsense manner she found reassuring.

"Yes and I'm not a man prone to hyperbole," Julian went on. "He always shamelessly gushed about you. I'd never seen him that way before. He didn't stop even when we harassed him about it. I think I was the worst. But lately he's been distant, moody…Not as much fun to be around, not at all like his usual self." He settled back in his seat, resting his head in the cradle of his large hands. "I want to see that deliriously happy side of him again. It sure would make things a lot easier around here."

"Is that right?"

Julian wore an expression that seemed to say, *so what are you going to do about it?*

CHAPTER 36

As Reese stepped out of the hospital into the bright, crisp fall morning, she ran smack dab into Adriana, who carried a cardboard box of kittens.

"Reese!" Again, Adriana was in full-out bohemian rhapsody gear, beaming and wearing another one of her clashing ensembles, including a skirt with a Native American-style pattern. In deference to the cooler temps she'd added boots (also scuffed) and a kaleidoscope-print poncho and cap. "It's so nice to see you again. How are you?"

"I'm good. And you?"

"Great!"

"And what have we here? More rescue critters?" Reese peered inside the box.

"Yes! A neighbor found them in her backyard. She kept them for a few days, but the mother never returned, unfortunately." Adriana's red lips turned downward for a moment. "We think she was killed."

"That's awful," Reese said, admiring the litter of squirming short-haired kittens of no particular breed.

"*Julian* will check them out for me," Adriana said. "I work *only* with *Julian, Lance* and two *other* vets now."

Adriana's declaration was so laughably exaggerated, she could forget about a second career as a secret agent or a professional actor. Gabriel's friends were going out of their way to make a case for him. She found it heartening. But persuasive?

"May I?" Reese placed her tote near her feet and lifted the kitten that kept trying to scale the box.

226

"I call that one Daisy," Adriana said. "The imp of the bunch, she's usually getting into something and agitating her brothers and sisters."

Reese cooed at the feisty kitten with the reddish brown coat. "Hi, Daisy, so you're a little firecracker." Another golden-wheat-colored kitten tried to follow her.

"I call her Rose, her sidekick and copycat, pun intended."

Reese cuddled the sisters as they meowed, sank their needle-like claws in her sweater and tugged at her heart. "They are *the* cutest things! Simply adorable!"

"They can be yours if you want them. They need good homes."

Before Reese responded someone inside Adriana's SUV tooted the horn.

"Is that a member of your menagerie trying to get your attention?"

Adriana laughed. "That's just Nathan, my boyfriend. His way of telling me to hurry along," she confided with a whisper as if she and Reese were old friends. "He's a dream. Wanna meet him?"

Nathan tapped the horn again.

"I don't want to hold you two up." Reese placed Daisy and Rose back inside the cardboard box. "Maybe another time, but I want to know more about these two scamps when you get a chance. Do you still have my business card?"

"I do. Will touch base when Julian's done looking them over so I can give you a full report."

"Sounds good." Reese enjoyed their easy rapport as she lifted her tote bag. Adriana's insta-chumminess could grow on a girl.

"Reese, I know this is none of my business. I don't enjoy dipping, but my sister is truly sorry for the way she behaved that night. I told her I'd met you and that I—"

"No need to say more." Reese wanted to bury that ordeal once and for all. "I'm glad you and I had a chance to chat again."

Nathan tooted the horn.

"Me, too!" Adriana said as she watched Reese head to the Beetle.

"See ya around!" Reese said.

"But not *too* often, right?" Adriana added.

Both women laughed.

As Reese slipped inside her car and secured the seatbelt, Adriana called out a last pitch. "Oh, and all kittens come with appropriate vaccinations! Just FYI!"

"Gotcha!"

CHAPTER 37

The following weekend Mayfair's Fall Fest kicked off with a perfect blue sky and brisk temperatures. The day of family fun started with a Halloween costume parade down Main Street. The route led to Gateman Park where a series of local bands played on two large stages. A costume contest for all ages and a Little Miss Mayfair pageant for tots took place on a third stage. Dozens of local merchants and artisans had set up tables. A kid's zone featured bounce houses, a petting zoo, a caricaturist, face-painting, games, and other activities. On an open patch of green, a group of boys played a pick-up game of football. The scent of fries, barbecue, corn dogs, cotton candy, and other eats filled the air.

Gabriel stood behind the long table with other contestants participating in the chili cook-off. He held up his third-place ribbon while he and Odette, who had won first place, posed for a photo with the other finalists.

"Third place is not bad for a newbie." Odette embraced her tall, gleaming trophy as if she were seconds away from frenching it.

"But first place is better," Gabriel said, reaching for her trophy. "Rematch next year."

Odette slapped his hand away. "Look, don't touch."

"That gives me plenty of time."

"Ah, measuring the drapes, eh? Bring it!"

"I have just enough room for that trophy on my mantel," he said.

"Have you seen Reese? She's around here somewhere." Using one hand to shield her eyes from the bright sun, Odette looked out at the immense crowd.

Of course Gabriel had seen Reese. Something in the air changed as soon as she'd shown up with her tablemate, the woman he'd taken to calling the "Tea Lady" because he could never recall her name. It was all he could do not to leave the judging table and dash over to say hello, but finalists had been instructed to stay close by for pictures and community newspaper coverage.

Reese, busy with her own setup, hadn't ventured over to the chili contest area. Gabriel prayed she'd check on her good friend Odette so he could see her, too.

After the day he'd comforted Reese in the hospital's parking lot, she had placed one of her signature cute thank-you cards inside his mailbox to show her gratitude for the flowers he'd left on her porch. He missed everything about the times they'd spent together, from their tag team roughhousing with his dogs to the jaunty swing of her ponytail when she ran. However, as promised, he didn't crowd her or try to force anything. She would view such gestures as "disrespectful" and "nuisance" behavior. He'd honored her wishes except for a couple of times. When he knew she was home, he might have aimed the dogs' Frisbees toward her backyard. That move gave him opportunities to see her again. Up close. He had to knock on her door and ask for permission to retrieve them, right?

When Gabriel wasn't at the hospital, he worked on his latest *Abraham & Zephyrus* book. The writing and illustrating kept him plenty occupied. And it was nice having his dogs all to himself. No shuttling them back and forth. He'd trained them for an upcoming all-breed dock dog competition at the annual Gray Hill Sheep Dog Trials. His family got to see a lot more of him, but he regretted missing the opportunity to introduce them to Reese. Lance and Julian had tried to cheer him up with choice tickets to pro football games. Still, he couldn't stop thinking about Reese and how bad he wanted her back in his life.

"They have all the pictures they need." Odette had read his thoughts. "Why don't you go grab a cupcake for dessert."

Yeah, well maybe he'd do just that. His patience had run out. What harm could it do to stroll over to buy a cupcake and say hello? It's not as if they were alone. Hundreds of people surrounded them.

With her hands on the back of his sweater, Odette gave him a playful-but-unneeded shove. "Go on. Get over there. Now!"

Gabriel left his empty Crock-pot behind with Odette and pinned his third place ribbon to his chest, a dork move he hoped Reese would find endearing. And from there, he hoped their conversation would fall back into the fun-and-easy flow they'd shared before he'd butted his nose in where it didn't belong. Maybe she'd ask about Apollo and Maximus. Gabriel could mention he had full custody of the dogs these days, without sounding as if he were working an angle, though he most certainly wanted to angle himself right back into her life. Maybe he could also just happen to mention she no longer had to endure his frequent exchanges with Adriana. Nothing and no one was worth jeopardizing his relationship with Reese…if she'd only give him another chance to prove it.

As he approached her table, Gabriel stopped to take her in. As usual, she dazzled. She wore a purple cashmere turtleneck sweater and jeans. The big bun atop her head accentuated her high cheekbones and large caramel-colored eyes. When she laughed at something Tea Lady said, his envy spiked. He wanted to be the one who made her smile. As he stood there, Reese's gaze met and locked with his.

When Reese smiled, relief flooded his body, and he stepped to her table. "It's great to see you."

"Ditto."

As they took in one another, Tea Lady got the hint. "Reese, gotta run to the Porta Jon. Be right back."

Gabriel rocked on his heels, hands in his pockets. *Thank you, Tea Lady!*

"Odette texted me," Reese said. "She told me you placed third. Not bad in a field of thirty. At least twenty are seasoned competitors in the event, according to Odette. Nice ribbon." She tapped the ruffled satin adornment pinned to his chest. "Congratulations."

"Congratulations to you too. Best specialty bakery in the DetoursMayfair.com competition. That's huge."

"Yes! But placing high in the chili cook-off is not too shabby."

"Next year is my year," Gabriel said. "I have a few ideas for tweaking my recipe to take it up a notch."

"I love it the way it is. It's to die for." Reese leaned closer. "Quiet as it's kept, Odette's chili is delicious, but so traditional. I think yours is much better because it has a nice Caribbean kick."

"In that case, I'll have to share the recipe with you," he added quickly.

"What happened to," she contorted her pretty features and formed claws with her hands, '*Zee cook, zee cook vill never tell. I vill die first!*'" she said mimicking his maniacal cartoon villain voice.

Gabriel laughed. "*Zee cook, zee cook vill…*," he started, then dropped the dopey voice. He spoke from the heart as he looked deep into her beautiful eyes. "I'll not only give you the recipe, but the sun, the moon, and the stars if you'll give me another chance to make you happy." Gabriel hadn't planned to get sappy or put her on the spot in a public place, but he loved this woman, and he'd tired of their present situation. They should be together, dammit! "I miss you," he continued, not bothering to keep the desperation out of his voice. Pride be damned. "I miss us. I want that back. I want us. I won't let you down again." Reese said something he didn't hear because he was so lost in his impassioned plea. "Wait," he finally paused. "Did you just say you miss me, too?"

"Who do you think texted first?" Reese asked. "I told Odette to send you this way."

"You did?"

"Yes, but…"

Gabriel's insides clenched again. "But what?"

"Maybe I should wait to see what you do to tweak that recipe. I'm looking forward to trying it."

"I'm thinking of tweaking it as soon as I return home as a matter of fact. How about I bring over a pot for dinner tonight?"

Reese's neat brows ran together. "Dude, aren't you chili-ed out already?"

"No, I could eat *my* chili for breakfast, lunch, and dinner."

Reese checked her watch. "Hmmm. Is six enough time?"

Dinner together? Progress! Thank you, God! Gabriel wanted to grab one of the pumpkins on sale at the table next to Reese's and spike it as if it were a football. "Yes, I mean, no. I don't do canned beans. Dried beans need to soak all night. I don't chance that quick-start cooking method."

"Oh," she said, eyes downcast. "That's a problem."

"Easily solved, if you don't mind Chinese instead."

"Chinese sounds fantastic!"

"So six?"

"I'll see you then. And oh, I have some new friends I want you to meet."

"Julian told me about them. Daisy and Rose?"

"You mean Lucia and Estella. After watching their antics, I've renamed them in the spirit of a certain classic sitcom's wacky redhead and her blond sidekick, who are always getting into trouble. It's just us girls now."

"Can't wait to meet Lucia and Estella."

CHAPTER 38

Gabriel arrived at Reese's house carrying bags with their dinner and a bottle of wine. Before they ate, Gabriel helped assemble the replacement climbing tree. The old one still had Sinbad's scent.

Reese had put away most of Sinbad's belongings and had the rugs and furniture professionally cleaned before she adopted her new cats.

Over their Chinese feast, Reese and Gabriel caught up on each other's lives while they were apart and discussed how they would move forward as a couple, focusing on open and honest communication. For the first time with him, Reese discussed her past struggles with "the need to please" and her difficulties being direct and open about her feelings.

Gabriel revealed his many failures to compartmentalize and establish proper boundaries with certain people in his personal life. "I still had such positive feelings about Adriana and the time we'd spent together, the friendship part we've had our entire lives. She's a great lady."

"Yes, I like her."

"I figured refusing to maintain the friendship was like admitting I still had romantic feelings for her, that I couldn't handle dealings on a more casual level. I knew I was done when we broke up that last time, but—"

"You had something to prove."

"Sounds odd, but yeah, I suppose. And there was probably a bit of having my cake and eating it too in there, I must admit, now that we're completely honest with each other."

Reese smirked. *Bingo.* Quinn had called that one.

"Yes, I wanted to help Adriana with a cause I believe in, but I suppose I also gave Luke's messy love life and what other people thought of the Camerons too much weight as well. I should've been living my own damn life."

"Luke? I don't follow."

"Luke makes his living playing many roles, and I played my one, the *good* son," Gabriel said. "Martin and Vivian Cameron raised us right, with good solid values, but Luke detoured, took his own path. For as long as I could remember, I've always believed I had to prove I was different. Meanwhile, Luke's not thinking about me, the family, or Mom's and Dad's standing on the usher and deacon boards at church, when he's feeding the tabloid machine."

"Most people know the majority of those tabloid stories are made up."

"I'm afraid in my brother's case, most of it isn't fabrication. And I've long felt some kind of way about it. High-minded and very quick to judge, if truth be told," Gabriel said. "I need to work on that. And Lance has said I sometimes behave like a meddlesome old woman."

Reese couldn't help considering how fired up Gabriel had become after learning about her and Darren.

"And speaking of Lance, I'm relieved you didn't go with the ol' birds of feather where my relationship with him is concerned. Lance has his baggage, too, especially with women, *but* he has a deep sense of loyalty. He's been a devoted friend to Julian and me—dependable, supportive, and easy to talk to. I figured you'd have a chance to get to know him and appreciate that side of him."

"Lance is quite a character. I like him."

"One day you'll meet Luke, too. Since junior high my brother has been... Let's just say Luke makes Lance look like a choirboy. Remember that day when we met at the mailboxes, and I pulled out all of Mrs. Cohen's tabloids? Luke's exploits had made the cover of at least two of them. Some of the screaming headlines about his latest... 'Cameron's Debauched Weekend Bender with a Bevy of Hookers and Porn Stars.' But you know what? He's a single man. Free to live his life and find his fun as he sees fit, as long as he's not hurting himself or anyone else. Living life in the glare of the spotlight can't be easy. And as much as I'd like it to be so, I'm not Mr. Nice Guy all the damn time."

"Surely you jest!" Reese chuckled. "But boy, do I know something about needing to be seen as the nice one all the time."

Going forward, Reese and Gabriel vowed to share their needs and expectations.

Before they could enjoy the leftover Lemon Lust cupcakes Reese had brought home from Fall Fest, they were all over each other again. Slow seduction? Fat chance after spending weeks apart. As they locked lips on the way to her bedroom, Gabriel had her undressed by the time they reached the bottom of the stairs. And soon he was also naked, except for the condom on his erection. With her bottom on a step he positioned himself between her open thighs and entered her, pumping with a fierceness that took her breath away. She clung to him, her fingers clasping his muscular shoulders, her teeth nipping at his neck. Barely missing a beat, he withdrew, flipped her around as if she were a rag doll (just the way she liked it!), and hauled her against his brick wall of a chest. They resumed their erotic dance with Gabriel picking up where he left off. No more talking. Just passionate moans and gasps. And the sound of heated flesh against heated flesh. Reese held on to the railing as he slammed into her again and again, each thrust lifting her off her feet. Gabriel's hand gripped her hip to keep her from falling as the other cupped her bouncing breast. Her hold on the railing soon gave way, the pleasure almost too intense. Both were slippery with sweat. Their frenzied coupling continued as if the aggressiveness and speed would compensate for the days they'd spent apart. Moments later they reached the peak together. She felt as if she were shimmering from the inside, before bursting into a shower of stars. They collapsed, winded. A heap of damp limbs on the wooden stairway, they erupted in laughter. Lucia and Estella, who had been playing on their new climbing tree, dashed over.

"Whew!" Reese said. "You did miss me, huh?"

"Yup," he said, planting a kiss on her forehead.

"And I missed you, too. Desperately."

"But...my lower back." Gabriel groaned, massaging it.

"At least you don't have splinters." Reese plucked one from her right butt cheek and her left elbow.

"Do, too."

"Do not."

Gabriel held up his palm. "Look.

"Aww, he has a owie," she cooed. "Let mama kiss it and make it better."

"I was hoping you'd say that." Gabriel perked up, cupping his penis. "I have an owie here, too."

Reese gave him a shove.

"You walked right into that one." Grinning, Gabriel held her close when they moved to relax on the plush rug at the landing. He reached for his sweater to cushion her head. Lucia clawed at Reese's now messy bun while Estella batted at the makeshift pillow.

"Sorry girls," Reese said, "you missed the show on the stairway. No command performances yet. Ow!"

Gabriel removed Lucia's claws that tangled in Reese's hair. Both cats took off toward the family room to get into other mischief.

Reese chuckled. "Who needs a bed when—"

"We have floors, walls, stairs, showers, and countertops." Her racing heart rate steadied. She nestled close to him and skimmed a toe along his leg, enjoying the hardness of his muscle and the tickle of the coarse hairs against her skin.

"And that hanging chair of yours in the guest bedroom looks interesting," he said, kissing her fingertips one by one.

"Now there's an idea!" Reese shot to her feet. She bounded up the steps toward the guest bedroom.

Gabriel, at her heels, snatched up his sweater and snapped it at her bottom. "Hey, I was only kidding! Damn!"

CHAPTER 39

One year later

Reese awakened and stretched, her nude body tangled in the sheets, with sunlight streaming through her bedroom windows. After slipping out to feed Apollo and Maximus at his place, Gabriel removed his clothes and then crawled back between the sheets. He lay on his side, admiring her face, which still bore traces of the makeup she'd worn with her costume. The night before, Reese had hosted a Halloween bash and dressed as a character from *Cats*, her favorite Broadway production.

At the foot of the bed, Lucia and Estella, now full-grown felines, tussled with each other as they'd often done as two-pound kittens. Though their weight had quadrupled in the past year, they remained in a healthy range because Reese had learned overindulging them with treats was not the best way to express her love.

"How did they get in here?" Groggily, Reese rubbed sleep from her eyes.

"Guilty." Gabriel lifted the hand that rested on her hip. "I didn't mean for them to wake you. I could watch you sleep for hours." He tapped her nose with its traces of black greasepaint.

"Exciting," she said dryly.

"I disagree." Gabriel kissed her neck and ran his fingers through her bed head.

"For the record, I'm still annoyed with you." With a pout, she pushed him away.

"You are? Hmmm. Baby, if that was annoyance you were giving me before we fell asleep I want more." He squeezed her bottom. "Let's go for enraged right now."

"You promised to dress like a character from *Cats* so our costumes would match. Same theme, dude," she added with a rap against his noggin.

"I said I'd *think* about it. And I did think about it, for about five seconds before deciding no can do."

Reese gave him another punch.

"C'mon now. You didn't actually think I'd agree to wear a skintight Spandex catsuit with a fur collar?"

"But you didn't wear a costume at all." Reese poked his pec. "Spoilsport."

"Did, too."

"*Did not.* A black tank top, jeans, and combat boots do not qualify as a Halloween costume, even if you shave your head and carry a photo of a tricked-out Dodge Charger."

"Hey, I was Vin Diesel in *The Fast & the Furious* franchise."

Reese gave him a reluctant smile. "But you did look smokin' hot last night."

"I have something for you. I hope it will make up for the costume thing." Gabriel took something off the nightstand.

"A ring pop? In strawberry. For me?" Reese gushed, playing along.

"I bought a ton of these for the trick-or-treaters, but this is an extra special one."

"With powers like the beans in *Jack & the Beanstalk*?"

"This one doesn't lead to an irate giant or a goose with golden eggs, but it's redeemable at any jewelry store."

"Any jewelry store?" Reese's eyes went wide.

"Because I want your real ring to be perfect, exactly what you want. You can choose from stock or do a custom design, that is, if you say yes."

"Oh, Gabriel." Reese's eyes misted. "Are you asking…?"

"Abso-freakin'-lutely." Gabriel placed her palm near his heart. "And for the record, I've never asked anyone this before. I held back all these years because I wanted to pop the question once, one time only, when I had gut-deep certainty it was right. The past year with you has exceeded my expectations. And I had high expectations when we got back together. You have made me happier than I ever thought possible. So, Reese Renita Sommers, will you marry me? You can take all the time you need to plan a lavish dream wedding with a splashy reception, *or* we can run off to Vegas and have a big reception with family and friends when we return, *or* we can invite everyone to Vegas *or* to some exotic locale."

"Decisions, decisions."

"It doesn't matter to me, as long as you say you'll be my wife. I want to spend the rest of my life showing just how much I love you. I'll do anything—"

"Except wear a skintight Spandex catsuit with a fur collar." Reese laughed through her tears.

"Yes, anything but that. So when you think the time is right and—"

"Stop." Reese interrupted. "I'm sorry, but...Whew! I need to get this out... I love you, too. And most importantly, I trust you with my life. I know this might sound silly. I've lost loved ones before. And I know people will say Sinbad was just a dumb cat, but to me he was so much more. You and I would've met eventually. I mean, you moved next door... And I know it sounds absurd, but I believe he brought you to me, a precious gift."

"Instead of a dead bird or mouse."

"Yes, my fur baby, the matchmaker. Hokey as it sounds, I think he wanted to make sure he left me in good hands. This past year with you has surpassed my expectations as well. I have renewed confidence in myself and in what I feel for you." Reese said, making his heart rate quicken. "I love you, but most importantly, I have confidence that what I have to offer is enough. *I'm* enough so I have complete confidence in what you feel for me."

"As you should."

"So...." Reese paused dramatically.

"Will you marry me?"

"Abso-freakin'-lutely. Gabriel Elijah Cameron, I will marry you." Reese let him push the chunky plastic base with its hard candy gem on her ring finger.

"Wait. I have one more thing for you." Gabriel reached toward the nightstand again and gave a small box to her. Reese opened it to reveal another sparkling charm for her bracelet.

"A heart."

"My heart. All yours."

"It's beautiful! And perfect!"

Gabriel had already given her charms to mark various milestones in their relationship so there was room for only one more. This new diamond-encrusted charm, larger than the others, would be the centerpiece. She placed it on her nightstand and covered his face with kisses. They rolled around embracing, causing too much of a ruckus for Lucia, who leaped off the bed. Estella wasn't far behind.

"I love you!" Reese cheered. "I love you! I love you!"

"I love you, too. I'll never tire of saying it, sweetheart. So," he stroked her thighs, "what time do you have to get to the shop this morning?"

"Linda's opening."

"Hmmm. How I love it when Linda opens," Gabriel said, his voice now husky with desire as his hand moved between her legs. "Now you can open for me."

Deep, tender kisses turned vigorous and heated. He maneuvered until she was straddling him. Her hips rolled and rocked against his erection.

The doorbell rang just as he reached for a condom on the nightstand.

"Let it ring," Gabriel said, now panting from arousal that nearly clouded all coherent thought. "They'll go away."

To more ringing and knocking, they resumed their kissing. Reese almost took him inside when she suddenly stopped.

"It's Quinn with breakfast," Reese said. "Got to answer that. I just remembered she promised to bring those rainbow bagels from Goldstein's Deli she's been raving about."

"No." Gabriel's biceps flexed, locking her in place when she tried to move. "You can't leave all this," he said, throbbing with the need to bury himself deep inside her, "for bagels?"

"I hear those bagels are the bomb!" She laughed. "And cute! Each one is a kaleidoscope of color."

"You're leaving bed for multicolored bread?"

Reese pecked his cheek and then, one by one, pried his fingers from her hips as he protested. "She promised to bring chive and onion cream cheese and smoked salmon, too. Yummers!"

"I can't," Gabriel groaned, covering his eyes with a bent arm. "This is torture. I can't watch your naked butt moving away from me now."

"I'm covering my naked butt." Reese scooted off the bed and donned a short silky robe.

Gabriel wasn't ready to get dressed or give up on his plan to have her that morning, but he threw on the bottom half of his "costume" anyway.

Stepping around remnants of last night's celebration —streamers, confetti, Mylar balloons in various states of inflation— the couple made their way downstairs. Lucia and Estella fought over the lace folding fan Odette had left behind. Their resourceful neighbor had dressed in an elaborate Marie Antoinette getup she'd made herself.

There was quite a commotion at the door. Two voices.

"Look what you made me do!"

"Woman, if you'd just released the box and let me be the gentleman that I am, it wouldn't have happened," said someone who sounded a lot like Lance.

Reese peered through the peephole. "It's Lance and Quinn."

"That I gathered." Gabriel peeked through sheer curtains covering one side window panel. A puddle of spilled coffee and multicolored bagels lay at their feet.

Quinn wore a baggy sweatshirt and weight lifting pants. Her hair was in her usual curly pouf. A visit to her favorite little hole-in-the-wall gym was obviously on the morning's agenda.

"Don't *'woman'* me." Quinn dropped the empty bagel box to latch her hands on her hips.

"I'm not sure why Lance is here. Oh, wait." Gabriel thwacked his forehead. "I forgot. Last night, I told him he could come by to pick up some golf clubs. Probably raced over here when he spotted Quinn."

Lance, who often copied Tiger Woods' golfing ensembles, wore a black cap, red polo shirt, dark vest, and black trousers. Mirrored sunglasses covered his eyes.

Reese pulled back the curtain on the other side window panel.

"I told you I could carry the box my-damn-self," Quinn said. "But oh no, you and your *'I insist'* and tug-of-war nonsense. I didn't need your help. What are you doing here? Shouldn't you be somewhere trawling your social media accounts and scheduling your next booty call?"

"Scheduling defeats the purpose," Lance said. "Impromptu, baby. Spontaneity makes it hotter. Besides, the beautiful booty caller, or I should say booty *callers*, the Tennyson Twins—"

"Bendy Cindy and Limber Kimber."

"Ah, so you follow their Post-a-Pic feeds, too," Lance said. "They left my place, oh, about an hour and a half ago."

Quinn clucked her tongue.

"But for *you*, I'd throw in breakfast in bed, a back massage, and door-to-door car service," Lance went on, pressing the hell out of Quinn's buttons, as he'd done at every opportunity for the past year.

"Only in my nightmares."

"Is that so?"

"Dream on, dude. With you? *Never-ever-ever-ever.*"

"Go on and add a few more *evers* to that."

"Ever-ever-ever-ever-ever."

Gabriel waited for Quinn to poke out her tongue at Lance, but she restrained herself.

"Ever-ever-ever-ever-ever," Quinn added on another long breath.

"Inspiration," Lance replied with a roguish grin.

"Never ever-ever-evers ad infinitum."

"*Ad infinitum*, you say?" Lance smirked, his rich baritone mocking. "Did she just test drive her Word of the Day? Cute."

"No, the Word of the Day is *blowhard*," Quinn tapped a finger against his chest, "as in a person who yaps way too much and way too loudly in an overly boastful manner, usually with very *little*," she glanced at his fly, "to back it up." She tsk-tsked him. "It's a pity actually."

"So, I've earned your pity?"

"Yes, because men who *are* about it, don't need to *talk* about it. Constantly. Now, put that in your pipe and smoke it."

"Oh, snap," Gabriel said. "Gauntlet thrown."

"That's our Quinn," Reese sang.

Lance removed his sunglasses. With a gleam in his gaze, he inched closer, his frame towering over Quinn's. "Speaking of pipe, as in when, how, and in whom I put mine. Remember this day. You'll eat those words."

"Ha!" Quinn held her ground, but tipped her head back to look up at him.

Lance's teeth caught his bottom lip, as he looked deep into Quinn's eyes, and gave her a slow, head-to-toe appraisal. His voice was low and sure, but carried through the door. "And I guarantee you'll beg for seconds… and more. And you'll call my name, my full name, Lance Garrett Donovan, and you'll tell me how much you love it…in languages you've never learned."

"And I'll even speak in tongues."

"Yeah, that, too," he said with a cool that underscored Quinn's fire.

"Dude, you're friggin' delusional!"

"Am I?" Lance's gaze never left hers.

Long, unexpected silence from a drop-jawed Quinn, suggested capitulation.

"Not quite sure, are you?" he said.

Quinn appeared to tip back in her sneakers, before firing yet another never-ever gibe that… fell flat. It was as if Lance's ridiculous prediction had jammed her circuits and blunted her sharp tongue.

"That's our Lance," Gabriel said.

But Quinn soon regained her equilibrium and on and on they went, childishly baiting one another.

As usual, the back and forth soon exhausted Reese and Gabriel.

"How long do you think those two will go at it this time?" Gabriel asked.

"Who knows? They set a record at your Fourth of July barbecue, but then they broke that one at the party last night. I'm hosting a big Thanksgiving dinner—"

"So I'm sure they'll square off again."

Reese reached for her phone on the nearby table. With Gabriel reading over her shoulder, she texted Quinn: *Sorry, gotta bend the sisters before misters rule today. Promise to call later with all the details. I have great news for you and the rest of the family!* She closed with two kissy-face emojis.

Gabriel found his own phone and texted Lance something similar, but without the emojis.

"I feel bad text shooing them away after we invited them here," Reese said.

"They'll get over it."

Again, Reese peered out at her sister, in rare form, razzing Lance again with fiery gusto. When the bickering pair's phones signaled they had texts both ignored them, too lost in their spat.

"Yeah, I think you're right." Reese faced Gabriel. "So, we stand here and wait? We could make coffee and breakfast."

"We could make coffee and breakfast… *or not.*" Gabriel opened her robe and slipped it off her shoulders to let it fall to the hardwood floor. He slammed her flush against him and swept her off her feet.

"Now," his fiancée wrapped her long legs around his torso, "take me back to bed."

"Yes, ma'am."

The End

ABOUT THE AUTHOR

Reon Laudat is the author of ten novels. She has a bachelor's degree in journalism from the University of Missouri-Columbia. As a features and lifestyle reporter, Reon covered the fun stuff—pop culture, fitness, television, and fashion. Her articles have appeared in newspapers across the country via the Gannett News Service. She resides in the Southeast with her family. Email her at reonlaudat@yahoo.com.

You can check in at www.reonlaudat.com, Facebook, Twitter, and Instagram.

Novels by Reon Laudat include:

Romance
The Flirtationship
Just Her Type
Welcome to Mistywood Lane
What a Girl Wants

Chick lit/ Women's Fiction Lite
The Mommy Group

Printed in Dunstable, United Kingdom

67065922R00143